ABERDEEN
CITY LIBRARIES
www.aberdeencity.gov.uk/libraries

Tel 732517

Return to . . . .
or any other Aberdeen City Library
Please return/renew this item by the last day shown. Items may also be renewed by phone or online

Cu 2/15

05 OCT 2015

17 - 3 - 16

19 - 5 - 17

Thirteen Weddings

Paige Toon

W F HOWES LTD

This large print edition published in 2015 by
W F Howes Ltd
Unit 4, Rearsby Business Park, Gaddesby Lane,
Rearsby, Leicester LE7 4YH

1 3 5 7 9 10 8 6 4 2

First published in the United Kingdom in 2014
by Simon & Schuster UK Ltd

ISBN 978 1 47128 295 9

Typeset by Palimpsest Book Production Limited,
Falkirk, Stirlingshire
Printed and bound by
www.printondemand-worldwide.com of Peterborough, England

This book is made entirely of chain-of-custody materials

For my husband Greg.
Bronte may not believe in
marriage, but I do.
You're my Nathan/Johnny/Luis/Ben/Joe/Leo
all rolled into one . . .

PROLOGUE

I am *nowhere near* drunk enough. I stare with a sinking heart at the sea of neon-wearing, tutu-donning, permed-haired Madonna-in-the-Eighties wannabes going absolutely hysterical on the dance floor below. A DJ is whipping them up into a frenzy as he hands out fluffy white tiaras to a frightening number of brides-to-be.

'WHO ELSE IS ON THEIR HEN NIGHT?' he shouts, and I cringe from the sound of screaming behind me.

'HERE! UP HERE!' Michelle yells at the top of her voice as she herds a red-faced, laughing Polly past me to the stairs. We've just walked in through the door on the upper level.

'GOOD LUCK, LADIES! ENJOY YOUR EVENINGS', the DJ shouts, and then the bright lights over the dance floor dim and the music cranks up. Michelle's moan at not getting downstairs quick enough is cut off by Polly's sudden squeal when she realises whose song is playing.

'IT'S KYLIE!'

She clutches at me with fevered delight and drags me onto the dance floor where I plaster a grin on

1

my face and do a reluctant Locomotion with my fellow countrywoman. I wonder how soon I can blame my jetlag and call it a night.

'I wish we'd dressed up', Michelle squeals with annoyance as an Olivia Newton-John lookalike in legwarmers shimmies past.

Michelle and I are not on the same wavelength.

I don't know her. At least, I didn't, not before tonight. I'd never met Kelly, Bridget or Maria before, either. Polly, on the other hand, I know well. But right now, I almost wish I didn't.

We've been friends since high school in Australia, but two and a half years ago she came to the UK to work and went and got herself engaged to a Pom. They're getting married next week, and unfortunately, I wasn't involved in the hen party planning, otherwise I would have made sure we were a hell of a lot drunker before dragging everyone to an Eighties club.

'Who's up for a shot?' Bridget yells before the song is out.

'ME!' I reply, darting off the dance floor. 'I'll give you a hand.'

We head to the bar. 'Shall we do tequila or vodka?' she shouts over her shoulder.

'Whichever's strongest!' I shout back, getting a look from a guy standing nearby. I smirk at him and he shrugs hopelessly in return. Hmm, he's a bit of a hottie, actually. His dark hair is a little longer on top and styled back off his face and he's

2

wearing black jeans and a light-coloured shirt with the sleeves rolled up.

'Here you go!' Bridget shouts, distracting my attention as she passes me a shot glass. Wow, that was quick. 'Cheers!' she says.

'Aren't we waiting for the others?' I ask.

She knocks hers back and winces. Apparently not. I raise my eyebrows and do the same. Urgh. Straight vodka. The barman lines up six more shot glasses and fills them up. 'I think you and I need extra ammunition,' Bridget says with a wicked grin, passing me three glasses and nodding in the direction of the others.

I glance at the hottie, but he's staring straight ahead, looking utterly fed up.

We reach the other hens and hand out the shots. A couple of the girls look a bit reluctant, but drink up anyway, and then A-ha's 'Take On Me' starts to play. It may be the vodka, it may be the fact that I love this song, or it may even be because there's at least one good-looking guy in this dive, but I feel like the night is looking up.

And then a cowboy dances into our circle and starts to gyrate against Michelle.

And – oh God – she lets him.

Bridget flashes me a 'WTF' look and I mirror her expression before taking in the scene. Boys are few and far between, but I can see two Michael Jacksons from 'Thriller', and a Michael J Fox from *Teen Wolf* in a yellow bomber jacket and impressively hairy werewolf gloves. A man-size can of

Bud beer is dancing enthusiastically with Batman and Robin a few feet away and his costume-enclosed face is hot and sweaty.

Suddenly I miss Jason. And I really don't want to.

My eyes involuntarily seek out the guy by the bar. He's still there, leaning back against a pillar with his legs casually crossed, playing with his iPhone. He looks totally out of place. I wonder what he's doing here? I bet he didn't come willingly.

I nearly jump out of my skin as Batman appears in front of me, the bottom of his masked face mostly taken up by a ludicrously cheesy grin as he starts to boogie on down in front of me.

I don't think so, buddy . . . I duck away from him to Bridget and she gives me the universal signal for 'another shot?' I nod eagerly.

'Anyone else want a drink?' I ask the others.

Polly and Maria opt for cocktails, but Kelly and Michelle decline.

Bridget and I head back to the bar.

'I'll get these,' I tell Bridget as she tries to flag down the barman. There are a few more people waiting to be served, but the bar is surprisingly not that busy. 'You want a cocktail as well as a shot?' I ask Bridget.

'Sure. Whatever you're having.'

'So how do you know Polly?' I ask her.

'Through work.'

'What do you do?'

'I'm a travel writer.' She sweeps her wavy, medium-length dark brown hair over her shoulder. 'I did a review on one of her hotel chains in Barcelona last year. She's sorted me out for a few freebies since.'

'Cool.'

'What can I get you?'

The barman has materialised in front of us so I lean across the bar and place our order.

'*Angry Birds?*' I hear Bridget exclaim after a moment and look over my shoulder to see that she's plucked the phone straight out of the hottie's hands. He gives her that cute, hopeless little shrug and she hands him back his phone in mock disgust.

'Anything to pass the time,' I hear him reply in a deep, gently sarcastic voice.

'What are you doing here?' she asks.

'Stag do.'

'Who's the groom?' I chip in, passing Bridget a shot glass.

He points at the dance floor with the hand holding his phone. 'Somewhere over there.'

'You don't feel like dancing?' I ask him as Bridget sinks her shot.

'Not drunk enough,' he replies.

'We can rectify that,' Bridget says flippantly, leaning past me to speak to the barman, who's currently shaking the shit out of a silver cocktail shaker.

'I'm never drunk enough,' he mutters to me.

'I'm Bronte,' I tell him, knocking back my own shot and grimacing. 'Yuck.'

5

'Alex,' he replies with amusement. His eyes are blue, I think, but it's pretty dark in here so it's hard to tell.

'We're on a hen night,' I tell him. 'My mate Polly's getting married next week.' I point her out. 'The blonde chick with her hair up in a ponytail.'

'You Australian?' he asks.

'Yep.' There goes my accent again, giving me away. 'I'm over for the wedding.'

'Where are you from?'

'Sydney.'

'Here you are,' Bridget interrupts with three more shot glasses.

I'm going to be off my face at this rate. *Clink!* Down they go.

The barman needs paying so I settle up, my head spinning.

I hear Bridget laugh as I try to juggle the four cocktail glasses and give up, passing one to her.

'Catch you later,' she says. I flash the guy a smile as she turns away and meets my eyes.

'Phwoar!' she mouths. 'He's gorgeous. Have you got a boyfriend?' she asks as we make our way back to the girls.

'Nope.' Not any more. 'You?'

'I've just started seeing someone,' she replies regretfully, adding, 'unfortunately, otherwise I'd be majorly on the pull tonight. You should get in there.'

I hand Polly and Maria their cocktails. 'I doubt

he's single,' I point out, humouring her, because even if he *is* single and interested, it would be too soon after Jason.

'She Drives Me Crazy' by Fine Young Cannibals is playing now. As I dance, the soles of my feet begin to burn. I knew I should have worn my trusty cowboy boots, but I bought a pair of electric-blue heels earlier and I couldn't resist. It's also been stupidly hot today, considering it's September and the UK should be cooling down. I don't know why Polly's always whingeing about the weather. I'm wearing a thigh-length fitted black dress and my long, light brown hair is styled in a loose fish-tail plait that drapes over my left shoulder. My eye shadow is dark green, glittery and probably smudged, and I'm guessing that my lipstick is long gone.

The Beer Can Man bumps into me and I don't even shove him away. The alcohol thrumming through my veins must be improving my state of mind. But, uh-oh, Batman's getting amorous ideas again. With a cheesy, sweaty grin, he starts to sidle his blue-Lycra-clad body over. Polly reaches through the throng and rescues me.

'I'm so glad you came!' she squeals in my ear, wrapping her arm around my neck.

'Me too.' I try to sound convincing.

'Especially considering how much you hate weddings.' She gives me an affectionate – albeit slightly violent – shake as if to knock some sense into me.

'I don't mind them that much,' I lie. At least she's getting married in a register office. 'Anyway, I couldn't miss yours, could I?'

'I would have killed you if you had!'

I don't doubt it.

'I can't believe it's been two and a half years,' she slurs. I always could drink her under the table, I muse with affection, before belatedly remembering she can be a really nasty drink. Hopefully not tonight. 'About time someone came to see me,' she adds.

Someone, not me specifically, I note.

'It doesn't seem that long,' I agree, taking a swig of my vodka, cranberry and grapefruit Seabreeze. The truth is, I barely recognise her. She's lost over two stone since getting engaged eight months ago. I was a bit taken aback when I saw her. She didn't look like herself.

'How's work?' Polly shouts in my ear. 'I feel like I've barely got to speak to you since you arrived.'

'It's good,' I tell her noncommittally. I recently got promoted to deputy picture editor at a weekly women's celebrity magazine called *Hebe*, named after the Greek goddess of youth. I used to work at a men's lifestyle magazine called *Marbles*, but my boss on the picture desk didn't appear to be going anywhere, so I had to move on to move up.

'Are you sure you don't mind staying at the hotel?' Polly asks me for the umpteenth time with a worried look on her oddly slim face.

'Definitely not,' I reassure her.

I flew in yesterday morning at the crack of dawn. I caught up with Polly for lunch – she's a manager at the hotel I'm staying in, which is near St Paul's Cathedral, just up the road. I spent yesterday afternoon sleeping off my jetlag, and then we went out for dinner last night in Soho with her fiancé, Grant, who's a structural engineer. He's good fun. Seems to really love my friend and, more importantly, seems to be able to handle her sometimes overly dominant personality, so that can only be a good thing. They only recently moved in together to a new-build one-bedroom flat near the river. Even though Polly offered to put me up on their sofa bed, I didn't want to cramp their style, not with so much else going on right now. So I plan to explore London for the next few days, although I wish I had longer because it's my first time here. On Wednesday I'll head with Polly and Grant to Grant's parents' house in Brighton. Grant's parents are hosting the wedding so I'll be able to help with the last-minute arrangements and spend some time with my old friend. I haven't even told her about Jason. She's been on at me to settle down for ages.

A few months ago my boyfriend of a year moved to Western Australia for work. He asked me to join him. He asked me a lot of things. But we weren't meant to be. We called time on our relationship three weeks ago.

Great. Now I'm not even in the mood for 'Footloose'.

'Just going to the loo,' I tell Polly before she can sense that anything is wrong. I squeeze through the crowd on the dance floor and emerge relatively free from assault. I shoot a quick glance at the bar, but the space in front of the pillar is bare. Oh well.

Polly and the others are by the bar taking a breather when I return, my feet stinging excruciatingly. I really need to sit down.

'Bronte!' Polly waves me over. 'What are you drinking?'

'I'll have another Seabreeze, please.' Hopefully alcohol will take the edge off the pain in my soles. An arm appears around my shoulders. I jerk away from the sweaty, red-faced guy staring down at me, but he grins drunkenly and hangs on for dear life.

'My best mate's getting married next week,' he tells me, slurring his words. 'This one here.' He puts his other arm around the guy to his left and drags him closer. 'He's . . . The best. Bloke. Ever.'

'Wow. Congratulations,' I say, deadpan, detaching myself from his pincer-like grip before he pulls me to the ground.

'I'm Nigel,' the drunk guys says, trying to sound serious and sober – and failing.

'We're on a hen night,' Michelle interrupts.

Don't encourage him, you idiot!

Nigel's eyes widen with amazement, as though this could possibly be a surprising thing in this venue. 'No. *Way?* Who's the bride?'

'Me!' Polly answers with a giggle, passing me my drink.

'What's your name?' Nigel asks her, stumbling into his pal. They're both dressed in short-sleeve check shirts and dark trousers.

'Polly,' she replies happily, as Maria, Kelly and Bridget join us. I slurp at my drink and stare on resignedly as they all introduce themselves. There are four of them – the groom is called Brian, but I switch off after that.

'ALEX!' Nigel suddenly shouts, right in my ear. I clap my hand over my ear and mouth, 'OW!' Then Alex – THE Alex – appears beside me. I watch with surprise as Nigel wraps his arm around Alex's neck. 'Where did you *go*, man?' he asks incredulously as he wobbles from left to right and then backwards and forwards. The strain of keeping him upright is showing on Alex's face.

'You're suffocating me,' Alex tells him with some effort. Brian helps extract Nigel and I have an image in my mind of one of those small, brown koala tourist toys that cling onto inanimate objects. 'This is Alex.' Brian, who appears marginally more sober than Nigel, introduces him. I notice Kelly and Michelle flash each other appreciative looks.

'Poppy's getting married next week,' Nigel butts in, indicating our blushing bride-to-be.

'POLLY!' Michelle and Kelly laughingly correct him.

'Oh right, cool,' Alex says to the group, feigning

interest. He slyly checks his watch while his friends fawn over Polly and the others.

'I saw that.' I gently elbow him in his ribs. He looks abashed. 'The shot didn't help?'

'No,' he replies with what I think is a genuine – although small – smile. 'I think I might need about ten more of those.'

'Your wish is her command,' I say wryly as I see Bridget getting the barman to line up shot glasses. Alex doesn't look convinced. 'So why are you so behind?' I ask curiously. 'Your mates are wasted.'

'I came along late.' Pause. 'Had to work,' he adds.

'On a Saturday? What do you do?'

'I, um, had to go to a photoshoot.' I can see he's reluctant to reveal this, but naturally I'm compelled to ask what it was for. 'Er, it was for a magazine,' he reveals, shifting from side to side.

'Really? I work on a magazine. I'm a deputy picture editor.'

'Are you?' He instantly relaxes, and I understand. Some people get all manic and overeager when you tell them you work in the media.

At that point, the others interrupt because it's 'shot time'. I don't need another one, but I chink my glass with Alex anyway and stealthily swap my full glass with his empty one as soon as he's done.

'You don't want it?' he asks.

'I've had more than enough,' I reply.

He shrugs and knocks it back and then 'Girls Just Want to Have Fun' starts to blare out of the speakers.

'LET'S DANCE!' Michelle screams, dragging Polly and Brian away. The others are all seemingly happy to follow, but Alex and I hang back.

'Still not drunk enough?' I ask him.

'No, but don't let me stop you,' he says.

'I need to sit down. My feet are killing me.'

He nods to the bench seat stretched across one side of the dance floor. My mood improves considerably as I follow him, staring at the back of his head. His dark hair curls around the nape of his neck. He's very different to his friends. They seem so . . . ordinary. I wonder how he knows them. He reaches the black-velvet-cushioned bench and flops down, leaning his head back against the wall. I take a seat beside him and cross my legs.

'Batman's at it again,' I comment as the super-hero wannabe gets up close and personal with a girl in a leopard-print miniskirt a few feet away. She looks very drunk, which probably suits him just fine.

'Christ,' Alex murmurs, as the girl plucks an ice cube out of her glass and licks it seductively.

I watch, goggle-eyed, as Batman sticks his tongue out and the girl rubs the ice cube along it. I snigger. 'If a guy wanted to score, this would be the place to come. The ratio must be ten to ninety.'

'Mmm,' he agrees.

'So what's your link to Brian?' I ask, making conversation.

'He's marrying my little sister.'

'Ohh,' I say, knowingly. 'I *see.*'

13

He glances at me. 'Why do you say it like that?'

'I wouldn't have placed you with them,' I tell him, belatedly realising that this could sound incredibly rude, even as I go on to say: 'They don't look like the kind of blokes you'd hang out with.' Eek. 'Whoops, sorry, that's the alcohol talking.'

He smirks. 'I'm still not drunk enough.'

'Go and get another shot, then.'

'I don't know how much longer I'm going to stay,' he admits, shoving a wayward sleeve back up past his elbow.

'Great, thanks very much,' I snap jokily. 'Leave me to fend for myself, why don't you. I'll probably have a werewolf humping my leg in a minute, but you go right ahead. Let him at me.'

He flashes me a sideways grin as he makes to get up. 'I'll go to the bar.'

'That's the spirit.' Yay!

'You want one?'

'I'd love another Seabreeze. I reckon if I stick to vodka-based drinks, I'll have less chance of passing out later.'

He looks amused and I feel a little jittery as I watch him pass through the crowd, then my attention is distracted by Batman trailing the ice cube up the inside of the girl's miniskirt. I look on with horror. Urgh, that's disgusting. He puts the ice cube back up to her mouth and she sucks it between her lips.

I barely even notice Alex return a few minutes later. There have been some developments.

14

'What's up?' he asks, giving me a quizzical look as he takes a seat next to me.

'Them,' I hiss. 'Look!'

Batman is pressed up against the girl's front and Robin is pressed up against her from behind in a superhero sandwich. She's smiling over her shoulder at Robin in what I'm sure she hopes is a seductive manner. She reaches around, pulls the toy gun out of his hands, puts it into her mouth, and pretends to give it a blowjob. Then I notice Batman's hard-on.

I shoot my head around to give Alex an incredulous look. His jaw has practically hit the floor and he looks so comical, I start to laugh. He meets my eyes.

'Fuck me,' he says with astonishment.

'I'm sure she would if you asked her to,' I quip. I look back at the superheroes. The girl has detached herself and is zigzagging off the dance floor in the direction of the toilets. Batman and Robin high-five each other and suddenly I feel sickened, not entertained.

'I hope she's going home,' I say, as Batman adjusts his crotch. 'Ew, that is so wrong . . .'

Repelled, Alex turns his face away towards me. I do the same, putting my hand up on the side of my face to shield us from view. He regards me with a playful smile and as I stare up into his eyes, my heart quickens. I let my hand drop and look back at the action on the dance floor. It's then that I spot Polly, standing stock-still and glaring

15

at me. I tense up as she storms over. I remember that she can be a really nasty drunk. How could I ever forget *that*?

'What are you doing?' she demands to know.

I inwardly sigh. 'My feet are killing me.' I kick up one electric-blue high heel, but she's already dragging me to my feet. 'What about Jason?' she barks in my ear, scowling down at Alex.

'We split up,' I tell her calmly, and while she looks stricken at first, her expression swiftly transforms into one of accusation. 'Why? For God's sake, Bronte, I thought he was The One? Why didn't you *tell* me?' Luckily I'm not looking for sympathy.

'I was going to fill you in after tonight,' I reply. 'Anyway, it's not a big deal,' I try to chill her out. 'But I do need a breather. These heels were a bad idea.'

She looks down at my feet and back up at my face, and I'm not at all convinced that she's going to let me off the hook, but then Starship's 'Never Gonna Stop Us Now' starts up and Michelle – my unwitting saviour – appears and pulls Polly back onto the dance floor. Deflated, I sit back down next to Alex.

'What was that about?' he asks.

I slurp my drink miserably. 'I hadn't told her I'd split up with my boyfriend.'

Pause. 'Oh.'

'I *hate* it when she's drunk. I can't tell you how many nights ended up with her flying off the handle in a drunken rage when we were back home

16

in Australia,' I rant. 'I thought she might have grown out of it.'

'When was the last time you saw her?' he asks.

'Two and a half years ago, before she moved here.'

'Oh.'

'It's not like we're best mates,' I continue full steam. 'But I've known her for donkey's years. She didn't even ask me to be a flippin' bridesmaid.'

'Oh, right.'

'Not that I wanted to be a bridesmaid.'

'No?'

'No. I think marriage is pointless and I bloody hate weddings and she knows it.'

'I see.'

'Sorry, I'm going on.'

He smiles. 'It's okay.'

'I'll shut up now.'

We fall silent for a bit.

'When did you split up with your boyfriend?'

Hmm, so he's asking *that* question . . .

'A few weeks ago.' I turn the interrogation around. 'What about you? Are you seeing anyone?'

He looks away. 'Nope,' he says shortly. I figure that's the end of the conversation, but then he elaborates. 'I split up with my girlfriend a few weeks ago, too.'

'Oh. I'm sorry.'

He shrugs, but doesn't meet my eyes. 'It's okay. Uh-oh.'

'What?'

He nods towards the dance floor. 'The girl's back.'

I look over to see her making her way through the crowds towards Batman and Robin. They're now dancing with a couple of nice-looking, reasonably sober girls. If these girls knew what the seemingly harmless superheroes had been up to with an ice cube, they'd run a mile. I sit there and cringe as I watch the wasted girl sidle up to the boys. They pretend not to see her.

'Doesn't she have any friends to take her home?' I ask worriedly.

We watch as the other two girls flash each other wary looks and move elsewhere on the dance floor. Obviously realising they've lost their chances, Batman and Robin revert to their original plan, locking the wasted girl in another sandwich. It's like watching the scene of a car crash – I can't tear my eyes away.

Suddenly, Alex's drink is in my hand and he's on his feet. He stalks over to Batman and takes him by his arm, firmly pulling him away. Batman stumbles slightly in surprise. I can't see Alex's face, but I see shame cloud Batman's expression and then he nods and reaches past the girl to tap Robin's arm. The girl wobbles drunkenly as the horny superheroes leave her be. Alex says something to her and she frowns, trying to process his words. Eventually she looks around and points up to the higher level where we came in. Alex takes her by the elbow and guides her off the dance floor.

Wow. I am so impressed right now.

There's a thump beside me and I turn with a start to see Bridget sitting in the space recently vacated by Alex.

'Polly's pretty pissed off at you,' she says flippantly.

'Is she?' My heart sinks.

'Wonder if it's time we should get her home.'

'Good luck with that,' I say wryly.

'You sound like you've been here before.' She cocks her head to one side and slurps her cocktail through a straw.

'Many, many times.' I sigh and get to my feet. 'We'll need to sober her up, first.'

I set off towards the bar. I'll get her a lemonade and lime. With vodka, it's her favourite drink, but I doubt she'll notice the alcohol is missing.

'Oi.' I feel a hand on my arm and I spin around to see that it belongs to Alex.

'Are you deserting me?' he asks reproachfully. 'I leave you alone for *one* minute.'

'I'm just getting Polly a lemonade,' I tell him with a smile as he lets his hand drop. 'Where's the girl?'

'I took her upstairs to her friends. They were just about to leave.'

'Good timing. That was really nice of you,' I say sincerely. He looks embarrassed by the praise. 'I'll be back in a minute,' I promise.

By the time I return to the bench seat, Polly is there, flanked by Alex and Bridget on either side.

'I got you another drink,' I say breezily.

'What is it?' Polly glares suspiciously at the drink in her hands.

'Vodka, lemonade and lime,' I lie.

She looks appeased. 'Good.'

Bridget and Alex smirk at me.

'*Why* did you split up with Jason?' Polly cries out of nowhere.

My eyes inadvertently flick towards Alex.

'When are you ever going to settle down? I thought things were going really well,' she adds bluntly.

'Yeah, well, things change.' I can't keep the touchiness from my tone.

'I doubt Bronte wants to talk about it now,' Bridget chips in reasonably.

Polly turns on her. 'How the hell would you know? You've only just met her!'

'Okay, time to go home,' Bridget snaps, leaping to her feet and dragging Polly with her.

'What? Why? I'm not ready!' Polly stutters.

'Yes, you are. It's nearly one o'clock, Grant's waiting up for you at home and he'll be properly jacked off if you barf all over your new carpet.'

I am *amazed* when Polly doesn't argue. Does that mean this night is over? I reluctantly get to my feet, feeling strangely disappointed.

'Stay,' Bridget insists. 'Finish your drink. I'll take her home.'

'What? No,' I reply, startled. 'I'll come.'

'Don't be ridiculous,' she waves me away. 'Your

hotel is nearby. I need to catch a cab home via theirs anyway.' She looks past me to Alex, then back at me with meaning. 'Stay,' she urges again. Out of the corner of my eye I see Alex hunch forward and rest his elbows on his knees.

The other hens have swarmed around us now. Maria and Kelly are talking about staying, too, but Michelle wants to catch a cab home with Bridget and Polly. She's Polly's only bridesmaid, after all: a friend from work.

'Do you want me to take you home?' I ask Polly, feeling guilty.

'No!' she exclaims. 'Go back to the hotel.' She grins, wobbling slightly. 'I asked the maids to leave some extra chocolates on your pillow. And anyway,' she pushes me away slightly then reaches back and locks her fingers around my wrist, 'Grant wants sex tonight.' She lets me go, turning to Michelle.

Too much information.

'Are you sure about this?' I ask Bridget.

'Absolutely.' She seems remarkably with it considering all the shots she's consumed.

We say our goodbyes and then Maria and Kelly head back onto the dance floor while I tail off towards Alex. Thankfully, he's still there. He looks up as I sit back down next to him.

'Staying?' he asks.

'Didn't want to leave you at the mercy of Batman and co.'

'I could take them on, no problem,' he says with exaggerated confidence. He stares at the throng on the dance floor. 'I haven't seen the lads for a while.'

Oh. Is he looking for an excuse to leave? 'Don't worry about me if you want to go and find them.'

'No, not at all,' he says quickly. 'Although I do feel a bit bad.' He glances at me. 'Not that bad, though.'

I narrow my eyes and peer through the crowd. 'Is that them over there?' I point and he leans his head close to mine to follow the line of my extended digit. We're so close I can smell his after-shave. Mmm, musk.

'Oh yeah, that's them,' he says.

'So . . . Brian, is it?'

'Yep. He's marrying my little sister Jo.'

'And do you approve?'

He shrugs. 'He's alright.'

'That's a glowing reference if ever I heard one.'

He laughs. 'No, he's alright. He's fine. I don't know him that well.'

'Tonight is supposed to be your chance to get to know him better.' I don't know why I'm pointing this out and encouraging him to leave.

He hesitates. 'Well, he's pretty off his face. I'm not sure I'm seeing him in his best light.' He knocks back his drink. 'I'll go buy them a round, make up for it.' He stands up.

'Get them more pissed?'

'Vodka, lemonade and lime, like Polly?' he teases.

I sit there for a bit on my own, crowd-watching and jigging my leg along to 'I'm Holding Out For

22

A Hero'. It's an apt song, considering my company. I mean Alex, obviously, not Batman and Robin. The next thing I know, Michael Jackson and Michael J Fox are sitting next to me.

'Are you here alone?' MJ asks with a lewd expression.

'Nope,' I reply. 'My boyfriend's just gone to get me a drink.' Not strictly true, unfortunately.

'Are you Australian?' Fox asks.

'Yep.'

'Why didn't you come as Kylie?' MJ demands to know.

'Didn't really feel like it.' They're not getting the hint. I'm not interested.

'Why not? You'd look so much hotter with blonde hair.' Fox reaches across and strokes my hair with his hairy werewolf glove.

'Get off,' I swat his hand away and he laughs, unfazed.

Idiot. I get up and bash straight into Alex.

'Whoa!' he gasps, holding two drinks aloft and trying to minimise spillage.

'Sorry!' My body is flush with his and I feel light-headed.

'You okay?' He steps back marginally and frowns past me at the guys on the bench.

'Yeah, I'm fine.' I jerk my head to my left and he follows me to a corner beside the dance floor. He hands over a familiar-looking cocktail. 'Seabreeze,' he shouts into my ear. 'And yes, it comes with vodka.'

I nudge him jovially. 'Thanks.'

'Were those guys harassing you?' We're closer to the speakers here and it's louder, so he has to lean into my ear to talk to me.

'No, just annoying. Told me I should have come as Kylie and that I'd look better with blonde hair.'

He looks horrified and shakes his head. 'You wouldn't.'

I laugh. 'No?'

'Definitely not.' He lifts the end of my fishtail plait and lets it drop back against my collarbone. He rests his elbow on a shelf jutting out from the wall. His shirt is slightly open at the top and from this angle I can see the smooth skin of his chest. He glances down at me and I quickly avert my eyes. I notice my feet have stopped hurting.

'When did you arrive?' he asks.

'Yesterday. I'm staying at a hotel up the road from here.'

'Oh right.' His eyebrows go up. 'No last Tube home dilemmas for you.'

'Where do you live?'

He looks momentarily fed up. 'I did live in Shoreditch, but I'm staying with my parents right now in Crouch End.'

I don't know where either place is.

'East London and North London,' he explains, seeing my look of confusion.

'Were you living with your girlfriend?' I ask, as understanding dawns on me.

'Yep,' he replies curtly.

I'm not sure he wants to talk about it, but I'm intrigued.

'Why did you split up?' I ask.

'Why did you and your boyfriend split up?' he bats back.

Fine, if he wants to play it that way. 'He moved to Western Australia for a job. He's a maintenance technician for a large mining company. The long-distance relationship wasn't doing it for us.'

'Didn't you think about moving there with him?' he asks.

'No. I have a good job in Sydney.'

'Sounds like it wasn't meant to be.'

'You're right. If it were, we would have made it work. But we were only together for a year.'

'Try eight,' he says drily.

'*Eight?* Is that how long you were with your girlfriend?'

'Yeah. We met in our last year at uni.'

'How old are you?'

'Just turned thirty. You?'

'Twenty-eight.'

He pushes his hand through his hair and rests his elbow back on the shelf. He has long, dark eyelashes. I wonder what his eyes look like in the daylight.

'So why did you split up?' I ask. 'You owe me,' I point out with a smile.

He shrugs. 'Just one of those things.'

'Not fair,' I complain at his lack of elaboration.

'We'd been growing apart for a while,' he

confides at last. 'I think she might be into someone at work.'

'Did she cheat on you?' I ask with a frown.

'I don't think so,' he replies. 'But I think she wanted to. She can do what she likes, now.' His jaw clenches and he takes a swig of his beer. 'Although we're *supposed* to just be on a break,' he says darkly.

'What does being "on a break" even *mean*?' I ask with irritation. 'Does it mean you've split up or not?'

He rolls his eyes. 'I hate that term, too. The truth is, she just wants to see what else is out there while I sit around waiting for her. *Then* she'll think about settling down.' He takes another angry swig of his beer.

'So don't sit around waiting,' I say. 'Do the same.'

My pulse races as he locks me in a direct stare.

I jolt at the sound of someone shouting his name, and turn in time to see Nigel coming our way with drunken purpose. 'We thought you'd gone home!' he exclaims. I look past him to see Brian dancing with Kelly and Maria? The other two stags appear to have left.

'Come and dance with us!' Maria shouts, excitedly beckoning me over.

Her dark hair looks remarkably glossy and unsweaty as it fans her pretty olive-skinned features. She's a professional hair and make-up artist and is doing Polly's make-up for the wedding, so I bet she knows all the tips.

26

'Come *on*!' Nigel urges, grabbing my arm with his hot, clammy paw and dragging me over to them.

Alex has no choice but to follow.

'Drunk enough yet?' I ask him with a grin as we reach the others.

Turns out we must both be drunk enough, because as 'Red, Red Wine' starts to belt out of the speakers, we both start to dance. I turn to face him, holding my drink aloft and singing along because it's hard not to. He grins down at me. It's a sexy, chilled-out song and my heart jumps when he puts his hand on my hip. I instinctively move closer to him. I'm eye-level with his lips and they're perfect, not too thin, not too full. I bet he's a great kisser.

'When are you going back home?' he shouts into my ear.

'Just under two weeks.'

He pulls back as his eyes widen. 'Long way to come for such a short time.'

'Work wouldn't give me any more time off. My new boss is a bit of a ball-breaker.'

'What?' He frowns and cups my head, pulling me closer so he can hear me over the music.

I feel the heat of his body seep into mine. The hairs on my arms are standing up. 'I'm going to Italy after the wedding.'

'By yourself?'

'Yeah. Rome, Florence, Venice, if I have time.'

His hand moves back to my hip as we continue

to dance. 'Red, Red Wine' ends and annoyingly, Yazz's 'The Only Way Is Up' kicks off. There goes our sexy dancing.

'You want another drink?' I ask him.

Maria winks one dark eye at me as we pass. 'You want anything?' I check with her and Kelly.

'No, thanks. Think we'll head off in a bit.' She jabs her thumb at Alex's departing back. 'He's a bit of alright.'

'Tell me about it,' I squeak in her ear.

At the bar, I chink my glass against his and take a sip, coyly looking up at him. He's standing quite close to me, my heels nestling between his Converse trainers. My stomach is suddenly aflutter with butterflies.

'See you later, Bronte!' Maria interrupts. Alex steps back as she and Kelly move in to give me a hug.

'Are you going to Grant's parents' house on Friday?' I ask Maria.

'Late afternoon,' she replies. 'Oh, I meant to ask, do you want me to do your hair and make-up for the wedding?'

She's making over the bridal party, but I didn't realise that included me.

'Really? Are you sure?'

'Yes. Polly asked me to ask you.'

So she does care, even if she didn't ask me to be a bridesmaid. 'That would be great.' I smile at her, before drily adding, 'I bet I look like a right state at the moment.'

'Nah, you look gorge.' But seemingly unable to stop herself, she runs her thumbs underneath my eyes. 'Now you're perfect. See you Friday. Bye,' she says brightly to Alex.

'I thought I was in for such a crap night.' Alex shakes his head with relief once she's gone. 'I'm glad I met you.'

'I'm glad I met you, too,' I tell him with a smile. He holds eye contact for a long moment.

'What colour are your eyes?' I ask curiously. It's still too dark to tell.

'Blue,' he replies. 'Yours?'

'Green.'

He staggers towards me as Brian stumbles into him.

'He's just been sick on the dance floor,' Brian gasps with some effort, trying to hold Nigel up.

I belatedly register the feeling of Alex's hand on my stomach.

'I'm going to take him home,' Brian says.

'Hang on a sec,' Alex says to me. 'I'll just see them into a cab.'

I take the opportunity to duck into the bathroom. My make-up isn't so bad. Maria must be a perfectionist. I touch up my lipstick and then return to the bar. Alex is nowhere to be seen. When he doesn't reappear after a couple of minutes, I start to think that he might not coming back. What am I doing, anyway? How is this night going to end? I've never had a one-night stand before, and I'm not going to start now. At

29

least, I don't think I am. Am I? Should I just go?

I see a flash of blue Lycra out of the corner of my eye, and then Batman is in front of me, smiling his smarmy grin.

'Hey, beautiful,' he says, even drunker than before.

'I'm not interested,' I reply in a bored-sounding voice.

'You don't even know what I'm going to say, yet,' he says, stroking my arm.

'Don't touch me!' I cry, batting him away. I know where his fingers have been tonight. He laughs, unfazed, and then he's stumbling backwards and Alex is between me and him, his hand on Batman's chest.

'Would you just fuck off?' I hear him yell.

Batman puts his hands up in assent and backs away. Alex turns around to face me and the look of fury on his gorgeous features takes my breath away. He takes two steps forward, hesitates only a second, but time seems to slow down, and then his fingers are tangled in my hair and his lips are on mine.

Jesus, he's amazing. To think I might have walked away from this. Shivers rocket up and down my body as our kiss deepens. He pulls away. No, no, no, don't stop. He's still so close, his eyes staring down at me as his chest rises and falls rapidly against mine. I slide my hand around his waist and feel the warmth of his body through the thin fabric of his shirt as I tug him closer. Then he's kissing me again and my world is spinning. He kisses so differently to Jason. Jason's lips were fuller, his kisses wetter and not always entirely pleasant. But Alex . . . Alex I could kiss for hours.

Someone whistles and claps and we reluctantly break away from each other to see that the venue is flooded with light. The music has stopped, people are leaving and a couple of guys leer at us as they pass.

Alex looks mildly embarrassed as he takes a step backward. I sigh and give him a little smile. Club night is over. And to think we were the last survivors, considering how little we wanted to be here at the beginning.

We join the crowds leaving as we file up the stairs and spill out into the cool night air. He checks his watch.

'How will you get home?' I ask as he glances up the street.

'It's too late for the Tube,' he replies. 'Cab, if I can get one. But I'll walk you back to your hotel first.'

'It's this way.' I nod to our left and we set off. We round the corner to see two forlorn-looking figures up ahead, flagging down a taxi.

Batman and Robin.

'All that effort and they still didn't get lucky.'

Alex strides on, his shoulders hunched against the cold. I fold my arms in front of my chest and hurry after him. My heels are starting to hurt my feet again.

On impulse, I hook my arm through his. After a moment, he takes his hand out of his pocket and wraps his arm around me.

'What are you doing tomorrow?' he asks as I cosy into his chest.

'Thought I'd do some sightseeing, maybe go to the Tower of London. I'll meet Polly for lunch if she's not too hungover. You?'

'My mum's doing a roast.'

'Nice.' I giggle. 'Gotta be some benefits to living at home, eh? Does she do your washing, too?'

He laughs. 'Yeah, she does, actually.'

'Bonus.' I grin up at him, but he's staring ahead.

'Is that it?' he asks.

I look further up the road to see the hotel canopy, the large green potted plants on the pavement lit by a warm glow spilling out of the glass doors.

'Yeah,' I reply downheartedly.

We walk the rest of the way in silence, coming to a slow stop where the darkness meets the light. Alex and I turn to face each other. He stares down at me for a long moment and then I step towards him and slide my fingers through the curling hair at the nape of his neck. I tilt my face up and his lips come down to mine. I kiss him back more fervently, desperately wanting to make the most of every second. His hand moves to the small of my back and he brings me closer. A dart of desire shoots through me, and I gasp, breathless through lack of oxygen. He pulls back, his pupils dark and dilated.

'Come inside with me,' I whisper, my heart speaking the words before my brain has time catch up and, potentially, intervene.

He nods and then my hand is in his and we're walking into the lobby together and he's punching the button for the lift. I keep my eyes trained on the doors, not looking over my shoulder at the reception desk in case one of Polly's colleagues recognises me and reports back to her tomorrow. The doors slide open and we step inside. I press the button for the third floor, and then we're kissing again and I'm trapped deliciously between the lift wall and his hard body.

I fumble about in my purse for my key card as we walk down the corridor to my room. My heart is beating wildly with adrenalin, but doubts are creeping in.

The green light on the keypad lights up and the door clicks. I push it open and turn to face Alex. The room is dark and my willpower is hidden in the shadows. I don't want to stop now. We kiss more slowly than before, my hands sliding under his shirt and across the soft skin encasing his hard muscles. He breathes in sharply as my fingers find their way to the waistband of his jeans, my thumbs brushing across the hairs that trail from his navel downwards.

I unbuckle his belt and his kisses become more frenzied. He finds the zip on the back of my dress and lowers it down. I slide it off my shoulders and thank my lucky stars that I wore nice underwear tonight. We dispose of the next few garments quickly and fall back on the bed in our underwear, our limbs tangling with each other's as we kiss.

'What the hell?' Alex mutters, his hand rustling on something on the pillow.

'Chocolates.' I reach behind me and sweep what must be half a dozen of them to the floor.

'You must be popular with the maids,' he whispers as he unclasps my bra. Then his mouth finds one of my nipples and I'm speechless with desire. His lips return to my mouth and I wrap my legs around him, pulling him against me. Oh wow, he *really* wants me. The feeling is mutual. Suddenly he freezes.

'What is it?' I gasp. Please don't stop now!

'I haven't got anything,' he says in a low, deep voice. 'I mean, I wasn't expecting . . .'

Shit! Condoms. 'No, me neither,' I admit, wanting to kick myself. 'I've never done this before.'

Our breathing is short and sharp.

'I . . . I'm on the Pill,' I say hesitantly. 'I haven't been with anyone since . . . I mean, I know I'm okay . . .'

'Me too. No one since . . .'

Neither of us says our exes' names out loud.

I tilt my head up and kiss him gently on his lips. He kisses me back, then pulls away.

'Are you sure?' he asks me quietly. 'We don't have to.'

'I want to,' I whisper. 'Don't you?'

34

I hear him smile, even though I can't see much in this low light. 'Yeah, of course.'

How can it possibly hurt to have one night of passion with a beautiful man?

I run my fingernails down his back and pull him into me, our mouths never breaking contact. The sensation is so intense it leaves me breathless.

I have no idea what time it is when I wake up. There's a dull throbbing inside my head as I roll over and come face to face with Alex, fast asleep beside me. I stare at him for a long moment, the dark hairs of his eyelashes curving like adorable miniature fans. He looks very peaceful when he sleeps, five o'clock shadow gracing his jaw and black, sexed-up hair. His face is lit by sunlight pouring in through a crack in the curtains. I prop myself up on my elbow and watch the whizzing, circling, silvery flecks of dust caught in the bright shaft of light.

Alex murmurs and I glance down at him.

'Wow, your eyes are *really* blue,' I say with surprise, my voice coming out sounding huskier than usual.

He smiles dozily up at me. 'What time is it?' His voice is thick with sleep and alcohol abuse.

'I don't know. I think it's late morning, judging by the sunlight.' I turn my head back towards the curtains. 'Look at the light shaft. The dust motes are like fairy dust. They're magical.'

He frowns. 'What are you going on about?'

'Can't you see them?'

'No.'

'Maybe you have to move out of the light to see how beautiful it is.'

'You're beautiful.' He reaches up and tucks a wayward strand of hair behind my ears.

I grin down at him. 'Aw, did you just deliver me a really corny line?'

He shrugs lazily. 'Might've done.' He cups my head and pulls me down for a kiss. I give him a quick peck, but resist taking it further.

'Let me go and brush my teeth.'

I slip out of bed, feeling self-conscious about the fact that I am as naked as the day I was born.

'Can you chuck me my phone from my back pocket?' he asks, oblivious to my insecurities. 'I'd better text my parents to let them know I'm alive.'

He watches me and I feel my face heat up as I dig around in his jeans pockets. I throw him his phone, he looks amused and then I duck into the bathroom and come face to face with my reflection in the mirror.

I look like a panda with a backcombing fetish. I untie my plait and run my hairbrush through my tangled mess of hair before cleaning away the make-up underneath my eyes. I brush my teeth, go to the loo and pull on the bathrobe hanging behind the door. Then I return to the bedroom.

Alex is sitting up in bed, staring down at the phone in his hands. He glances up at me and his expression makes me halt in my steps.

'What is it?' I ask uneasily.

He rakes his hand through his bed hair and looks down at the phone again. I see that the hand holding it is shaking slightly. He looks wrecked.

'What's wrong?' I ask again.

'Zara . . .' His voice sounds croaky. 'My . . . My girlfriend, ex-girlfriend . . .'

So that's her name. 'Yes?' I nod quickly, impatient for him to spit it out.

'She wants to meet me for lunch.'

'Oh.' I sit down on the bed and bounce slightly.

He rubs his hand across his mouth, but doesn't look at me.

'Do you still love her?' I ask gently, swivelling to lie belly-down on the bed, facing him.

'I think so, yeah,' he says quietly. His eyes are shining when they meet mine. Nausea sweeps through me.

'Are you going to go?'

He shakes his head, then pauses before shaking his head again. 'I don't know.'

'What else does her text say?'

He hands me his phone and sighs deeply as I read it.

I think I made a mistake. I miss you. Will you meet me for lunch?

I take a shaky breath as I hand him his phone. 'What do you think?' he asks.

'What do *I* think?' I reply, taken aback.

'Sorry, I don't know why I just asked that.' He rubs his face with his hands. 'Fuck.'

A wave of pity rushes through me. 'Well . . .' I start.

He looks up hopefully, as though I might have some pearl of wisdom to dispense.

'. . . I'm going home in less than two weeks. It's not like we're going to see each other again,' I say nervously.

He stares at me directly and I have no idea what's going through his mind, but then his face softens and he shakes his head again, looking away.

'You're right. Of course you're right.'

He climbs out of bed and I avert my gaze as he pulls on his boxer shorts and jeans. I watch him sadly as he does up his shirt. He sits on the bed beside me to put on his shoes and socks. I feel flat.

He looks across at me and I'm pretty sure that the feeling is mutual.

'It was nice meeting you,' I say with a small smile.

He pulls me towards him and touches his forehead to mine. It's such a tender gesture, I have to fight the urge to kiss him as he slowly withdraws. He squeezes my fluffy-robe-clad arm and stands up, pushing his fingers through his hair with frustration before clamping his hands behind his head. 'This is so weird.'

I force a light laugh. 'Yeah, it is a bit.'

He shakes his head and lets his arms drop to

his sides. He takes a step forward and as I look up at him, he touches his thumb to my cheek and frowns.

'I really like you,' he says hopelessly. 'I can't believe that I'm never going to see you again.'

I sigh and stand up, then I wrap my arms around his neck. His arms snake around me and he buries his face in my neck and holds me tightly.

'You'd better go.' My voice sounds muffled against his chest.

I feel him nod and then he breaks away and strides over to the door.

'See you,' he says, casting me one last look with his very blue eyes before he goes out of the door.

There's a lump in my throat and I try to swallow it, but I can't. I sit down on the bed and cover my face with my hands, fighting back tears. Turns out I'm not cut out for this one-night-stand business, after all.

A YEAR AND A HALF LATER

CHAPTER 1

'Argh! For flipping, frig's sakes . . .'

'*What?*'

'Fucking fuck!' I exclaim, succumbing to my urge to swear as I come to a sudden stop on the cold, grey pavement underneath the Centre Point building.

'What *is* it?'

I glare at Bridget who's giving me a very perplexed look.

'I *knew* I'd forgotten something!'

Bridget sighs. 'What did you forget?'

'The flipping . . . *argh!*'

I turn on my heel and storm off in the opposite direction.

'Shall I let Simon know you're going to be late?' she calls after me.

'Yes please!' I call back, beyond irritated with myself. Bloody goddamn whatchamecallits. I can't even think of the name for them, but I need the bastards for the photoshoot this morning. I glance quickly at my watch. I'm going to be *so* late.

I step up my pace, hurrying down the stairs into Tottenham Court Road Underground station, trying not to get knocked flying by the tide of people coming towards me. Will I ever get used to the sheer volume of people in this city? It's rush hour and everyone is coming into central London, not leaving it. I swipe my Tube pass and go through the turnstile and step onto the escalator.

I don't know why I glance over at the other escalator – the one that's carrying all of its passengers up – but I do. And my heart almost stops when I see him.

Alex.

I freeze, staring in disbelief as his blue eyes lock with mine and instantly widen. The escalators continue to carry us way too quickly past each other in the wrong direction. My heart pounds as I hold up my hand in a silent gesture asking him to wait at the top. He looks freaked out as he tilts his head away from me, facing forward. I turn and run the rest of the way down the steps, and join the crowds of people merging at the bottom of the 'up' escalator. Screw this. I queue-jump, push and duck my way to the front and begin to climb up what soon feels like the longest escalator in the world. Legs aching and out of breath, I hurry off at the top and look around wildly, trying to spot him. Someone bumps into me and I barely notice. Another person crashes into me.

'Watch it!'

Where is he? My eyes flit over the dozens and dozens of commuters, but I can't see Alex.

Hesitantly I walk towards the turnstiles, still

looking all around for him as more and more people shove against me. How I hate London at this moment! What do I do? Give up? Or go outside to see if I can spot him there? On a whim, I swipe my Tube pass and then I face another dilemma. Which exit? There are six. I make a snap decision for Oxford Street and join the hordes climbing the stairs and spilling out onto the teeming pavement.

There are people *everywhere*. My heart jumps as I spot a dark-haired man, but it's not him. Nor is he the next dark-haired man I see, nor the next. He's gone. I've lost him. Again.

Unable to believe it, I turn in a daze and re-enter the Tube station, my heart sinking further with every step I take into the depths of the Underground.

My head is spinning as I stand by the tracks, waiting for my Northbound train towards Edgware. I check my watch: 9.35 a.m. If he works nearby, maybe I'll see him again. It occurs to me that I could wait outside alternate exits every day until he emerges out of one, but that would probably lose me my job, and I'm already going to irritate my new boss by being late. Plus that sort of behaviour would be completely obsessive and I've never had stalker tendencies.

I stand back as the Tube whooshes along the line, waiting beside the doors as dozens of commuters pour out. I climb on, take a rare seat, and let memories of Alex wash over me.

I never stopped wondering what happened to

him. I regretted letting him walk out of my life without any way of us contacting each other. Even after I returned home, I would find myself scrolling through the names on magazine mastheads to see if I could spot an 'Alex'. I didn't know his surname and stupidly never asked him which publication he worked for. I was curious to know if he got back together with his girlfriend. When I heard about the picture editor job at our sister magazine in London, he was one of the people who first crossed my mind. Polly, Bridget and Alex.

Polly thought I'd be crazy not to jump at the opportunity to come over to the UK for a year, and Bridget encouraged me too. I'd kept in touch with her after the blast we had at the wedding reception. I was drowning my sorrows about Alex and she was my partner in crime again. I hated admitting it, but he'd got to me.

I was surprised when they gave me the job. I'm still surprised. My publisher, Tetlan, sorted out my one-year work visa, and within two months I had packed up my life in Sydney and flown to the other side of the world. Bridget offered me a room in her new flat in Chalk Farm – she's no longer with the guy she was seeing a year and a half ago – and coincidentally, this week she's freelancing for a magazine on the floor below mine.

I inwardly sigh. Why didn't he wait for me at the top? Were my hand signals not clear? Was it actually *him*? Of course it was. Did he recognise me? Doesn't he remember who I am?

I'm so deep in thought that I almost miss my stop. Outside on the pavement, I pick up a snappy-sounding voicemail from my immediate boss, Nicky.

'Simon's just told me you're going to be late. You're going to miss the briefing meeting now, so go straight to the studio in Kentish Town and start setting up. Call me when you get there. And for God's sake, don't forget the feather boas!'

She sounds pissed off. I'm *Hebe*'s picture editor, but she's the picture *director*, a position that we didn't even have at the *Hebe* office in Sydney. So in a weird way, I haven't even been promoted. I still answer to one other person in the pecking order before the magazine's editor, Simon, who interviewed me alongside Nicky via video conference call. I like him a lot – he's popular with everyone – but I belatedly realise I've probably put Nicky's nose out of joint by letting Bridget notify him of my lateness instead of her. Bridget has freelanced for Simon in the past so she knows him.

Bridget's flat is a ten-minute walk from the station and is on the middle floor of a cream-painted three-storey Georgian terrace. It has two medium-sized bedrooms, one shared bathroom, and a modern open-plan kitchen and living space. It's bright and airy with large sash windows looking out onto trees. It's March right now so the branches are bare, but it's only a matter of time before we'll have a leafy green view. Despite its size, which is much smaller than the house I shared in Sydney, I love it. It feels very English. I pay rent direct to Bridget's dad, who bought the flat recently as an investment. Bridget's parents are divorced and I haven't yet met her mum, but her dad popped over the day after I arrived to see if he could help with anything. He couldn't – I had already unpacked my one meagre suitcase – but I appreciated the gesture.

On my first weekend here, Bridget and Polly took me shopping at Camden markets and we bought a few items for my new bedroom: a yellow lampshade, a string of green and white fairy lights, a rug for the floor, a couple of posters. It's still a fairly sparse space, which is why I'm even more annoyed at myself for managing to forget to take the bags of flipping feather boas hanging on the coat stand.

Considering I've only been here for three weeks, I already feel like I'm on my way to becoming a Londoner. I gave myself a week to settle in and get over my jetlag before starting work, and in that time I sorted myself out for a Tube pass and took train rides all over London, getting to know my new city. Halfway through my first week, I went to meet Polly for lunch at the hotel I stayed in; seeing it again gave me a funny feeling in the pit of my stomach. I never told her about Alex, but I confided in Bridget. I don't know why – I've known Polly for years – but I had a feeling she would judge me, and Bridget, well, I didn't think she would. I was right.

I call Nicky when I arrive at the studios.

'We're on our way,' she snaps. I presume she's in a cab. 'Is the photographer there yet?'

'No, I'm the first to arrive.'

'Sort out the catering for lunch and we'll be with you in twenty. Did you remember the feather boas?'

'They're what I had to go back home for,' I point out patiently.

'Fine.'

She ends the call. I exhale loudly, realising I've been holding my breath. My boss at *Hebe* in Sydney was a bit of a bitch and I'm not entirely convinced that I haven't jumped from the frying pan into the fire. Nicky was charming when she interviewed me, but maybe I'm seeing her true colours away from Simon.

We're shooting the four judges from a primetime reality TV show and the theme is 'cheese', hence the colourful feather boas. Phil, the photographer, arrives after ten minutes – a weary-looking man in his mid-forties who looks like he's had a few too many late nights. The make-up artist arrives next, and I jolt with surprise when I recognise her olive skin tone and glossy dark hair.

'Maria?' It's one of Polly's hens!

'Bronte?' she exclaims with surprise.

'How *are* you?' I walk over to her and give her a hug.

'I'm great!' She pulls back.

'I didn't know you did hair and make-up for this sort of stuff?'

'Yeah, I do it all.' She shakes her head, still taken aback at seeing me again. 'What are you doing in the UK? Do you work at *Hebe*?'

'Yeah, I started a couple of weeks ago. Packed up and left Sydney.'

'Wow.'

'Have you seen Polly recently?' I ask.

'No, I haven't seen her for months.'

That strikes me as a bit strange, considering she came to the hen night. I assumed they must be close. 'Hey, I was just about to make coffee. Do you want one?'

'Sure, that'd be great.' She smiles warmly.

My phone rings on my way to the kitchen. It's Nicky.

'We're two minutes away,' she says. 'I'll need help getting the props out of the cab.'

'Sure,' I reply, but she's already gone. I frown at my phone and stuff it back into my pocket, then I traipse down the studio steps to the street. I stand outside for what feels like forever in the cold spring air, thinking regretfully of my warm coat up in the studio. So much for Nicky only being two minutes away. Actually, she said 'we'. She must be bringing Russ, the writer who's doing the interview.

A cab pulls over and I see Nicky in the back, leaning forward to pay the driver. I stand back as she climbs out, followed by someone else. My heart stops, everything feels like it's moving in slow motion, and then Alex is standing before me.

CHAPTER 2

'This is Alex Whittaker, our new Art Director,' Nicky says offhandedly. 'Simon thought he should come along to the shoot.' We stare at each other in shock, his blue eyes intense with recognition. He looks paler than I remember him, but maybe that's blood loss to his face. I bet my Aussie tan has retreated, too.

'Bronte Taylor, my deputy,' Nicky continues her casual introduction, then addresses me specifically. 'Can you get the props out of the cab?' She's completely oblivious to the fact that I'm frozen and not from the cold. 'We'll go up.' She indicates for Alex to follow her and he hesitates only a moment before doing so. No acknowledgement of me, no 'Hello, how have you *been*?' No 'Holy shit, it's YOU!' Nothing. I'm lost for words myself.

'Come on, love, I haven't got all day,' the cabbie moans. I come to with a start and climb into the back of the cab, dragging out five colourful sunshade umbrellas, a medium-sized fake palm tree and then box after box, dropping them onto the pavement. A spark of irritation ignites inside me. Why didn't Nicky and . . . whoa, it was Alex!

Alex! I was going to complain that they didn't help carry anything up the stairs, but I'm thrown again by the understanding that Alex is here. He's *Hebe*'s new Art Director.

'Are there many more boxes?' Maria asks on my return. 'Let me give you a hand.'

'Sure. Thanks.' Nobody else is offering.

'Your Art Director looks familiar,' she muses on our way downstairs, and my stomach lurches as I remember she saw us getting very cosy at the club. 'I feel like I've seen him before.'

'Maybe you met him at another job.' My tone sounds surprisingly even.

She shrugs. 'Must've done.'

She picks up a box, ready to drop the topic, but I panic. What if she places him? It would be beyond awkward if she blurted anything out in front of Nicky.

'Can you keep a secret?' I ask quickly.

She looks baffled, tilting her head to one side as she shifts the box in her arms. 'Yes?'

'Please don't say anything.'

She shakes her head quickly. 'I won't. What is it?'

'Alex . . .'

'Oh!' Her eyes widen and I know that she's got it before I need to elaborate.

'At the hen night!' she cries, nearly dropping the box.

'Shh!'

'Sorry!' she squeaks.

'I haven't seen him since, and for some reason he's choosing to pretend that he doesn't know me.'

'What a bastard,' she says crossly.

'Huh. Yeah.'

I pick up a box and, to my relief, she doesn't interrogate me further.

The TV judges arrive soon afterwards and then it's all go, the studio becoming a hive of activity as we – although mostly it's just me – get the set ready with the colourful props: umbrellas, plastic neon bar glasses, the fake palm tree and strings of fairy lights. Maria has brought a rail of colourful clothes with her and Nicky is going through the items and assigning them to the various TV stars while Maria begins on hair and make-up. Phil is setting up his photography equipment and Alex . . . He was talking to one of the judges a minute ago, but I can't see him now . . .

'Hey.'

I nearly jump out of my skin when I realise that he's right behind me.

'Hi,' I reply curtly.

'I had no idea . . .' His voice trails off.

'No, me neither.' I give him an awkward smile. I haven't forgiven him for failing to acknowledge me earlier, but maybe he's trying to make up for it now.

'How are you?' he asks quietly.

'I'm fine.' I shrug and look around. 'I'm good.'

'When did you . . . How . . . What happened?'

'You mean how did I end up here in front of you?' I ask.

He nods.

'I applied for a job and got it. I'm here for a year. I started at *Hebe* two weeks ago, arrived from Oz the week before that.'

'Wow. Where are you living?'

'Chalk Farm. I'm staying with Bridget. You might remember her.'

'Bridget?' He frowns. 'Oh, "shot" Bridget!'

'Yeah. "Shot" Bridget.' My expression softens. 'We stayed in touch after the hen night.'

I glance across at Maria, but she's busy applying foundation to one of the already astonishingly orange female judges.

'That's Maria,' I whisper. 'She was at the hen night too.'

He looks knocked for six.

'I know. Weird, right? But she won't say anything,' I quickly add.

He exhales in a rush and I regard him with curiosity. It's so strange seeing him again. But I don't get it. I don't understand his behaviour. What's the big deal if we've met before? 'Was that you on the escalator this morning?'

I know it was, but I want him to admit it.

He looks down and kicks his foot lightly against the palm tree. 'Yeah.'

'Why didn't you wait at the top?' I shake my head, perplexed.

'Bronte!'

We snap to attention at the sound of Nicky's voice.

'Yes?'

'Have you got the catering under control or what?'

Alex folds his arms uncomfortably. She has no right to talk to me like I'm some minion. I almost reply angrily, but it would look unprofessional in front of everyone here.

'I'm on it,' I call back.

Alex steps backwards and lets me go.

The rest of the morning is excruciatingly awkward. Alex barely speaks to me and I barely speak to anyone. Russ, one of the features writers from *Hebe*, arrives towards the end of the shoot, and Nicky breaks away from scrutinising Phil's digital shots on a laptop to come over to me.

'Russ is here now to do the interview.' She flicks her medium-length light blonde hair back off her face and regards me with cool blue eyes behind her red horn-rimmed glasses. 'Alex and I are going to head back to the office. You can bring everything back later in a cab with Russ.'

Great. So I'll be tidying up on my own. 'Okay.'

She turns away and smiles charmingly at everyone. 'Thanks for a great shoot, guys!' She theatrically air-kisses each of the four judges, then Phil, before turning to Alex. 'Ready?' she asks him, waving goodbye to Maria, who's still packing up her make-up bag.

He glances at me with confusion. 'Is Bronte not—?'

'No,' she cuts him off. 'She's staying to clear up. We should get back.'

Alex looks uneasy, but doesn't argue. It's his first day in the office, after all. Nicky turns on her heel and she and her skinny butt leave the building, closely followed by a man who I have spent a huge number of days dreaming about in the last year and a half.

'You alright?' Maria asks me with concern.

'I feel a bit weird,' I tell her honestly.

'That *was* weird,' she agrees. 'You both seemed tense.'

My eyes shoot up to look at her. 'Do you think—?'

'No,' she cuts me off. 'No one else would have noticed. It was just me, because I knew.'

She doesn't even fully know what she knows, but I think she suspects we slept together, and well, she'd be right.

'Do you want to go for a quick drink?' she asks sympathetically. I glance over at Russ. He'll be at least another half an hour, maybe more, with the interviews.

'Sure, yeah, okay, that'd be nice.' I smile at her gratefully.

We go down the road to the first pub we come across and order a couple of Cokes, taking them to a booth seat by the window. It smells of stale booze and years of pre-ban cigarette smoke ingrained in the flocked wallpaper and swirly red and brown patterned carpet. I sip my Coke miserably.

'Do you want to talk about it?' Maria asks me, her warm brown eyes full of compassion.

'I don't really know what to say,' I mumble. 'I never thought I'd see him again.'

'It must have been a shock.'

'The oddest thing is that I saw him on the Tube escalator this morning.'

She looks incredulous. 'No way?'

'He was coming up, I was going down. I motioned for him to wait at the top, but he didn't.' I feel embarrassed by this revelation and dejectedly rest my chin on my hand.

'No wonder you're freaked out. Then I go and turn up, too. Talk about weird coincidences.'

I regard her across the table. 'I don't believe in coincidences.'

She smiles and delivers a quote in a regal-sounding voice: 'There's no such thing as coincidence. Just God's hand in a greater plan.'

I smile at her wryly. 'I don't believe in God, either.'

'What about Einstein?'

'What about him?'

'Well, as Albert Einstein himself said, "Coincidence is God's way of remaining anonymous."'

I grin at her. 'I still don't believe in God.'

She rolls her eyes, giving up on me. 'So what are you going to do now?'

'Go back to the office and act like I've never met him before.' The thought makes my heart clench painfully, and the emotion takes me by surprise. I barely knew him. It was one night. It shouldn't be too hard to move on from this. 'Where are you off to after this?'

'I'm meeting up with a friend. She's getting married this weekend and I'm doing her make-up.'

'Cool. Where do you live?'

'Golders Green.'

'That's a few stops up from Chalk Farm, right?'

'Yeah. Have you been?'

'No. I only arrived from Oz three weeks ago.'

'Aah. Well, it's a nice neighbourhood, and Hampstead is not far, where there are lots of lovely little shops, restaurants and cafés. Definitely worth a visit, and it's great hanging out on the Heath in the summer.'

I glance out of the window at the grey sky. 'Summer feels like a long way away.'

'It'll be here before you know it.' Pause. 'And then it'll be gone again, just as quickly.'

I snort with amusement. 'Well, I'm not here for the weather.'

She smiles across the table at me. 'How's your job?'

I can't help hesitating and her face falls.

'What? You're not happy?'

'I'm being such a misery guts today.' I sigh heavily. 'I'm not too sure about my new boss,' I admit. 'But maybe she just takes a bit of getting used to.'

'I didn't think much to the way she spoke to you at the shoot,' Maria empathises.

'No, neither did I,' I reply glumly. 'Oh well, I'll just have to get my job satisfaction from elsewhere.'

'Like where?'

'I like taking photographs,' I admit. 'I prefer being

behind a camera than trawling through pictures of paparazzi shots of celebrities' wobbly bits.'

'Have you done any freelance work?'

'A little. I've done portraits of friends' babies and that sort of thing, and I've done some birthdays and a few events.'

Her face lights up. 'What are you doing this weekend?'

'Er, nothing . . .'

'Rachel is going to kiss me!' she exclaims excitedly.

'Who's Rachel?'

'My flatmate. She's a wedding photographer and her assistant has just completely let her down for this wedding we're doing this weekend. Can you help out?' she asks quickly.

My head prickles with panic. A wedding? 'I'm not sure. I mean, I might not be good enough.'

'Rachel would handle all the tricky shots. You'd just be her back-up.'

'I don't know,' I say hesitantly. I believe in marriage as much as I believe in God.

'It pays well. Why don't you just come over and meet her? Bring a portfolio of your work?'

'I don't suppose it could hurt,' I respond. It's not like I couldn't use the extra money.

'Brilliant!' She beams from ear to ear and I wonder what the hell I've got myself into.

CHAPTER 3

The red-painted front door whooshes open and a pretty woman in her mid-thirties with brown eyes and blonde ringlets beams at me.

'Bronte!' she cries. 'Thank you so much for coming!'

'Hello!' I recognise her instantly. So *this* is Rachel . . . 'You did Polly and Grant's wedding,' I say, juggling my laptop under my arm as she ushers me past her into the cramped hall.

'That's right,' she replies, closing the door behind me. 'When I was a weekend warrior.'

'Weekend warrior?'

She smiles at my confused look. 'A part-time wedding photographer. I've *finally* left my accountancy job and gone full-time.'

'Wow, that's great.'

I remember her well. She was friendly and approachable and everyone felt relaxed around her. I still haven't seen Polly's wedding photos, but I'd put money on them being fantastic.

'Can I get you a drink? We've just opened a bottle of white,' she says.

'I'd love one.'

She leads me into a cool and cosy kitchen styled like a Fifties diner with pastel shades of blue, pink and cream. Maria leaps up from the kitchen table, leaving behind two large glasses of white wine and a stack of large black, square books.

'Hey!' she says happily. 'I'm so glad you could make it.' She gives me a friendly hug.

'Thanks,' I reply as a long-stemmed wine glass finds its way into my hand.

'Maria said you've just arrived from Australia?' Rachel says as we sit down.

'That's right. About three weeks ago.'

'And you've done some events?'

'A few,' I reply uneasily, feeling compelled to elaborate. 'No weddings, though, I'm afraid, although I have done some portraits for friends.'

'Any documentary-style photography?' she asks, worry lines appearing on her forehead.

'Um, well, I've taken quite a lot of pictures at friends' birthdays and I did an awards ceremony once.' Back when I worked at *Marbles*, my boss let me have a go at some boring industry awards.

'Have you got anything to show me?' she asks.

'I didn't bring my portfolio with me from Australia, but I've got a bunch of shots on my laptop.'

Maria smiles encouragingly while Rachel clicks through the images. I watch her nervously, feeling the pressure.

'How's it going at work?' Maria asks.

61

'It's okay.'

'Have you seen much of Alex?'

'Not really. He's been in and out of meetings.'

The glass-walled meeting room is right opposite my desk so I've had a perfect view of Alex steadfastly ignoring me since getting back to the office after the photoshoot yesterday.

I notice Rachel pausing on the occasional picture, taking time to study it. My nerves intensify and I take a large gulp of my wine. I love photography and I want her to be impressed.

'This is great,' she says finally, looking pleased.

'Really?'

'Perfect. Just the sort of thing I'm after.'

I exhale with relief. 'So what will you need me to do exactly?' I ask. 'I mean, I have a camera.' I invested in one when I started getting some freelance work. 'But I'm not sure my two lenses will be good enough.'

'No need to worry. My assistant, Sally, will be happy to lend you her kit.'

'Are you sure she won't mind?'

'Not at all.' Rachel tuts. 'She owes me, dropping me in it at the last minute like this.'

'Why did she pull out?'

'Her boyfriend wants to take her away for the weekend.'

Rachel can't be very happy about it. Maria gives me a pertinent look, answering my unspoken question.

'Where is the wedding?' I glance at Maria.

'It's near Cambridge, about an hour away, in a village a few miles from where I grew up,' she reveals. 'We can all travel up together in Rachel's car on Saturday morning.'

'Great.' I look down at the stack of books on the table and Rachel notices.

'These are some of my weddings.' She picks up the book on the top and hands it to me. The cover says 'Pippa and John' in swirly script on the front and there's a beautifully romantic shot of a groom dipping a bride backwards while planting a gentle kiss on her lips. Rachel talks me through her work, explaining how a wedding package tells the story of the wedding from the getting-ready part, sometimes all the way to the last dance. It's a far cry from the traditional leather-bound albums that you usually see of fifty formal, stiff-looking photographs of the wedding party in various staged poses. Rachel's books are packed full of natural photographs of relaxed and happy people enjoying what looks like the best day of their lives.

'I'm so glad you like it.' Rachel smiles warmly when I tell her how impressed I am. 'I learned everything I know from a wedding photographer called Lina Orsino. She and her partner Tom work as a team. Eventually I hope to have the same set-up – a partner, rather than an assistant – but one step at a time.'

'Sounds great,' I say. 'So what will you need from me?'

She leans forward and I sit up straighter. 'The

service will take place around the corner from the bride's parents' house, so you can come with Maria and me for the bride preparation shoot and hang out, see how I do things. Then, you'd need to go to the church ahead of time to take photographs of the little details. People rarely appreciate how much goes into a wedding, but we do, and we need to capture it for posterity. So take photos of the flowers, the candles, the church . . .'

My heart jumps, but I force myself to listen carefully, wishing I'd brought a pen and paper. Actually . . . 'Do you have a pen and paper?' I ask.

'Sure!' Rachel looks pleased as she gets up from the table and hunts them out. Maria gives me the thumbs-up and I shift self-consciously as Rachel sits back down.

For the next hour, I take notes as she fills me in. Eventually I say goodbye, realising the wine has done nothing to quash my steadily growing nerves. The fee she is paying me is substantially more than I earn in a day at work, which is fantastic, but this feels like such a big responsibility. I really hope I don't screw it up.

On Friday, I'm in the small kitchen adjoining the *Hebe* office making tea for Nicky and Helen, the deputy picture editor. Helen is a moody little cow and I keep catching her giving me dirty looks, but I don't know why.

I squeeze the tea out of Nicky's teabag and dump it in the bin. I miss Sydney. Thank goodness for

Bridget – I'd be lost without her to hang out with every night, watching crappy TV and dissecting our days over wine and microwave meals. We're going to the pub tonight after work for a few drinks – not many; I have to be up early. Tomorrow's going to be a long day.

'Hey,' I hear a voice say and turn around to see Russ coming into the kitchen.

'Hi,' I reply with a smile.

I like Russ, *Hebe*'s deputy features editor. He was cracking me up on Monday in the taxi back to the office, telling me all the judges' dodgy secrets. He's a bit of a gossip, I think, but good fun. He's tall at about six foot two, of medium build, with short ginger hair and a fair few freckles. He reminds me a little of Ed Sheeran – he's pretty cool.

'You coming to the pub tonight?' he asks as he moves past me to fill up the kettle.

'I can't. My flatmate wants me to go to the pub with her.' I pass him the teabags.

'Bring her along. The more the merrier,' he says casually.

I lean against the worktop, in no rush to get back to my icy colleagues. 'Who else is going?'

'Pete and Lisa from news, Esther, the features editor, will probably come along for one. Zach from production and Tim on the art desk usually come. I don't know about Alex.'

The sound of his name makes me tense up.

'What about Helen and Nicky?' I ask, trying to sound casual.

'Nah, not likely. Nicky never socialises with us minions, and Helen spends every spare second up her boyfriend's arse – not literally,' he adds, flashing me a cheeky grin.

I'm taken aback by his openness, but try not to show it.

'How are you finding things on your desk?'

'Er, it's okay,' I say weakly.

'Helen being a bitch?'

He gives me a knowing look, not fazed by my surprise. 'She went for your job,' he reveals.

'Oh?'

'Simon didn't think she had enough experience.' He pauses before adding, 'Although I'm not sure Nicky agreed . . .' He lets his voice trail off, stopping short of saying that Nicky wanted to promote Helen to picture editor instead of employing me.

'I see.' Now it all makes sense. I'm guessing Simon made the final call and that put my two most immediate colleagues' noses out of joint. No wonder I'm feeling the chill.

'Don't let them get to you,' Russ says with more compassion than I'd expect from an almost total stranger, and a bloke at that. 'Everyone knows how bitchy they are. Well, everyone except for Simon.' He rolls his eyes. 'Bitchiness is not on that guy's radar.'

I'm still surprised he's talking to me so openly, but I can't say it's not welcome after two weeks of feeling completely alone at work.

'Come to the pub,' he urges, picking up his mug.

'Alright, I'll see if Bridget fancies it.'

'Not Bridget Reed?' he checks as we walk out of the kitchen together.

'Yeah, the very same.'

'Oh, Bridget will definitely be up for the pub with us lot,' he says with a grin.

'You know her well?'

'Not that well, but I've seen her play enough drinking games at various work dos to know that she'll fit right in.'

I laugh as I pass him, completely forgetting that I'm right by Alex's desk until his brilliant blue eyes lock with mine over the top of his computer. I quickly avert my gaze.

'Cheers, Russ, see you later.' I break off to go to my desk.

Russ is right of course: Bridget is not about to turn down a chance to be sociable.

Next week's issue of *Hebe* has been put to bed by five p.m. so I join the crowd pulling on their coats and mingling by the door. Alex's seat is empty – he's over by Simon's desk, signing off the last of the page proofs. Helen and Nicky walk by together, completely ignoring the rest of us as they talk.

'Have a nice weekend!' Russ calls after them jovially and they both start with surprise.

'You too,' Nicky calls back uncomfortably.

Helen gives Nicky a look as she pushes the button for the lift. They both stand there in silence until the lift arrives.

I catch Russ's eye. 'Miserable cows,' he says under his breath, flashing me a grin. I try to keep a straight face. 'Bridget meeting us there?' he checks with me.

'Yeah, they're still going to press.'

Bridget is freelancing at monthly travel magazine *Let's Go!* this week.

'Bridget Reed?' Lisa, the news editor, asks, having overheard.

'The very same,' I reply with a smile. Does *everyone* know Bridget?

'There go my plans to have an easy one,' she mutters.

'I'm definitely having an easy one,' I say firmly.

'Good luck with that,' Russ says wryly. 'Tim, are you coming or what?' he snaps suddenly.

Tim, the art editor, is hovering over his computer.

'Yep,' he replies shortly, glancing up at Russ. He's rocking the geek chic look, with black-rimmed glasses and shaggy dark hair. 'Done,' he murmurs, grabbing the coat hanging over the back of his chair. I glance at Alex in time to see him turn away from Simon, rustling A3-sized pages in his hands.

'You coming for a drink?' Tim calls to him.

'Erm . . .' he checks his watch. 'Where are you going?' His eyes flit towards mine.

'Just to the pub across the road,' Tim says.

'I might meet you over there.' My heart jumps and then plummets. I try to convince myself that I don't care either way.

I fail spectacularly in my efforts, spending the next twenty minutes at the pub glancing at the door in case Alex walks in. I'm curious to see him in a social situation again – this week at work has been strange.

'Hey, guys!' Bridget calls cheerfully as she arrives. 'Who's up for a drinking game?'

Everyone groans theatrically.

'Bronte?' she asks teasingly. 'You want a shot?'

'Don't even think about it,' I warn. 'I'm fine with beer. I have to get up early tomorrow.'

'What are you doing?' Lisa, who's a petite redhead, asks with interest, as Bridget gathers orders from the rest of the table and heads off to the bar.

'I'm going to a wedding.'

'Nice!' she says.

'Whose?' Esther, the features editor, asks, over-hearing. She's striking and extremely tall at almost six foot, with shoulder-length dark brown hair.

'I have no idea.' I smile at the look on her and Lisa's faces before explaining. 'I'm assisting the wedding photographer.'

'Wow. Have you done a lot of weddings?' Lisa asks.

'No, this is my first.'

'How exciting!' Esther nudges Pete. 'You should get Bronte to do your wedding in July.'

'Steady on.' I hold my palms up. 'I might not be any good at it. I'm absolutely shitting myself at the moment,' I admit, making everyone laugh.

Bridget comes back over with our drinks, plonking a beer in front of me.

I'm sure she'll be trying to get me to do shots before the night is out. I *will* resist!

'Hey, here's Alex,' Tim says. I stopped watching the door once Bridget arrived.

'Hi,' he says, dropping his bag loudly beside the table. He freezes and I glance up at him to see that he's noticed Bridget.

'Howdy. I'm Bridget,' she says smoothly, holding her hand out to him. 'Who are you?'

'Alex,' he replies with a slight frown as he hesitantly shakes her hand. 'Can I get anyone a drink?'

No one needs one so he heads to the bar. I give Bridget a WTF look over the table and she suppresses a grin. Alex seems to have recovered by the time he joins our table, pulling up a seat between Lisa and Tim. I can't see his face very well from here, which suits me just fine.

'How's your first week been?' Lisa asks him.

'Good. Just settling in, seeing how everything works,' he replies in that warm, deep voice of his. Unfortunately I can hear him very well and I let out a small sigh at the sound. Why has he put this distance between us? Fine if he doesn't like me. Cool if he's seeing someone else. But can't we be friends? Why is he being so standoffish?

'What are you up to this weekend?' Lisa asks, and I realise her question is directed at him. I wonder if her job on the newsdesk helps her excel at small talk.

'Er, just hanging out with my girlfriend,' he replies.

A dark feeling washes over me. Not that I didn't have my suspicions.

'Well, fiancée,' he clarifies.

The dark feeling violently intensifies.

'How lovely! When are you getting married?' Esther asks warmly.

'December,' Alex reveals, as I pick up my beer bottle and take a swig. I have to force myself to swallow. I can feel Bridget's eyes on me, but I keep mine trained on the table.

'When did you get engaged?' Lisa presses on while I inwardly cringe. Do we have to hear the gushy details?

'Couple of months ago,' he says, shifting in his seat. He doesn't want to talk about this, either. Maybe it's because I'm here; maybe it's because he's quite a private person. I got that impression when we met, but really, I don't know him at all. I'm a fool to think that I did.

'Let's play a drinking game!' Bridget erupts and everyone groans again. 'Come on, you *Hebe*s are so boring!' She shoves against Russ and he moves aside to let her out.

'Bronte, come help me carry the shots.'

'I am not doing shots,' I reiterate.

'Yeah, yeah, whatever. Come and help me anyway.'

I cast my eyes wearily at the ceiling, but silently thank her for the distraction.

*　　*　　*

71

The next morning, I'm up and out of bed early. I have a headache, despite my attempts to remain sober, but it's not too bad. Bridget, however, is decidedly worse for wear.

'Hey,' I whisper, poking my head around her door.

A strangled moan comes from the bed.

'I brought you pills,' I tell her with a smirk.

She gingerly sits up in bed and reaches for the water, glugging some down with the headache tablets. 'Why, oh why did you let me drink those shots?'

'*What?*' It's an outrage!

She purses her lips. 'I meant to tell you, there was a message on the landline from your mum.'

'What did she say?' I ask warily.

'She said she was just touching base with you. Wanted to say hello.'

Nothing important, then.

'Have a good day,' she says. 'Good luck with it.'

Anxiety surges through me and then the door buzzer goes and Bridget clamps her hands to her head. 'Shut them up!'

'I will.' I laugh. 'I'll see you in the morning.'

'Good luck.'

'Thanks.' I'm going to need it.

CHAPTER 4

'How are you feeling?' Maria asks the bride, Suzie, as she applies foundation to her pale complexion.

'Nervous,' Suzie admits.

I'd be nervous, too, if I was about to legally bind myself to another person for the rest of my life. Mind you, there's always divorce if it doesn't work out.

'That's a good sign,' Maria says encouragingly. 'I think nerves help you to feel more connected to the day.'

Is that what she reckons? Well, I'm nervous as hell. And I'm not sure I want to feel connected to this particular day.

'You're looking radiant,' Rachel says gently, taking a photograph.

I'm sitting in the corner, just watching and trying to keep out of the way. Rachel moves over to the wedding dress, which is hanging behind the door. 'Can you adjust the curtains to soften the light?' she asks me.

I get up and close the net curtains a little, as Rachel moves in to photograph lots of tiny, delicate lace flowers across the bodice. I'm looking forward to seeing how Suzie looks with it on.

I watch as Rachel takes some shots of the bride's shoes and her gran's wedding ring sewn into her garter. Suzie's mother comes in with cups of tea for us all. The atmosphere is very relaxed, which is not what I was expecting.

The doorbell rings to announce the arrival of Suzie's only bridesmaid and the energy levels ramp up a notch. She's a sweet, friendly girl, but over the course of a short space of time, the chilled atmosphere becomes charged with electricity as we draw closer to the big event.

'Time for you to go,' Rachel says to me quietly with a smile as Maria puts the finishing touches to the bride's make-up.

My nerves return as she sees me to the door.

'So don't forget to get the details,' she says. 'The flowers, the candles, the organ . . .'

A little dart of fear zips through me.

'The Order of Service, the stained-glass windows . . .' she continues.

I recover quickly and shake my head. 'I won't forget.'

'Try to get the groom arriving if he's not already there, and as many of the other guests as you can. Don't specifically ask guests to pose for shots, but do take any that they ask you to.'

'I remember,' I say, nodding quickly now.

'And do your best to get his reaction,' she urges solemnly.

'I will,' I promise.

'Just do your best,' she says again, this time with a reassuring squeeze of my arm. I sense she's as nervous about my abilities as I am.

The church is a mere three-minute walk from Suzie's parents' house along a pavement slick with dew. There was a frost when we arrived this morning, but it's burning off now in the late March sunshine. The blue sky is streaked with wispy white cloud. It's been overcast and freezing this week. Could Suzie and Mike be the luckiest bride and groom on the planet? I breathe in the crisp spring air and listen to the sound of birdsong coming from the nearby trees. I pass a tiny chocolate-box thatched cottage behind a low hedge lined with bright yellow daffodils and impulsively start to click off some shots. This is such a pretty, picture-postcard old English village. I round the corner and the grey-slated church spire comes into view, gleaming in the sunlight.

I move out of the light and into the shadow of the stone church, walking with trepidation along the winding asphalt path to the porch. I take a deep breath and try to calm my jitters.

Get it together, Bronte. Get it together. I stop on the path and close my eyes, bracing myself.

'Hello!' a cheerful voice says. My eyes shoot open and I see a well-groomed usher waiting in the porch, holding a stack of sheets.

'Hi,' I reply quickly.

'Bride or groom?' he asks brightly.

'Photographer,' I tell him and he smiles.

'Great.'

I force myself to smile back as I pass by him into the church. It's the first time I've been inside one for years – Polly and Grant got married in a register office. I inhale the cold, damp air in short, sharp breaths. The musty smell is making me feel light-headed. How can churches smell so similar, even when they're oceans apart?

It's okay. It's okay. I look around. The church is vast and chilly, with a grey stone floor, cream limestone walls and enormous, arched, stained-glass windows.

There are already a dozen or so guests seated in the pews, talking quietly amongst themselves in hushed and reverent tones.

My dad used to say churches are like libraries. But he was wrong. They're nothing alike. I like being in libraries.

Rachel has already met the vicar, but she asked me to introduce myself. I feel a surge of relief when I see that she's a woman. She welcomes me warmly.

'I'll be staying down the back,' I promise her, relaxing slightly. 'I won't get in your way.'

Rachel told me that vicars tend to like her because she doesn't use a flash and disrupt the service, nor does she run all over the place like a lunatic. Because there are two of us, she can remain static up by the pulpit.

The weight of responsibility helps me to focus. I can do this. I can.

The groom is not yet here so I get busy capturing the details. The camera sounds loud to my ears at first, and I wince with every click, but it gets easier after a few shots. I capture the pretty flower arrangements – white daffodils, hyacinths and roses with acid green guelder-roses – suspended from the ends of the pews and the sunlight streaming in through the stained-glass windows. I force myself into the chancel and snap some shots of the larger flower displays and the gleaming silver candlesticks on the altar table. My heart is in my throat as I quickly click off a few shots of the organ with its polished golden pipes and all-too-familiar layers of black and cream-coloured keys. Then the groom arrives so I step down from the chancel into the nave, exhaling the breath I didn't realise I was holding.

Mike is in his mid-twenties like Suzie and Maria, and he's tall and slim with short brown hair. Maria told me that Suzie met Mike at university and next week they're setting off to go travelling for a year. This wedding is also effectively their leaving party and our photographs will be a strong link to home for them over the next twelve months. It's even more important that we do them justice.

I focus my attention on Mike and get a lovely shot of him sharing a moment with his mum, which ends with her kissing him on his cheek and laughingly wiping away the lipstick mark. I sheepishly step forward to introduce myself and wish him luck.

The church is filling up, but the hushed quality remains and when Suzie's mother appears, I know that the bride must be on her way. I've set up Rachel's monopod – a tripod with one leg – out of view behind the pulpit, like she asked me to. She shoots with minimal but top-notch equipment. She explained that her 85 mm F1.2 – the Holy Grail of lenses – lets in so much natural light that she doesn't even need to use a flash until the first dance, and only then so she can freeze the action on the dance floor.

I take some shots of Suzie's mother and then go to wait in the porch. I take a calming deep breath. This is okay. I'm doing okay.

After a few minutes, Rachel comes into view. Suzie, her father and her bridesmaid, who's wearing a dusky-rose-coloured, vintage-style lace dress, have walked here from Suzie's parents' house and I watch with a smile as Rachel snaps away without losing her footing as she moves backwards.

Suzie looks jaw-droppingly beautiful. Maria has curled her golden-blonde hair into perfectly wavy curls and left it down. A delicate lace, flapper-girl-style headpiece takes the place of a traditional veil, with a large, white silk flower on the left-hand side. Her long, slim-fitting skirt is made of white lace, and as I noticed before, dozens of small lace flowers have been sewn all over the strapless bodice.

Rachel turns and comes towards me over the wet grass.

'Good luck!' she whispers loudly. 'Don't forget

to get his reaction!' she stresses again as she hurries past me into the church.

'I won't,' I promise, but she's already gone.

I hold my camera up to my face and look through the viewfinder as Suzie and her entourage come towards me. I snap away as I back into the church to the sound of the organ playing.

A cold flush washes over me. The music fills up my head and reverberates through my body and for a moment I feel like I'm going to faint.

I force myself to focus. Hurrying over to the other side of the church, I try to block out the haunting music as I look for Mike at the front. Rachel stressed to me that this is my most important shot of the day. Once Suzie has entered the church, my one and only goal is to get Mike's reaction to seeing his bride. Rachel says that this shot of the groom – and her own corresponding shot taken from the front of the bride locking eyes with the man she's about to commit to spending the rest of her life with – is the one many couples have said they treasure the most. And now it's up to me to get my half of it.

The organist starts to play the rousing strains of Wagner's 'The Bridal March' and I steel myself to concentrate. I zoom in on Mike up at the front as he slowly turns around to watch his bride come down the aisle. Then someone lifts an iPad over their head and completely obscures my vision. Shit! The bridesmaid passes by and I dart to my left to find an unobstructed view of the groom. Out of the corner of my eye I see a white blur move past. I click away as Mike's expression softens, his eyes fill with tears and I know that I've got it: I've done my bit. Happiness bursts inside me.

I wouldn't say I actually enjoy myself after that, but it does get easier and it helps that I have a job to do. I take some beautiful long shots of the bride and groom at the altar, framed by the green and white flowers hanging from the end of every second pew. I stop cringing at the sound of my shutter, and zoom in to get the occasional candid shot of guests dabbing their eyes and a couple of cheeky little children peering over their parents' shoulders at me. Mostly I keep out of the way and let Rachel do her bit from the front.

All too soon, it's my turn to take centre stage again. I need to get the bride and groom coming down the aisle as man and wife, and I feel like I can hear my heart pounding over the sound of the 'Wedding March' as Mike and Suzie head happily in my direction, stopping to be congratulated by their friends and family as they go. Soon they're past the last pew and I snap away as I back out of the heavy wooden doors into glorious daylight and watch them swing shut. Then Suzie and Mike burst through and Mike punches the air, yelling, 'YES!'

As he kisses her right in front of me, I try to contain my laughter and capture every joyous millisecond.

The other guests quickly follow, and then Rachel is with me.

'Did you get it?' she asks.

I assume she's referring to the groom's reaction and I nod happily, light-headed with blissful liberation. I did it. I got through it.

She laughs, misreading my reaction. 'Did you have fun?'

'Yes.' Tears prick my eyes. In hindsight, I think I almost did.

She pats my arm. 'I'm so pleased to hear it. But it's not over yet,' she reminds me with amusement.

The hard part is.

The reception is being held at a fancy pub just up the road, so I go on ahead while Rachel covers the shoot outside the church. There's a buzz in the air as the excited, friendly staff put the final touches to the table settings and fill tall flutes with champagne. I stand for a moment and look around, taking everything in. The pub has a shabby chic vintage feel to it, with stripped floorboards, open log fires, flocked wallpaper and paintings hanging from the walls. The tables are covered with white lace tablecloths and are centred with white and green flower displays in rustic white and silver painted pots. One staff member is going around lighting tealights and putting them in silvery green glass candle holders dotted around the tables. There's a vintage birdcage on a table near the door for people to post wedding cards through, and beside it are three cakes on individual cut-glass cake stands. They vary in height and colour and have thick ruffle-style piped icing in pink, pale yellow and white. Sprays of tiny white flowers adorn them.

The whole effect is stunning.

After I've taken enough shots of the inside details, I move outside to the garden where a twenty-metre white marquee has been erected on the grass. A small bar has been set up inside and a member of staff is putting down a silver tray full of wine glasses brimming with a peachy-coloured cocktail. I could do with one of those. I take some photos, keeping my eye on the doors, until finally I see the wedding party start to arrive.

The rest of the waiting staff have gathered in the marquee, and we all clap when Suzie and Mike come towards us. Suzie blushes adorably and takes two flutes of champagne.

'Cheers!' She and Mike chink glasses and she giggles while he smiles lovingly at her.

I continue taking candid camera shots while cocktails and canapés are served until I feel a tug on my arm. I look down to see Suzie's gran's watery blue eyes peering up at me from under her purple hat.

'Got any good ones?' she asks.

'Absolutely.' I smile at her. 'They're gorgeous, aren't they?'

She nods with satisfaction and I take a picture of her. She bats my arm away and I laugh. Rachel interrupts.

'Time to do the group shots.' She hands me a piece of paper with the various group shots requested by the bride and groom: his family, her family, wedding party, friends. It's my job to gather everyone together, which is tricky and tiring, but various friends and relatives help me hunt out the guests we need.

Afterwards we need to take Suzie and Mike for a private shoot – no hangers-on allowed. Rachel needs the bride and groom's full attention and wants them to be as relaxed as possible without a host of friends and family looking on. So we steal them away to the sunny green field behind the pub and shoot some atmospheric pictures of them walking hand in hand through the long grass. They hug and kiss like pros without complaining. Job done.

'We can have a break before the speeches,' Rachel tells me, leading me inside the pub. The guests are getting seated ready for the wedding breakfast to start, and I flash a grin at Maria as we pass by her table. She's here as a guest now, sitting with a group of young people. I eye her glass of champagne with envy.

A moment later, we're in a small office beside the kitchen and Rachel is putting a glass of fizz in my hand.

'Really?' I ask with surprise. I didn't think we'd be allowed to drink on the job.

'Of course. One's not going to kill us. And you totally deserve this.'

'Aw, thanks.' We chink glasses and I take a sip, but her face is serious.

'Honestly, I don't know what I would have done

without you today.' She perches her bum against the desk.

'You haven't seen my pictures yet,' I joke. 'I hope they're okay,' I add nervously.

'You're welcome to come over to mine tomorrow and help me process them if you like?'

'I'd love to!' And I genuinely would. I'm dying to see the fruits of our labours. I thought I'd have to wait weeks, like the bride and groom.

A waitress appears at the door with two plates. 'Hungry?' she asks.

'Starving,' Rachel replies, moving from the desk so the waitress can put the plates down.

'Enjoy,' she says brightly. We call our thanks after her as she leaves the room.

I look down at the smoked salmon starter. It's part of our contract that we get fed, but I wasn't expecting wedding food.

'Yum.'

The break is a welcome one, but it will be over far too quickly. I've had to be friendly and professional all day, and now I find I can't stop yawning.

'The speeches are next,' Rachel says, giggling at me as I don't even bother trying to stifle what must be about my twentieth yawn. 'They should perk you up. This lot seem like a good bunch, so I suspect their speeches will be half decent. I've heard some rubbish ones, I can tell you.' I smile and she continues. 'Then it's cut-the-cake time – a bit boring, but a box we need to tick – and after that, the first dance. You can let your hair down and have a few

84

drinks with Maria once that's over. I'll cover the last dance, and drive us home. It's been a long day.'

'I don't know how you do it and still seem so perky,' I admit.

'Lots of practice,' she replies with a grin. 'And I bloody love weddings. I think you're either a wedding photographer, or a photographer who does weddings. Some people might not think it's very cool to be a wedding photographer, but I think it's much nicer to have someone who genuinely loves weddings to photograph their big day.'

I have to agree with her, even if I fail on that front.

She beams at me and tucks into her starter.

I'm on a strange high in the car on the way back to London, and it has nothing to do with the few drinks I've had.

'That was such a great day, thank you so much for asking me to help out,' I say. Maria is staying at her parents' house tonight, so it's just the two of us.

'I'm so pleased you enjoyed yourself,' Rachel says.

'If Sally ever lets you down again, please give me a shout. I'd love to help out.' I seem to have forgotten how hard I found it initially.

'That's really good to know,' she replies with a smile.

I look out of the window and yawn loudly. I'm asleep before we reach Chalk Farm.

CHAPTER 5

I'm still yawning on Monday morning when I go into the kitchen to make tea for my moody picture desk colleagues and myself. I spent most of yesterday at Rachel's place going through the photographs and helping her to process them. I was very curious to see mine. Rachel seemed happy with how I did, considering it was my first wedding. There were certainly some good shots there, but I made my fair share of mistakes, too. Hopefully I'll learn from them. She put a teaser shot of Suzie and Mike – one of them walking hand-in-hand across the green field – onto the internet to keep everyone going. Rachel's website is linked to Facebook and already guests have been commenting on it, and Suzie herself has left a lovely message thanking us for our hard work. Other guests will no doubt start to post their own photos today, but at least there will be one professional shot to counterbalance the Instagram ones, which inevitably will feature half-closed eyes and unflattering angles.

The door swings open and I cast a smile over my shoulder, expecting to see Russ, who was making a move to follow me when I walked past. My stomach contracts when I see that the person who's joining me instead is Alex. He looks on edge at the sight of me.

'Hi,' I say weakly.

'Hey,' he replies and I wonder for a moment if he might turn around and go back to his desk, but he doesn't.

'How was your weekend?' I ask in an attempt to make small talk. I could really do with some of Lisa's skills.

'Good,' he says, reaching into the cupboard for a couple of mugs. 'Yours?'

'Great.' The kettle boils and I fill up my three mugs then refill it with water, flicking it back on again.

'Thanks,' he says, leaning back against the worktop and looking awkward. 'What did you get up to?'

'I had a—'

He cuts me off. 'Oh, you had a wedding, didn't you?'

'That's right,' I reply.

'How was it?'

'Amazing.' I can't help beaming.

'I thought you didn't like weddings?'

How does he know that? Oh! I ranted about it when we first met! I try not to show my surprise that he remembers.

'I don't. But I love taking photos.'

'Really?' He looks interested. 'Me too.' We have

a common hobby? 'What camera have you got?' he asks.

'It's a Canon 60d, but I used Rachel's assistant's kit on the weekend and she's got a better model. What about you?'

'I've just bought a Nikon d7000.'

I stare at him blankly.

He smirks. 'It's not pro-level, but it's fine for me.'

The kettle boils, and as he moves past me in the cramped space, I unwittingly breathe in his aftershave. I'm hit with a memory of him kissing my neck in bed.

I turn away and concentrate on fishing the teabags out of my mugs.

'So how did it go?' he asks a short while later, leaning back against the counter again and regarding me directly while his tea brews.

'Pretty well, I think.' Boy, his eyes are blue. 'But I did make some mistakes.'

He smiles warmly. 'What like?'

'I messed up the focus on a few occasions. One time I thought I was focusing on the groom, but I ended up getting his aunt in the foreground. The shot of her would have been great, but she was blinking, so Rachel said she might be able to steal her eyes from another shot and Photoshop them in.'

He laughs and my insides go all jittery. 'No way? Does she do that sort of thing?'

'All the time.'

'Well, that doesn't sound too bad,' he says

commiseratively, passing me the milk and sugar and turning back to his own tea.

'I struggled with camera shake, too,' I add, reluctant to draw a line under the conversation. 'Especially towards the end of the night.'

He glances at me. 'Was the room quite dark?'

'Pretty dark, yeah.'

'No tripod?'

'Rachel has a monopod. But no, I didn't use it and I probably should have.'

'Rachel's the wedding photographer?' he asks.

'Yes. She's lovely.'

'I'm curious to see these shots now.' His smile makes my heart flutter. He is so gorgeous . . .

I inwardly slap myself around the face. 'What about you? What did you get up to at the weekend?'

'Er, it was my girlfriend's dad's birthday so we went out for a pub lunch.'

He sounds uncomfortable talking about his fiancée, and I'm not sure I want to hear about her either, but I've got to get over that if we're going to be working together. I don't want it to be awkward.

'Congratulations on your engagement, by the way,' I force myself to say.

A flicker of some emotion passes over his face, but I can't decipher it. 'Thanks.'

'What's your fiancée's name?'

'Zara.'

'Aah.' He's just confirmed that he's marrying the girl he was on a break from when we met.

He gives me a small, knowing smile which makes me feel a little funny inside, and then Russ bursts into the kitchen, startling us both.

'Wassup!' he shouts, clapping me on my back. 'How was the wedding?'

'Great, mate,' I tell him brightly, finding his energy endearing.

'You great big galah,' Russ teases at the sound of my Aussie-ism.

'That's the worst Australian accent I've ever heard.' I shove his arm.

'Oof!' he cries, going overboard. 'You lot are doing Lisa's nut in today.'

'What do you mean, us lot?'

'You Australians. You and your bloody time differences. Lisa got in this morning to find a message from some tourist Down Under saying that he spotted Joseph Strike with his bird today, hugging a frigging koala with a proper big baby bump. If he's got pictures, it could be next week's cover story, but she can't get hold of him because he called from work and now he's already buggered off home, lazy bastard.'

I shake my head with confusion. 'Who had the baby bump? Joseph Strike's girlfriend?' Actually, she's technically his fiancée, and Joseph Strike is a British actor who's huge in Hollywood.

'No, the koala,' he says, adding, 'Dur! Of course I mean the girlfriend.'

I ignore him. 'Where was the photograph taken?'

'Some conservation park.'

'Do you know which one?'

He frowns. 'I think he said Adelaide.'

My eyes light up. 'My friend works at a conservation park in the Adelaide Hills. I wonder if it's the same one? Want me to call her and ask her if she saw anything?'

'Christ, yes! Do it!'

'Catch you later,' I say to Alex.

'Sure,' he replies.

Russ follows me back into the office like an eager puppy dog and for a moment I think he's going to hang over my desk while I make the call, so I quickly put a stop to that.

'I'll come and speak to you in a bit,' I promise, forcing him to reluctantly walk away.

I first met Lily when she covered for me at *Marbles* magazine in Sydney, the place I worked at before *Hebe Australia*. We became friends when she left Sydney to go to South Australia with her boyfriend, turning down the chance to apply for my editorial assistant job when I was moved over to the picture desk. My parents live in a small beach town about an hour and a half south of Adelaide, so we hook up when I go home to visit. She's a budding wildlife photographer, and I've used some of her photos in *Marbles* in the past, but she also works with her husband Ben at a conservation park in the Adelaide Hills.

'Hello?' A male voice answers in a warm, Aussie accent.

'Ben?' I ask. 'It's Bronte.'

'No way? *Lily!*' he calls, covering the receiver. '*It's Bronte!*'

'*No shit?*' I hear my friend exclaim in the background.

'She was just about to email you,' Ben speaks into the receiver, sounding amused. There's a scuffle and then Lily comes on the line.

'Joseph Strike,' she says. 'Am I right?'

'Yes, you freaking are. Did you see him?' I ask eagerly, as Nicky glares at me from beside Helen on the other side of the desk. She probably thinks I'm making a personal call.

'I got pictures.'

'No!' I gasp. 'Does she have a baby bump?'

'Clear as day,' she tells me. 'I got a brilliant one of him with his hand on her tummy.'

'Wow! Can we buy them from you?' Helen also glances up, eyeing me over the top of her computer.

'Ooh, I don't know . . . How much do you think they're worth?' she asks cheekily.

I laugh. 'Who would have thought you'd become a pap.'

Nicky is still watching me with annoyance. I've piqued her curiosity, and I suspect she hates being kept out of the loop.

'I did ask their permission first,' Lily reveals.

'Did you?' I'm amazed she had the nerve. Joseph Strike is such a big star.

'Yeah. His chick and I compared bumps.'

'What?' I exclaim. 'Are you telling me you're pregnant?'

'Yes.' She laughs gleefully. 'Four months.'

'Oh, that is so lovely!' My pitch goes up an octave. 'I'm so excited for you! Is Ben pleased?'

'Ridiculously.' I can tell how happy she is and want to talk more about it, but Nicky is shooting me daggers. 'Anyway, Joseph didn't mind having his picture taken at all. They're such a lovely couple,' she gushes. 'So, do you want to see them?'

'Yes, please. Have you shown them to anyone else?'

'Don't be daft. You were the first person I thought of.'

'Aw. I really, really appreciate this.'

'My pleasure. Give me your new email address and I'll send 'em over.'

I do, promising I'll call her once I've spoken to my boss.

'What was all that about?' Nicky asks irritably as soon as I hang up.

'What did she say?' Russ interrupts. He must've been watching me like a hawk to get across the office this quickly.

I answer his question first.

'She's got pictures,' I reply with excitement. 'She's sending them over.'

'You're a genius!' He shakes my shoulder.

'Who's got pictures of what?' Nicky interrupts, scowling.

'Bronte's friend in Australia has pictures of Joseph Strike's fiancée's baby bump.'

'She's pregnant?' she asks with surprise.

'Apparently so.' Russ gleefully shakes my shoulder again and pulls up a spare seat from the production desk behind me. He nods at my computer. 'Have they come in yet?'

I click on my inbox to check. Nicky gets up and comes around to my side of the desk. Helen follows, and then Lisa appears.

The name Lily Whiting pops up in my inbox. I nervously click on the link.

'Oh my God!'

'That's amazing . . .'

'Wow.'

'Awesome.'

My colleagues coo and relief surges through me as I elatedly scroll through the five pictures Lily has sent. The first could absolutely make the cover: Joseph Strike in shorts and a slim-fitting cream T-shirt which reveals the definition of his perfect abs, smiling down at his fiancée as he places his hand on her unmistakeable baby bump. The last picture is of Joseph holding a koala and by the time I get to it, half of the women in the office have gone gooey at the knees. About a dozen people are crowded around my desk. I feel a little like a celebrity myself.

'Who's the hottie he's with?' Esther asks, leaning in to get a closer look.

'That's Ben,' I tell her. And she's right: Ben is hot. Tall, blond and sexy, even in his khaki conservation park uniform.

Simon, the editor, eventually breaks up the

gathering. 'Okay, everyone back to work.' My colleagues reluctantly head off. 'Bronte, can I have a word?'

I'm nervous as Simon leads me into the back office, but he just wants to know everything about Lily and his chances of securing an exclusive. He's delighted to discover that she used to work at *Marbles* under his friend Jonathan's leadership.

'Hopefully she'll show some loyalty,' he murmurs. I don't point out that I think she's more likely to show loyalty to me than to a magazine. He means no harm by the comment.

'Can you call her back now and offer her a price?' he asks.

'Sure.'

We agree a figure and he pushes the phone across the desk to me. I realise he wants me to ring her right now, in front of him, to secure the deal. Pressure!

'I need to grab her number from my mobile,' I say, hesitantly getting up from the table.

I feel Nicky and Helen's eyes on me as I come out of the office.

'What's going on?' Nicky asks.

'I'm just going to call Lily and try to secure an exclusive.'

'Oh, right,' she says a little snootily and I can't help but feel a thrill at getting one over her. I imagine she's used to having all the limelight, but she's been nothing but a cow to me since I started.

Alex grins at me as I return to my desk. It warms

my heart. Maybe there's hope for us as friends after all. I grab my phone and return to the back office where Simon is impatiently tapping his fingers on the desk. A few minutes later, we have our exclusive and Simon is more excited than I've ever seen him.

'I've got to go and tell Clare,' he says with a grin, referring to his boss, the publisher. 'We'll need to increase our print run.' He pats me on my back. 'Well done, Bronte. Absolutely fantastic.'

'Thanks.'

I'm bursting with pride as I come out of the room. Russ and Lisa jump up from their desks.

'Did you secure them?' Lisa asks quickly, worry etched across her forehead.

I nod. 'Yeah.'

'Woo-hoo!' Russ calls, clapping.

'Fantastic!' Lisa enthuses. 'We'd better see if we can buy the tourist's shot, too, pip the tabloids to the post.'

'I'll do that.' Nicky swiftly appears at my side. 'Lisa, can you get me his details? I'll call him from home tonight. I don't want to miss another day with the time difference.'

Russ furtively rolls his eyes at me, but I don't really mind Nicky cutting in. Whatever floats her boat.

By Thursday, Nicky has moved on from being defiant and defensive and has settled on looking deflated. She hasn't managed to get hold of the man – his phone keeps going to voicemail – and

Simon suspects one of the tabloids will be running the shots on Sunday. He doesn't seem too fazed. *Hebe* comes out on a Tuesday and he's confident we'll be able to ride the crest of the publicity wave. Our pictures will undoubtedly be stronger, because Lily is a professional photographer, and we'll have more of a story because she also relayed everything Joseph said to her. We can effectively sell the piece as an exclusive interview. Simon is expecting a huge uplift in sales.

Nicky's mood is not helped when Simon calls to me on Thursday afternoon. He's standing over Alex's computer with Clare at his side. 'Do you want to see the cover?' he asks me with an easy smile.

Alex leans back in his chair while I make my way over there, feeling Nicky's eyes boring into my back. I feel a little daunted by Clare. She's super-confident, straight-talking and has the respect of everyone in the company. She and Simon get on like a house on fire.

Alex has an image of the cover open on his computer screen. The shot of Joseph Strike tenderly touching Alice's baby bump takes pride of place. The bright pink magazine colours are striking, and the cover-line shouts out:

Joe speaks: 'I can't wait to be a dad!'

'What do you think?' Simon asks me.
'It looks great,' I reply.

'Well done, Bronte,' Clare says. 'I heard you're responsible for this.'

I try to fight off the blush, but it's no use. 'Thanks.' My voice comes out sounding croaky, and I notice the corners of Alex's lips turn up.

'Have you seen the article?' he asks me, diverting attention away from my embarrassment. He clicks on his mouse to bring up five more pages of a news article with the rest of the photographs.

'Fantastic,' I say, speaking of the piece in general. I'm not about to read the content with Clare and Simon standing behind me.

Simon smiles warmly. 'Well done again,' he says.

'No worries.' I back away and return to my desk, keeping my head down. I can feel Nicky's discontent oozing from her like poison.

Simon lets us leave early the following day.

'Coming to the pub, Bronte?' Russ calls across to me. It's Friday, so it's pretty much a given, even if I don't want a big one.

'Sure.'

'Have you got the skinny celebs feature sorted?' Nicky interrupts.

I waver. 'I've got most of them.'

'How many is *most* of them?' Her tone is as cold as ice.

'I've got five so far. The deadline isn't until Tuesday, right?' I double-check. What's the rush?

'Who knows what will come up on Monday,' she points out.

She's just being difficult. I'm confident I'll have all of the pictures ready by Tuesday, even if I have to work late on Monday night. And it's only for a feature, which has longer lead-times.

'I'll have them ready on time,' I say calmly, gathering my things. I'm not going to let her bully me into working late on a Friday when it's completely unnecessary.

'You'd better,' I hear her mutter as I walk over to the others waiting by the door.

'You coming?' Russ asks Alex.

'Yeah, just finishing up.' He smiles brightly at us as he grabs his coat.

'Bridget coming out tonight?' he asks me on our way across the road.

'I'm seeing her later. She worked from home this week,' I explain.

'You two going out for a big one?' he asks as he holds open the pub door and lets me pass through into the warmth.

'Nah. We're going to my friend Polly's place for dinner.'

'Drunken bride-to-be Polly?'

'Yeah,' I reply, casting him an inquisitive look.

He nods, letting the conversation drop as we reach the bar. We place our orders and then Lisa turns to me.

'Did I seriously hear Nicky asking you about those skinny celebrity pictures?' she asks me.

'Yep,' I say resignedly.

'What a stupid cow!' Russ exclaims. 'I don't know how you work with her.'

I make no comment. I'm beginning to wonder that myself.

'What's this?' Alex chips in, overhearing. 'Has she been giving you a hard time?'

'She's fine.' I shake my head. 'I can handle it.'

He lets it lie when the barman comes over to take our order.

'What's everyone up to this weekend?' Lisa asks.

'Nothing much,' I reply.

'No weddings?'

I laugh, half-heartedly. 'No. The other assistant is back on the job, now.'

That thought makes me feel strangely subdued.

I leave after an hour, taking the Underground to Polly and Grant's apartment in Borough Market, near London Bridge. Polly's waiting in her doorway when the lift opens, a glass of sparkling wine in her hand.

'Hey, you.' She grins, hugging me before handing over the glass.

'What a great place,' I enthuse, taking in the whitewashed floorboards and the large warehouse-style windows with a view of the river. The flat is fitted out with minimal furniture, but there's barely enough room to swing a cat, let alone house a toddler, so I gather they're not planning on having a baby any time soon.

'Bridget's just texted to say she's on her way

from London Bridge,' she says, directing me to the sofa.

'Oh, I must've just missed her. She'll be busting to get out after being cooped up at home all week.'

'How are things going with her?' Polly asks as she sits down beside me.

'Really well.' I grin. 'She's a blast.'

She smiles and nods, but her eyes look strangely dull. 'How are you?' I ask, a little thrown by her expression.

'I'm fine,' she says breezily, crossing her legs.

I was a bit taken aback when I saw her again a few weeks ago. She's put on all of the weight she'd lost for the wedding and is even larger than she was when we lived in Australia.

'How's Grant?' I ask.

'He's good. He's been really busy at work lately.' Her lips turn down.

'Oh no.' Are things not all rosy at home? 'Will that calm down soon?'

'I hope so.'

I spy a familiar-looking black book on her coffee table. 'Are these your wedding pics?' I ask excitedly.

She beams. 'Yeah.'

'Can I take a look?'

'Sure.'

I reach down and pick up the book, flicking through the pages.

'These are beautiful,' I say to Polly, who stares at the photos over my shoulder.

'I look so thin,' she says listlessly and I glance at her.

'You looked gorgeous then and you look gorgeous now.'

She seems flat. 'Grant says he hardly recognises me in those pictures.'

My face falls. I don't really know what to say. 'Had you lost weight when he proposed to you?' I ask carefully.

'No. I was as fat as I am now,' she replies bluntly.

'So you know that he loves you for the way you are. He proposed to *you*, Polly.' I point at her. 'Not the Polly in these pictures.'

Her eyes cloud over. 'I kind of wish he married me, too.' She indicates herself. 'Rather than *her*.' She nods at the book.

I smile sympathetically and make a mental note to pass on this advice to any future brides I come across. Don't lose weight just so you look good in your wedding photos – you might not recognise yourself later.

'I hope Polly's alright,' I say to Bridget on the way back to the station.

'She seemed a bit down,' Bridget agrees.

Grant arrived as we were finishing up our dessert, looking a little worse for wear. He called Polly soon after Bridget arrived to let her know that he was working late so not to wait for him, then he texted an hour later to say that he was going for a quick drink. A quick drink which turned into several, from the way he was slurring. Polly was not impressed, so we decided to leave them to it.

My phone rings just as we're walking into the station. I dig it out of my bag and frown when I see that it's Rachel.

'Hello?'

'Bronte! Thank flip you answered!'

'What's wrong?'

'What are you doing tomorrow?' She sounds breathless and panicked and my heart jumps.

'Nothing!' I say hastily. 'Why?'

'Sally isn't well and I've got a wedding to do in Buckinghamshire. Can you help out?'

My heart swells. 'I'd love to!'

CHAPTER 6

All hell is breaking loose. The murderous cries of a child who has been woken up from her nap pierce me to my very core. And I'm not the only one: Veronica, the poor bride, looks close to tears as her not-quite-two-year-old daughter Cassie clings to her and lets rip.

'Let me take her so you can finish getting ready,' Veronica's mum Mary says gently, but as she reaches down to the screaming ball of fury masquerading as a child, Cassie's screams reach new levels of hysteria and she clings onto whatever she can. A second later, Veronica's cries join the mix – Cassie has her fingers tangled in Veronica's hair.

'Mum, leave her!'

Mary lets go and Cassie buries her face in her mother's chest.

Rachel told me that Cassie was a happy, bright little thing the last time she was here, but today she woke up with a raging temperature and has been physically attached to Veronica all morning. Maria had to work around her, starting with Veronica's hair before moving on to her make-up.

Eventually, Veronica put Cassie down for a nap, but judging by the screaming now, that might have been a mistake.

I look out of the window to see that a taxi has arrived. 'That's probably for me,' I say to Rachel. 'I'll see you there.'

She nods, worriedly.

The wedding is taking place in a village in Buckinghamshire, near the River Thames. It's a wet and windy day and I arrive at the church just in time to see the arch of flowers fixed over the gate collapse.

Someone shouts as I run to pick it up, wincing at the cold wind and rain slashing my face. I hear the thudding of footsteps and a flash of black morning suit as one of the ushers reaches me.

'Shit!' he gasps as I struggle to hold up the arch with Sally's heavy kit bag strapped over my shoulder. 'Kev! Give us a hand!' he shouts towards the church. Another usher hurries towards us, shielding his dark hair from the rain. A couple of guests arrive handily equipped with large umbrellas, but we're wet through by the time we've re-attached the flowers and entered the church. It's then that I realise the first usher was actually the groom.

'Let me get you a towel,' I tell him, fighting off the heady sense of foreboding as I force myself to walk through another vast, cold and damp church to look for the vicar. I find him in the vestry, just off the chancel. I take a deep breath and try to steady my swirling nerves before knocking on his open door with a clammy fist.

'Excuse me,' I say shakily.

He looks up with annoyance. He has a shaved head and gauges in his ears and is wearing white ceremonial robes. He doesn't look like any vicar I've ever seen. It helps.

'I'm—' I have to clear my throat. 'I wonder if you have a towel? The groom has got himself a bit wet,' I explain apologetically, my voice wavering.

'Do I look like a towel dispenser?'

His tone takes me aback. 'I'm sorry,' I say, my hackles going up. 'It's just that the flower arch fell down and—'

'Who are you?' he interrupts haughtily, spying my kit bag.

'I'm the assistant photographer,' I reply.

'You'd better not be,' he humphs, getting to his feet. He's quite short, only a little taller than me, but I'm five foot seven. 'I don't allow photographers in my church.'

His comment throws me and for a moment I think he must be joking, but I soon realise from his expression that he's not.

'But I—'

'This service is about God. I won't have your lot detracting from what we're all here for.'

Panic sweeps through me. 'We won't get in your way, I promise.' Do Veronica and Rachel know about this?

106

'You're right,' he says, eyeing me coldly. 'You won't.'

'But—'

'You'll find some paper towels in the bathroom just outside the emergency exit on the west wing of the church,' he says, cutting me off.

I turn and leave, figuring I'd better sort out the groom before I attempt to tackle the vicar.

The vicar will not be moved. I explain that there are two of us so we won't disrupt the ceremony. I tell him that we never use flash inside the church. I ask if we can photograph the bride's entrance and the bride and groom's exit. I've never wanted to be inside a church so much in my life, but he says no to everything.

Finally I ask him if I can photograph the inside of the church and the bride's arrival. He sniffily agrees.

I take the groom, Matthew, aside and tell him. I managed to catch some fun shots earlier of him and his usher, drying themselves off. He was laughing then, but now he shakes his head miserably. 'Veronica will be devastated.' He thinks for a moment. 'Let me talk to him,' he says determinedly.

He stalks off and I watch him sadly, doubting that he'll have any luck. I get to work photo-graphing the church, the vicar's attitude helping to distract me. The chill from the air seeps straight through my skin and into my bones and I'm shivering by the time I finish.

A disheartened Matthew joins me in the porch. I manage to cheer him up a bit and take some good photos of him and the windswept guests arriving, laughing from underneath their umbrellas. A black and silver two-tone Bentley turns into the road while I'm there. Good timing: it's the bridal car. Anxiety sweeps through me as I run around to Rachel's door.

'The vicar said no photographs,' I whisper urgently.

Her face falls. 'None at all?' she checks with me.

'We can capture her entrance, but that's it until after the service.'

'Shit,' she mutters, her shoulders slumping. 'I asked Veronica to double-check with him but she didn't, obviously.'

Veronica looks weary but beautiful as she climbs out of the classic car under the shelter of the driver's large, black umbrella. She's wearing a long cream-coloured gown with three-quarter-length lace sleeves and lace skirt overlay. Her dark blonde hair is half tied back and curled into loose waves and she has pearl earrings. She's not wearing a veil and the dress has no train, coming to an inch above the ground. Her cream shoes peek out from beneath the hem.

'Let me break it to her,' Rachel whispers.

I nod and plaster a smile on my face as I look at Veronica.

'You look stunning,' I tell her. She returns my smile, but hers is shaky, too.

Mary lifts Cassie out of the other side of the car. The toddler is clutching a ratty pink blanket and sucking miserably on a blue dummy with a cartoon picture of a yellow duck on the front. Not the usual accessories for a flower girl. She whinges to be put down and wriggles out of her grandmother's grasp, running to her mother and clutching her leg. Veronica looks exhausted and I feel a wave of pity for her. Her pre-wedding experience has been a far cry from Suzie's. She's not a bride; she's a mother in a white dress.

I crouch down on the ground. 'You look like a fairy princess,' I tell Cassie, who regards me with misery. I grin and poke my tongue out at her, clicking off a couple of shots, just as she begins to smile. Hopefully her mother will also smile in the future when she sees these pictures, even if today has been anything but perfect.

My yawning starts the moment I'm buckled into the passenger seat of Rachel's car. She laughs at me as she starts the ignition.

'That was a tough one,' she says, pulling away from the kerb.

'It was great.' I smile sleepily, surprised at the truth of the statement.

'You enjoyed yourself?' she asks with genuine curiosity.

'Yeah, I did,' I reply. 'I think Veronica and Matthew had a good day in the end.' Even if I think marriage is pointless, they seem like a nice couple and they deserve to be happy. 'Okay, the stuff at the church was hard,' I qualify. 'That vicar was a nightmare.'

'Urgh, wasn't he?'

'I hope we don't come across another one like him again,' I say without thinking. Sally will be back for the next wedding so there's no 'we' about it. The thought makes my heart sink.

'Without a shadow of a doubt, we will,' Rachel replies, not appearing to notice my slip-up.

CHAPTER 7

'Good morning,' Alex's warm voice cuts into my thoughts first thing on Monday morning when I'm in the kitchen.

'Hi,' I reply. He was chatting to Tim when I walked past and I'm sure he must've seen me come this way.

'How was your weekend?' he asks cheerfully.

'Great. I went to another wedding,' I tell him with a smile, relieved to see that he's clearly comfortable around me now.

'Did you?' He looks confused. 'I thought that was a one-off?'

'It was supposed to be, but Rachel's assistant called in sick at the last minute, so I helped out.'

'That's cool. How was it?'

'Amazing. Well, actually, it was a total nightmare at first. The bride and groom have a toddler and she was sick, so that made things difficult, and then the vicar was a total arse and wouldn't let us take pictures of the service.'

'No way?'

'Yeah. Really mean. The bride was in tears. And it poured down and was so windy, everyone got soaked.'

'It does sound like a nightmare!' He leans back against the wall and folds his arms.

'It was, but it was amazing too. Rachel is just *so good* at what she does. She got this fantastic shot of the pair of them later, in the rain under an umbrella. So stylish.' I saw the teaser shot yesterday. It's beautiful.

He grins. 'How was camera shake?'

I smile. 'I think I'm getting a bit better.'

'And no need to borrow Auntie's eyes from another shot?' he asks teasingly.

I laugh and shake my head. 'I don't think so. Although, actually, I did shoot the bride and groom after the ceremony and in some pictures the flowers look like they're sprouting out of the bride's head. Rachel said she'll have to fix those ones in Photoshop.'

He looks amused and a familiar skittish sensation swamps my stomach. This is not good. And now my tea has stewed. 'Whoops.' I fish out the teabags. 'Nicky hates it strong.'

'Maybe she should make her own, then,' he says drily.

'Mmm.'

He flashes me a conspiratorial look, intensifying the edgy feelings.

'So what did you get up to?' I ask, trying to sound casual.

'Not a lot. Pottered around at home, went out with some mates for a few drinks on Saturday night.'

'Your girlfriend was away, right? I mean, fiancée,' I correct myself.

'Yeah, she was in New York for work.'

'What does she do?'

'She works in advertising,' he says in a monotone.

'Oh right. Cool.'

He shrugs. 'She likes it.'

'That's the important thing.'

Okay, so we're not entirely past the awkward stage. I make a move to pick up my mugs.

'What about you?' he asks. 'Do you reckon you'll be doing any more wedding photography?'

'I'd love the extra work. I could certainly do with the extra cash.' My lips turn down. 'But Rachel's assistant is back now. Maybe I'll see if I can hook up with another photographer.'

'That'd be good.' A thought seems to come to him. 'Zara and I still haven't sorted out a photographer for our wedding in December.'

He's not asking me to do it, is he? That would be taking this new-found familiarity a bit far.

'Do you really recommend Rachel, then?' he asks.

My face breaks into a smile. Phew. 'Yes, definitely. She's incredible. Do you want me to get you her contact details?'

He grins. 'That'd be great. Thanks.'

We walk back into the office together.

'Ah, the new issue is here,' he says as I put my mugs down on my desk.

He grabs a Stanley knife and slices through the plastic vacuum-packed wrapping, studying the front cover while I go back over to him and pick up a copy for myself.

'It looks great,' he says, glancing at me.

'Bronte! Can you bring one to me?' I hear Nicky call.

'And me!' Helen adds.

I do as they ask and then settle down to read the latest issue of *Hebe*. Drinking tea and reading the current issue is probably my favourite part of a Monday morning – we all do it.

'How are you getting on with those skinny celeb pictures?' Nicky cuts into my thoughts.

'Fine,' I reply, glancing up at her.

'I'm sending Helen on the *Dragons' Den* shoot this morning, so I'll need you to get on with the mark-up.'

The mark-up is one of those super-dull accounting jobs which involves trawling through every page of the magazine, marking down which picture came from which agency and how much each one cost. It's so we know our picture expenditure for each month and it's very, very boring, but it ensures we don't overpay anyone. It's usually the assistant's job, not the picture editor's, and it's by no means urgent. But judging by Nicky's face, it's not up for discussion.

I put down my magazine and get on with my work.

I'm lonely that following weekend. Rachel is doing a wedding with Sally, and Bridget has gone to a leaving party in Cambridgeshire with her friend Marty. She invited me to go with them, but I don't know the people who are leaving: a friend of hers who nearly died last autumn when she was hit by a car, and her American-Cuban boyfriend who's apparently keen to take her back to Key West where they met. I wouldn't have felt comfortable gate-crashing, even though Bridget said the boyfriend had to be seen to be believed. She really needs to get herself a man.

As for me, I haven't been with anyone since . . . . Well, I haven't had a boyfriend since Jason, but I haven't *been* with anyone since Alex.

He's been thoroughly pleasant to me this week and I'm starting to think we could be friends, even though my heart still hurts a little sometimes when I look at him. I'll get over it. He came for a quick drink on Friday night, but left early to go for dinner with Zara. I wonder what she's like.

I passed on Rachel's details and they're meeting up this week. I hope it works out for both of them. I thought a lot about Rachel on Saturday. Sally had better not be taking her job for granted.

'When are you meeting Rachel?' I ask Alex on Monday morning.

'Tomorrow lunchtime. She's coming into town.'

'Is it just you going?' I don't know why I asked that.

'No, Zara's coming to meet us.'

'Cool. Rachel always likes to meet the bride and groom together. Get ready to dazzle her with your proposal story.' I try to inject some enthusiasm into my voice. I don't feel enthusiastic. 'She'll want to hear all the gushy details.'

'Oh. It's not very exciting. We just decided to get married.'

'What?' I exclaim. 'You didn't give your girlfriend of almost a decade a proper proposal?'

He frowns and then gives me a quizzical look. 'You remember how long we've been together?'

I shrug. 'Yeah. I wasn't that drunk,' I add and my face heats up under his amused gaze.

The truth is, I remember everything about that night – the fact that he and his girlfriend have been together since university is just one detail of many. That's not to say I wasn't surprised myself when he remembered I didn't like weddings.

'Back to it, then,' I say, rather than taking the conversation further.

Late on Tuesday afternoon, Clare comes into the office. 'Can we gather?' Simon calls to everyone, so we get up from our desks and congregate in the middle of the room.

'I have some sales information,' he says, and from the look on his face, it's good.

It turns out, last week's Joseph Strike baby bump issue saw our sales shoot up by over 50 per cent. Everyone gasps and bursts into spontaneous applause at the news.

'Thank you to everyone who worked on the article,' Simon continues. 'But special thanks to Bronte for acquiring those stunning pictures *and* the interview.' I try to contain my blush as everyone looks at me. 'If you don't already know, Bronte's friend works at the conservation park where these shots were taken. In fact, her friend took the pictures herself. She could have sold them to anyone, but she sold them to us. So thank you, Bronte.'

'Well done, Bronte,' Clare chips in.

My colour deepens as everyone claps again – some more enthusiastically than others. I notice Nicky roll her eyes at Helen, who smirks, but even that doesn't bother me. Warmth washes away my embarrassment as the sweet, eager editorial assistant, Sarah, appears with four bottles of champagne and everyone cheers. She pops one of the corks and starts to pour champagne into plastic disposable glasses, handing the first glass to me. 'Here you go, honey,' she says with a smile.

'Thanks.' I started out as an editorial assistant, too, so I have a lot of respect for her, knowing how much work goes into keeping an office as large as *Hebe* running smoothly.

'Cheers, B.' Russ appears at my side.

'Cheers.' I grin at him.

Nicky and Helen and a few others return to their desks with their glasses, and Russ gives me a significant look. Lisa, Tim and Zach huddle round us. It's nearly home time.

'Cheers,' Alex says, joining the group. 'Well done.' He nudges me good-naturedly.

'Thanks.' My treacherous face heats up again. 'How did your meeting with Rachel go?' I ask him, winking comically at Sarah as she pulls out her iPhone and starts to snap off a few photos.

'Really good.' He nods.

'Did she show you any of her work?'

'Yeah, she brought in a couple of her books.' He shakes his head, impressed. 'They're fantastic. I love her documentary style. I think it's the way we should go.'

'It's so much better than the old way, isn't it?' I say.

'Definitely. Much more natural. I hate posed crap.'

'Me too,' I agree. 'What did Zara think?'

He cocks his head to one side. 'I think she liked it. She's quite traditional, although you'd never know it. I'm going to have a chat with her tonight. We should get Rachel booked in as soon as possible.'

I am so curious to know what Zara's like. I wonder if I'll resist the temptation of asking Rachel next time I see her.

Fat chance.

'Does she have anyone else lined up for December?' I ask.

'Not yet, but you never know. I'm sure there are others out there who have left it as late as us to book a photographer.'

'You're lucky. She only left her job quite recently so I don't think this year is too crazy busy for her. She's already got dozens booked in for next year.'

'I'm not surprised. Thanks again for her details.'

'No worries.'

Easter comes and goes and I fall into an easy routine at work and outside of it. Nicky seems to have moved on after her grudge and while I don't think the tension will ever truly be gone, she, Helen and I function fairly well.

Bridget returns to cover for the recently departed features editor on *Let's Go!* so I catch up with her regularly for lunch, and she joins our Friday nights at the pub. Alex usually comes for a couple, but always heads off earlier than the rest of us. He's booked Rachel now for his wedding, and I'm pleased it all worked out.

One Friday night at the beginning of May, I go out for a girls' night with Bridget, Maria and Bridget's friend Marty. We bar-hop and end up at a club, where we dance the night away. Later, Maria and I sit on a bench seat and giggle as we try to ignore Bridget and Marty getting cosy with two random boys on either side of us. We're all single, and if there were more good-looking boys in the vicinity, I'd be making the most of it, too. As it is, I'm happy just hanging out with my friends.

'How's Rachel?' I ask Maria.

'She's good,' she replies. 'She's got a wedding tomorrow.'

'You're not doing the make-up?'

'No, the bride is using her friend.'

'Uh-oh, big mistake!' I exclaim, tipsily.

'Tell me about it.'

'How's Sally getting on?'

Maria pulls a face. 'She's alright.'

'Oh?' That didn't sound too promising.

'Between you and me, I don't think she's really cut out for this wedding photography business.'

This fact shouldn't make me feel happy, but it does.

'Well, tell Rachel that I'm happy to step in if she ever needs me.'

'I will,' Maria promises. 'She thinks you're amazing.'

My heart swells. 'Does she?'

'Absolutely!' Maria enthuses. 'Much better than Sally.'

'Has she said that?' I ask with surprise.

'Not in so many words. Rachel's far too nice, but I know what she thinks.'

I ponder this for a little while, before asking the question I've resisted for so long. 'Did she tell you she's doing Alex's wedding in December?'

'No?'

Damn. That means I can't ask about Zara.

'How do you feel about that?' she asks carefully.

I shrug. 'It's fine. I suggested he call her. She's

great and he's a friend, so why wouldn't I hook them up?'

She says nothing for a bit, before asking, 'Is he?'

I frown. 'Is he what?'

'A friend?'

'Of course. Things are cool between us now.'

She smiles. 'Well, that's good.'

'Yeah.'

Rachel calls me that Sunday.

'Hey you,' she says warmly. 'I was wondering if you'd like to come over sometime and see the books for Suzie and Mike and Veronica and Matthew?'

'Yes, please. How are they looking?'

'They're great. I've used a lot of your shots. You really did such a good job on both days.'

'Thank you.' I'm genuinely touched.

'Have you thought about doing any more wedding photography?' she asks tentatively.

'Yes,' I reply with a sigh. 'If you can recommend anyone who might need an assistant, please do.'

She pauses. 'It's just that . . . Well, I have a little bit of a problem with Sally.'

My heart skips a beat. 'Really?'

'She wasn't enjoying herself yesterday. I know she's madly in love with this new man of hers, and that's lovely.' I don't get the feeling Rachel thinks it's *that* lovely. 'But she just wanted to be somewhere else and everyone could see it.'

'Oh dear.' I try to sound sympathetic while my heart races.

'I was wondering . . . I need to speak to Sally first,' she clarifies, 'but would you be interested in taking over some of her weddings this year? Just to give her a break so it's not so full-on?'

'I'd love to!' I gush.

'Really?' she asks hopefully.

'I would love to!' I say again and she laughs.

'Well, I have a wedding coming up next weekend in Scotland, and in a few weeks there's one in the Lake District. Sally is massively dragging her heels about being away from her boyfriend so much. I really need someone who's enthusiastic and keen.'

'I'm enthusiastic and keen!' I pipe up, unable to stop myself.

'I'm so pleased to hear it,' she replies. 'Can I call you back later once I've spoken to her?'

'Definitely!'

CHAPTER 8

We're about half an hour into our flight to Glasgow when I finally give in to my curiosity and ask Rachel about Alex and Zara.

'How did it go with Alex?'

'Good.' Rachel nods. 'We're all booked in for December.'

'What was Zara like?'

'You haven't met her?'

'No, he hasn't brought her out to pub night yet.' Surely it's only a matter of time.

'She was nice,' she says with a shrug. 'She wasn't overly enthusiastic about my style of photography, but maybe she was just pondering which way to go. Alex seemed keen.'

I should have known Rachel would be diplomatic. I'm not going to get a completely honest reaction from her. She continues to flick through her magazine. Conversation finished?

Nup. Can't let it lie. 'What does she look like?'

Rachel looks up and purses her lips, thinking. 'She's tall, slim, attractive.' She shrugs and looks down at her magazine.

'What colour is her hair?'

She glances at me. 'Blonde.'

'Up? Down? Long? Short?'

She gives me a funny look. 'I think it was long because it was pulled up into a bun.'

'Maybe she used one of those donut things,' I muse.

'Maybe.' Now she's looking at me weirdly.

'What was she wearing?'

She gives a half-laugh and shakes her head, before launching into the detail I require. 'Well, if I recall correctly, she was wearing a very well-fitted and no doubt expensive navy suit with a white shirt. And she had black horn-rimmed glasses and dark red lipstick. And killer heels.'

'Horn-rimmed glasses? Urgh, she sounds like Nicky.'

'Who's Nicky?' Her brow furrows.

'My evil boss.'

'Well, Zara didn't seem evil,' Rachel clarifies. 'Just a little reserved with her compliments. I'm sure she's perfectly nice.'

Sounds like a bit of a bitch, if you ask me. I don't say that out loud.

The Loch Lomond hotel where the bride, groom and immediate family are staying is super-pricey, so Rachel and I have opted to stay at an inn twenty minutes away. It's late Friday night by the time we arrive in the car we hired at the airport so we head up to our rooms.

The next morning, we go to the hotel where the bride, Karmen, is getting ready.

'Karmen's family is Turkish,' Rachel explains as we walk along the hotel corridor, 'although she's lived in London most of her life.' She knocks on the door of their suite. Before I can ask what the Scottish connection is, the door swings open and a large woman beams at us.

'Come in! Come in!' she cries in a Middle Eastern accent, stepping aside for us. 'I'm Karmen's Auntie Bora.'

We squeeze past her large frame in the doorway and walk into a big bridal suite crammed full of people. 'The photographers are here!' Karmen's aunt announces to much excitement.

I soon discover that Karmen's family is *huge*. In every way imaginable.

'Hello!' Rachel says warmly, going to hug the person who I'm assuming is Karmen. She's very, well, shall we call it voluptuous.

No need to dispense the 'don't lose weight before your wedding' advice here.

At first, I'm slightly overwhelmed by the chaos, but everyone is a lot of fun and Karmen seems relaxed and happy as she jokes around with her five bridesmaids, two flower girls, one pageboy, mother and four 'aunties' – not all of whom are related, apparently. The make-up artist looks less relaxed as she tackles one boisterous bridesmaid after another. Karmen opted to use a local girl recommended by the hotel, but she could have really done with an extra pair of hands. If only Maria were here.

There are many people in the room, but the one person attracting even more attention than the bride is the smallest: four-year-old pageboy Devrim. At one point he clambers onto Karmen's lap and practically swings from her fluffy white robe.

'Devrim, get off!' she squawks as he hooks his fingers onto her bra and pulls.

Whoa. One of the many aunts rushes in and extracts him. Someone's had too much sugar this morning. There are platters of pastries everywhere and the make-up artist has to work around Karmen eating hers.

'Want to come next door with me to shoot the dress?' Rachel asks, indicating a door off the suite.

I nod eagerly and the silence that greets us is blissful.

'Got any headache tablets?' I ask.

She giggles, then stops in her tracks when she spies Karmen's *enormous* white dress hanging from the doorframe.

'Oh dear,' she says with a sigh.

'What's wrong?' I ask.

'Don't get me wrong, I love a big dress, but this is strapless.'

I'm confused. Suzie's strapless dress was beautiful. 'What's wrong with that?' I ask.

'Busty brides and strapless dresses don't mix. She'll be hoiking it up all day and night. It will ruin countless pictures.' She sighs again. 'Avoid overhead shots. I'll be Photoshopping out nipples, you mark my words.'

'Let's just hope Devrim doesn't unleash the puppies again,' I say.

The hotel is licensed to hold wedding ceremonies, so it's only a short walk across the sprawling grounds to the building where the wedding is taking place. I don't know what I expected, but the family of the groom, Luca, is Italian – there's seemingly no one of Scottish descent at this entire Scottish-based wedding. Luca's side of the family are a lot of fun, too. Big in numbers but not in body size, Luca and his ushers are mostly short and skinny. I wouldn't have placed him and Karmen together in a million years.

It's a grey and gloomy day, but the over-excited, often oversized guests arriving in colourful outfits make a nice juxtaposition to the dark skies.

Rachel texts me to tell me to look out for a blue and white Fiat 500. Who's driving? And why a Fiat? Must be the Italian contingent. The grooms don't seem to get very involved in wedding plan-ning, but booking the bridal car usually comes top of their list of priorities.

Even though I've been warned about the car, my mouth falls open when it pulls up. Karmen's olive-skinned face can be seen in the front passenger window, pressed up against the glass amid a cloud of white fabric.

Recovering quickly, I start to snap away, trying

to keep a straight face. Rachel and a host of cackling bridesmaids dressed in purple, worryingly strapless gowns, appear on foot a moment later. The chief bridesmaid struts over to the Fiat and opens the door.

'Out you get, love!' she shouts.

There's a flurry of movement as Karmen's white dress shivers and shakes, but Karmen herself remains firmly rooted in the car.

'Come on, we're late!' another bridesmaid hollers.

Another flurry of movement, followed by: 'I can't! I'm stuck!'

Rachel flashes me a look and I try to keep a check on my building hysteria as two bridesmaids pull on Karmen's arms and legs. Finally she bursts out of the tiny car.

'Ta-dah!' she shouts joyously, her tuck shop lady arms wobbling wildly as I laughingly snap away. At least she's a good sport.

Karmen's mother and aunts go into the venue, and after Rachel has got a few shots of Karmen and her massive posse, she heads inside, too. The music pipes up and the flower girls take their places at the front of the queue, followed by Devrim the pageboy and then the horde of purple bridesmaids. Karmen's beaming face turns into one of shock as Devrim races out of his position and runs up to her to swing from her dress. Luckily one of the bridesmaids intervenes before I can act on my impulse to clap the little urchin over his head. The flower girls walk into the room and he follows at a run, dressed in his mini pinstripe suit. I hear the sound of numerous oohs and aahs. Looks can be deceiving, my friends.

Now for my part. The groom. Everywhere I look, my view is obstructed by a sea of smartphones. Surely this was easier before the digital age? I manage to find a spot with an unobstructed view, just as Luca turns around. His face goes red as he sees his bride and his eyes fill with tears.

The sight warms even *my* cold, cynical heart.

After the service, it's time for the ubiquitous confetti shot. Everyone gathers around the bride and groom while Rachel counts to three and then:

'Ow!' Karmen hollers, clamping her hands over her eyes. 'Who threw rice at me?' she squawks.

Rice?

'Foreign weddings are a minefield,' Rachel mutters.

The bridesmaids help to cram Karmen into the front passenger seat of the Fiat while Luca hops into the driver's seat. The uncle who threw the rice at Karmen looks red-faced as his niece rubs her eyes, but as the door closes, she peers out at us from her white cloud and beams. I wonder if Luca will be able to find the gearstick under all that chiffon.

Rachel and I run as fast as we can, just managing to beat the bride and groom to the main hotel building, and our next couple of hours are manic as we shoot the wedding party on the lush green lawns of the hotel with Loch Lomond as a back-drop. It is so beautiful here, and when there's a break in the clouds that lets the sun shine through, we can't believe our luck.

'That's our teaser shot,' Rachel says with a grin, as Luca and Karmen stand arm-in-arm, staring at the view. They really are a sweet couple.

Later, everyone moves from the ballroom, where the wedding breakfast took place, into the adjoining dance hall for the live entertainment and dancing. I get an awesome shot of Devrim standing behind one large guest in a scarlet red dress. With the colour as a backdrop he looks brilliantly evil, especially when his peanut brain gives him the idea of pinching her bottom. She jumps and I move away, stifling my giggles. I may be immature, but it amuses me to no end.

'What are you laughing at?' Rachel asks me with a grin as the other guests mingle.

'Devrim. What a little shit.'

'Tell me about it,' she says drily. 'There's no way I'm having kids at my wedding.'

'Aw, kids are okay. I think they add to the atmosphere. *If* their parents keep them under control . . .'

'Not much of that going on around here,' Rachel comments as we both spy Devrim's mother laughing, completely oblivious, while Devrim pops out from underneath Karmen's billowing skirt. The poor bride looks a bit harassed.

'Ooh, hello there,' Rachel says breathily. She's

looking at the small stage set up behind the dance floor, where a guy with sandy-blond, shaggy hair and a short-ish beard is perched on a stool. He's holding a guitar. I shoot my head around to gape at Rachel and she smirks back at me.

One word: Phwoar.

He starts to strum his guitar, and when he sings into the microphone in a deep, sexy, soulful voice, I almost forget we have a job to do. Rachel is also staring, rapt. I nudge her and we both laugh at each other. She unzips her kit bag and gets out her speedlites because it's almost time for the first dance.

'I might just get a few of him with Sally's 85,' I tell Rachel nonchalantly. She gives me a significant look and I flash her an innocent grin as I move through the crowds to the side of the stage. I raise my camera to my face and stare at him through the viewfinder. He's even hotter up close, and I'm mesmerised. I have to remind myself to take my photographs. His lips brush against the microphone when he sings, but when he pulls away to focus on his guitar, his shaggy hair falls down across his forehead and partially obscures his face. I decide to move around to the other side of the dance floor where I might be able to see him better. I turn around to check out the stage, and at that point he looks straight at me and my heart skips a beat. Photographing him now is going to be a touch excruciating. I'll do it anyway – it's my job. At least, that's my excuse and I'm sticking to it.

His eyes follow me as I take my place to the right of the dance floor. A smile plays about his lips while he strums an acoustic section. I can't keep a straight face as I shoot him, and then he's singing again and his focus is on his music.

Rachel appears at my side. 'The hottest wedding singer I've ever come across, period.'

The song draws to a close, and when Guitar Guy makes an announcement, it comes out in an Australian accent. Rachel and I glance at each other with unbridled glee.

'I just want to say congratulations to Karmen and Luca. I wish you all the best. Ladies and gents, let's hear it for the bride and groom. The first dance . . .'

Rachel nudges me excitedly. 'He's Australian!'

'I heard!' I'm a little gobsmacked. I wonder where he's from and what he's doing in Scotland.

The crowd on the dance floor parts and Karmen and Luca take their positions in the centre. Guitar Guy starts to play 'Love Cats' by The Cure as Karmen and Luca throw themselves into an hilarious choreographed routine. Suddenly Devrim runs onto the dance floor, trying to steal the show. But he goes completely arse up and bangs his head. Everyone watches in horror as his face goes red and he starts to scream the room down. His mother – at long bloody last – runs to his aid and takes him out. I think everyone here is in agreement: serves the little bugger right.

Guitar Guy stops playing, Karmen looks crest-fallen, and then he announces in his warm accent, 'Shall we start again?'

Everyone laughs and cheers, Karmen and Luca attempt their routine from the beginning and every single person in the venue gets into the swing of it, singing along and clapping.

After the first dance, we're done. We haven't been paid to stay for the evening do, so we seek out the bride and groom to say goodbye.

'Do you really have to go?' Karmen asks with dismay. 'Stay and have a few drinks. Let your hair down.'

'Yes, go on,' Luca encourages as Rachel glances at me. I give her a hopeful look.

'I suppose we could catch a cab back to the inn and return to collect the hire car in the morning?' It's not like we've got anything better to do for the night.

'Yes!' I agree eagerly.

'Yay!' Karmen exclaims.

Karmen asks the bartender to put all of our drinks on the house, and Rachel promises to take some more photos in return, although there's no pressure. All in all, it's a win-win situation.

Rachel and I grab a couple of glasses of wine and decamp to a table near the stage.

'Do not let me lose this,' she says after a while. She indicates her kit bag. 'I once misplaced my compact flash cards for ten minutes and nearly had a heart attack.'

'I'm not surprised!' I can't even bear to imagine how I'd feel if I lost the tiny little cards that hold thousands of pictures. An entire wedding: gone. I think I'd die if that ever happened to me.

'Maybe I should go and lock what we're not using in the room next door?' Rachel says.

'Might not be such a bad idea. Want me to go?'

'It's okay. You nip to the bar. I'll hang onto my 200 and speedlites.'

'Cool. I'll keep Sally's 85.' Less chance of camera shake. Alex would approve, I think with a smile, before shoving him from my mind.

She goes, while I stay and watch Guitar Guy for a little longer. He's playing a quirky, cool, stripped-back version of Billy Idol's 'Dancing With Myself'. He meets my eyes again, but this time he holds the contact for a good few seconds. I'm having a hot flush by the end of it as I fight the urge to look away. Then I realise he probably does this to all the girls and I feel a bit silly. I get up and go to the bar.

When I come back, he's no longer playing. Music is blaring out of the speakers instead and I feel a wave of disappointment. I wonder if that's him done for the evening.

A pint of beer is suddenly plonked on the table and I look up to see the man himself grinning down at me.

'G'day,' he says. 'Mind if I sit down?'

'G'day yourself,' I reply with amusement. 'Go for it.'

He pulls out a chair and slumps into it. 'A fellow Aussie, hey? Or are you just really good at accents?'

'Right first time.' I hold out my hand. 'I'm Bronte.'

'Lachie.'

It's pronounced Lockie, but I know it's short for Lachlan. It's a pretty popular name Down Under.

His handshake is warm and firm and he smiles as he stares at me directly. Full of confidence, isn't he?

'What are you doing in Scotland?' I ask, keeping my tone neutral and friendly. I'm not falling for your charms, buster, even if they are considerable.

'I like it here.' He shrugs. 'I'm travelling around a bit, gigging and doing a few weddings when I get a chance.'

'Do you play for a living?'

'I wish. Nah, I do a few odd jobs here and there. Don't know how much longer I'm going to be here.'

'In Scotland?'

'Yeah, and in the UK generally. I've gotta head back home at Christmas and I still want to see Europe. What about you?'

'I'm living and working in London. I'm here for about a year.'

'Cool. Wedding photographer?'

'No. I have a full-time job. I do the occasional wedding at the weekend.' I look up to see Rachel approaching. 'With Rachel,' I say with a smile as she reaches us.

'Hi there!' She tries to contain her considerable delight as she sits down on the other side of Lachie.

He introduces himself with another handshake before leaning back lazily in his chair so he doesn't block her out from the conversation. He's wearing a light-grey T-shirt which isn't tight enough to outline what's underneath, but his arms are toned and muscular so I'm guessing his body is pretty fit.

'So you're an Aussie, too?' Rachel asks with a smile.

'Yep. Born and raised in Perth.'

He's from Western Australia, then, the other side of the country from me.

'You?' he asks me.

'I grew up in South Australia, not far from Adelaide, but I've been living in Sydney.'

'Cool.'

'And Rachel is from . . . I don't know where you're from actually,' I say with a frown, my attempt to include her backfiring.

'I grew up in Bath,' she reveals. She notices our blank faces. 'Neither of you knows where that is, do you?'

'Nope,' I reply.

'Nup,' he says.

'Bloody Aussies,' she mutters and I have a flash-back to standing in the kitchen with Russ and Alex the day I asked Lily for the Joseph Strike pictures.

Lachie grins and downs a third of his pint before banging it back on the table. 'Better get back up there. Four songs. Keep my seat warm for me, would ya?'

Rachel sucks the air in through her teeth as he strolls back to the stage. 'He is *so* hot.'

'Shit-hot,' I agree. 'But doesn't he know it,' I add drily.

We watch him as he picks up his guitar and nods at the DJ in the corner. The song from the speakers dies down and he starts to play Arctic Monkeys' 'I Bet You Look Good On The Dancefloor'.

'How old do you reckon he is?' I ask, silently instructing my eyes to peel themselves away from him. They're being very disobedient.

'Mid-twenties?' Rachel replies. 'Too young for me, that's for sure.'

'As if!' I exclaim. 'How old are you?'

'Thirty-six.'

'So?'

She laughs. 'Toy boy.'

'He could be thirty-six himself, for all we know.'

'Ha! Unlikely,' Rachel scoffs.

'Let's talk about something else,' I say determinedly. 'I get the feeling he doesn't need help puffing up his ego.'

We manage, with some effort, to not pay Lachie an astounding amount of attention until he joins us again.

'Have you guys finished working now?' he asks.

'Technically, yes,' Rachel replies. 'Karmen invited us to stick around for a few drinks so we'll take some more photos in a bit when everyone's loosened up.'

'Have you done a lot of weddings?' He glances at me when he asks this.

'I've only done three, but Rachel has done gazillions.'

'About fifty,' she clarifies.

'Cool,' he says.

'You?' I ask him.

'About the same.'

'That many? Sorry, how old are you?'

He grins. 'Twenty-four.'

'Twenty-four? And you've done nearly *fifty weddings*?'

'More or less.'

'Wow.'

'That's impressive,' Rachel agrees.

'How old are you guys?' he asks us.

'Thirty-six,' Rachel replies with a screwed-up nose.

'Twenty-nine,' I reveal. That makes us both too old for this little upstart.

But he doesn't look put off in the least. 'When are you turning thirty?' he asks me with an easy grin.

'Next month.'

'Are you?' Rachel interrupts.

'Yeah. But I don't want a big celebration.'

'Screw that,' Lachie says, turning to Rachel. 'I hope you're gonna do something.'

'Do you sing at thirtieth birthday parties?' she asks him pertinently.

'Christ, yeah, I'll do anything,' he replies with a

cheeky grin, looking back at me with a raised eyebrow.

This boy has more confidence than Johnny frigging Jefferson. He's a wedding singer, not a rock star, for crying out loud.

Rachel checks her watch when he goes for his final stint. 'How much longer do you want to stay?' she asks. 'Another half an hour?'

'Sure,' I reply. 'Whatever suits you.'

'Okay, I'll book a cab.'

Lachie joins us again as we're preparing to leave. 'You're going already?' he asks with a frown.

'Yep. Flying back to London first thing. Are you done for the night?'

'I'm never done for the night.' He winks at me – he actually winks. Rachel laughs.

'Can I hitch a lift with you?' he asks.

I shake my head, bemused. 'You don't know where we're staying.'

'Yeah, I do. You're at The Hare.'

Rachel's surprise matches my own. 'How did you know that?'

He grins. 'Saw you checking in.'

'Come on, then,' Rachel says, casting her eyes at the ceiling. How did we miss him?

We go and gather our kits and coats from the room next door. Lachie slings his guitar case strap over his shoulder and follows us. He rides in the front of the taxi, chatting amiably to the Scottish driver the whole way back to the inn. The sound of their easy-going voices sends me to sleep. I jolt out of my slumber when the door opens and look up with stinging eyes at Lachie smiling down at me.

'Wakey-wakey, sleepyheads,' he says.

I glance across at Rachel to see her yawning. 'I'm knackered. I'm going straight to bed,' she says with tired but certain determination as she gets out of the car.

'You'll come and tap a beer with me in the bar, won't you?' Lachie asks me with a frown. 'Come on,' he urges when I dither. 'One won't kill you.'

'When have I heard that before?' I say wryly, climbing out. He barely moves backwards for me so I find myself looking up at him. I didn't realise how tall he was earlier – he was sitting down for most of the time. He must be about six foot two because my eyes are in line with his broad chest. I notice that he's still only wearing a grey T-shirt with his guitar strap hung over his shoulder.

'Aren't you cold?' I ask as we wander into the inn.

'Nah. I'm hardcore,' he replies, glancing down at me. 'Cop a feel.' He holds his arm out to me. 'Still really warm.'

'I'm sure you are,' I reply drily, refusing to indulge him. He doesn't seem fazed by my lack of bicep-fondling as we walk inside.

'Well, good night,' Rachel says in the lobby.

'Nice to meet you,' Lachie replies.

'You too.' She smiles at him then turns to me.

'See you in the morning for breakfast at nine? I should be back from getting the hire car from the hotel by then.'

'Okay, thanks,' I reply with a smile, still undecided about whether I should just head upstairs to bed myself.

'Don't even think about it.' Lachie shoves me towards the bar area.

'Hey!' I complain as he puts his hand on my shoulder and steers me through tables of punters. I stumble ahead of him until we reach the bar and he lets me go.

'I'll get us a table,' I say as I spy one coming free by the window.

He comes over with a bottle of red wine and two glasses.

'Australian,' I comment, noting what he's chosen.

'Adelaide Hills,' he points out, jabbing his forefinger in my direction.

I can't help smirking. 'Good choice,' I concede, plonking the bottle back down on the table between us.

'So how did you come to be a wedding singer?' I ask as he glugs red liquid into my glass. I can't help looking at his tanned, toned arms.

He shrugs. 'I'm not just a wedding singer.'

'Nothing to be ashamed about,' I say.

'I know,' he replies, more seriously. 'I used to busk all the time and then when my older cousins and sisters got married, it became a bit of a thing for me. Word spread, the money was better than busking, so I kept it up.' He picks up his glass and chinks it against mine. 'Cheers.'

'Cheers,' I reply, taking a sip. 'Mmm. Nice.' I put my glass back down. 'So how do you know Karmen and Luca?'

'I don't. Luca's . . . Let me see if I can get this straight. Luca's aunt's husband's son works at the pub in Edinburgh where I work and sometimes gig, so he put me forward.'

'Right. So you live in Edinburgh?'

'At the moment. Not for much longer. Figure I might head to London after this.' He scratches his beard.

'It's that easy?'

'I work in a pub. It's a cash job. Anything's easy if you put your mind to it.'

And if you have enough confidence, I think to myself.

'What about you? Where do you work when you're not photographing weddings?' He leans forwards and rests his tanned forearms on the table.

'I work for a magazine.' I shift and try to cross my legs over my bulky kit bag. I can't risk anyone nicking my camera equipment so I'm keeping it close.

'Really? Which one?' he asks with interest.

'It's called *Hebe*.'

'No shit? My sisters love that magazine. I bet you know all the gossip.'

'People always say that, but there's not as much

behind-the-scenes gossip as you'd think. All the good stuff goes in the magazine. If the rumours were actually true, you'd know about them. How many sisters do you have?' I take a sip of my red wine.

'Four.'

'Wow. Any brothers?'

'Nup. Just me, the baby, the golden boy.'

He's quite sweet, actually. Talking to him is certainly easy.

'You got any siblings?' he asks.

'No. Only child.'

'Aw.'

I shrug and turn the conversation back around. 'How old are your sisters?'

'My oldest sister Bea is thirty-three, Maggie is thirty-one, Tina is twenty-nine and Lydia is twenty-six.'

Maybe that's why he feels so comfortable with older women. Not that I'm *that* much older than him. Jeez.

We chat and make our way through the bottle of wine until the lights go on.

'So how did you come to be a wedding pho-tog-rapher's assistant?' he asks with an easy smile, making no attempt to leave, even as the bar empties out around us.

'Rachel was stuck. I've done a little freelance photography so a friend put us in touch.'

'You enjoy it?'

'Um . . .'

He hooks onto my hesitation like a fish on a fishing line. 'It's not for you?'

'I like photography,' I explain. 'And I have enjoyed photographing the three weddings that I've done. I just don't believe in marriage. Or God. And I hate churches,' I find myself admitting. The wine has loosened me up.

He puts his glass down a little too loudly on the table. 'Isn't Adelaide nicknamed the City of Churches?'

'Yep.' Just my luck.

'Why don't you believe in marriage?'

'Why bother? If you want to be together, be together. If you don't, don't. Why make it legal? Why swear, under the eyes of God, to stay together for the rest of your lives? Which brings me onto my next issue with the whole shebang – who believes in God anyway?' I pull a face.

He shrugs. 'I don't know. I mean, I sort of do.'

'Do you?' I stare at him with surprise.

'Yeah.' His lips turn down and he cocks his head to one side as he regards me from across the table. 'I mean, I believe in something. I don't know what's out there, but there's gotta be *something*.'

I screw up my nose. 'Why? Why has there got to be something out there?'

'I don't know. I just think there has to be.'

'It's not exactly the most convincing argument I've ever heard,' I tease as the bar staff start putting on their coats. I nod at them, then smile at Lachie. 'We should go. Let them get off.'

He nods and scratches his beard, then folds his arms and stares at me. The posture makes his biceps bulge.

'Which room are you in?' I ask, feeling oddly nervy as I reach behind me to grab my coat and stand up.

'Yours?' he says cheekily, looking up at me.

'Ha! In your dreams.'

He grins and gets to his feet, picking up his guitar case and slinging it over his shoulder. 'Are you seeing anyone?'

I can't believe the cheek of him! 'No!' I exclaim. 'That still doesn't mean I'm sleeping with you!'

He shrugs. 'I'll just crash on your floor, then.'

'Are you for real?' I tut and make my way out into the lobby. I can sense him behind me, but as I start to make my way up the stairs, I realise he isn't following. I turn around on the stairs and look down at him in confusion.

'Isn't your room upstairs?' I ask with a frown. He's standing at the bottom, looking a little less confident than before.

He shrugs. 'I don't have one.'

My mouth drops open. 'Hang on, you said you saw us checking in . . .'

'I was having a drink in the bar. Doesn't mean I'm staying here.'

'Where are you staying, then?' I ask incredulously.

'My friend's car is in the car park.'

'*What?*'

He laughs lightly. 'I'll sleep in my friend's car. I borrowed it to drive here from Edinburgh.'

'Are you serious?' I sit down on a step with a bump.

'Yeah. It's no biggie. I've slept rough before.'

'Were you really just expecting me to sleep with you?'

He leans against the wall and smiles lazily up at me. 'A guy can hope.'

I shake my head at him with amazement. 'I'm sure you've had no trouble at all picking up plenty of pretty bridesmaids over the years, but you've made a mistake thinking I might be that easy.'

His lips turn down and he shrugs, but he's unfazed by my comments.

'I barely know you,' I say with a frown. Alex flashes into my mind. I barely knew him, either. And look where that got me.

'I'm not that scary, am I?' he asks.

A thrill darts through me at the sight of him standing there, staring up at me with his sexy, cheeky grin. He really is obscenely hot.

I shake my head and get to my feet. 'Are you seriously going to sleep in a car?'

'If I hadn't hitched a ride with Luca's mates to the wedding, I'd be sleeping on the pavement.'

'Well, that's something, I suppose,' I say drily, looking up the stairs.

'Night, then.'

I almost shout at him to wait, but I can't.

No. I *won't*. I won't go there again.

'Bash on my window in the morning before you go,' he calls over his shoulder. 'Check I'm still alive.'

I turn and stare after him, but he flashes me an easy grin. 'Just kidding. Catch you later, Bronte. Come say bye before you set off.'

He pushes through the inn door and I watch him go, not doing a thing to make him stay.

CHAPTER 9

I don't say goodbye to Lachie before we leave the next day. I find his borrowed car – a battered old red hatchback looking slightly steamed up in the car park out the back – and I peer through the window to see him huddled in a sleeping bag on the back seat. I can't bring myself to wake him up.

He's still on my mind on Thursday afternoon when I'm in the office filling my glass from the water cooler.

'Hey,' Alex says, joining me.

'Hi,' I reply, breathing in his divine scent and sighing a small sigh.

'Busy?' he asks.

'Yeah.' I pick up my glass and he fills his. 'Helen's not in today.'

'Bronte, you are going to have to go on the shoot this afternoon,' Nicky interrupts, coming over to me.

'Really?'

'Yes. I'm too busy,' she says bluntly. 'I've got a meeting with Clare and Simon and I have to prepare . . . Oh, I'm just busy, alright?' she snaps, storming back to her desk.

'It's fine. I'm more than happy to go,' I reply calmly, following her.

She no doubt would have asked Helen if she were here. She's sent her on more shoots than me since I started, which is disappointing, because I really enjoy them.

'Take these,' Nicky says curtly, picking up a stack of papers and practically throwing them at me.

I scramble to gather them up before they go everywhere.

'Is everything alright?' I glance up to see Simon frowning at Nicky.

Her face breaks into a smile. 'It's fine,' she says charmingly. 'Just gathering everything together. I'm going to send Bronte on the shoot this afternoon so that will be fun for her and I'll have more time to prepare for our meeting in the morning with Clare.'

'Great,' Simon says smoothly.

Nicky's smile slips from her face and she glares at me as he turns away.

She is such a bitch.

'Are you coming too?' I ask Alex with surprise as I wait for Russ beside two boxes of props at the door. Russ is conducting the interview.

'Sure am.'

'Guys, I'm going to have to meet you there,' Russ calls. 'Esther needs me to write something up for the next issue.'

149

Alex and I make our way outside to hail a cab. He opens the door for me and climbs in afterwards, while I direct the driver to take us to London Bridge.

'Nicky still giving you shit?' he asks, sitting beside me. 'You seem a bit down.'

'She's just being her usual self,' I say resignedly. 'Nothing I can't cope with.'

'I've barely spoken to you this week. Did you have a wedding on at the weekend?'

'Yeah.' My face lights up marginally. 'In Scotland, actually.'

'So are you doing more weddings with Rachel, then?'

'A few more, yes, when Rachel's assistant Sally can't make it. Don't worry, I'm sure Sally will be doing your wedding in December.'

'Why should I be worried? I'd rather you did it, actually.'

'Would you?'

'Yeah.' He shifts slightly. Maybe he's having a rethink. 'Rachel said you're really good.'

I smirk. 'Despite my sometimes soft focus and the occasional need for Photoshop?'

He laughs. 'You're obviously not that bad. She raved about you.'

'Really? Aw. Well, we'll see, I guess. December is a long time away.' But I'm still quite certain I won't want to do his wedding. 'How are the preparations going?' I ask.

'Fine. Well, Zara's doing most of it. She's leaving

it to me to organise the car and the music. Oh, and the photographer.'

I smile at him. 'Rachel told me the groom always gets to do the car and the music. What are you planning?'

'I don't know. DJ, I guess. But I don't want a crappy DJ who does shit wedding music, so if you have any suggestions . . .'

'I'll ask her. I'm sure she knows people.' I pause for a moment as I think of Lachie. 'I met a really good wedding singer at the weekend, actually. Aussie. Played the guitar. Cool stuff, not cheesy at all.'

'You sound enthralled.'

I laugh. 'I was a bit.'

'I'm not sure I like the sound of him,' Alex says wryly.

'Well, I wouldn't know how to get hold of him if I tried,' I reply. Who was it who got him the job? Luca's cousin's auntie's . . . No, that can't be right. Oh, I give up.

It's six o'clock by the time we finish the shoot, which involved photographing a bunch of cool kids from a hot new British TV show on London Bridge. I was pleasantly surprised when Maria turned up to do the make-up. I hadn't had any input in organising the shoot at all.

'Are either of you going back to the office?' I ask Russ and Alex as Maria gathers the last of her things.

151

'Yeah, I need to,' Russ replies.

'I'm going to head home,' Alex tells me.

'Can you drop the props back?' I ask Russ. 'I might go see my friend who lives nearby.'

Polly texted me last night to say she was bored working the graveyard shift so I could surprise her if she's home.

'Yeah, that's fine,' Russ agrees.

'Do you want to come and see Polly with me?' I turn to Maria.

'Sure. I haven't seen her for yonks.'

'Why has it been so long?' I ask her, calling bye to the boys as we walk off.

'I don't know. I suggested meeting up a few times after the wedding, but she always said she was busy. I don't really know her that well, to be honest. I was a bit surprised when she invited me to her hen do.'

'Well, I'm glad that she did,' I say.

'Me too.' She smiles and hooks her arm through mine.

There's a lot of surprise flying around when we arrive at Polly's flat. Polly is surprised to see us, Maria is surprised at how much Polly's appearance has changed since she last saw her – I can tell by her expression – and my surprise is reserved for the fact that Polly is already two thirds of the way through a bottle of wine.

'Where's Grant?' I ask, eyeing the bottle – and my friend – with concern.

'He's at work.' Polly waves her hand at me dismissively. 'Work, shmerk. Always at work.' Polly pours us each a small glass and tops up her own. 'I'll get us another bottle,' she says, bumping into the corner of the coffee table on her way to the kitchen. 'Ouch!'

I have a feeling she's already drunk more than one bottle. I glance at Maria and then cautiously follow Polly. 'Don't open another,' I say. 'I only want one glass.'

'You're such a party pooper!' she squeals. 'Get with the programme, B!' she adds in an annoying American accent.

'I don't really want much to drink either,' Maria says, coming to my rescue.

Polly glares at each of us in turn and then stumbles slightly into the worktop.

'Are you alright?' I ask worriedly.

She puts her hand over her mouth and suddenly looks a little pale. My eyes widen in shock and then she staggers out of the kitchen. The sound of her vomiting into the toilet reaches me before I reach her. I rub her hunched back and sigh heavily.

When she's emptied the contents of her stomach, she slumps back on her heels, groaning miserably.

'Can you take over?' I ask Maria, who's standing in the bathroom doorway.

She nods reluctantly. I go into the kitchen and set about making some coffee. We need to sober her up.

When I'm done, I swap places with Maria again. 'Come on, let's go back to the living room.'

'Grant,' she mumbles, not moving from her position in front of the toilet bowl.

'Grant?' Is she trying to tell me he's the problem?

'Get him,' she adds.

Maybe not, if she wants him here. I give Maria a wary look, but Maria just shrugs uncomfortably, not really sure what to do.

'Grant!' Polly prompts, glaring at me.

I sigh and hunt out her phone, dialling Grant's number. There's no point arguing with her. I've been here with her before.

'What is it now?' Grant snaps as a greeting.

'It's Bronte,' I say calmly.

'Bronte?' He sounds surprised. 'What are you . . . Where's Polly?'

'I'm *with* Polly,' I say.

'Has she been drinking again?' he asks in a monotone, before I can explain.

'She's pretty plastered. Are you far away?'

He groans. 'I'll come home now. I'll be there in half an hour.'

I relay this to Polly.

'He's going to kill me.' She staggers to her feet. I follow her into the living room.

'Polly, what's wrong?' I ask with concern, handing her a cup of coffee as we sit on the sofa. 'Is everything okay with Grant?'

'Nope.' She hiccups. 'Marriage is *hard*,' she says loudly, hiccupping again. '*Hard.*'

'Why? Has he done anything to hurt you?'

'Hurt me?' She scoffs. 'Sorry, have you met my husband? He's the sweetest guy that ever lived.' Her sigh is broken up by another hiccup. 'He's just never here. And when he is, he's always moaning at me. He doesn't ask me to go out with him and his friends. He doesn't find me funny any more.'

I'm not surprised, if she's been regularly drinking herself into this state. 'Have you talked to anyone about this? I mean, you know you can talk to me about Grant any time,' I stress. 'But do you think you should see someone about your drinking?'

She lets out a bitter laugh. 'You're acting like *you* don't have any problems. My mum saw your mum up the mall the other day.'

My insides contract and my face burns like acid as she continues.

'She said you never call her, never—'

'Shut up!' I cut her off, my body wracked with tension. She looks at me in a slight daze. 'Just shut up,' I say again, feeling the weight of Maria's shock resting on me as I shoot to my feet.

A key in the lock distracts us. The door opens and Grant comes in, his face a picture of dismay.

'For fuck's sake, Polly,' he mutters.

'Don't you speak to me like that!' she erupts, her face contorting.

'Shhh!' he hisses. 'The neighbours are going to go ballistic if you kick off again!'

'Hey, hey,' I say reasonably.

'I think it would be best if you guys left,' Grant says without taking his eyes off Polly.

Maria gets up, looking uneasy.

'Sorry,' he mutters as he waits by the door.

'It's okay,' I reply, following Maria through it to the landing outside the flat. 'Maybe she should just get some sleep,' I suggest.

He nods. 'I'll put her to bed.'

'I'm not a child!' she snipes, overhearing us.

'You're tired, Pol, you've been doing the graveyard shift,' I point out through the open door.

She seems to consider this a fair argument, even through her booze haze.

'Thanks,' Grant whispers.

'Why don't you give me a call?' I reply in a low voice. 'If she needs help, don't try and do this on your own.'

He nods and I can hear his heavy sigh as he closes the door on us.

CHAPTER 10

The next day is Friday and I plan to catch up with Bridget over lunch. She has continued to freelance for *Let's Go!* while they interview for a new features editor. She's been asked to apply for the job, but she's not sure she wants to be tied in to work at a magazine full-time after the freedom of freelancing. I'm trying to convince her it would be fun for us to commute in together every day.

I pick her up from her office and then we both walk downstairs. Alex comes out of the lift as we step into the vast, cream-marble-lined lobby.

'Hey, Bridget,' he says.

'Howdy,' she replies. 'How's it all going at *Hebe*?'

He continues to join us for Friday night drinks, but he never stays late. I wonder if he's coming out tonight.

'Good. Sales are up.'

'Must be your excellent art direction,' she says with a teasing smile.

I lead the way out through the revolving doors and take in several things at once. Guitar music, singing, a small crowd of people on the pavement and . . . Lachie. Lachie standing there wearing a green jacket and a beanie hat pulled over his shaggy blond hair. His eyes light up when he sees me and his face breaks into a massive grin, then he stops his rendition of 'You Can't Always Get What You Want' by The Stones and starts to play 'Wake Me Up Before You Go-Go' by Wham. Bridget crashes into me.

'Oof! Sorry!' she says to me, then gasps as Alex, I assume, bumps into her. My attention is on Lachie. He sings the jaunty song with a look of sheer joy on his face. I mirror his expression and then I start to laugh because I can't actually believe it. Bridget appears on my left and Alex on my right.

'Phwoar,' Bridget says, not yet realising that this is the Lachie I told her about.

'Do you know him?' Alex asks me with confusion as I start to bounce a little on the spot. Lachie is literally singing the song to me.

'Yeah.' I nod happily. 'That's Lachie. The wedding singer I told you about.'

The song is infectious and a few people start clapping along when Lachie really gets into the swing of it. I laugh with delight and applaud madly when he finishes. He lifts his guitar strap over his head and holds his guitar by the neck as he strides over his open, coin-spattered guitar case to get to me.

'Hey!' he says warmly, engulfing me in a hug.

'What are you doing here?' I pull back and beam up at him as his guitar bumps against me. He's just as gorgeous as my memory had led me to believe.

'Thought I'd stalk you,' he replies with a cheeky look.

'But how did you find me?' I'm confused.

'You told me you worked at *Hebe*.' He nods past me to the building.

'I can't believe it.' I shake my head in amazement. 'Are you in London now, then?'

'For now.' He grins down at me.

Bridget nudges me and I come to with a start. 'Sorry, this is Bridget.'

'Hello,' she says in a flirty voice that has me pursing my lips.

'And this is Alex,' I add.

'G'day,' Lachie says, warmly shaking both of their hands.

'Catch you later,' Alex says to me immediately afterwards with a slightly furrowed brow. He glances at Lachie once more.

'Bye.' I flash him a small smile then turn to Lachie as Alex crosses over the zebra crossing. The people around us have dispersed. 'Bridget and I were just going for some lunch. You want to come?'

'Sure.'

As he scoops up the coins from his case and packs his guitar away, Bridget mouths something thoroughly indecent to me. I bet *she* wouldn't think twice about jumping into the sack with him. The thought is not an entirely pleasant one, which is a bit dumb considering I've had my chance and turned him down.

We go to a local brewpub in the heart of Covent Garden and traipse downstairs to the tables in the basement. Lachie entrusts me with his guitar while he and Bridget go to get the drinks and order our food. I'm reluctant to leave them alone together, but I know what I'm having and Bridget is yet to decide. I carry the guitar over to a table in the corner. It's heavier than I thought it would be. The black case is scuffed and well-worn and I feel strangely on edge as I prop it against the wall. This guitar must mean a lot to him.

Bridget and Lachie laugh as they bring the drinks over.

'I cannot believe you made him sleep in his car!' Bridget exclaims as Lachie slides into a booth seat opposite me.

'I told you that already,' I brush her off with mild annoyance as she sits down next to him, rather than me. Duplicitous cow.

'Yes, but that was before I saw him,' she says, not appearing to feel self-conscious in the slightest.

Lachie looks thoroughly entertained by her praise, lifting up his pint glass and chinking it against my Diet Coke and Bridget's cider. I wouldn't dare drink during a work day, even if it is a Friday. I don't need another reason to piss off Nicky. She was in a foul mood when she returned from her meeting with Simon and Clare, the publisher, earlier. Helen's still off sick so I've been the bullseye in her dartboard of irritation.

'Where are you staying in London?' I ask Lachie.

'Dunno. I've only just arrived.'

I stare at him. He has nowhere to stay?

'I thought you might like to make up for past mistakes,' he adds. Bridget's eyes light up, my mouth falls open with disbelief, but before either of us can speak, he chuckles. 'Just kidding. I'm crashing at a mate's in Camden.'

'Damn,' Bridget says, looking disappointed.

'As if we have room at ours anyway,' I mutter at Bridget.

'He could have had the sofa,' she replies with a shrug, while Lachie grins. 'Or mine's a double,' she adds, taking a casual mouthful of her cider.

'So's mine,' I point out flippantly.

'Finally we're getting somewhere,' Lachie chips in.

I roll my eyes at him. 'When did you arrive?'

'Yesterday.'

Yesterday and he decided to come and find me today? I'm strangely touched. 'Have you got a job?'

'Not yet. My mate says there's something going at a pub in Camden where he works. I'm dropping by there later.'

'Busking in the meantime?'

'That's the plan.'

The waitress brings our food over so we chat between mouthfuls until eventually it's time for us to head back to work.

'I've just got to nip to the chemist,' Bridget says, peeling off. 'See you soon, I hope,' she says to Lachie. Thankfully her hormones have levelled out over the course of lunch.

'For sure.' He gives her a quick hug and I see her place her hand strategically on his chest. I inwardly sigh as she gives me an ecstatic smile.

'I'll walk you back to work,' Lachie says.

'See ya,' I tell Bridget, turning away.

'Hey, hang on a sec.' Lachie calls her back. 'Have you got any plans for her birthday?'

Bridget looks confused. 'What birthday?'

'It's your thirtieth next month, right?' He looks down at me.

I nod, reluctantly. I wasn't planning on making a fuss, let alone give an almost-stranger any say in the matter.

'When?' Bridget gasps.

'The twelfth,' I tell her. 'I wasn't planning on—'

'Bloody hell, Bronte!' she snaps, looking genuinely cross. 'You know I'm not back from Key West until the fifteenth! How the hell could you have failed to mention this when I was booking my flights?'

'It's not a big deal,' I say weakly. She's going out to visit the friends who left last month – apparently they've set up a B&B – I was hardly going to put a spanner into her plans.

'Of course it's a big deal! It's your thirtieth! It's a HUGE deal!'

I was kind of hoping to turn thirty without anyone noticing . . .

'We can celebrate when you get back,' I say calmly. 'It's only a couple of days.'

'We'll celebrate next weekend,' she decides.

'Can't. I've got a wedding in the Lake District.'

'This weekend, then. Shit! There's not enough time to organise anything! I can't believe you are doing this to me.'

'We'll talk about this later,' I say firmly. 'Coming to the pub?'

She screws up her brow. 'Of course.'

'Silly question.'

'Which pub?' Lachie asks as we set off back towards my building, dodging the tourists.

'The one across the road from work. Come if you like,' I say without thinking, then instantly wonder if it's such a good idea. I can't see why it would be a problem.

'Cool, yeah, I might do that.'

'Well, here I am.' I look up at the glass-clad building where Tetlan UK's multiple magazines are housed.

'Have a good arvo,' he says.

'Are you really coming out tonight?' I check.

'Why not? Got nothing better to do.'

'Weren't you going to drop in on the pub to see if they have any work?'

'I'll drop in on your pub across the road instead. I'm not fussy.'

Free and easy, just like he said.

★   ★   ★

I'm grinning that afternoon as I stand by the photocopier. Alex comes over to me. He's wearing a dark blue denim shirt with the sleeves rolled up and the colour really brings out the blue in his eyes.

'So what's he doing here?' he asks.

'Who? Lachie?' I ask casually. I know exactly who he's talking about.

'Yeah.' He folds his arms while I muck around with the settings on the copier.

'He said he was going to come to London,' I reply. 'And he did.'

'What are you trying to do?' he asks me with a frown, nodding at the machine in front of us.

'Double-sided A3,' I reply.

He moves closer and presses a couple of buttons, then hits the start button.

His aftershave drives me slightly insane. What can I do about that?

'You coming for a drink tonight?' I ask.

'Yeah. Zara's away this weekend.'

'So you're up for a big one?' I tease.

'Might be,' he replies with a conspiratorial grin.

I don't know if Lachie will turn up. I don't actually know for certain if I'll ever see him again. I have no way of contacting him if he doesn't appear – no change there, of course. But I do know that he came to find me today, so I'm confident that he'll stick to the pub plan.

And there he is, sitting on a stool and drinking

164

a pint of beer when six of us wander across as a group after work.

'Hey!' he says cheerfully.

'Not working behind the bar, then?' I ask as he gives me a friendly hug.

'Nah. Nothing going at the moment.'

'Oh well, there's still Camden.'

'Exactly. Hi,' he waves at my colleagues. I look over my shoulder to see pleased expressions on Lisa and Esther's faces and slightly disgruntled ones on the faces of Russ, Tim, Pete and Alex.

'Everyone, this is Lachie,' I say, adding, 'a fellow Aussie,' as if that will do as an explanation. We Aussies stick together, and all that.

Bridget walks through the door before anyone can say another word.

'Hello, *Hebes*!' she shouts, to my amusement, then, 'Lachie? What are you doing here?'

'Bronte invited me.'

She gives him a hug. 'Impressive work, flatmate.' She punches me on my arm.

'Who wants a drink?' Alex interrupts.

'Hi!' a bubbly voice calls from behind us.

I look over my shoulder to see that Maria has arrived.

'Hello!' I cry, turning around to give her a hug.

'Hey, Maria,' Russ says, putting his hand on her lower back. 'Can I get you a drink?'

'Hang on, I thought I was buying this round?' Alex asks with confusion.

'I'll get mine and Maria's, you and Bronte can do what you like,' Russ decides.

I turn back to the bar, feeling Lachie's knee against my leg. I shift slightly towards Alex, but our elbows touch and I tense and instinctively move away again.

A couple of drinks later, I've lightened up considerably. We've all relocated to a table and Lachie is going down a storm with my female colleagues. He's wedged in between Maria and Lisa, who switched seats when I went to the loo, leaving the chair beside Alex free.

'I thought you said he didn't play cheese,' Alex comments, turning to look at me with his stupidly blue eyes.

'Sorry?' I give him a puzzled look, distracted by Maria playfully restyling Lachie's hair.

'You said he played cool stuff, not cheese.'

What's he going on about? He hasn't heard Lachie play. Oh, hang on. Wham at lunchtime. 'Are you talking about "Wake Me Up Before You Go-Go"?'

'Yeah. Doesn't come much cheesier than that.'

I laugh. 'That was an insider joke.'

He regards me with uncertainty, and as his eyes widen slightly, I realise he might be jumping to conclusions. Oh well.

'You guys need to help me here,' Bridget says loudly, making everyone at the table turn to stare at her. 'It's Bronte's thirtieth birthday in a few weeks.'

I interrupt with a groan, leaning back in my seat while several pairs of eyes land on me. 'I'm going away the weekend after next for two weeks and I will miss it,' Bridget says crossly, as though we're all to blame. 'So I'm thinking we'll bring the celebrations forward. What's everyone doing next weekend?'

'I've already told you,' I interject just as Maria starts to say that she can't. 'I've got a wedding in the Lake District then. Maria has, too.' I smile across at her. 'I don't want a big bash.' I turn back to Bridget.

'That's what I was thinking!' Bridget says with worrying excitement. 'How about a group of us go up to the Lake District with you? My aunt has a little cottage in Keswick, which is not far from where your wedding is taking place, right?' She doesn't wait for me to answer. She's obviously done her research. 'We could stay there, otherwise we could camp. There's a campsite just across the lake.'

'That's a wicked idea,' Russ enthuses.

'I'd be up for that,' Lachie chips in.

'I'm free,' Lisa says.

'I can't,' Esther tells us with disappointment. 'It's my dad's fiftieth.'

Tim can't either, and Pete thinks his fiancée, Sylvie, might have already made plans for them. Alex has said nothing, but I know that the answer will be no, anyway.

'Alex?' Bridget asks him directly. 'What about you?'

'Maybe.'

I glance at him with surprise. 'Zara's away,' he explains. 'So I don't see why not.'

'She goes away a lot, your missus, doesn't she?' Russ says.

'A fair bit,' Alex agrees.

'So what do you reckon?' Bridget asks and I snap to attention when I realise her question is directed at me. 'We'll gate-crash your wedding. Just kidding,' she says when she sees my face. 'You can do your bit in the daytime and we'll help you celebrate at night. Yeah?'

'We'll probably be done by eight-ish,' I tell her thoughtfully.

Her face lights up. 'In that case, perfect! We can go up Friday night, straight from work, celebrate Saturday night, and play on Sunday before heading back in time for work on Monday. What do you think?' she asks the table.

'I think it's a brilliant plan,' Maria speaks for everyone.

CHAPTER 11

I call Polly on Sunday and I'm relieved when she answers. I thought she was avoiding my calls. She tells me she's going to see Grant's parents the following weekend, so she can't come to the Lake District. Bridget mentioned inviting them as well, but it's probably a good thing they can't come if Polly's trying to stay off the drink. I tell her I've been worried about her, but she brushes me off in her usual manner, accusing me of overreacting and claiming that what Maria and I saw was just a slip-up. I reiterate that I'm here for her if she needs me and leave it at that.

The following Friday night, a group of us congregate at the office to drive up to the Lake District for my fourth wedding – and my thirtieth birthday celebrations.

Rachel is taking Maria, Russ and Lisa, and Alex, who is the only other one of us who actually has a car, is taking Bridget, Lachie and me.

We're going to try and hook up at a motorway service station for a bite to eat and drive the rest of the way in convoy.

'Thanks for giving me a lift, bro,' Lachie says to Alex.

'No problem,' he responds, although he seemed less than thrilled to be taking my new buddy. He tried to persuade Russ to travel with him, but he was keen to travel with Maria. The pair of them seemed to hit it off at the pub last week – so much so that Maria played less with Lachie's hair and more with Russ's as the evening wore on.

'I don't know if that will fit in the boot.' Alex nods at Lachie's guitar as we walk through the dingy underground car park to his blue Alfa Romeo Brera.

'If not, it can come in the back with me,' he replies.

'One of my bags can come in the back with me, too,' Bridget says. So she's sitting next to Lachie, hey? Not that I mind sitting in the front with Alex.

Lachie has a backpack slung over his shoulder. Alex's bag and tent are already in the boot. He's borrowed a second tent from his sister and her husband, who I met at the hen night.

That seems like a lifetime ago.

Rachel, Maria and I already had a B&B booked, but the others are staying at Bridget's aunt's place tonight, then tomorrow they have to move to a campsite across the lake because a new weekly rental is coming in. Russ and Lisa are also bringing tents and Maria and I are playing things by ear. We might crash in a tent if there's room, otherwise we'll go back to our B&B with Rachel, who has shown no interest at all in sleeping on the ground when there's a perfectly good bed waiting and already paid for. She's promised to join us for drinks around the campfire after the wedding, though.

'Are you planning on playing that much?' Alex nods at Lachie's guitar as he pops open the boot to see if it will squeeze inside. It won't.

'We're gonna have a campfire, dude. Gotta have songs around a campfire.'

Alex frowns and takes my bags from me, kit bag included. He manages to find room for them somehow.

'Your friend is a little uptight,' Lachie mutters, his breath in my ear as he climbs with his guitar into the passenger seat behind me.

'Ooh, it's a bit squashy,' Bridget says as she joins Lachie in the back.

'Snuggle in close, Bridgie,' Lachie replies. Such a typical Aussie man, dishing out nicknames. 'You can rest your pretty little head on my shoulder.'

Alex flashes me a look and I mirror him, both of us knowing that Bridget will be only too happy to oblige. He navigates us out of the car park and straight into London at rush hour. Lachie starts to sing along to the radio, Alex turns the sound up and I smile to myself and let him concentrate on driving.

Two hours into our journey, Lachie and Bridget are both fast asleep; Lachie's head is tilted back on his headrest and Bridget's head is on one of his broad shoulders. I twist to face Alex.

'So Zara didn't mind you coming away this weekend?' I ask him. He glances in his rear-view mirror and turns the radio back down, satisfied that Lachie won't be singing along in the near future.

'No, why would she?'

I shrug. 'I don't know. That's good, though,' I add awkwardly.

'What's the deal with him?' Alex frowns, jerking his head towards the back seat.

'What do you mean?' I ask.

'What's he doing here?'

'I told you, I met him a couple of weeks ago at a wedding in Scotland.'

'And he just came to London and hunted you out?'

'I obviously made an impression on him. He's found a job in a pub in Camden.'

'It's a little obsessive, don't you think?'

I laugh. 'He's just being friendly, you dork, cut a girl some slack. It doesn't mean anything. It's not like he's in love with me,' I add in a self-deprecating voice.

'I don't know. He seems pretty used to women falling at his feet.'

'Who cares what he's used to?' I reply. 'I'll do what I want. And anyway, I'm single, he's single, what does it matter?' His jaw twitches as he stares straight ahead out of the windscreen. 'What's your problem with him?' I ask, not getting a reply. 'You just need to get to know him better,' I decide.

'How well do *you* know him?' He glances across at me, and I can hear the accusation in his tone.

'What are you asking me?' I reply, a chill spreading inside me as he looks back at the road. As if he has a right to ask me anything.

He glances at me again. 'Have you slept with him?'

Wow. I didn't expect him to be so upfront. Thankfully irritation overcomes my surprise.

'What's it to you if I had?' I bite back.

'Nothing. It's none of my business,' he says blandly, indicating to overtake a lorry. 'You can sleep with whoever you want.'

I stare at him with shock and anger. 'Is that what you think I do?' I ask coldly. 'Go around having one-night stands with people?'

He shrugs. 'Forget it.'

I glare at him for a moment longer, before instinctively turning around to look at the back seat. When I do, Lachie's half-open eyes are staring right back at me. He closes them again, leaving me to wonder if I'd just imagined him eavesdropping on our conversation.

CHAPTER 12

'I couldn't believe it when I woke up this morning. Wayne said to me, not this morning, obviously, because you're not allowed to see each other on the morning of the big day, but he's said to me in the past, he's said, "The weather is shit in the Lake District. Shit!" he said, but he's wrong. Look at it! Look out there!'

'It's beautiful, isn't it?' Maria says warmly, while Rachel snaps away.

'Absolutely stunning,' Becky, our excessively chatty bride continues. 'And to think he wanted to get married in London. London! Boring old London instead of here? I'm so glad I stuck to my guns. So glad.'

'Just hold still for a moment,' Maria says gently.

'I'll head off to the register office,' I whisper to Rachel. She nods with amusement.

Wayne agreed to marry Becky because she told him it was now or never, that's what we've been hearing. Both in their late thirties, the couple have been together for twelve years with no sign of a proposal. She wants children; he wants an easy

174

life. She decided it was time to make his life difficult or call it quits.

I still have no idea why she'd bother.

Wayne and I appear to share the same sentiment.

'What's with all the flowers? I told her to keep it simple,' I overhear him complaining to his mother, who looks like she's gone to a real effort, judging by the size of her hat and her matching lilac silk suit.

'It's her big day,' Wayne's mother says reasonably. 'She's waited a long time for this.'

'It's ridiculous. We don't need to get married to be together.'

Can't say I don't think he has a point. But it's a little late to be trying to convince anyone else on that matter . . . Wayne is still looking cranky and I don't want to shoot him with a black look on his face.

'Doesn't your mother look lovely, Wayne?' I prompt, hoping he'll glance at her and smile.

But instead he shocks me by saying, 'I don't want any photos. Get that thing out of my face!'

'Wayne!' His mother gasps, looking horrified. But he storms off.

Oh dear. We've got a tricky one here.

I do what I can, shooting him from afar with a zoom, but I barely get a single shot of him not scowling.

Thank goodness for the flowers, I say. They give me something to focus on. Masses of pinky-purple hellebores, blue delphiniums, muscari and corn-flowers are attached to the gilded aisle chairs with purple ribbons, and huge displays adorn every other surface. I think they look stunning.

When Becky arrives, she's like a beaming ray of sunshine. I hope some of her happiness rubs off on her husband-to-be. I thought she might have gone for something a little more understated, seeing as they're getting married in a register office, but to my surprise she has opted for a full meringue. She's not slim, but she hasn't made the strapless mistake. Her gown has a flattering V-neck, structured bodice with decent-sized shoulder straps, and there are crystal and pearl beads scattered attractively around her waistline just above a billowing white skirt. Her auburn hair is up in a bun and she's wearing diamanté drop earrings.

Rachel gives me a delighted thumbs-up.

'I love it when they go for the big dresses,' she says, making to move past me. 'How's everything here?'

'Er, okay,' I say.

'What is it?' She looks concerned.

'I think we've got a bit of a reluctant groom.'

We both look over at Wayne to see him checking his watch. He's wearing a nice enough suit, but it's nothing special. Not in comparison to the effort Becky has made.

'Don't worry, we'll get some good shots later,' Rachel assures me.

I've set her up at the front, so all she has to do

is start shooting. *The Princess Bride*'s 'Once Upon A Time . . . Storybook Love' begins to play out of a small stereo and I bite my lip. It makes a nice change from 'The Bridal March', that's for sure.

Becky begins to walk down the aisle and I ready myself to capture Wayne's reaction. But he's not turning around; his eyes are trained on the registrar. The guests coo and gasp as Becky passes them and then the curiosity must get to Wayne because he starts to swivel. Snap. His mouth falls open with shock. No smile. He stares at his bride-to-be in disbelief. He obviously had no idea she was going for a big dress. He pulls himself together and re-adjusts his face, but my heart sinks on her behalf.

To my surprise, Becky doesn't seem particularly fazed about her reluctant groom as the day proceeds. She's having the time of her life. Rachel and I drive along a scenic, winding road to the reception venue. The lake is on our right, visible above a grey stone wall dotted with splats of greeny-brown moss. To our left are tall, leafy trees, and beneath them the forest floor is covered with green grass and feathery ferns unfurling upwards into the sparse sunlight.

Waterfall slivers cut through the mountains like scars, and the mountains themselves are impressive, their colours smudged with greens, mauves, browns and greys. Scraggy gorse bushes cling to the slopes, bursting with yellow flowers. The rhododendron flowers are vibrant in colour: bright orange, pink, red and yellow.

When we arrive, we decide to make the most of the gorgeous weather by shooting the group shots in the garden. But when we're setting everyone up, we realise there's no groom. I find him around the back of the hotel, talking on his phone.

'I don't want to be in any photographs,' he snaps as soon as he sees me.

'But we're doing the group shots,' I plead.

He ignores me. 'Yeah, thanks,' he says into the receiver in a downhearted voice. 'Got me ball and chain now, never mind.'

Rachel and I are relieved when we finally get a break.

There's a stone bench under the trees by the lake so we take time to have a breather. The evening air is mild, but the bench is cold underneath us. Through the trees I see four familiar-looking people walking along the path on the other side of the lake. One of the guys is blond and wearing a black beanie, the other is dark-haired, and there are two girls.

'Is that the others?' I say aloud, jumping up and moving out from under the trees. I wave and the guy who I'm assuming is Lachie waves back. 'Do we have time to go and say hi?' I call to Rachel.

'Go for it,' she replies, firmly rooted to the bench. 'We've probably got half an hour. I'm going to chill here for a bit.'

'Okay, no worries.' I hurry along the path, my kit bag heavy on my shoulder and my camera clonking against my stomach until the faraway faces become more and more distinct. I grin at Lachie as he runs the last twenty metres towards me. The last thing I expect is for him to pick me up and swing me around so I squeal when he does.

'Put me down!' My head is spinning by the time my feet are planted on the pathway, my camera smacking against my gut. 'Oof!'

'How's it going?' he asks, laughing and blocking me as I try to hit him. He's wearing a white, slightly holey T-shirt and a beanie which is completely unnecessary in this weather.

'Urgh, it's all a bit shit, actually.'

'What's up?' Alex asks with a frown as he, Bridget and Lisa reach us.

'The groom is a total tosspot,' I reply to everyone's amusement. 'What are you guys doing here?'

'That's the campsite there,' Lachie says, twisting around to point behind him.

'That's so close. The reception is just across the lake.' I jerk my head to my right, indicating a distant whitewashed building. 'I could practically walk here later.'

'It'll be too dark.' Alex shakes his head authoritatively. 'I'll come and pick you up in the car.'

'Or I could walk you,' Lachie interjects.

'It's okay, Rachel's driving,' I tell them with a smile, turning to Bridget. 'How's your tent?' I ask her. She's just had her hair cut into a stylish blunt bob and she looks fantastic.

'You want my honest answer?' That sounds ominous.

'Yes?' I reply tentatively.

'I can't believe I ever suggested this.'

I laugh. 'Why?'

'I don't think I'm a camping sort of girl. The tent is so small!' She pulls a disgusted face. 'And my bed is so hard!'

'Have you never been camping before?' Lachie asks, looking down at her with amusement.

'No.'

'No?' I ask, perplexed. But she was so keen on the idea! 'Then why did you suggest it?'

'I didn't know my aunt was going to be booked out,' she grumbles.

'Have my bed at the B&B if you like. I'm happy to camp.'

Her mood visibly improves. 'Really?'

'Sure.' I scan the meadow behind them. 'Where are Maria and Russ?'

'They're up at the tents,' Lisa reveals with a mischievous look.

'Did you know they got it on together last week?' Bridget questions me with narrowed eyes. 'After the pub?'

'Did they?' I reply with surprise. 'Wow.' I wonder why Maria didn't mention it. Felt a little self-conscious, I imagine. I look for Rachel under the cluster of trees in the distance. 'I need to get back.'

'We'll walk with you,' Alex says. He and I fall into step with each other. The warm sun beats down on my neck and shoulders. I'm wearing

180

smart black trousers and a navy-blue shirt and my light-brown hair is up in a ponytail.

'You want me to carry that for you?' Alex asks, nodding at my heavy kit bag.

'I'm alright,' I brush him off.

'Go on.'

I comply, sliding it off my shoulder and into his proffered hand. 'Thanks.'

He nods at my camera. 'Can I see some of your shots?'

'Sure.' I turn my camera on and scroll down as we walk. We pause on a small grey stone bridge curving over a bubbling brook and I tilt the screen his way.

'There's a fish!' Lisa cries, while Bridget takes off one of her shoes and complains about a blister.

Alex moves his head closer to mine. I return my attention to my shots, breathing in his scent as I do so. 'I messed up the exposure on these ones,' I remember as I skip through the signing of the register.

'The bride and groom silhouettes look good, though,' he comments, touching his hand to mine so I slow down.

'Rachel manually exposes when she shoots in front of a window, so she will have got what she needs,' I tell him, noticing the slight waver to my voice. 'Check this out.' I go back to the pictures of the groom before the service.

'Bloody hell,' he exclaims, pulling the camera closer to his face. 'What a miserable twat.'

'I know.' I laugh and look up at him.

Rachel joins us. 'Hey, guys,' she says, nodding towards the reception venue and then at me. 'We should get back.'

'Sure,' I reply.

'How much longer do you think you'll be?' Alex asks me.

'Not long, thankfully. We've just got to tick the first dance box and then we'll be done.'

'Is there a pub nearby?'

'There's one next door.'

Alex spins around and walks backwards for a few steps, facing the others. 'Why don't we go for a couple of beers and wait for Bronte?'

'Good plan,' they concur.

Alex spins back around and flashes me a sidelong smile. 'Then we could all walk back together.'

CHAPTER 13

'I need a drink. A big one,' Rachel says. 'Damn, I'm driving,' she remembers.

Rachel and I join the others at the pub as soon as we can. It is such a relief to be done with that day.

'Why don't you leave your car here and walk back with us?' Alex suggests. 'I can give you a lift here in the morning.'

'Thanks, but I'm kipping at the B&B. You can have your terrible night's sleep, but I've got a bed to go back to.'

We take our drinks to the table where the others are sitting.

'Bronte!' Lachie exclaims when he clocks me. He's already had a few and his effervescent personality is practically bubbling over.

Rachel sits down and Alex sets off to hunt out another chair.

'She doesn't need one,' Lachie calls after him, pulling me onto his lap. I gasp with surprise. Then he buries his face in my neck and laughingly kisses me over and over, just above my collarbone.

'Argh!' I squeal. His beard tickles. 'Stop it!' I manage to spit out, smacking his thigh.

He stops kissing me, but he keeps his warm arms hooked around my waist and smiles up at me, his light blue eyes twinkling. What a flirt.

Alex averts his gaze from us and sits down, picking up a pint glass.

'What's Zara up to this weekend?' I ask, trying to include him. I don't want him to regret coming.

'She's—'

'Who's Zara?' Lachie interrupts before Alex can reply.

'His fiancée,' I tell him over my shoulder.

'Really?' He says it with total surprise, looking past me to Alex. 'You getting married, mate?'

'Yep,' Alex replies shortly.

'When?' he asks.

'December.'

'You gonna get Bron to do your wedding?' Lachie rests one hand lightly on my right leg.

'Rachel's doing it,' I say hastily with a smile in her direction.

'Well, if you need an awesome wedding singer, you know where to find me,' he says cheekily, jigging me up and down on his knee.

'Would you stop that?' I slap his thigh again. He's wearing scruffy denim jeans.

'I'll keep you in mind,' Alex replies drily. 'She's in New York for work,' he answers my question, trying to ignore the person whose knee I'm sitting on.

'Again?'

He nods.

'Does she go there a lot?'

'Every few weeks.'

'You must miss her,' Lisa says, listening in.

'Yeah.' He shrugs.

'Ever thought about moving to New York?' Lisa asks.

My heart skips a beat.

'Aah, not really,' Alex replies, meeting my eyes again. And then Lachie buries his face in my neck once more and I'm distracted fighting off his ticklish kisses.

We head back to the campsite while it's still light enough to see. Bridget, with her sore feet, hitches a lift with Rachel, but the rest of us are happy to get some fresh air.

'What's the story with your mate?' Lachie asks me in a low voice, nodding ahead at Alex, who's walking next to Lisa and talking about work. Alex asked me a similar question about Lachie on the way up here.

'What do you mean? There's no story,' I say innocently.

'What's going on between you?'

'Nothing,' I exclaim under my breath, keeping my voice low so no one can hear us. 'You heard him. He's getting married in December.'

He thinks for a minute before speaking. 'If you don't mind me saying, things seem a little tense between you two. It's like you've got history.'

Now I really am tense. 'I *do* mind you saying, and I'd appreciate it if you kept your mouth shut.'

He digs his hands into his jeans pockets, but the ensuing silence doesn't last for long.

'Do the others know?'

'Know what?'

'About your history?'

'What history? I didn't say we had any history!'

Lachie gives me a look, and for once there's no trace of amusement on his face.

I take a deep breath and give in. I think he'll keep my secret safe.

'If you really want to know,' I say quietly, 'Alex and I met a year and a half ago when he was on a break from his girlfriend. Something . . . happened,' I leave him to fill in the blanks. 'I didn't expect to ever see him again.'

'And now he works with you?'

'Yes.'

'Fuuuuuck,' he says slowly.

'That's one way of putting it.'

'Never mind, Bronnie, I'll take your mind off him.' He wraps his arm around my neck and pulls me close.

Bronnie? 'Oh, stop.' I push him away and Alex looks back at us, hearing the commotion. I force a light laugh and he returns to his conversation with Lisa. 'I don't need anyone to take my mind off him, thanks,' I say under my breath. 'There's nothing between us, and I'm happy being single right now, anyway.'

'Just trying to be helpful,' he says quietly. I glance at him to see if I've hurt his feelings, but I can't tell. His expression is too hard to read.

The path turns to a grey stone one, and small clouds of dust puff up around Alex's Converse trainers as we walk. I take out my camera and start to click off some shots. This view around us is breathtaking. Majestic mountains slant across each other and the beech trees are still lime green with fresh new leaves, undarkened by the summer sun. Bluebells peek out of the grass amid the ferns, and I almost short with laughter. This is so perfect it looks staged. If I saw a film with a set like this, I'd think it was a tad overdone.

I turn and click off a photo of Lachie, then call to the others to spin around. Alex pushes his hair off his face. He looks gorgeous in black jeans and a dark grey long-sleeve T-shirt pushed up to the elbows. I do think he has sexy forearms.

Oh dear. I really shouldn't be thinking such thoughts.

We leave the dry path and climb a slight hill to get to the campsite. The green grass is shaggy and wet underfoot and my boots squelch through the bog. Lachie leaps like a goat over the muddiest patches, helping the rest of us to navigate our ways. We reach a sturdy wooden gate attached to a chunky, moss-covered stone wall and pass through it into a forest of pine trees.

The others have already set up their tents and built a fire, so now all they have to do is light it.

Russ and Alex take control. The fire crackles into life in the centre of a large log circle meant for sitting on. Four tents surround the circle, facing the fire. Lisa is in one, Alex and Russ are staying in another, Lachie has a small one-person tent to himself and Bridget was supposed to have the fourth tent before she decided to sleep at the B&B. Maria and I have agreed to swap with her.

Lisa brings a couple of bottles of Prosecco out of her tent with disposable glasses, and Maria emerges two seconds later with bags of popcorn and marshmallows. Then Bridget appears from behind her tent with a cake, lit with candles. Lachie follows, strumming his guitar.

'Aw!' I cry, as everyone sings 'Happy Birthday' to me. There's a number '30'-shaped candle on the top, and the flame flickers as Bridget steps carefully around the fire towards me. My eyes mist up and I blow out the candles, touched by the effort everyone has gone to.

'Thank you,' I say meaningfully, giving Bridget a clumsy hug around the cake she's holding.

'Happy birthday, Bronte.' Russ steps over a log to give me a kiss on my cheek.

'It's not her birthday yet,' Bridget reminds him. 'Don't forget it's on the twelfth. I can't believe I'm not going to be here for you.'

'Don't be silly. You'll be having a brilliant time,' I say.

'Where are you going?' Lachie asks her.

They chat about Key West while everyone settles

themselves on log seats around the fire. I sit between Russ and Lisa, with Alex on the other side of Russ. Russ and I talk about work and he slags off Nicky on my behalf, then we move on to trying to get information out of Alex about Simon's plans for a redesign. After a while, Russ gets up to go and sit next to Maria and Lisa joins in a conversation with Rachel beside her.

'I didn't know Nicky was still giving you a hard time,' Alex says, shifting to close the gap between us.

'Not always,' I reply, holding out my hands to warm them on the fire. 'It's no big deal.'

'It doesn't sound good,' he says with concern.

I glance at him to see him staring at me, the orange glow from the fire lighting one side of his face and casting shadow across the other. His eyes are dark in the low light, his hair black and pushed back from his face. My heart flips and lands with a dull thud. I can't be feeling like this about him.

'Who wants a song around the campfire?' Lachie interrupts loudly.

'Yeah!' all the girls reply.

Alex drags his eyes away from mine and sighs quietly as Lachie starts to play an acoustic version of Daft Punk's 'Get Lucky'.

I look over at the girls' rapt expressions and then see Russ give Alex a resigned look.

'You've got to admit, he's a damn good singer,' I comment.

'Mmm,' Alex grunts his reply. 'I heard too much of this song last summer.'

'What sort of music do you like, then?' I ask with amusement at his jealousy.

'Oh, I don't know,' he says casually. 'Kylie, Starship, T'Pau . . .'

I laugh and he grins. 'As long as it's from the Eighties, I love it,' he jokes.

'Now I *know* that is not true,' I point out with a significant look.

'I never said I didn't like Eighties music.'

'True,' I admit. 'Do you?' I ask with surprise.

'Not really,' he replies with a chuckle. 'Although I don't mind UB40.'

We danced to 'Red, Red Wine'. My head prickles at the memory.

Lachie sings about being up all night to get lucky, his eyes locking with mine. He grins at me and I smile a small smile back before looking at the fire.

'I wouldn't go there,' Alex warns quietly.

'What?' I look at him to see the torn expression on his face.

He shoots a quick glance at Lachie. 'Nothing,' he says under his breath. I jolt as he gets up abruptly and walks away from us.

'You alright, mate?' Russ calls after him.

'Just going for a leak,' he replies flatly.

I stare at the fire, confusion muddling my brain.

Later, when all of the alcohol has been drunk and all of the snacks devoured, I see Maria huddled over with Lisa. Rachel called it a night a while ago, Russ and Alex have gone to gather some more wood, Lachie has picked up his guitar again, and Bridget is on the phone to the taxi company.

'Oi!' I hiss at Maria. 'What's going on?'

'Just discussing sleeping arrangements,' she replies with an embarrassed smile. She turns back to Lisa. 'Are you sure?'

'Hang on, who's sleeping where?' I whisper loudly.

'Maria and Russ are in one,' Lisa tells me while trying to keep a straight face. 'And I'll go in with you, if you're still staying?'

'Yep,' I nod.

'Bridget's going back to the B&B,' she adds.

'No, I'm not,' Bridget says loudly, ending her call. 'I can't get a cab.'

'Oh,' I say, finding it hard to take her disappointment seriously. 'Bad luck.'

'In that case, do you two want to go in together?' Lisa asks us. 'Lachie can go in with Alex and I'll have the one-person tent,' she decides with a smile.

'Hang on, what's going on?' Alex reappears, overhearing the last part of our conversation. Lachie stops playing and listens.

'Can Lachie go in your tent with you?' I ask.

'Why?' His brow furrows.

'Russ and Maria are going together . . .' I say with meaning.

'Oh!' He cottons on, but doesn't look too happy about his new tent partner.

'I don't mind sharing with Bronnie,' Lachie says with a wink. He's clearly in two minds about what my pet name should be. Bron or Bronnie?

'You're in a one-person tent. Bron*te* won't fit,' Alex points out firmly, emphasising the second syllable of my name.

'She's only little,' Lachie says. 'We can cuddle up,' he adds cheekily.

'You don't give in, do you?' Bridget laughs.

'Just trying to be helpful, Bridgie,' he says cheerfully.

'No, you can come in with me,' Alex tells him decisively. 'Why doesn't Bronte have the one-person tent, seeing as it's her birthday,' he suggests.

'Good idea,' Lisa agrees.

'I don't care where I sleep,' I say to Alex. 'But I really hope you have a spare sleeping bag.'

'I could keep you warm,' Lachie says.

'Yes, I have a spare sleeping bag,' Alex says loudly, ignoring him.

'Just give me a shout if you get cold,' Lachie chips in.

'Would you leave her alone?' Alex exclaims.

I *think* he's joking.

Finally, after quite a lot of kerfuffle, I'm settled in a tent. Lachie and Alex are sniping at each other in the tent next door, and Bridget is complaining in the tent next to them. On my other side, Russ and Maria are giggling quietly. After what seems like forever, everyone quietens down and I roll over on my side on the hard ground. A bird makes a racket in the trees.

'What the fuck was that?' Lachie's voice pierces the silence.

'A pheasant,' Alex says wearily. 'The forest never sleeps,' he adds in a mock wildlife documentary-style voice, making me purse my lips.

Russ and Maria whisper to each other and try to stifle their giggles and then silence descends once more.

I'm just drifting off when I hear the sound of them kissing.

'At least someone's getting some,' Lachie mutters.

'Shut up!' Alex snaps.

The rest of us laugh. I fall asleep to the sound of Maria and Russ 'getting some'.

The next morning I wake up early with a sore head and a full bladder. I slept in my clothes so all I have to do is pull on my boots and unzip the tent. The air is damp and the fire is long gone, a circle of ash set within a ring of logs. I straighten up and stretch my arms over my head, yawning, then I set off towards the toilet block.

After kicking myself for failing to bring so much as a toothbrush, I re-emerge and see Lachie and Bridget approaching. He has his arm draped around her neck and for a moment I think I've missed something, but then I realise he's only being his usual friendly self.

'Bronnie!' he says jubilantly, letting go of Bridget

and ruffling her hair. She bats him away with annoyance, looking thoroughly fed up.

Her new blunt bob has not fared well overnight. She looks like she's wearing a birds' nest. 'Are you okay?' I ask her with a grin.

'No, I'm flipping exhausted,' she snaps, but her lips are pursed so I know she's not completely serious. She walks past me into the toilet block and Lachie opens his arms up to me. I smile and step into his embrace. His arms close around me and I rest my face against his warm chest.

'How did you sleep?' he asks, his voice muffled against my hair as he rocks me slightly.

'Fine,' I murmur, feeling stupidly content.

He really is so sweet and friendly and tactile, and yes, flirty too, not just with me, but with everyone. I like him, though. A lot. I'm glad we're friends.

I pull away and look up at him. 'You?'

'Same. I can sleep anywhere.' His light blue eyes are tired and his shaggy blond hair looks even more just-slept-in than usual. 'I don't think Maria and Russ got much shut-eye,' he adds with a raised eyebrow.

'No? I fell asleep after the kissing started.'

'They make a funny couple,' he comments, mystified.

Physically, they're opposites – Russ is tall with red hair, pale skin and freckles, and Maria is short and curvy with olive skin and dark glossy hair.

'They seem to get on.'

He laughs. 'They certainly do.' He lets me go. 'See ya in a bit.'

When I get back to the tents, Alex is awake and building another fire.

'Morning,' I say warmly.

'Hey.' He gives me a sleepy smile.

'Would you mind running me over to the B&B so I can brush my teeth and change my clothes?'

'Sure,' he replies. 'You want to go now?'

'That would be great. When you're ready.'

'You are so going to have a shower, aren't you?' Bridget butts in, arriving back in time to hear the tail end of our conversation. 'That's cheating!'

'You can come with me,' I tell her.

'Bloody brilliant idea,' she says, scrambling back into her tent to grab what she needs.

Maria entrusts us with checking out and bringing her bags back. She has no desire to leave Russ – she's got that flush of new love about her.

Back at the B&B I have a quick shower and get changed in the bathroom while Alex and Bridget lie propped up on the bed, watching TV. I emerge feeling a million times better.

'It's all yours,' I say to Bridget.

'Cheers, big ears.' We swap places, but as soon as Bridget locks the door to the bathroom, Alex passes me a large brown envelope.

'What's this?' I ask, confused.

'Open it,' he urges, his eyes crinkling at the corners.

I lift the flap and reach into the envelope, pulling out a mock-up cover of *Hebe*. I'm the cover star, winking cheekily at the camera and holding up a plastic glass.

I gasp and cover my mouth with my hand as I take it all in.

'Bronte turns 30!' yells the headline, and there are other, funny little in-jokes and coverlines about camera shake, Photoshop and Friday nights at the pub. I recognise the picture as one of the shots Sarah, the editorial assistant, took when we were celebrating the Joseph Strike baby bump issue.

'Did you do this?' I ask, touched beyond belief as he nods, smiling at my reaction. People get mock-up covers like this if they resign, not for something like a birthday.

'I wanted to give it to you last night, but . . .' He shrugs.

There was too much else going on.

'Thank you,' I whisper.

'You're welcome,' he replies gently. 'Now, is there anything you want to watch?' he asks as I continue to stare at the cover.

'No, I'm good,' I say, carefully placing it between us on the bed. I lie down on my side, facing him. 'I'm just going to rest my eyes.'

The morning's mist has burnt off and now sunshine is coming through the window, spilling across the bed. I bask in the warmth and feel content. Out of the blue, a horrible dark feeling washes over me and my eyes shoot open. Alex is still watching the telly, his arm draped across his tummy and his chest rising and falling with slow, steady breaths. I look up at his face, but he's fixed on the television. Déjà vu hits me hard and I realise that we lay on a bed in this same position under the window on the morning after we'd slept together.

Perhaps sensing my gaze, he glances down at me, his blue eyes lighter under the sun's rays. He gives me a curious look.

'I'm tired,' I say, trying to ignore the darkness I'm feeling. 'Did you get much sleep last night?'

'No,' he replies. 'Your friend kicks.'

'Does he?' I smirk. 'Sorry about that.' I know he's not really cross, but I feel bad. 'Do you wish you hadn't come?'

His brow furrows as he looks down at me. 'Of course not. Why would you say that?'

'Just, I don't know . . .'

He shakes his head. 'It's been fun.'

I roll over onto my back. 'You wouldn't have rather stayed at home in peace and quiet, being able to sprawl out in your lovely, big double bed?'

He gives me a pointed look. 'No,' he says resolutely.

I grin. 'Good.'

He keeps eye contact for a long moment and the dark feeling inside me turns into jitters. He looks like he's about to say something but the sound of a hairdryer starting up in the bathroom seems to jolt him to his senses. He returns his gaze to the TV.

'What?' I ask, my curiosity too great to let it lie.

He glances down at me again, his expression grave. 'I'm sorry about what I said in the car on the way up here.'

'Oh. Don't worry.'

'I know you don't go around . . .' He lets his sentence trail off. I don't go around having one-night stands with people.

'No,' I confirm.

'And if you like him, well, that's cool.'

His lips may be curved upwards, but his smile doesn't feel sincere. Still, he's trying to be nice.

'Okay. Thanks,' I say quietly.

He looks back at the TV and I close my eyes as the dark feeling returns.

CHAPTER 14

'Honestly, they were a frigging nightmare.' I'm at work ranting to Alex about my latest wedding.

'Rachel reckons it's a phenomenon. The Rise of The Useless Bridesmaid, she calls it,' I tell him. 'They were *utterly* useless. All they cared about was getting drunk and having a good time. They even changed out of their dresses for the evening do.'

'Really?'

'Yeah. They had on these beautiful, Fifties-style dresses, all in different shades of blue, and they took them off and put on some awful clubbing outfits that barely covered their arses. If I was the bride, I would have gone spare. Not that I'd ever want to be a bride. But honestly, I've never seen anything like it. They were completely selfish. Didn't care about their friend at all. I was the one who had to carry her train and bouquet half the time. Rachel even helped her go to the loo.'

Alex laughs. 'It sounds awful.'

'Honestly, I hope Zara's got some nice friends, because those girls were useless.'

After the tension in the Lake District a couple

of weeks ago, I've been making a concerted effort to talk about Alex's fiancée more. It seems to be working. We're much more relaxed around each other.

'She's not having bridesmaids,' Alex reveals.

'Isn't she?' Doesn't she have any friends?

'She's having a couple of little flower girls instead.'

'Oh, right. That will be nice.' The flower girls on the weekend were almost as bratty as the bridesmaids. The bride indulged them by letting them wear fairy wings at the last minute.

'How did your birthday drinks go?' Alex asks.

'Stupidly,' I tell him, not amused. 'We ended up at Lachie's pub doing shots before hitting a club.'

'Guess you only turn thirty once,' Alex points out.

'I felt so sick on Saturday.'

Luckily Rachel didn't mind. In fact, she was sympathetic. Sally had let her down again – flu, this time, allegedly – so I stepped in at the last minute.

'What are you *doing*?' I jump at the sound of Nicky's irate voice. She's obviously come to find me because I've been away from my desk for so long. 'Simon wants to see you,' she snaps, glaring at me.

'Be there in a sec,' I tell her as she spins on her heels and walks out again. 'I wonder what that's about,' I say worriedly.

'I think I know,' Alex whispers. 'It's nothing bad,' he adds with a reassuring smile.

I take my tea and return to the *Hebe* office.

'Ah, Bronte,' Simon says, spying me. 'Can I have a word?'

He nods at the meeting room near my desk. I nervously follow him in there.

'As you know, we're doing a redesign.'

'Yes.'

'I need to take a small team of people out of the office for the next three weeks to work on it and I'd like you to come from the picture desk.'

My heart lifts. 'Really? Not Nicky?' I check.

'No, Nicky's got enough on her plate,' he says smoothly.

'Okay, great.' Wow! I wonder who else is going. 'Is there anything I need to do to prepare?'

'Nope. Friday will be our last day in the office, so try to tie up any loose ends. Esther, Pete, Alex, Mike and Teagan will be coming, too.'

That's all the department heads from Features, News, Art, Production and Style. I'm the only one who is not a department head. How weird. Not that I'm complaining.

'Great.'

He stands up, meeting over.

I walk out of the room and catch Alex's eye. He smiles at me, but I keep a straight face because Nicky's watching me. I sit back down at my desk, trying to ignore the sound of her slapping her paperwork around.

'I don't know why,' Alex insists on Friday night at the pub.

Russ thinks he has the answer to why Simon has asked me to be involved in the redesign instead of Nicky. 'It's because she's crap,' he says. '*And she's a silly bitch*. I'm going to miss you guys, though. It's going to be quiet in the office.'

'Aw,' I say, ruffling his hair affectionately. 'Are you catching up with Maria later?'

'Yeah, I'm meeting her at Lachie's pub.'

'Cool.' I turn to Alex and Pete. 'Are you guys coming out?'

'Can't. Sylvie's mum is over from America,' Pete says. Sylvie is the American girl he's marrying next month.

'Last-minute wedding preparations?' Lisa asks him.

'Yeah, just enough time for her to put her two pence in,' he confirms.

'What about you?' Lisa turns to Alex. 'Camden?'

'Not tonight,' he replies. 'Zara's parents are here from Devon for the weekend, too. Wedding dress shopping,' he reveals.

'How exciting,' I say, trying to sound like I mean it.

'So when are we going to meet this bird of yours?' Russ asks. 'You should bring her out one Friday night.'

'Yeah,' he says, noncommittally. 'Maybe.'

I know that it would probably be a good idea for me to put a face to her name.

But it doesn't feel like a good idea.

* * *

'What can I get you?' Lachie asks me with a grin when we arrive at the Camden pub. 'Shot of tequila?'

'No!' I say firmly. 'I've got a wedding tomorrow. Last week nearly killed me. I'll have a lemonade, please.'

He grabs a glass down from above the bar and fills it up from the soda gun. 'What time are we heading off?' he asks.

'Heading off where?' I'm confused.

'To the wedding.'

'What wedding?'

'The wedding tomorrow. You know I'm coming, right?'

'Are you?' I ask with surprise. 'How did that happen?'

'Rachel called me on Wednesday. They decided at the last minute to get a live act and she recommended me.'

'Oh, cool. That was nice of her.' I didn't know Rachel even had his number.

'So?' He puts my drink in front of me.

'What? Oh, what time are we setting off?'

He nods, amused. I'm still a little thrown that Rachel didn't tell me about this.

'Nine, I think. Didn't she say?' I get my purse out and hand over a fiver.

'Yeah, but I forgot. Thought I'd ask you tonight.' He goes to the cash register and returns with my change.

'Are we picking you up?' I ask.

'Yep.'

'What's this?' Maria asks, overhearing.

'Did you know Lachie was coming to this wedding tomorrow?' I ask her.

'Yeah,' she replies. 'Rachel said.'

'How late do you think you'll be back tomorrow night?' Russ asks her.

'I was thinking about staying up there, catching up with my parents,' Maria replies.

He looks disappointed. I guess he wants to spend time with her this weekend. 'You could come if you like?' she suggests.

'What, and stay with your parents?'

'Well, no, they'd go mental.'

'Would they?' Bridget asks with surprise as Lachie gets on with serving a group of girls who have just come in.

'Yeah, they're really strict,' Maria says. 'Catholic.'

'Where are you from?' I realise I've never actually asked Maria this before.

'Spain,' she replies. 'Well, my parents are. I've lived in Britain all my life. My grandfather still lives near San Sebastian.'

'Oh, I love northern Spain,' Bridget says. 'Do you have loads of holidays there?'

'We usually get over there in the summer. They have a villa which they rent out.'

'Nice!'

'So if I can't stay with you . . .' Russ's voice trails off, bringing Maria's attention back to the weekend.

'Well, okay, maybe I'm not really thinking

properly. I only have to do this wedding in the morning, then we could go say hi to my parents and travel back down with the others. You can stay at mine and Rachel's. Just don't tell my parents you've been doing that,' she adds quickly.

From what I've been hearing since we went to the Lake District, Russ has practically moved in.

'I'm a bit scared,' Russ says in a small voice.

'Don't be scared. They'll love you.' She squeezes his arm. He smiles down at her and I glance at Bridget, who rolls her eyes at me. I smirk and walk around the lovebirds so I can chat to my flatmate. I pull up a stool next to her and sit down.

'There are far too many pheromones flying round at the moment,' she says. 'Check out Lachie.'

I look over my shoulder to see the group of girls at the end of the bar flirting with him as he gets their drinks. He seems to be lapping up the attention.

'I bet he could go home with a different girl every night if he wanted,' she muses.

'Mmm,' I reply, averting my gaze as I sip my drink. 'He probably does. Can you imagine how many bridesmaids he's shagged over the years?'

'Too many to count,' she agrees drily. 'I still would, though.'

I snort with laughter at her typically casual comment.

'Wouldn't you?' she asks with a smirk.

'Becoming another notch on Lachie's bedpost would be the last thing I need,' I tell her with absolute certainty.

CHAPTER 15

Rachel, unlike Alex, does not have a problem with Lachie singing along to the radio. I sit in the back, squeezed up against the door as Maria and Russ smooch beside me.

'So just to give you a bit of an update,' Rachel says loudly, and I realise she's talking to me. 'The groom's uncle is a part-time wedding photographer.'

I cling onto her headrest and pull myself out of my tight corner to speak to her. 'Why isn't he doing the wedding?'

'I don't know. Maybe Nina and Seb just want him to enjoy the day,' she replies.

Nina and Seb are the bride and groom.

'Or maybe he's shit,' Lachie butts in, swivelling in his seat to look at me, then at Rachel.

'Maybe,' Rachel says, glancing at him. I can't see her face, but I can hear the smile in her voice.

'Apparently, he has vowed to make our lives difficult,' she adds.

'What?' I scoff.

'I *think* he's joking. I *hope* he's joking,' she corrects herself.

★　★　★

206

He's not joking.

'That's a big lens for a little girl.'

I'm assuming this is the uncle, because he's carrying a massive professional camera around, photographing the same details in the church as I am. I'm trying not to let him put me off.

'Aah, a Canon,' he says. 'I'm a Nikon man, myself.'

I honestly couldn't give a toss.

'Bob,' he says, holding his hand out.

'Uncle Bob? Are you being serious?' I ask with a grin. Bob's your uncle . . .

'Afraid so. What lens are you using?'

'35 prime.' It's good for portraits and I'm hoping the groom is about to arrive.

'Really?' he pulls a face. Just then, the groom does come into the church.

'Excuse me,' I say, but Bob crouches slap bang in the middle of the aisle and calls for his nephew.

'Seb! Come here, lad. Just stand there, would you? Flash us a smile. Great!' *Click, click, click.* I can't believe the cheek of the man.

'Sorry, can I just . . .'

He doesn't budge. 'Gorgeous, my boy. Turn a little to your right. Hand on your hip. Perfect.'

I give up. I don't want posed shots anyway. I continue capturing the details until Bob moves on, and then I surreptitiously take some nice, natural shots of Seb chatting to his mother and his best man before going into the chancel.

I falter at the sight of the pipe organ. It's not as

big and daunting as some of the ones I've seen recently. There are only two keyboards – or manuals, as they're called – and just over two dozen shining silver pipes. Some of the largest organs in the world have as many as seven keyboards and over twenty thousand pipes. The pedalboard, which is the wooden keyboard played by the feet, is scuffed and dirty from use. The yellowing, curling-edged sheet music is laid out and ready for the entrance of the bride, and several of the stops – the cream-coloured knobs that control the sounds for each keyboard – have been pulled out and are already in position.

I notice my breathing has sharpened as I stare at the instrument. I shouldn't feel so affected by wood, metal and plastic. It's actually faintly ridiculous. I force myself to walk over to it and run my fingers across the keys. My pulse rate jumps up a notch, but I stay there a while longer before letting my hand drop to my side. Then I pick up my camera and start shooting. By the time I've finished, I feel relatively peaceful.

As luck would have it, sunlight is streaming in through the church doors when Nina, the bride, arrives. She's wearing a white gown of chiffon and silk with pleats over her bodice and a halter-neck lace detail. Her floaty, chiffon A-line skirt billows out into a bell shape and is scattered with white sequins. She's also wearing a veil and the light shines straight through it, making her look like an angel. Her three bridesmaids, stunning in long, floor-length gowns in varying shades of pink, from pastel to rose, hover behind her, but she's central and serene in the shot. And then Bob bumps into my elbow.

'Beautiful,' he says, snapping away. I stare at him in disbelief. Is he for real? Thankfully I've got my shots, but what is he thinking?

He doesn't improve during the church service. Sometimes he blocks my view and he doesn't even turn off his focus beep, so every time he takes a picture during the ceremony, his camera beeps and the vicar looks up the aisle at us. I want to shout, 'It isn't me!' but I don't think that would go down too well.

He's even worse when we're doing the group shots at the reception venue. He stands to Rachel's right and gives directions to the wedding party. 'Hold your bouquets like this, girls,' he calls to the bridesmaids. 'Right here, just above your hips.'

Rachel is having none of it. 'Sorry, that's not how we work. No, just look natural,' she calls to the group. 'Don't put them on your hip.'

'Why not?' he has the cheek to ask her.

'It's too formal,' Rachel says firmly but calmly. 'We don't do formal.'

Now no one seems to know what to do. The bridesmaids look at each other awkwardly, not sure where to put their bouquets.

'Throw your arms around each other,' I call, so they do, and Rachel snaps away quickly while Bob looks totally put out.

Rachel always takes the bride and groom away from other guests for their private shoot, so we are disappointed when we see Bob and his wife sneaking off after us, his wife tottering behind him in her heels with his camera bag and two glasses of champagne. But because Bob is Seb's uncle, and because Seb and Nina don't say anything, we can't really tell him to bugger off. So we have to make do with him hanging over our shoulders, taking his own shots and generally making our lives difficult, just like he promised he would.

'Don't let him get to you,' Rachel says calmly when we retire to the kitchen for a break after the speeches. 'He's obviously an old-school photographer. Let him do his thing and we'll do ours. At the end of the day, Seb and Nina booked *us*, not him.'

I'm glad she's so calm about it.

'I wouldn't even take a professional camera to a friend's wedding,' Rachel says later in the car on the way home.

'Wouldn't you?' Russ asks, his arm draped around Maria's shoulders. From their body language, I'm guessing their visit home went well.

'Not unless I was asked to,' she says. 'I think it's completely disrespectful.'

'That must've been so off-putting having him standing over your shoulder like that,' Maria comments.

'I hated it,' I admit. 'You didn't seem bothered

210

in the slightest,' I say, pulling myself forward to hang over Rachel's shoulder.

'There are always going to be a handful of wedding guests who have cameras as good as yours. But you've just got to chill out, let it go, worry about your own angles. The bride and groom have chosen us because they like our style and the finished product. It's always going to look better as a package than anything anyone else is going to do.'

'I wish I had your confidence,' I say.

She laughs. 'When you've done as many weddings as I have, not much fazes you.'

'How many weddings have you done?' Russ asks her.

'Getting up towards sixty.'

'Wow,' he says. I've still only done six.

'Always the wedding photographer, never the bride,' she says drily.

For some reason, that makes me think of Alex.

CHAPTER 16

'This is cosy.' Alex stands in the doorway and looks around the small conference room – our makeshift office for the next three weeks, just north of Oxford Street.

'I'll say,' I reply, watching as an IT guy hooks up my computer. I got here early and they haven't finished setting up.

'Are you going to be long?' he checks with the IT guy.

'Twenty minutes, at least,' comes the curt reply.

'Come and get a coffee with me?' Alex suggests.

'Sure, okay.' There's not much else I can do, and we are early. 'How are the wedding plans coming along?' I ask as we walk down the stairs. We're on the third floor.

'Well, I think. Zara's doing most of it. She's good at organising stuff.'

'Has she got a dress yet?'

'She went shopping on Saturday with her mum.' He gives me a meaningful look as we wander out through the lobby. 'Came back looking pretty happy.'

'That's a good sign. I forgot you said they were staying. Do you get on well with them?'

'Yeah.' He shrugs, holding the door open for me. 'I've known them so long now.'

I jerk my head in the direction we need to go and we set off along the pavement. It's a cool morning, but the sky overhead is bright blue. It might be park weather at lunchtime.

'I can't believe you've been together since uni. That's impressive.'

'Mmm. So tell me about your weekend.' He changes the subject as we walk into the café, the scent of freshly brewed coffee filling our nostrils. There's nothing like it.

'Another wedding. This one was a nightmare.' I fill him in on Bob's your uncle and he's laughing by the time we reach the front of the queue.

'So Lachie went too?'

'Yeah, and Maria and Russ.'

'Those two are getting close,' he comments.

'I'll say. Meeting her parents and everything.'

'Good for them.'

'Yep.' Another two bite the dust.

My time with the redesign team flies by. During one brainstorming session I suggest we launch a brand-new section called Celebrity Houses, which involves the picture desk first having to broker the deal and then going to shoot whichever celebrity has agreed to have photos of their home splashed across the pages of *Hebe*. Sometimes this will involve overseas travel by one of the team – possibly me – to America or wherever the celebrity

213

lives, which in turn means a much bigger Picture budget. Simon takes me with him on his meeting to convince Clare, and I'm on top of the world when she agrees to allocate Pictures more money. Then I have to follow through on my suggestion, which involves buttering up various PR people and eventually going to shoot hot young A-list actress Nelly Lott at her plush home in the country. Alex comes with me and if it weren't for his very impressive skills of persuasion, I'm not sure we would have ever got her to agree to let us shoot her in bed, wearing comfy but highly unsexy PJs and looking all dishevelled and bleary-eyed. Simon is delighted with the pictures and gets me working on setting up the next shoot straight away.

There are so few of us that we tend to spend our lunchtimes together, when we're not out shooting celebrities. I get to know Pete, the news editor, really well. He often comes to the pub on Friday nights, but I haven't spoken to him much before. Esther, Russ's boss on the features desk, and Mike from production usually join us, but Teagan from the style desk spends her lunches shopping on Oxford Street, and Simon tends to keep to himself. I think he likes to put a little distance between himself and his employees.

On our last Wednesday in the redesign office, it's a stinking hot day and the five of us – Esther, Mike, Pete, Alex and I – are eating sandwiches and hanging out in nearby Cavendish Square in the sunshine. This afternoon Clare is coming by to run through our redesign ideas so she can give us feedback before our main presentation to her on Friday. We'll present to the team on Monday when we're back in the office. I'm a little nervous – it will be the first time Clare has seen my Celebrity Houses shoot.

Alex and Pete are reminiscing about the time they worked together at a Sunday supplement. It turns out the two of them are old friends.

'When was this?' I ask, trying to take my mind off our publisher.

'A couple of years ago,' Pete replies. 'Before *Hebe*.'

'You worked at a Sunday supplement before joining *Hebe* too?' I ask Alex.

'Yeah,' he replies, flicking a handful of grass at Pete.

So that's why I never saw Alex's name on magazine mastheads after I went back to Australia. The memory of me trailing through all of those glossy magazines makes me feel sombre.

'It's your last day of work tomorrow.' Esther nudges Pete, bringing my attention back to my colleagues.

'Yep,' he replies with a grin.

'Are you looking forward to being a married man?' she asks.

'Can't wait,' he tells her, with total and utter sincerity.

Unusually, I find his response heartwarming. 'Are all of Sylvie's family coming over?' I ask.

'Yeah. Quite a few of them are already here and others arrive tomorrow.'

'Nice that she wanted to get married in the UK instead of in the States,' Esther muses.

'She says this is her home now,' Pete replies with a small, happy shrug.

'It should be a great weekend,' Mike says decisively. 'My girlfriend has been planning her outfit for weeks.'

'Aw, are you going?' I ask Mike.

'Yep. You guys are, too, right?' Mike checks with Alex and Esther.

'Sure am,' Esther replies with a smile.

'Mmm-hmm,' Alex says, not meeting my eyes as he continues to pull up grass with his fingers. Does he feel bad that I'm the only one here who hasn't been invited?

Pete's eyes shift to mine and I force a bright smile. 'Who have you got doing your wedding photos?'

'Er, a couple called Lina and Tom,' he replies, probably feeling bad that I'm not even doing his pictures. Those names sound familiar.

'Lina and Tom . . . Her name's not Lina Orsino, is it?' I ask.

'Yes.' Pete looks taken aback. 'How did you know that?'

'She's Rachel's mentor. Rachel often talks about her. Apparently she taught her everything she knows, so she must be amazing. Will you say hi to her from us?'

'Sure,' Pete replies with a smile.

★　　★　　★

216

Later, when we're all packing up for the day after a brilliantly positive meeting with Clare, Pete takes a call from his fiancée. I pat him on his back and give him the thumbs-up to wish him good luck before setting off. I'm halfway down the stairs when I hear his voice.

'Bronte, wait!' he calls out. He catches up with me, a little out of breath. 'What are you doing this weekend?' he asks as I wait on the second-floor landing.

'Er, nothing,' I reply, puzzled. I'm not working so I was just planning on hanging out with Bridget.

'Would you like to come to my wedding?' he asks hopefully.

My brow furrows. I'm confused. Is he asking me because he feels bad for leaving me out?

'We've just had a cancellation,' he explains in a rush. 'Sylvie's American cousin has appendicitis so he and his wife have had to cancel. I'd love you to come if you're free.'

I waver. He seems to genuinely want me to join them.

'You can bring someone. Everyone else is,' he goes on to say.

It dawns on me that Alex will be going with Zara. Do I really want to meet this woman in the flesh? No.

'Go on. I know there's still space at the B&B where the others are staying,' he says.

Just say no.

'Go on,' he urges, good-naturedly. 'I feel like you're an old friend too after all these lunchtimes.'

I can't help but smile at him.

This is a bad idea. You don't want to meet her.

'Thanks, that's so sweet. I'd love to.'

I swing by Lachie's pub on the way home. He hasn't answered my text or panicked phone call, so I'm hoping he's at work. I smile with relief when I see him wiping down the bar top. His face breaks into a grin.

'What are you doing here?' he asks me.

'I've come to ask you for a favour,' I say, hopping onto a stool. 'What are you doing this weekend?'

He shrugs. 'Nothing much. Busking, probably.'

'Are you working on Saturday night?'

'I don't have to. Why?'

'Will you come to a wedding in Yorkshire with me?' I ask quickly.

'Whose wedding?'

'Pete's. You've met him at the pub. He's just invited me to his wedding and I can bring someone. The Yorkshire Moors are stunning, apparently. It'll be fun.'

He looks amused. '*You* want *me* to escort you to a wedding?'

Annoyingly, I blush. 'As a mate,' I hastily point out, looking down at the bar top before meeting his eyes with a hopeful look on my face.

He straightens up and continues to wipe down the bar.

'Who else is going?' He glances at me.

'Um, Esther, who I think you've also met, a guy from work called Mike, and . . . Alex.'

'Alex is going.'

It's not even really a question.

'Yes.'

'And Alex's fiancée?'

Shit. He's cottoned onto me.

I shrug nonchalantly. 'I would have thought so. Everyone is bringing someone.'

He looks straight at me. Once more, my face heats up. 'And *you* want *me* to bring *you*,' he says slowly.

'Sure,' I say weakly.

'Okay.' He continues with his cleaning up.

'You'll come?' I double-check that's what he's saying.

'Yeah. Why not?' He gives me a significant look, but I decide to talk about something else rather than interrogate him about it.

CHAPTER 17

I 'm trying not to ruin my manicure as I stare out of the window at the lush green scenery flashing past. I have a strong desire to bite my nails, and I haven't wanted to do that since I was a teenager. We're on an early morning train to York and I'm sitting opposite Lachie. Alex and Zara are driving Esther and her boyfriend, and Mike and his girlfriend drove up last night. We were lucky to get reduced rates on our last-minute train fares.

I glance at Lachie, who's staring at me calmly. He's wearing a well-fitted white shirt which is slightly open at the collar, and black trousers. He said he didn't have a suit, but I can't imagine anyone minding too much.

'You seem nervous,' he comments.

I screw up my nose. 'I don't really like weddings.'

He laughs half-heartedly. 'What are we doing coming to this one, then?'

I purse my lips at him. 'I don't know, to be honest.'

'You're an odd one, Bronte . . . What's your surname?'

'Taylor.'

'You're an odd one, Bronte Taylor.'

I grin at him, relaxing slightly because he tends to make me do that. 'Why am I odd?'

'You don't believe in marriage . . . You don't believe in God . . .'

'I know. Miserable bitch, aren't I?'

He grins. 'Yet here you are, working as a wedding photographer.'

'It's a strange world,' I concede.

'And coming to a wedding which you really could have said no to,' he points out.

I shrug and look out of the window again.

'Have you met Alex's missus?' he asks. His question makes me tense up.

'Nope,' I reply flippantly. 'That's about to be rectified, though, isn't it?' I say with saccharine sarcasm.

He doesn't smile at me. It freaks me out when Lachie gets that serious look about him.

'What's your surname?' I ask.

'Samson,' he replies. 'Nice change of subject,' he adds.

I poke my tongue out at him.

I'm wearing a silk cocktail dress which is fitted around my waist and kicks out into a flirty A-line with a just-above-knee-length hem. The shoulder straps, side panels and back of the dress are black, but the front centre is cream with a cream bow detail just below my bust. It's very pretty. I picked it up in the sale yesterday lunchtime, when I was having last-minute anxiety about going through with this. I'm wearing my hair off to one side in a fishtail plait and my nails are painted cherry red.

Lachie and I are catching a bus straight to the wedding in a little village in the Yorkshire Moors so we're carrying small overnight bags with us. We managed to get a room at the B&B Pete mentioned. Just the one. Lachie can't believe I agreed to share with him at long last, but I've told him in no uncertain terms that either he's sleeping on the sofa, or I am.

There's an accident on the way and the traffic is backed up for a mile along the country road so we're cutting it fine by the time we arrive at the church. It doesn't help my already swirling nerves.

I've chosen to come to a wedding, a wedding of someone I don't really know that well, I'm about to meet someone I really don't want to meet, and I don't even have a camera to take my mind off things.

The wedding bells are ringing as we hurry up the hill to the church, just two of them, slowly, in different pitches: *Ding-dong. Ding-dong. Ding-dong.*

The stone church tower is visible from a distance through the old market town, but as we climb a set of stone steps between a shop and a cottage, the rest of the beautiful ancient church comes into view. I notice a young male photographer wearing a white shirt, black trousers and waistcoat waiting at the top of some steps outside the church. I wonder if it's Tom, Lina's partner. And then he nods behind us and we see the bridal car down on the road.

'Jesus Christ, we're late,' Lachie mutters as we hurry into the church past the vicar waiting in the porch. He looks to be in his mid-thirties and he has a slightly balding head.

He gives us an amused look. 'Is He here too?' he asks sardonically. 'That's a good sign.'

I purse my lips and Lachie coughs to cover up his laugh and then the familiar damp, cold, musty smell hits my nostrils and I instantly feel a little dizzy.

Lachie slides into the last pew on the groom's side and puts our overnight bags at his feet.

I sit down and close my eyes for a moment, trying to gather myself.

'You okay?' he whispers and I snap my eyes open.

'Fine,' I reply. 'Just feel a bit faint.' I force myself to take some deep breaths. Is Alex here? My breath catches as I spy him, a few pews in front of us. He's sitting with Esther and her boyfriend, and on his left is a girl with light blonde hair. My stomach lurches and my fingers automatically seek out Lachie's hand. He glances at me with surprise, but doesn't comment. His grasp is warm and comforting. I wonder if he's noticed that I feel cold and clammy.

'This place is incredible,' Lachie says with awe, looking around. I follow his gaze upwards to see paintings on the walls. One is of St George slaying the dragon, another of St Christopher carrying Jesus Christ as a baby.

'Medieval frescoes,' Lachie whispers, bringing

my attention to the short history of what I soon discover is a Norman church included on the Order of Service. High above our heads, the vaulted church ceiling is made of oak.

I notice Pete up near the pulpit, shifting from foot to foot. He's not speaking to his best man or the two ushers. He looks nervous and my heart goes out to him, momentarily distracting me from how ill at ease I feel.

I hear the familiar sound of a shutter going off and look over my shoulder to see a short, curvy woman with long, curly dark hair holding a camera with a long lens. Lina? She has a quick word with the vicar and hurries up the aisle. I follow her with my eyes, intrigued to see in action the woman who taught Rachel everything she knows. She says something to Pete, who frowns and nods. His best man steps forward to ask him something. I wonder if everything's alright.

I look over my shoulder again to see a flash of white in the porch. Well, Sylvie's here, so I assume if there is something wrong, it's nothing to do with her. There's more clicking as Tom photographs the bride, her father and bridesmaids.

It's strange to attend a wedding as a guest. I feel like I should be standing in Tom's position, in the porch with the bride. It's been a long time since I've been in a church in anything other than a work capacity.

I look around again, taking in the scene. The flowers are all pink peonies, hanging from the end of every second pew and tied with long, pink satin ribbons. Up at the altar, more peonies are packed into long-stem vases. And then I'm not looking at pink peonies. I'm looking straight into Alex's deep blue eyes. A jolt rockets through me.

He smiles at me and I force a small smile back at him. My eyes flicker to the back of Zara's head before returning to Alex's. His expression sobers. I force myself to turn to speak to Lachie.

'I wonder what's wrong?' I whisper.

He frowns, staring straight ahead. 'Something to do with the music, I think.'

The vicar appears at the front of the church.

'Sorry for the delay,' he says with an air of theatrics. 'I'm afraid the organist is stuck in traffic.'

A collective murmur comes from the pews.

'We'll begin as soon as we can,' the vicar assures us, before returning to the porch.

The hushed, reverent silence evaporates as people start to chatter amongst themselves. I can pick out several American accents coming from the other side of the church.

I hear the vicar talking to the bride behind us in a quiet but audible voice. 'I'm afraid we'll have to start without him if he's much longer. I have a christening this afternoon.'

'Shame you didn't bring your guitar,' I say to Lachie.

'Hmm. "The Bridal March" is one song I *don't* know,' he replies.

★   ★   ★

225

'Give me your hand . . .'

His fingers dance over the keys, his feet shifting across the pedals as he slides from side to side across the four-foot polished wooden stool. I watch, enraptured, as the music fills my head and my heart. Surely this is the most powerful, awe-inspiring sound in the world? The bass vibrates right through my tiny body, sending shivers down my spine.

'It's not as hard as it looks.'

'I don't believe you.' My voice is small. I'm small. I'm just a little girl.

'I can teach you if you're willing to learn,' he says . . .

I jolt out of the memory, ripping my hand from Lachie's and pressing it to my chest.

'What is it?' he asks with concern. 'What's wrong?'

I shake my head quickly.

'Is it Alex?' he asks urgently.

'What?' I shoot my head around to look at him, the shock of his question knocking me to my senses. 'No!'

'Then what?' he asks, perplexed.

'I can play the organ,' I blurt out.

His anxiety transforms into astonishment. 'Can you?' he asks with surprise.

I'm surprised myself. Why did I just tell him that?

'Can you play "The Bridal March"?' he asks.

I hesitate only a second before nodding.

'Will you volunteer?' he checks, glancing towards the front at Pete.

'It's been a long time,' I say, my voice wavering. What's got into me? Why am I offering to do this? 'But I think I remember.'

'Do it,' he urges, nudging me out of my seat. I start to move, but I freeze halfway to my feet. 'Go on,' he says, gently pushing me. In a surreal daze, I straighten up. 'Do you want me to come with you?'

'Please'.

We go to speak to the vicar under the porch. I flash Sylvie a nervous smile.

'You can play "The Bridal March?"' he checks with disbelief when Lachie reveals my hidden talent. 'On a pipe organ?'

I nod, words at this moment failing me. I'm beginning to think I need to be committed.

'Fantastic!' he cries. 'Do you know any hymns?'

'Not well.' My voice sounds shaky.

'Well, at least we can get this show on the road,' he says eagerly. 'Even if we have to sing the hymns acapella.'

He leads the pair of us down the aisle and under the intricately carved wooden rood screen into the chancel. The organ is on our left: two keyboards and approximately two dozen golden pipes. I should be able to handle this, I think with more confidence than I feel. I slip off my high heels and slide onto the long wooden stool, resting my bare feet lightly on the already treadworn pedalboard.

Lachie crouches down at my side. The sheet music is open to 'The Bridal March', but I know it by heart. I switch the organ on and while I wait for the electric motor to push air into the bellows, I adjust the stops – the cream-coloured knobs that control the sounds. If this were 'The Wedding March', I'd be pulling out more stops to create an even bigger sound, but 'The Bridal March' is more subdued. I think I'm ready, but boy, it's been a long time.

I hear the vicar address the congregation. 'We've got ourselves a volunteer!' he cries. 'It turns out, one of the guests can play the pipe organ!'

No going back now . . .

I look down at my feet to check they're resting on the right keys – I'll stick to pedals C, G, F and D, and my right foot will also need to regulate the volume. I'm only going to use one keyboard. This will be a dumbed-down version – I'm not about to risk trying to play like a pro.

My heart is racing and I brace myself. I can do this. It's just like riding a bicycle.

'Are you okay?' Lachie asks me.

I don't meet his eyes, but I nod. I take a deep breath and place my fingers on the keys.

'Ready when you are,' Lachie says, looking past me down the aisle.

The sound that comes out of the pipes as I gently press down almost takes my breath away. It fills up my head, fills up my heart, just as it did when I was a little girl.

I can do this.

It's almost as though my limbs are moving on autopilot. As my fingers work the keyboard in front of me, my feet move over the pedals at ground level. As Sylvie reaches the top of the aisle, I pull out the eight-foot flute stop so the organ changes to a brighter sound. The piece is over before I know it.

My fingers still resting in position on the final keys, I look up at Lachie, my eyes shining. He's staring down at me with wonder in his eyes.

'Wow,' he whispers.

I look up at the gleaming golden pipes and they turn blurry as my tears spill over. No one here will ever know how big a deal this is for me. It's momentous.

'You can return to your seats, now,' the vicar calls with amusement in his voice.

It startles me into action and I slide off the stool and Lachie hauls me to my feet and guides me towards the nave.

I step out from the chancel into the church and feel all eyes on us as the congregation breaks into spontaneous applause. I catch Alex's eye and he looks blown away.

Pete beams at me, as does his bride-to-be, and then I hurry, with my face down, back to my seat. Lachie slides into the pew after me. My face is burning as the applause dies down.

A man yells, 'Sorry I'm late!' from behind us and we look over our shoulders to see an unassuming man in a green jumper and brown corduroy trousers burst into the church. 'I'm here, now. Oh!' He spies the bride at the front.

'Aah, our organist has arrived,' the vicar explains to the bride and groom and the rest of the congregation. 'Looks like we won't have to sing unaccompanied to the hymns after all.'

Lachie takes my hand and squeezes it. I close my eyes and rest my head on his shoulder, suddenly more exhausted than I've ever been in my life.

Forty minutes later I find myself hurtling towards my next hurdle. The service is over and we're standing outside in the churchyard, surrounded by higgledy-piggledy gravestones and listening to the sound of all seven church bells jubilantly ringing in unison. It's time to meet Zara. Alex brings her over to us while Pete and Sylvie are meeting and greeting their guests.

After the challenge in the church, I should feel ready to do anything, but ice freezes my insides as I see them coming our way.

She's tall and very skinny, with long, dead-straight, very pale blonde hair. She's pretty, but her features are a little sharp, her nose straight and her jaw severe. She's wearing a structured, expensive-looking knee-length dress in apricot-coloured chiffon and her skin is pale with no hint of a tan.

'How the hell did you learn how to play the organ?' Alex exclaims as he reaches us, distractedly shaking Lachie's hand.

I force a light-hearted laugh. 'I had strange hobbies as a child.' My fingers seek out Lachie's and I lock my hand in his.

I notice Alex glance down at our tangled grasp before meeting my eyes with a puzzled look on his face.

He indicates his fiancée. 'This is Zara. Zara, this is Bronte and Lachie.'

'Hi.' I give her a bright smile.

'Hello,' she replies with a tight, reserved one. She holds out her hand and when I shake it, her fingers are cold and thin.

There. It's done now. A face to a name. And whatever I felt for him should shrivel up and die. It would be about bloody time.

'Bronte works at *Hebe*,' Alex tells her.

'Oh, right,' she says, feigning interest as she gives Lachie a perfunctory handshake, too. She slides her arm around Alex's waist.

Lina calls everyone over to do the confetti shot so Lachie and I make our way towards her, our hands still entwined. I realise I may be sending Lachie mixed signals, but the truth is, I need him. I need his support. I hope he doesn't mind giving it to me without strings attached.

'Most people don't just play the pipe organ as a hobby,' he murmurs in my ear as he squeezes my palm.

'I did,' I reply casually, willing him to drop it. He does. For now.

★　★　★

Lachie has always been tactile, but tonight I don't discourage him. The reception is taking place at a nearby hotel, and he and I sit at a table with Sylvie's American relatives. My *Hebe* colleagues are sitting nearby, but Lachie and I are a late addition to the table plan so I guess we're taking the seats that were assigned to Sylvie's missing cousin and his wife. I can't say I'm not relieved. I don't think I'd be very good at making pleasant conversation with Zara. I feel much more relaxed here with Lachie and people we barely know. The wine is sliding down easily and the food is delicious. I've been watching Lina and Tom at work and I'm having a surprisingly good time being on the other side of a camera for a change. I didn't think I would.

I'm blaming the company of my laid-back Aussie mate.

'Thanks so much for coming with me,' I say to him later, after the speeches. We've moved outside to a marquee in the hotel garden where the evening's entertainment is being set up. It's only a matter of time before my colleagues find us. I find that thought weirdly unwelcome.

'No worries,' he says. His eyes look a lot darker in this dim light and as he stares down at me, warmth floods my stomach. 'It's been enlightening.' He seems surprisingly sober considering all the wine we drank at dinner. His lips crook into a smile. 'Bar's open. I might switch to beer.'

'Good plan.'

He grabs my hand and leads me to the makeshift bar, letting go when we reach it. I feel momentarily bereft, but then his hands are on my hips and he's standing behind me, trapping me in front of the counter.

'Two beers, please,' he says to the bartender.

His touch is very distracting.

It's time for the first dance so we wander over to the dance floor. A live band are sitting on a small stage and as Sylvie and Pete take the dance floor, I notice Sylvie has removed her long cream-coloured bridal skirt and is wearing a shorter cream skirt with layers and layers of pale pink ruffles underneath. It reminds me of the peonies from the church and table settings. Sylvie's bouquet was made up of a dozen tightly packed peony balls, and there are peony heads cascading down the side of the three-tiered cake, too. I've noticed you can often describe a wedding from the flowers, and this one has been true to form: pink, soft and feminine.

The band launch into The Temptations' 'My Girl'. The band are good, but, 'Not as good as you,' I say in Lachie's ear. He takes a swig of his beer and smiles at me around the mouth of his beer bottle. All of a sudden, I feel light-headed. I drag my eyes away from his and force myself to watch Pete and Sylvie's fun, choreographed routine. I notice Sylvie's bridesmaids standing in a group off to one side of the dance floor. Their dresses are the colour and style of peonies, too, layers of pretty pink ruffles coming to just below their knees. They're giggling and talking to each other and staring our way. My stomach tightens. I look up at Lachie, but he hasn't noticed the attention. Or maybe he has. Maybe he's ignoring it.

The first dance comes to an end and the band launch into Nina Simone's 'My Baby Just Cares For Me'. A few other people take to the dance floor.

'Still not drunk enough,' I hear a familiar voice say and I spin around to come face to face with Alex.

I giggle. 'I'm wasted.'

'Are you?' He looks past me to Lachie.

'Where's Zara?' I ask.

'Bathroom,' he replies. 'She's not feeling that great. I don't think we'll be staying for long.'

I try to appear compassionate. 'Oh no. I'm sorry.'

'You're staying at the same B&B, right?' he asks.

'Yeah.'

'So we'll see you at breakfast?'

'For sure.'

I hear a girl say, 'Fancy a dance?' and look behind me to see that one of the pretty pink peony brides-maids has accosted Lachie. He glances at me.

'Go for it,' I encourage him.

The gleeful girl drags him onto the dance floor. I watch with amusement as he starts to spin her. So he can dance as well as sing.

'So he can dance as well as sing,' Alex says my thoughts out loud. 'You don't mind him doing that?' he asks me.

'Doing what? Dancing with other girls?'

He nods, his eyes narrowing as he tries to read my mind.

'No.' I shrug. 'He's his own person, he can do what he likes.'

'So you and he are not . . .' His sentence trails off.

'Together? No,' I confirm. 'We're *still* not,' I add with a pointed look. We weren't together the last time he asked me, either.

I cast my eyes over at Lachie who seems to be having a pretty good time.

Zara appears at Alex's side. 'Can we go?' she asks him.

'Already?' His brow furrows.

'I'm tired,' she replies, squeezing his waist. She glances at me. 'It's been a long week.'

'I bet.' I nod sympathetically, but really, I have no idea what her life is like or why she feels like she's had a long week.

'Okay,' Alex agrees. 'See you in the morning,' he says to me. 'Say bye to Lachie for us.'

'I will.'

We smile at each other and he lightly touches his fingers to my hand before following Zara out. I watch them go with a sinking heart, then I neck the rest of my beer.

'Have they gone already?' Lachie asks with a frown as he joins me again.

'Yeah, Zara's tired,' I reply sardonically.

'What a lightweight,' he jokes. 'She doesn't have much go about her, that one.'

'I know!' I say eagerly, keen to gossip. 'She's a bit weird, I thought.'

'Very uptight,' he agrees with me. 'Stuck up her own arse. And skinny.'

'Far too skinny. And cold, I thought.'

'She *was* cold, wasn't she?' he concurs.

'Like death warmed up!'

He chuckles at me and I like him more with every sentence that comes out of his gorgeous lips. His lips *are* gorgeous, actually. I find myself staring at them.

'So what was the deal with you in the church?' he asks.

My heart jumps.

'You seemed a little freaked out,' he continues.

'I don't like churches,' I find myself admitting.

'Why?'

I shrug. 'I have a fear of them. It's called ecclesio-phobia. Look it up.'

He gives me a weird look. 'Are you serious? You have a fear of churches?'

'Yes.'

'Yet you take photos at weddings.' He says this slowly, like he can't actually believe the words that are coming out of his mouth.

'Call it therapy,' I reply, but I don't feel as flippant as I sound.

'Are you having me on?' he asks with a frown.

'No.' I can't help smirking. 'I do have a genuine fear of churches.'

'But . . . *Why?*' he asks, perplexed.

I shrug. 'I don't know.'

'But something must have happened—'

'Is your beard itchy?' I interrupt him, reaching up to stroke his jaw.

He catches my fingers and I breathe in sharply. His eyes are staring steadily back at me and my pulse quickens.

'No,' he says, letting my hand go. 'I'm used to it now.'

'So,' I say, turning away from him and trying to sound normal. 'How was your bridesmaid?'

He chuckles. 'My bridesmaid? Which one?'

I glare at him. 'The one you were dancing with.'

He laughs. 'She was good. A good dancer,' he elaborates.

'How many bridesmaids have you had, then?' I ask the question that has so often been on the tip of my tongue.

He laughs again, but his demeanour has turned cheeky. 'Ask me no questions, I'll tell you no lies.'

'Why would you want to lie to me? I don't care,' I say with a shrug.

That seems to take him aback. 'You really don't care?' he asks with a frown.

'Nope.'

'Not even a little bit?' He raises one eyebrow.

'Not at all.'

'Wait.' He puts his bottle down firmly on a table behind him. 'You're telling me that you don't even care a tiny, weeny little bit how many bridesmaids I've had sex with?'

His words make my head prickle a touch, but I refuse to give him the satisfaction. 'You can shag whoever you want,' I say flippantly as my stomach clenches. I don't really want him to shag whoever he wants. Why am I encouraging him to? I'm starting to think I have sadomasochistic tendencies.

He stares at me, no trace of a smile on his gorgeous lips. 'So you wouldn't care if I went over there right now and kissed her.' He points at the bridesmaid he danced with earlier. 'And took her home with me,' he adds, leaning down to look me right in the eye.

I waver.

'Shall I?' he asks purposefully. I can barely hear his voice over the live band, but I can read his lips.

I look back up at his eyes and I swear the hot and cold flush that ensues is almost on a par with some of the ones I've had in various churches over the last few months. His blue eyes stare back at me, challenging me, his face inches from mine.

I've had too much to drink. I'm finding him obscenely attractive and his defiant attitude is turning me on.

'Shall I?' he asks again.

I ever-so-slightly shake my head.

'No?' He pulls back marginally to question me, but instead of waiting for my answer, he grabs my head and pulls my mouth onto his. I kiss him back, deepening our kiss instantly. Oh God, he is divine. He puts his hands to the small of my back and I become aware of us moving. Goosebumps spread across my skin as we emerge from the marquee into the cool night air. He wrenches himself away from me and gives me a look that is so damn sexual I go weak at the knees. He grabs my hand and stalks determinedly across the flat, smooth lawn. We reach a greenhouse and he goes inside, tugging me behind him. The smell of damp earth and tomatoes fills my senses and then he's kissing me again. I push my fingers through his hair and hold his face steady as he hoiks my legs up around his waist and bumps me against the door.

'Careful,' I murmur into his open mouth, imagining us both crashing through the glass. His fingers find the zip on the back of my dress and then he's sliding the straps off my shoulders and tugging down the front of my bra. As his lips seek out my nipple I throw my head back and gasp.

My head is so hazy. I feel delirious with desire and more than a little bit drunk. As his lips find mine again he lowers my feet to the ground and slides his hands up the inside of my skirt. His fingertips are just skimming the waistline of my knickers when it occurs to me to wonder just what the fuck it is that I am doing.

'Lachie, no wait, stop,' I say, trying to find his wrists so I can still his wandering fingers. He kisses my mouth again as though he doesn't hear me. I turn my face away and grab his arms. 'Stop,' I say again, more firmly.

He breaks away from me, his breath coming in short, sharp gusts. 'What the— What's wrong?'

'I can't. Stop.'

He lets me go instantly and I quickly smooth my skirt down and hook my straps back over my shoulders.

'You can't stop?' he asks. 'Or you can't. Stop.? I think you should work out exactly what message it is you're sending, because those words can be taken two ways.'

He knows exactly what I mean, judging by the angry look on his face. He's just being difficult.

Maybe angry is the wrong word. But he doesn't look at all happy.

'I'm sorry.' I shake my head and wobble on my heels slightly as I try to zip up my dress. It isn't easy. 'My head's all over the place and I know you know I have feelings for someone.' I don't want or need to say Alex's name out loud. 'I just can't. I've had too much to drink. I'm confused.' And I don't want to have a fling with Lachie if I'm only going to end up getting hurt again. He's too young, too flirty, too playful. I can't imagine him in a serious relationship. Not that I want a serious relationship, but I don't need to be having a one-night stand with him, either.

He scratches his head. 'Shall we call it a night?'

I nod. 'I think that might be a good idea.'

Forty minutes later after a tense taxi journey, we find ourselves standing in a room that is barely

240

bigger than the double bed it's accommodating. There's certainly not room for a sofa.

'I don't know about you,' he says, 'but I'm sure as hell not sleeping on the floor.'

I give him a withering look.

'I'm not,' he says nonchalantly.

'In that case, I will,' I say.

'Don't be so pig-headed, Bronte,' he snaps. 'Jesus, I'm not going to fucking touch you if you don't want me to.'

'I don't want you to,' I say bluntly.

He glares at me and starts to unbutton his shirt. I catch a glimpse of his tanned, toned chest before I avert my gaze. 'I'm going to get ready for bed,' I say, heading into the bathroom with my overnight bag.

I'm too weary to even be angry at the girl I see staring back at me from the mirror. I change out of my clothes into my PJs and brush my teeth, not even bothering to take off my make-up. When I go back into the room, Lachie is lying on his side facing the wall. I slip between the sheets and switch off the light.

CHAPTER 18

I won't switch it on. I daren't make a sound. My fingers lightly trace the keys, darting left and right as the tune plays inside my head. I thought he'd be here, but he's not. It's quiet, so quiet. But I'm not scared. I'm never scared here.

Dad will be cross if he finds out I've come alone. But Mum is crying again and I'm so sick of seeing her cry. I needed to get out of the house. I needed to come here.

I hear a noise and my fingers freeze in position. I'm all ears as I listen for the noise again. It comes a second later, but I don't know what it means. It's a human sound. It sounds like someone is in pain. Fear clutching my stomach, I slowly rise to my feet. Half of my brain tells me to stay hidden, but the other half is overridden with curiosity. I peek slowly around the corner in the direction of the altar. A dark sickness overcomes me. I don't know what I'm seeing, but I know what I'm seeing is wrong.

'No!' I jolt awake, gasping for air as a cold sweat rushes over me. I'm sitting up in bed and I can't get enough oxygen into my lungs. There's movement beside me in the darkness and out of the blue I remember where I am: in bed with Lachie.

'Are you okay?' he asks in a deep voice that is croaky from lack of sleep. It must be the middle of the night because it's still pitch black outside from what I can tell.

'Just a bad dream. It's fine.' I slump back onto my pillows and try to calm my breathing.

It was just a dream. Just a dream, I repeat inside my head.

Only some dreams are born out of reality.

There's movement beside me and I think he's rolling over onto his side again. It all comes back to me. Our kiss, well, kiss*es*, and quite a lot else that went on between us, too. I'm such a screw-up. I've probably lost Lachie as a friend, and all because I couldn't keep my stupid hands to myself.

I close my eyes and sigh heavily.

'What was it about?'

His voice makes me jump. I thought he'd turned away from me, but he turned towards me instead.

'Nothing,' I murmur.

'You shouted, "No".'

'Did I?' He heard me?

'Come here,' he says and to my surprise he slides his arm underneath my shoulders and pulls me against him. His chest is bare and I tense up, but then I realise I haven't lost him as a friend and that makes me relax. I rest my head in the crook of his arm and lay my right arm across his chest while he holds me snugly in place. He strokes my hair with his left hand and after a while my breathing begins to regulate.

I fall back asleep like that, in his arms.

We must have broken apart in the night, because when I come to, I'm lying alone on my side of the bed. I glance across at him. He's breathing slowly and steadily and is still in the depths of deep sleep. I turn away and stare morosely up at the ceiling.

I haven't had that dream for a very long time. It must've been the organ. I shouldn't have played the organ.

I climb out of bed and walk disconsolately into the bathroom. I can't bear to look at myself as I pull a navy-blue and white maxi dress over my head and slip on some sandals. I need to get out of here. I need to clear my head.

Pausing at the door, I look at the sleeping figure of Lachie lying in the bed. The sheets have slipped away from him and I can clearly see the muscle definition on his broad back. He held me in the night when I needed comfort. I have a strange urge to return to the bed and slide my hand across his ribcage. I really need some fresh air.

I leave him a note:

Gone for a walk. B x

I take a chance on turning right as I come out of the B&B and set off down the country lane.

It's a beautiful, crisp sunny morning and soon the lane goes through open fields. Sunlight spills across the hills, highlighting the plough lines created by farmers' tractors.

What a strange day yesterday was. I met Alex's fiancée and I feel slightly sick about it. I've felt quite close to him recently, but now I just want to put a whole lot of distance between us. Zara's not a faceless name any more, and I don't like that, but it had to happen.

Then there was that whole thing with the organ – I still can't believe I did that. I never thought I'd play an organ, ever again, let alone in a church with an audience. That could have gone so horribly wrong.

And then there was Lachie. I sigh heavily. What was I thinking? I was drunk. My throbbing head is proof of that. But that's no excuse. He's flirted with me for ages – he's a flirt, that's what he does. I don't think I expected him to take it further, and I certainly didn't think I'd let him. Did we almost have sex? It was *him* who kissed *me*, right? Or did I kiss him?

Embarrassment floods me and my face burns. Suddenly I want to run. I break into a jog down a wide dirt track cut right through a wheat field. The hill slopes downwards and I lift up my long dress and gather momentum as I go. It's liberating. If anyone saw me they'd think I looked like a loony, running along through a field in a long dress like something out of a Jane Austen novel. The thought makes me laugh out loud, which makes me look even more crazy.

Eventually, I come to a stop and hunch over on the path, out of breath and completely unfit. There are cracks in the soil that are so wide and deep it's almost like the whole world is splitting apart. I stare into the depths of the darkest cracks and imagine seeing right through to Australia. I'm suddenly overcome with homesickness and out of the blue, I burst into tears. I'm completely alone, no one will see me, no one will hear me cry. And as far as I can tell, that's a good thing. I force myself to keep walking, even though I'm a blubbering mess. I should call my mum. I've been avoiding her for so long, ringing only on Saturday evenings when I know she'll be out. I always leave a message, telling her I'm really busy and that I'll try her again another time. I never, ever do.

I sniff and wipe away my snot, the thought making me feel morose rather than sad. I wish Maria were here. She'd have a tissue.

I haven't seen her for ages. I know she's still seeing Russ, but he tends to go and stay with her in Golders Green, rather than her coming into town. I have a wedding next weekend which she's doing too, so we'll catch up soon enough. I assume things are still going well between her and my *Hebe* colleague.

I take a left when I come to another field, figuring I'll walk a triangle back to the B&B. I set off uphill. Spider webs shine in the light, and the long, silky threads twist and shimmer in the breeze as they drift across overgrown blades of dew-crystallised grass. I stomp along the path, wrecking tiny homes and habitats as I go. I've calmed down by the time I've reached the top of the hill. I pause for a moment and breathe in the fresh air while staring at the view, and then I set off on the last leg of my triangle, back to the B&B. I'm walking along, humming to myself, when I see a dark figure on the other side of the hedge. I nearly jump out of my skin. The figure stops walking in the other direction and turns to look at me through the foliage.

'You scared the shit out of me!' I exclaim, seeing Lachie's eyes staring at me.

He grins. 'Sorry.'

'What are you doing?' I ask him.

'Felt like a walk myself.'

'Oh. Did you?'

'Yeah. How do I get to you?' He indicates the hedge.

I smile and point back to where I've just come. I passed a gap a moment ago. I wait for him to join me.

'All good?' he asks with a grin, his light blue eyes twinkling as he catches up to me.

I'm relieved. This is not going to be weird.

'So I finally got into your bed but not into your knickers,' he says.

I spoke too soon.

I hit his chest and he laughs and wraps his arm

around me. 'Just kidding, Bronnie. You alright?' He peers down at me with amusement.

'Yeah.' I shrug. We set off along the path, but my thoughts are jumbled. Eventually I can't keep them to myself. 'What were you planning on doing, anyway? Were you just going to shag me without any thought of protection?'

'No, I carry a condom in my wallet.' He frowns as if to say, 'Duh!'

'Of course you do,' I mutter, slipping out of his embrace.

'What? Are you having a go at me now?' he asks incredulously. 'For practising safe sex?'

'Not at all,' I say smoothly. 'I'm sure you practise safe sex *a lot.*'

'So now you're accusing me of being easy.' He grins down at me.

'Aren't you?' I don't smile back.

'Depends on your definition,' he says cheekily.

I tut. 'I can't believe I let you kiss me,' I mutter.

He steps in front of me on the path, catching my hips at the same time to bring me to a stop. 'Do you want to do it again?' he asks sexily, staring down at me.

The bastard's question makes my face heat up.

'Would you cut it out?' I snap, shoving him to one side and storming off.

'I'm just teasing,' he calls as he hurries after me.

'Well, don't. I'm not in the mood.'

He puts his hands in his pockets.

'So . . . Yesterday was bizarre,' he says.

I half laugh. 'You're telling me.'

'Do you really have a church phobia?'

I'd completely forgotten I'd told him that. I try to appear unbothered. 'I don't like them, no.'

'I thought you were having me on, but you knew the name for it and everything.'

'Ecclesiophobia.' Pause. 'I might have been exaggerating about having a full-on phobia, but I definitely don't like churches.'

He studies me thoughtfully as we walk.

'How did you learn to play the organ?' I know he's confused. Will it really hurt to tell him?

'My dad taught me.'

'Your dad?'

'He was a church organist.'

'Was he? Wow.' He falls silent, but not for long. 'I thought you were freaked out about meeting Alex's chick.'

I snort, relaxing slightly. 'It wasn't the most fun thing I've ever done,' I admit, even though I totally brought it on myself.

His expression softens as he glances at me, and then he pulls me in for another hug. I let him.

Breakfast is being served when we reach the B&B, so we go straight into the small dining room. Alex and Zara are sitting at a table by the window and the sight makes my heart hurt a little.

'Morning,' Alex says with a smile, looking over at us.

'G'day,' Lachie replies.

'Hi,' Zara and I say at the same time. She's wearing skinny blue jeans and a pristine white jumper and her blonde hair is pulled back into a tight ponytail. She takes a sip of her tea from a china teacup and gently places it back on the saucer. The room is filled with the gentle clatter of cutlery and crockery.

Lachie pulls out a chair for me at a spare table and sits down opposite me. I'm surprised by his chivalry, but I fight the impulse to tease him.

'Good night?' Alex asks us.

I can't help glancing at Lachie. 'Yeah,' I reply with a shrug, willing my face to stay the same colour. 'You?'

'Pretty good, yeah,' he replies.

'Are you feeling better?' I ask Zara, trying to be friendly.

'Hmm?' She looks confused. Alex gives her a look. 'Oh, I'm fine,' she brushes me off.

Esther and her boyfriend join us. 'Good morning,' Esther says brightly, taking a seat at the table next to us. 'How's everyone feeling?'

'Well, I have a headache,' I reply ruefully.

'Oh dear,' she says sympathetically. 'Have you got any ibuprofen?'

'No.'

'I have. I'll get them for you after breakfast.'

'Thanks.' I smile at her.

The B&B owner comes over to take our order and then goes back to the kitchen.

'What time are we setting off today?' Esther asks Alex.

'Soon, if that's alright?' he replies.

'Sure. How are you guys getting back to London?' she asks Lachie and me.

'Taxi to the station, then train.'

'What happened to you last night?' she asks with a frown. 'Mike was looking for you. He wanted to see if you needed a lift back here.'

'Oh, did he? That was nice of him,' I say innocently, trying to ignore the smirk on Lachie's lips. I purposefully press my foot onto his toes under the table. He sniggers, which doesn't help.

Later, on the train, he and I sit side by side facing the direction of travel. He has his arm around me in his usual laid-back, comfortable manner and I'm leaning into him, feeling incredibly content.

'Thank you for coming with me,' I say, staring out of the window in a slight daze.

'Anytime,' he murmurs, brushing a few loose strands of hair back from my face. His touch is soothing, but it belatedly strikes me that I shouldn't be encouraging him. Reluctantly, I pull away.

'I'm sorry about last night.' I find myself saying.

He doesn't comment so I turn to look up at him.

'Forget about it,' he says seriously, staring down at me. 'No harm done, right?'

I look back out the window. 'No,' I say quietly. 'No harm done.'

CHAPTER 19

Maybe something is going around, or maybe the events of the weekend have caught up with me, but on Monday morning, I just can't get out of bed. Whatever I'm feeling, it goes way beyond exhaustion. I feel weary to my bones.

I call in sick and spend the morning in bed, trying not to over-think everything that happened at the wedding. I miss Australia and the simplicity of my life in Sydney – back when I was a deputy picture editor and not much else. Calling my mum would cure my homesickness. Bridget told me she rang again on Saturday. I know I'll probably be quite content to stay on the other side of the world if I speak to her, so with a sigh, I pick up the phone and dial her number.

It's weird returning to the hustle and bustle of work the next day after three weeks in a different office. Yesterday, Simon presented our redesign ideas to the rest of the team, and from what I hear, they went down well. We'll start implementing the new look magazine immediately with the longer lead time Features and Style pages this week, and then next week will be our first live News week. We're using the Nelly Lott shoot as our first Celebrity Houses feature, and I'm already working on setting up the next. I'm back to earth with a bump because Nicky literally throws work at me, so I have no choice but to hit the ground running. It's probably a good thing. After meeting Zara, I now find myself naturally steering clear of Alex. I catch him giving me odd looks a couple of times, and he even comes over to my desk on Thursday to ask if I want a cup of tea. I lie and tell him I'm detoxing, flashing him a quick smile before getting on with my work. The week is a struggle, and on Friday night I make my excuses and head straight home. I have a wedding the next day, and it's a big one. From the way Rachel talks about it, the groom's family own half the county.

Rachel calls me early the next morning. I've never heard her sound so panicked. 'I can't. I just can't. I've been throwing up all night. I can't risk it. Imagine if I passed this on to them? I could throw up all over the bride! Oh, Bronte, you're going to have to do this on your own!'

'But . . .' Oh shit! 'What about Sally?' I ask helplessly.

'She's on holiday.'

'Lina and Tom?'

'No, they passed this wedding on to me because they couldn't do it. You'll be fine!' she insists. 'Maria

253

will be there for moral support. She's insured on my car so she'll drive you both there. Maybe she can get the groom shots. We'll have to give them a discount, but I don't know what else to do.'

'Okay. Okay. It's going to be fine,' I say with a voice that I hope doesn't give away my underlying hysteria.

'Where's Rachel?' Binky, the bride, asks in an incredibly posh accent, when the man – butler? – announces our arrival.

'Didn't she call?' I ask nervously, going into the opulent sitting room where the white-silk-robe-clad bride is sitting at a small wooden table by the window and sipping tea from a china teacup.

'The phone's been ringing off the hook all morning. Mummy probably pulled the plug out of the socket.'

'Oh. I see. Well, I'm afraid Rachel is not very well.' I try to sound sympathetic. 'But it's okay. I can handle the photographs, and Maria will assist me once she's finished with your hair and make-up.'

A second door to the room opens and a woman whooshes in. She's middle-aged and handsome, and carries herself with an air of entitlement. 'Who are you?' she asks haughtily.

'I'm Bronte,' I say warmly, extending my hand. 'I'm Rachel's . . . colleague,' I decide to say at the last moment. I'm not sure meagre 'assistant' will go down too well in this situation.

'Where's Rachel?' the woman asks, giving me an unpleasant look as she waggles my fingertips. I guess my whole hand is not worth bothering with.

'I'm afraid she has a sick bug.' I come right out and say it.

'Urgh.' The woman snatches her hand away as though I might be a carrier.

'Oh, Mummy, what are we going to do?' Binky erupts melodramatically, clattering her teacup onto her saucer and standing up.

'Mummy' rushes to her side. 'It will be fine, darling. We'll get through it.'

'Bronte really is an excellent photographer,' Maria chips in helpfully. 'Rachel sings her praises to me on a daily basis.'

I smile at her.

'How many weddings have you done?' Binky asks me, anxiously pressing her fingers to her face.

'Oh . . .' I screw up my nose.

'Too many to count,' Maria answers for me.

I think this might be my seventh, although I have been to eight weddings so far this year, including Pete and Sylvie's. Still, even eight really doesn't sound like a lot.

'Shall we make a start?' Maria asks pleasantly.

'Ears, I suppose so,' Binky's mother says.

Ears? Oh, she means 'yes'. Honestly, this lot would fit right in at Buckingham Palace.

Binky and Charles, her husband-to-be, are getting married in Ely Cathedral. Stretch limousines take

255

us from Binky's country manor in Cambridgeshire for a three o'clock start.

The bride is looking timelessly classic in a long, fishtail gown of white lace. Tiny diamantés and pearls have been sewn into her straps and around her waist and she's wearing sheer white gloves. Her dark hair has been styled in an intricate, tightly curled topknot and she's wearing pearl-drop earrings, dark red lipstick and thick black sweeping eyeliner. She looks like a Forties starlet and could have stepped straight off the set of a film.

It would be almost impossible for me to mess this up. She's going to look amazing no matter what I do.

Ely Cathedral, known locally as 'the ship of the Fens' because of its prominent shape that towers above the surrounding flat and watery landscape, is a magnificent Norman cathedral which is unlike anything I've ever seen. The driver tells me a little bit about it on our way to the venue – Binky's mother shoved me at the front to sit with him. I welcome the brief respite – this morning has been hard work. Maria is in another car, travelling with the five bridesmaids, but as soon as we arrive, she'll be assisting me. She had to be convinced to step into my shoes. To say she wasn't keen is a complete and utter understatement. Eventually Rachel's bribery convinced her. I believe she's agreed to do the washing up for the next six months and I know she is paying Maria a substantial amount, too. If we can just get through today, everything will be okay.

I'm using Rachel's kit bag and Maria has mine. Half of my equipment is Sally's, anyway, but I plan on investing in a couple of new lenses soon.

When the cars pull up, I usher Maria inside to capture a few shots of the groom. She has played around with Rachel's cameras in the past, but I tell her that, if she is in doubt, to use centre point focus and a higher F stop. I'm sure Rachel would rather see well-taken photos than have Maria experiment and end up with no sharp shots. But I'm sure she will be fine.

I snap away at the bridal party on the neat, manicured lawn with the cream stone cathedral as a backdrop, before hurrying inside. I take a sharp intake of breath. It's a very long way to the altar.

Ely Cathedral is vast, cold and beautiful, just like any other church I've been in but on a *much* larger scale. Considering its size, it's odd that it doesn't freak me out like the other smaller churches have. I glance up at the painted nave ceiling as I hurry along the aisle. I plan to capture the details after the service, but I'm unable to resist taking a few shots as I go. The cathedral is open to tourists, but the section up at the front has been roped off. A sea of green and white flowers cascade from the end of every pew.

I set up my monopod behind the lectern and take a few shots of the groom with the vast expanse of the cathedral behind him. He's wearing a black morning coat with a light grey vest and a burnt-orange-coloured tie. I keep Rachel's 24-70 mm on so I can flick between the nearby groom and his bride coming up the aisle. I'm too nervous to risk a lens swap at this late stage. The sound of the organ crashes through the vast space, the bass reverberating through my entire body.

I shake my head violently and force myself to focus. Here comes the bride.

It's a long walk for Binky, her five bridesmaids and two flower girls, but they seem to enjoy every second. I've never seen a more coherent-looking wedding party: each of the bridesmaids is wearing a long fishtail gown of burnt orange and they're all slim and attractive and of roughly the same height. The two flower girls look as sweet as sugar in white lace dresses with matching orange sashes. I wonder if Binky has any ugly friends. Somehow, I doubt it. And if she does, it's clear the poor girls were never going to make the bridal party. This group appear to have been chosen on the grounds of their own perfection.

I was looking forward to being up at the front in Rachel's usual vantage point, but it's a little disappointing. The cathedral feels too big and I'm not sure the bride and groom or guests feel that connected to the service. There are no tissues being dabbed to eyes, very little emotion on any of the faces. At one point I find myself paying more attention to a group of Japanese tourists photographing the Octagon.

As soon as the service is over, I run as fast as I can down the side of the pews to catch the bride and groom coming up the aisle towards me. It's all for show, though – we're in no rush to leave this beautiful cathedral, so once they reach the end of the roped-off area, they turn and go back to greet their guests.

I'm almost out of space on the compact flash card I'm currently using so I kneel on the floor and get a tiny black case out of my kit bag, swapping the cards over.

'Got any good ones?'

I stifle a sigh as I look up at the middle-aged, oversized American tourist staring down at me.

I can't resist. 'Nah, to be honest, I'm having a bit of an off day.'

'What?' Her face falls and then breaks into a grin. She laughs at me. 'You Brits are so funny,' she says, waddling off.

Actually, I'm Australian.

I pick up my kit bag and go and find Maria. We shoot dozens of candid camera shots inside the cathedral before taking the guests out onto the lawn for the group shots.

The group shots are like nothing I've ever known. The politics at this wedding surely rival anything ever seen in the Houses of Parliament. Binky's father is estranged from her mother. Grandmama Beatrice can't bear to be within a one-mile radius of Cousin Ernest. Aunt Rose and Uncle Bertie haven't spoken to each other in three years. We've been given strict instructions to not even dare try to put any of these guests in the same groups, and we have a list as long as my arm of all the shots that Binky and Charles require.

I have a pounding headache by the end of the group shots, which I'm sure only alcohol will cure. Thank goodness for Maria helping me. I'd be lost without her.

'Do you need a card?' I ask her.

'I'm getting a little low, yes,' she says.

'May as well refill before we go to the reception.'

I take my kit bag off my shoulder and open it up, looking for the little black case that carries all of the cards. It's not there. I unzip my kit bag fully and scramble through the contents. It is definitely missing.

Flu symptoms wash over me in the space of mere seconds: I go hot, I go cold, I feel feverish, sweaty and clammy, and then I feel like I have the onset of Rachel's sick bug. I've done it. My worst night-mare has come true. I've lost the compact flash cards. That's a whole wedding: gone.

'What is it?' Maria asks as I feel like I'm going to pass out.

'I can't find the compact flash cards!' I whisper urgently.

'Is everything alright?' I look up to see Charles peering down at me.

'Yes, everything's fine,' I say breezily.

'The cars are waiting,' he says.

'We'll be there in a minute,' Maria tells him as I hurriedly zip up my kit bag.

'Right away, ears?'

'Ears?' Maria asks.

'*Yes*, he means *yes*,' I hiss at Maria. Where are they? Where the hell are they?

I dash back into the cathedral and try to retrace my steps. When did I last see them? A sudden brainwave comes to me. '*Got any good ones?*' Ears! I mean, YES! It was when that woman distracted me! I run back to the top of the roped-off section and look wildly around. No sign of a little black case. I fall to my knees, fearing I might stay there forever if I don't find these damn cards, but then I see it, the case, underneath a chair. I swear, I almost look up at that beautiful painted nave ceiling and say thank you to God Himself, I am so relieved. I quickly check to make sure the cards are inside and then run out of the cathedral. I give Maria the thumbs-up, beaming at her as though I've won the lottery, and climb into the limo, ignoring the scowling faces of all the people I've kept waiting.

That was close.

Never has a break been more welcome. I'm a little bit giddy with all of the adrenalin as we eat our cheese and pickle sandwiches. No fillet steak for us paupers.

'Of all the weddings to have to do solo,' Maria mutters. 'I'm not even sure Rachel has had one as full-on as this before.'

'What about the family politics?' I exclaim. 'What a nightmare that was with the group shots.'

'It's such a shame people can't heal things for the sake of their children,' she says.

'Mmm.' I tuck into my sandwich with gusto. 'How are you?' I ask between mouthfuls. 'I haven't seen you much recently.'

'No.' The corners of her mouth turn down. 'I've just been keeping to myself, chilling out at home with Russ.'

'How are things going with you two?' I ask.

She nods, looking down at her plate. 'Great,' she says, but her voice cracks. I watch with alarm as her face crumbles and she bursts into tears.

'What's wrong?' I ask with horror, clambering to my feet so I can get around to the other side of the table to comfort her.

'Oh God, I wasn't going to say anything,' she cries.

'What is it?'

'Please don't tell anyone. Rachel and Russ are the only ones who know.'

'I swear, I won't say a thing.' I shake my head vehemently.

She looks at me, tears spilling out of her warm brown eyes. 'I'm pregnant,' she says.

I stare at her in shock. 'Are you sure?'

She nods, tearfully. 'Ten weeks.'

I pause for a moment, thinking.

'Lake District,' she mumbles, her face turning bright red.

I don't know what to say. We heard them *making a baby*? 'What are you going to do?' I ask.

'I don't know. Oh, Bronte, my parents will disown me!' she wails.

'Of course they won't,' I snap, slightly impatiently. Who does that, these days?

'You don't know my parents. They've been trying to marry me off for years. They think I'm still a virgin.'

'Well, they're going to get a little shock, then, that's all. People have had babies out of wedlock before.'

She shakes her head, and for the first time I realise how pale she is. 'You really don't have any idea what you're talking about.'

CHAPTER 20

The wedding is so awful that I actually can't wait to tell Alex about it on Monday morning, but to my disappointment, he's not there.

'Where's Alex?' I ask Tim, his colleague on the art desk.

'Not in.'

'Oh.' I was hoping he'd be coming with me to the Celebrity Houses shoot today. We're photographing the pantomime villainesque star of a reality TV show at his home in Wimbledon. 'Is he sick?'

He shrugs. 'Personal problems.'

He doesn't come in the next day, and by Wednesday, I'm quite worried about him. I jump when I return from the kitchen to see him sitting at his desk, staring at his computer.

'Hey!' I say warmly. 'Are you okay?'

He meets my eyes, but his face is washed out. He looks exhausted. 'Yeah,' he says quietly, without a hint of a smile. 'I'm fine.'

'Have you been sick?' I can't help asking, even though I'm not sure he wants to talk about it.

'Er,' he looks down, moving some proofs across his desk. 'Yeah. Not that great.'

He definitely doesn't want to talk about it. I respect his wishes and go and get on with my work. Nicky is on holiday this week so I'm standing in for her. Helen is much nicer when she's in the deputy role and we have a freelance assistant doing holiday cover.

'It's a boy!' Simon calls out to anyone in the vicinity before I sit down. 'Joe Strike's had a baby boy.' A moment later, people are crowded around his desk, ooh-ing and aah-ing, me included.

Joseph Strike's management company has put out a press release together with a single publicity shot of Joseph and his fiancée cradling a beautiful little baby.

'Alex?' Simon looks over his shoulder, but Alex isn't with the colleagues crowded around his desk; he's still sitting behind his computer, staring at his screen in a daze. 'Alex!' Simon calls, making him jolt upright. Simon jerks his head, motioning for him to come over, as *Hebe*'s other workers disperse.

'Bronte, stay here,' Simon commands as Alex joins us, looking pale-faced and unwell.

'Joe Strike's had his baby,' Simon says. 'I want them on the cover of the new redesign issue,' he adds determinedly. 'Lisa?' he calls to our friendly news editor, who is acting news director in Pete's honeymooning absence. 'Let's have a chat.' He pushes out his chair and leads the three of us into the meeting room. I grab a notepad on my way past my desk. Simon maps out his plans for the issue while Lisa and I nod and make suggestions. Alex stays oddly quiet.

The next two days fly past. I've been trying to source pictures of Joe and his fiancée and we're running the baby bump photos again. The management company has released an exclusive shot of the happy couple and their baby son to us at a hefty price – all of the money is going to charity. I'm on a high as I work. I enjoy my job so much more when Nicky isn't around, and even Helen is impressing me with her new fired-up attitude. I'm thriving on the extra responsibility, organising shoots and going along to art-direct a couple of important ones with high-profile celebrities. The only problem is Alex, who seems like a wreck. As Nicky's stand-in, I'm supposed to work more closely with him, so when shoot photos come in, I print them out on contact sheets and we edit them together. I also need to regularly check pictures on his screen to make sure they look sharp enough on the layouts – the resolution on digital photos from readers is often not good enough to print. Each time I'm more or less alone with him, I ask him if he's okay, and each time he barely meets my eyes as he tells me he's fine.

On Friday he leaves as soon as he can. I watch him go with a heavy heart. I wish I knew what was wrong.

I have a wedding myself the next day, so I don't

go out on Friday night, either. I haven't seen Lachie for two weeks, although I've texted him a few times to keep things friendly. I know he's working as many shifts as he can to try and bring in some extra money. He's taken to busking in Camden when he's not working at the pub so he doesn't waste money on Tube fares into Central London.

In the car on the way to the wedding in Guildford, Rachel tells me that the bride's parents are divorced.

'Urgh,' I groan. 'The last wedding's politics were a nightmare. Those group shots were the most stressful part of the day.' I didn't tell her that I nearly lost the compact flash cards.

'Even more stressful than thinking you'd lost the compact flash cards?' she asks wryly, casting me an amused look from the driver's seat.

I look suitably bashful. 'Did Maria tell you?'

She laughs. 'Yes. Don't worry, I've done it myself. It's a total nightmare, isn't it?'

'One of the worst things I've ever experienced,' I admit. I'm not sure how accurate that statement is, but it certainly felt pretty awful at the time.

'I've attached the carry case to a clip inside my kit bag now, so they won't come loose again.'

'That's a good idea,' I tell her. I pause a moment. 'How's Maria?' I ask. I haven't seen her since the last wedding. She hasn't answered my calls – only my texts, to say that she's still trying to work things through. Russ has seemed almost as subdued at work as Alex, but Maria asked me to keep quiet so I won't say anything to him.

'She's . . . not great,' Rachel says carefully.

'Has she told her parents, yet?'

'She's telling them this weekend.'

'Oh, if only I'd known. I would have wished her good luck.'

Mind you, I think she's going to need quite a lot more than my good luck wishes.

'At least she has Russ with her for moral support.'

'Russ is going with her?' I ask, taken aback. I don't know why I should be surprised – Russ is a nice guy – but from the sounds of it, this is going to be one heavy conversation. And they're still only in the early throes of their relationship. It's a lot of pressure to place on new love.

'He insisted,' Rachel replies with a significant look.

My ninth wedding of the year is taking place in a village church on the outskirts of Guildford with a reception in the gardens of a local country estate.

Louisa, the twenty-seven-year-old bride, has two dads. Her parents split up when her mother was still pregnant with her, so she has a stepdad who raised her from the age of one, and a biological father who she has grown close to in the last ten years. She says the most upsetting part about this whole wedding process was trying to choose between them. And then she realised she didn't have to.

There's barely a dry eye in the house as she walks down the aisle with a father on each arm. The two men smile proudly – there's not an ounce of animosity between them – and the groom, Carl, looks as though he's going to burst with pride. I capture his glowing face and then straighten up and brush my tears away.

Yep, they've even got to me. Who would walk me down the aisle? The thought is stifled before I can ponder it when I remember that I'm never getting married. My cynicism slots back into place.

I'm back in a smaller church again after the magnificence of Ely Cathedral, but this time nothing feels quite as sinister, nor as cold. Perhaps it's because it's high summer – it's August now – or perhaps it's just because my stint with the organ a few weeks ago has proven to me that I can handle just about anything.

The country house where the reception is being held is not quite as grand as anything you'd see on *Downton Abbey*, but it's not far off. The elderly couple who own the place have had to rent it out for functions because it's falling into a state of disrepair. The lady of the house does not appear to be happy about this turn of events. She certainly doesn't seem keen on the paupers who are traipsing about her land. When we go to do the bride and groom shoot inside the house, she gets herself in a bit of a tizz.

'Watch your shoes on that rug – it's a hundred and fifty years old! Be careful of that vase – it's a family heirloom! Don't stand on that balcony – it's five hundred years old and it might collapse!' She even seems annoyed when I brush away some cobwebs. The eccentric old dear makes me think of Miss Havisham.

It's a relief to return to the great outdoors. In spring the sound of birdsong filled the air, now in summer, it's all about the insects. Bees and wasps buzz around the nearby orchard trees and the sunshine is hazy from dust and pollen drifting through the air from the adjoining fields.

Guests bask in the sun with glasses of champagne in their hands, and everyone seems reluctant to move inside to the marquee when it's time for the wedding breakfast to be served. Rachel and I stay outside and sit on some weathered stone steps leading down to the rose garden. Rachel turns her sun-kissed face up to the sky and I do the same.

'This is bliss,' I say, pulling my skirt up to my thighs in an attempt to tan my legs. The air smells of freshly mown grass and I can see a large, dark eagle-type bird circling and soaring on the thermals far above. It makes a mewing sound.

'Buzzard,' Rachel says.

Is that what it is? A butterfly flits past us.

Rachel looks across at me. 'That was a nice service. I like church weddings. I don't do many of them these days.'

'You don't do many church weddings?' I check.

Almost all of the weddings I've done have been in churches.

'No. They're mainly register offices and licensed venues. Sally hasn't done a single church wedding all year; you've been getting them all.'

'Oh.' Lucky me. 'How are things going with Sally?' I ask.

'She's okay.' She nods. 'Still with her boyfriend.' She smiles wryly. 'I think she's happy that you're doing today, although she did seem to enjoy last week.'

'Did she?' I didn't even know Rachel had a wedding.

'Might have had something to do with the wedding singer,' Rachel adds sardonically, rubbing her thumb over a patch of moss on the steps to bring it loose.

I smile. 'Who was that?'

She looks momentarily confused. 'Lachie. I thought I told you.'

'No.' I shake my head and force a little laugh. 'That's nice. Did you get him the job?'

'Yeah. It was a bit of a last-minute thing.'

'That was nice of you.' I can't seem to think of any other adjectives. 'Sally liked him, then?'

'Yeah.' She rolls her eyes. 'Bit hard not to, isn't it?'

'Mmm.' Bet she thought he was better than 'nice'.

'What's that?' she says suddenly, her ears pricking up.

'A fire alarm!' I exclaim, scrambling to my feet.

Turns out, the kitchen equipment is just one more

thing that needs updating in this decrepit mansion. The fire is quickly contained with minimal damage, but a bright red fire engine screams down the country lane regardless, causing all sorts of excitement, not least amongst the female guests and children. Not one to waste a photo opportunity, I convince four buff firemen to hold our bride aloft with the fire engine as a backdrop while Rachel laughingly clicks away. Finally they return Louisa to her feet to a chorus of cheers. Rachel winks at me.

I catch up with Polly the next day. Grant is at the cricket so we meet for Sunday lunch at a pub in Borough Market. She suggests we get a bottle of wine, and isn't too pleased when I say I don't feel like drinking alcohol. In the end, she reluctantly opts for a soft drink, too.

'How are you?' I ask.

'I'm okay,' she replies.

It's the first time I've seen her since Maria and I dropped in on her unannounced. I've tried to meet up with her on a few occasions, but she's always claimed to be busy.

'Do you miss home?' she asks outright.

'Sometimes.' I don't want to get into a conversation with her about Mum like last time so I bat the question back at her. 'What about you?'

'I miss my parents and my sister. I miss my friends. I know you're here, but I miss everyone else. I don't have any history here.'

'It was always going to be hard, putting down your roots in another country.'

'I thought Grant would be enough for me.'

'I don't think one person can ever be enough, can they? That's a lot of responsibility to place on one set of shoulders.'

'Yeah, well, he's useless anyway,' she grumbles.

'Are things still not going well between you?' I ask cautiously.

'I barely see him,' she replies. 'He's always at work or out with his friends.'

'Does he still not ask you to join him?'

'Occasionally,' she says. 'But he doesn't like me drinking.'

I look down at the table.

'I don't have a problem,' she tells me defensively.

My eyes lift to meet hers. 'Polly, you've always had a problem.'

She scoffs. 'Don't be ridiculous. Like you don't drink? Come off it.'

'I usually know when enough is enough,' I reply. 'Okay, sometimes I make mistakes, but I've never been abusive.'

'I don't get abusive,' she snaps.

I give her a look. 'You often get abusive. You just don't remember it in the morning.'

She glares at me.

'And I don't drink in the daytime when I'm on my own,' I add quietly.

'I'm not drinking now,' she says, indicating her glass of cola.

I don't say anything.

'He thinks I need to go to AA meetings,' she says with disbelief.

'Is that such a bad idea?'

'It's ridicu—' her voice cracks and '—lous' comes out sound choked.

I reach across and take her hand. She shakes her head to ward off the tears.

'Why don't we catch up more,' I say gently. 'I'd like to get to know Grant better. Why don't you bring him out with Bridget and me so he gets to know your friends, and it's not always on his terms? It might make you feel a little less isolated.' I'm thinking it would also help if Grant got to know *me* better. Maybe it would help if we joined forces. He shouldn't have to do this on his own, but I understand that he might not want to ask for my help if he doesn't know me that well.

She sniffs and nods. 'Maybe.'

CHAPTER 21

On Friday, Russ comes over to me, practically vibrating with anticipation. 'Are you coming for drinks tonight?'

'Er, yeah, maybe one or two.'

'Fuck that. It's going to be a big one.'

'Really?' I give him a perplexed look. 'Why?'

'You'll see.'

He grins and I look over my shoulder to see him go straight over to Alex's desk. I see Alex nod before I turn around again to face my computer. My phone buzzes to let me know I have a text message. I smile when I see it's from Lachie asking if I'm out tonight. I reply that I am and he tells me he's coming into town and will see me at six p.m. He usually works on Fridays. My pleasure is quickly crushed by nerves. It feels like ages since I've seen him and the sudden memory of our kiss makes my face heat up. I press my hands to my cheeks to cool myself down and then another text message comes in. I snatch it up, wondering what he's got to say now, but it's from Polly:

Grant up for drinks tonight. See you at that pub across the road from your work?

Oh. I slump back in my chair. When I suggested getting to know Grant better, I was thinking more of a pub lunch one day, not a night out drinking with my work colleagues. That's the last thing Polly needs. But she knows I go out every Friday, so what can I say? I bite my lip, reply, 'Cool, I'll see you later,' and pray for the best.

I don't usually bother, but late that afternoon, I duck into the bathroom and apply a little extra mascara and lip gloss. Russ, Alex and the others have gathered by the door when I re-emerge.

'There you are,' Russ exclaims, grabbing me and pulling me to him for a rough but affectionate hug.

We all walk across the road together as a group. Maria and Rachel are already sitting at the bar.

'What are you doing here?' I ask, pleasantly surprised as I give Rachel a hug, followed by Maria. 'Hello!' I say warmly to Maria.

'Maria dragged me in,' Rachel tells me with a playful glint in her eye. Maria seems positively glowing. What's going on?

'G'day.'

I hear his deep Aussie voice and feel his hands on my hips a second later. I spin around and smile up at Lachie. He grins down at me with amusement in his eyes and then he lets me go to greet

Maria and Rachel. He kisses them both on their cheeks and I feel a little put out that he didn't kiss me. I push the thought to one side as Alex appears beside me.

'Drink?'

'I'll get these,' Russ interrupts with a grin.

'What?' Alex and I say at the same time. Russ rarely offers to buy a whole round.

'Go and get a table,' he urges.

I sit next to Alex on a bench seat against the wall. Lachie pulls up a chair opposite. Lisa, Esther and Tim also sit down, blocking Alex in on his other side. There's no Pete – he's still on his honeymoon. I don't know what time Polly and Grant are coming. Bridget also said she'd join us later if we're still out – she's meeting up with a friend for dinner straight from work.

We might need a bigger table.

I look across at Lachie. 'Have you trimmed your beard?' I ask. He looks different, although he's still wearing his usual scruffy denim jeans and a black T-shirt.

He rubs his hand over his jaw. 'Yeah. Finally got around to it.'

I smile at him. 'You didn't have to work tonight?'

'Got the night off.' He grins up at Rachel and leans back in his seat as she pulls out a chair at the end of the table.

'Yeah, well done,' she mouths significantly as she sits down between us.

I'm confused. Did Rachel invite him here? Why?

Is she interested in him? Is he interested in her? I know it's none of my business and it really shouldn't bother me, but bugger that: it does. And then Russ is bringing over a tray with two bottles of sparkling wine and a load of champagne glasses. I stare up at him with astonishment.

'What on earth is going on?' I ask, looking around at my *Hebe* colleagues' equally confused faces.

He looks like the cat that got the cream. Rachel and Maria are definitely in on it, but Lachie just shrugs at me. He seems to know something is going on, but I'm not sure he knows what. Russ pops the cork and keeps us waiting while he smugly takes his time pouring the fizzing liquid into several glasses. Then, ensuring everyone has a glass, he stands behind Maria, who's sitting on the other side of Lachie, and puts one hand on her shoulder.

'I propose a toast,' he says.

Maria looks like she's going to burst with happiness. She glances up at him and Russ's face grows momentarily serious as he smiles down at her, gently chinking their glasses together. 'To my future wife.'

'What?' I stare at them in disbelief, as does almost everyone else around the table.

'Maria and I are getting married next month,' he tells us with a huge grin as he sits down beside her.

I nearly fall off my chair.

★　　★　　★

Maria's parents flew off the handle when she told them she was pregnant, but their suggestion that Russ make an honest woman of her was not met with the derision Maria expected from the soon-to-be father of her child. In fact, the more Russ thought about it, the more he *wanted* to put a ring on her finger. Both Russ and Maria realise that everyone will think they're being too impulsive – Russ's parents and brother have already been trying to talk them out of it. But at the end of the day, Russ told them this is his decision, and they say they'll support it. Maria is due in January, and she wants to wear a white dress before she starts to show.

'It's not long to get organised,' I say, wanting to be pleased for them but doubting their sanity. 'Have you made any plans?'

Maria laughs at the horrified look on my face. 'We're keeping it simple,' she says, smiling lovingly at Russ. 'In fact, we're going to get married in northern Spain at my grandfather's villa.' She returns her gaze to each of us in turn. 'And we were wondering if you'd all be up for coming?'

A murmur passes around the table, but she continues. 'The flights to Bilbao are super-cheap. We'll put on a minibus to the venue, and we can all squeeze into the villa and adjoining apartments. My grandfather has blocked it out for us on the weekend of Friday the twelfth to the fourteenth of September.'

Craziness, but what the hell. 'Count me in,' I

say with a grin. 'Who's going to do your photos?' I ask, flashing Rachel a look. She grins back at me.

'We were sort of hoping you guys might consider doing the photos as a wedding present.' Maria glances sheepishly between us.

I laugh. 'Definitely.'

'I think that's about the one weekend I'm not doing a wedding,' Rachel replies.

'I know,' Maria says with a cheeky grin. 'I checked your wedding diary.'

Rachel laughs. Then Maria smiles hopefully at Lachie, who's sitting to her right. 'And we also wondered, if we paid for your flights, and of course we'll cover yours too,' she quickly says to Rachel and me, continuing before I can tell her no, 'would you consider doing the entertainment?'

Lachie chuckles. 'Yeah, why not. I'll ask for the time off work.'

'We'll *all* have to ask for the time off work,' Alex says, leaning forward and resting his elbows on the table beside me.

Alex will come?

'It's only one day, and it's a Friday, so most of the issue will have gone to press. Hopefully Simon won't mind,' Russ says. I hope he's right. 'And obviously partners are invited, too,' he says to Alex and the others.

Maria lets out a little squeal of delight and eagerly claps her hands as she sees her plan coming together.

'Who's going to do your make-up?' I ask her teasingly. She rolls her eyes at me and then collapses into giggles. It's hard not to get swept up in her excitement.

By the time Polly and Grant join us, we've moved on to talk about something other than babies and weddings. I get up to give them both hugs and kisses, cringing slightly as I smell the alcohol on Polly's breath. They must've gone for drinks beforehand.

Polly hasn't met Lachie or my colleagues, although she does know Rachel and Maria. I make the introductions, everyone shifts along so they can squeeze a couple of chairs between Lachie and Rachel, and I sit back down without thinking much more about it. And then I see Polly frowning at Alex.

'Have we met before?' she asks him.

Oh no, I forgot to warn her not to say anything!

'You were at my hen night!' she squeals, suddenly placing him.

'Steady on,' Russ interrupts, confused. 'Alex was at your hen night?'

'I wasn't at *her* hen night,' Alex brushes him off. 'It was my sister's husband's stag do.'

'Were you there, too?' Lisa asks me directly.

'Mmm-hmm.'

'I didn't know you guys had met before you started working at *Hebe*,' she says with a frown. Trust the person from the newsdesk to cotton on.

'Yeah,' I reply casually. 'Weird, hey?'

I can sense Alex's tension beside me. Someone kicks me under the table and my eyes shoot up to meet Lachie's. He leans forward.

'I've just booked my ticket back home.'

My stomach falls. 'Have you? For when?'

'December. Back in time for Christmas.'

'Oh, right.' This doesn't feel like happy news.

'Are you going back for Christmas?' he asks me.

'No, my visa doesn't expire until March.'

'Not that she'd go home for Christmas anyway,' Polly says with a smirk.

'Why not?' Alex asks casually as I take a large gulp of my wine and start to cough it back up. He pats my back.

'Are you going to Perth?' I ask Lachie, my eyes watering from the effort of speaking. I want to get the question in before Polly can speak again.

'Yep,' he replies, crossing his arms.

'Are you from Perth?' Polly asks him with surprise. Her eyes shoot towards mine and her expression turns mischievous as she looks back at him. 'Do you know anyone called Jason?'

'No, I don't know any Jasons,' Lachie replies, confused.

'Don't be ridiculous, Polly,' I snap, wishing she'd never come. 'Perth is a big city.'

'Who's Jason?' Lachie asks.

'He was my—'

'Fiancé,' Polly finishes my sentence with an impish grin.

'Fiancé?' Maria asks me with amazement as Alex turns sharply to look at me. I can feel Lachie's eyes on me from across the table, too, although luckily, the rest of my colleagues are deep in conversation about something else at the other end of the table.

'He wasn't my fiancé,' I wave her away, my face burning as Alex's eyes bore into me.

'He wanted to be, though,' Polly says, seemingly enjoying my discomfort as she polishes off her drink in record time. Grant shifts beside her.

'Thanks for that, Polly,' I say, my voice dripping with sarcasm. 'Now the whole world knows about my disastrous love life.' I slide out from the bench seat and stand up. 'Anyone for a drink?' I ask through gritted teeth.

'Ooh, yes please,' Polly says.

I ignore her and stalk over to the bar, hearing the sound of a chair scraping across the floorboards behind me. Lachie joins me.

'Your mate's a bit of a handful,' he comments drily.

'She pisses me off sometimes,' I mutter, unable to keep a lid on my anger.

'I kind of got that feeling,' he says. 'And she's the one you flew halfway around the world for to come to her wedding?'

My face softens slightly. 'Yeah. I don't know why.'

He purses his lips together as the bartender comes over. 'Three beers,' he says. 'Russ and Alex are empty,' he tells me. I didn't wait to find that out. 'What are you having?' he asks me.

I need something strong. 'Vodka, lemonade and lime,' I tell the bartender. 'Actually, make it a double.'

'Anything for Polly?' Lachie asks drily.

'And a lemonade and lime,' I call after the bartender. 'No vodka!'

'So why *did* you come to her wedding?' Lachie asks, bringing my attention back to him.

I sigh. 'Some bizarre, weird sense of loyalty coupled together with the fact that I had always wanted to come to the UK. It was the excuse I needed, and she said she really wanted me to be there.'

We walk back to the table together. I wink at Grant as I give Polly her glass. He looks confused. 'No alcohol,' I mouth. He just looks more confused. I give up. If he can't lip-read, that's his problem.

Alex shifts in his seat as I squeeze back past the others to sit down next to him again. Everyone is chatting amongst themselves. Polly and Grant are reminiscing with Rachel about their big day, Lachie joins in on a conversation between Maria and Russ, and to Alex's right, Lisa, Esther and Tim are discussing work. Normality seems to have resumed at our table. My relief is short-lived.

'You were *engaged*?' Alex murmurs under his breath. He gives me a freaked-out look.

'No,' I say determinedly. 'We weren't.'

'But he proposed to you?'

'Yes, and like I told you, I don't believe in marriage.'

'But he proposed to you. He obviously thought you did. You must've been close.'

'Why does this matter to you?'

'I'm sorry, I just . . . I didn't realise it was that serious. I thought you were only together for a year.'

'We were.' He fell . . . fast.

'Was I a rebound thing?'

I cannot believe he just asked me that. Here. With all of these people around. I stare at him in shock before answering his question with a question. 'Was I?'

He shakes his head resolutely. 'No.'

'That makes two of us, then,' I whisper. His eyes sear into mine, like they're carving their way right into my soul. A shiver rockets down my spine and I know I should look away but I can't. We hold eye contact for only a few seconds but it feels like minutes. It physically hurts to snap myself out of it. Shaken, I reach for my drink and take a large gulp.

Wait. Something's not right. I take another sip. Oh no. I've given Polly the double vodka. I stare with dismay as she takes a massive gulp.

Lisa, oblivious to my inner turmoil, uses her small-talk skills on Polly and me. 'How long have you two known each other?' she asks.

'God, forever,' Polly replies, her voice ramping up a notch. She's well on her way to being off her face and deeply unpleasant. Grant looks awkward beside her and my heart goes out to him.

'Since primary school, right?' I come in on the conversation, hoping to defuse it.

'So you lived just outside of Adelaide too?' Lachie asks Polly.

'Yep! But I followed Bronte to Sydney as soon as I could.'

'When did you go to Sydney?' Lachie asks me. Alex, beside me, is staying very quiet, but I'm as aware of his presence as I would be of a furnace.

'When she was seventeen,' Polly says with a grin before I can get the words out.

'Almost eighteen,' I point out.

'That was young,' Lisa comments.

'She couldn't wait to get away from her parents.'

'Polly!' I say sharply.

'Oh, stop being so touchy,' she belittles me. 'You're thirty. So what about your dad? Get over it!'

I feel sick. She's made me feel sick. Why am I even friends with this person?

'I couldn't wait to get away from my family, either,' Lachie says, coming to my rescue. 'But that was because I have four older sisters.'

'No way?' Maria turns to him, but not before shooting me a perplexed look. 'How did you survive?'

The focus moves away from me, as I'm sure was Lachie's intention. I feel Alex shift beside me, and a moment later his hand is on my lower back. I instinctively tense up, but as his thumb moves up and down, I know he's trying to comfort me. I take a deep breath and shakily exhale.

'Did you know your mum has a boyfriend?' Polly's words spear my moment of peace and I'm instantly racked with tension again. Alex's hand stills.

I shake my head at her, confused. 'I don't . . . What do you mean?'

She continues in her too-loud voice. 'My mum said she's got a man.'

'She can't . . . She wouldn't . . .' I stutter as the blood drains from my face. Everyone around the table is listening now and it's excruciating.

'She takes him to church and everything.'

My stomach lurches. 'You can't . . . You must have that wrong. My mum wouldn't . . . He must be a friend.'

'Nope,' Polly says definitively. 'Mum said they're way more than friends. *Everyone* is talking about it,' she adds pointedly.

'Maybe this is a conversation you should be having with Bronte in private.' Alex's authoritative tone cuts through the silence. His hand is flat against my back, pressing firmly.

Polly looks a little shocked. She wobbles slightly on her chair as she regards him. Then she laughs as though she's absolutely outraged.

'I think we should go,' Grant says quietly.

'What?' she screeches at her husband, before turning her accusing stare back to Alex. 'What are you doing here anyway?' She waggles her finger between the two of us. 'Are you two fucking each other?'

There's a collective gasp around the table as everyone stares at her in disbelief.

'Right, that's it,' Grant says, angrily pushing his chair out from the table. 'We're going.'

He hauls her to her feet but she smacks his hand away. 'I'm not going anywhere!' she snaps.

'I'm leaving. And you're coming with me,' he says firmly.

'I'm not leaving,' she slurs drunkenly, sitting back down again. 'If you want to be a party pooper, be a party pooper. I'm staying here with my friends.'

I slide out from the bench seat position and stand up, squeezing past Rachel.

'Come on,' I bark, tapping her shoulder.

Lachie also stands up. Polly looks over her shoulder at me as if I'm from another planet.

'Get up,' I raise my voice at her while Grant turns away from us and rakes his hands through his hair in a despairing gesture.

Polly shakily gets to her feet. I grab her arm and try to march her towards the door, but she furiously wrenches away from me. 'What are you doing?' she hisses.

'Come on, Polly,' Lachie says calmly, his hand on her back. 'We're all going home now anyway.'

'What?'

'It's late,' he says.

'It's early!' she screeches. 'You're all a bunch of wusses!'

By now, we're outside the pub. I flag down a

passing black cab. The driver regards Polly warily as Grant tells him their address and I almost think he's going to reconsider, but Lachie opens the back door and ushers Polly inside.

'You okay, mate?' he asks Grant, who nods tersely and makes to climb into the car. But Lachie puts his hand on his chest to hold him back. 'Do you need some help getting her home?'

'No, no, it's fine,' Grant replies curtly, while I fight back tears.

'Maybe you two should speak tomorrow?' Lachie suggests to both of us.

Grant hesitates, not meeting my eyes as he nods again. Lachie lets him go and he climbs into the cab.

Alex comes out of the pub doors, just as the car is pulling away from the kerb. 'Are you alright?' he asks me with concern.

I nod quickly, but there's a lump in my throat now. 'Sorry,' I mutter, looking away. I really, *really* need to cry. 'I'm going to go home.' I see a cab's yellow light through blurry vision and impulsively flag it down.

'Hey,' Alex says gently, his hand on my forearm. 'Don't go yet.'

I shake my head quickly. He shouldn't be touching me. He should be keeping his distance, not being kind and making me like him too much. Lachie crosses his arms over his chest, but keeps a safe distance. 'I have to,' I say in a croaky voice. 'Will you tell Bridget I'm sorry I missed her when she arrives? Chalk Farm, please,' I say to the cab driver through his open window. I open the door and climb in, pulling it shut behind me. I scoot across the seat and look out of the opposite window as tears start to roll down my face. I can't bear to look at either of the men standing on the pavement as I hurriedly brush them away.

As the driver sets off around the corner towards the tall, concrete and glass office building that is Centre Point, anger mixes with my grief. At that very moment, I despise Polly. She never makes me feel good about myself. She's a taker, never a giver. I feel bound to her because she's one of a very few links to my childhood. Sometimes I wish I could smash those links with a sledgehammer and set myself free. My anger dissolves as my bottom lip wobbles dangerously.

Then someone pounds on the window on the opposite side of the car and I nearly jump out of my skin. I whip my head around and stare in shock at Lachie. He holds my bag up and I suddenly realise I have no money on me whatsoever.

'Is he with you?' the cab driver asks acerbically. We're waiting at the traffic lights near Centre Point.

'Yes!' I exclaim, leaning across the car to open the door. 'Thank you!' I try to take the bag from him, but he slides into the car beside me and shuts the door.

'What are you doing?'

'Hitching a ride,' he says, out of breath. He must

have run like Usain Bolt to catch up with me. 'Can we go via Camden, mate?' he says to the cab driver.

'Thank you,' I say quietly, taking the bag from him, but not meeting his eyes as the cab sets off again.

He hesitates before speaking. 'Alex wanted to come.'

My heart soars, but the feeling is short-lived.

'Did he?' I ask with a wavering voice.

'Yeah.'

'Why . . . didn't he?' I ask.

'I didn't think it would be a very good idea,' he says in a monotone.

I stare down at my hands. 'No, probably not.' Lachie knows that I have feelings for Alex. I told him myself. He swivels to face me, but I can't meet his eyes. 'I don't know what I'm going to do about her,' I murmur, steering the conversation towards Polly.

'You need to host an intervention,' he says matter-of-factly.

I look at him with a frown. I'm not sure I know what he means.

'You need to get Polly's friends and Grant together to convince her that she's got a drink problem. She needs professional help.' He shrugs. 'A mate of mine back in Oz was the same. Binge-drinking, laying into everyone, never remembering it in the morning.'

'She doesn't remember anything in the morning,

either,' I say. 'But whenever I say anything to her, she shoots me down.'

'That's why you do it with others. Bridgie, Grant, anyone else she's close to.'

'Michelle,' I say aloud, thinking of her bridesmaid. I wonder if she and Polly are still close? I could call the hotel and ask her. The thought makes me feel exhausted.

'She'll be okay,' Lachie assures me. 'I'm not saying she'll be instantly cured. In fact, she's almost certain to carry on drinking, but it's the first step to convincing her she's got a problem. She'll probably start to recognise the signs in herself.'

I sigh heavily. I don't feel like I've got the energy for Polly after what she said tonight.

Lachie slips his arm behind my shoulders. 'Come here.'

I shuffle against him and rest my head on his shoulder as his arm encircles me, but I don't find the gesture as comforting as I have done in the past. I think of Alex putting his hand on my back and the look in his eyes when he asked me if he was a rebound thing. The thought makes my heart flutter. I squeeze my eyes shut, but the memory intensifies. I sit up straight again, not wanting to be consoled by Lachie. I bite my lip and stare out of the window. Lachie doesn't seem to know what to say so we ride the rest of the journey to Camden in silence.

'Just up at the traffic lights, mate,' Lachie says

to the cab driver, getting a note out of his wallet. He looks at me. 'Come for a drink with me?'

I shake my head. 'I can't.'

'If you want help, I can help you,' he says. 'I'll even call Grant for you if you like.'

I smile downheartedly at him. He is beyond nice. 'Thanks,' I say quietly. 'But I just can't deal with Polly right now. I know that's wrong.' My throat closes and my eyes well up. 'I'm her friend and I should be there for her. But I just can't right now.' I quickly brush my tears away.

'Come for a drink with me,' he urges again as the cab driver pulls over.

I shake my head. 'I should go home.'

Home? Nowhere feels like home.

He sighs heavily and pats my leg, then gets out of the car and pays the driver. 'I'll see you soon,' he says through the open door.

'Thanks for bringing me my bag,' I tell him.

'No worries.' He shuts the door and my heart feels heavier than ever.

CHAPTER 22

That night, I get a text message as I'm drifting off to sleep. Curiosity getting the better of me, I wearily unplug my phone from its charger and peer at the screen in the darkness. My heart jumps when I see it's from Alex.

You awake?

I am. Instantly. I sit up in bed. What's he doing texting me late at night? Does Zara know he's texting me? Has he told her what happened with Polly and me earlier? It occurs to me that I should ignore him, but my fingers are already typing out a reply.

Just. Thanks for trying to help. See you Monday.

I stare at the screen, feeling on edge as I wait to see if he replies. He does.

Did Lachie catch you up?

My head buzzes as I reply.

Yes. Dropped him off in Camden on way home.

I want him to know this. I also know that I shouldn't want him to know this.

I hear the front door open and shut. Bridget is home. She clatters about in the hallway for a bit before opening my door.

'Bronte?' she whispers into the darkness.

'Hi,' I reply, reaching over to switch on my bedside light.

'Hey,' she says sympathetically. She comes in and sits on the edge of my bed. 'I heard about tonight.'

I groan inwardly. 'Did you?' And then my phone starts to vibrate. I snatch it up and freeze. Alex is calling me. 'I've got to get this,' I tell Bridget with startled urgency. 'Hello?' I say into the receiver, willing Bridget to leave.

'It's Alex.'

'I know,' I breathe.

'Can you talk?' he asks. He sounds different and I wonder how much he's had to drink.

'I'm with Bridget,' I tell him. 'Alex,' I mouth at her.

'Do you need to go?' he asks.

'No. Hang on.' I look up at Bridget. 'I'll come and talk to you in a sec,' I promise.

She gives me an odd look before getting up to leave, shutting the door firmly behind her.

'I'm here,' I say into the receiver. My pulse has sped up. 'Where are you?' I ask.

'At home,' he replies.

'Is Zara with you?' I almost choke on her name.

'No, she's out tonight,' he replies thickly.

So she doesn't know he texted, let alone called. There's an awkward pause as I contemplate this.

'I just wanted to check you got home alright,' he says gruffly. But he already knows that I did. He texted me.

'I'm here. I'm fine.'

'I was worried about you,' he says. I think he's pretty wasted.

'I'm okay,' I reply, wondering where this conversation is going. 'A bit embarrassed.' I switch the light off and slide down in bed, pulling the covers up to my chin. 'What did the others say after I left?'

'Not much. Bridget was concerned about you when she turned up and you'd gone.'

'She's just arrived home.'

'Oh, right. Yeah. She didn't stay that long.' Pause. 'Do you know what you're going to do about Polly?' he asks.

'Lachie thinks we need to host an intervention. He had a friend in Australia with a similar problem,' I add. 'I guess I'll give Grant a call this weekend.' The thought fills me with dread. I barely have the mental strength to deal with myself, let alone Polly.

'What Polly said about your mum. You never talk about your parents.'

Maybe it's the darkness, but I find myself opening

up to him. I sigh heavily. 'I didn't have a very good childhood.'

'Why not?' His deep voice is comforting.

'My parents weren't happy. They shouldn't have been together, but they were too stubborn to split up. At least, my mum was. I think my dad would have got divorced if she'd let him. He was too weak.' My voice is almost a whisper.

'I'm sorry,' he says.

'Are your parents happily married?'

'Er, yeah, they are.' He sounds reluctant to admit it.

'That's good. You have good role models.'

He says nothing for a while. But it's true what I've said. Zara is lucky. The thought hurts and it suddenly feels surreal that we're having this late-night conversation at all.

'Are they why you don't believe in marriage?' he interrupts my thoughts.

I bite my lip. 'I guess so,' I admit.

'That's sad.'

I don't want to talk about this any more. 'What about you?' I shift under the covers, suddenly feeling cold. 'I've been worried about you lately.

'I'm okay,' he says quietly.

'Is everything alright with—' I can't believe I'm asking this question. '—Zara?'

He sucks in a sharp breath and exhales loud enough for me to hear. 'Yeah,' he emits the word halfway through his exhalation. 'We're alright.'

That sounds completely ominous. To my distress,

a spark of hope ignites inside me. I finally find my voice. 'Has anything . . . happened?'

He groans softly. 'Uh, we had a bit of a scare a week or so ago.'

'What sort of scare?'

'She thought she was pregnant.'

A dark feeling settles over me.

'She wasn't,' he says quickly. 'But, I don't know, it sort of threw us.'

I feel sick. 'In what way?'

'She wanted to bring the wedding forward. I thought we should postpone it.'

His words take a moment to sink in. He thought about postponing their wedding? The nausea turns into jittery nerves.

'What did you decide?' I'm almost too scared to ask.

'We didn't have to. She wasn't pregnant.'

'So the wedding is still on?'

His reply doesn't immediately come. 'Yeah,' he says, half-heartedly, and my eyes inadvertently shut. With real effort, I steel myself.

'I can't believe it about Russ and Maria,' I force brightness into my tone.

'Yeah. Pretty nuts.' He still sounds flat.

'Listen, I'd better go and speak to Bridget, but thank you for calling,' I effuse unnaturally.

'Okay,' he says slowly.

'See you Monday.'

'Sure.' He seems averse to ending the call.

'Bye.' I almost throw my phone at the wall.

Instead I throw it onto the bed, which is not nearly as satisfying. I rub my hands over my face in frustration. What was all that about? Was I just drunk-dialled by an almost married man? I wrench back the covers and get out of bed, too worked up to sleep. I go and knock on Bridget's door.

'Everything alright?' she asks wryly. She's in bed, reading a book.

'No.'

She looks surprised. 'What's up?' She puts her book down. 'What was Alex doing calling you at this hour?'

'That's a very good question,' I say sarcastically.

She shakes her head. 'He still likes you, doesn't he?'

I collapse onto her bed. 'I don't know. Sometimes it feels like there's still something between us.'

'And you still like him?'

'I'll get over it,' I mutter. 'It'll help when he gets married. He thought he'd got Zara pregnant.' I fight back tears as I look up at the ceiling.

'Really?' Bridget says.

'That would have put me off him,' I laugh bitterly.

'I could never fall for a married man,' she says.

'No, me neither,' I'm quick to point out.

'There's nothing more off-putting than a man who's deeply in love with another woman.'

'I couldn't agree with you more. But that's the thing. Alex doesn't seem to be deeply in love with Zara.'

Bridget looks worried at my revelation.

I explain. 'He just told me that Zara wanted to bring the wedding forward when she thought she was pregnant. But he wanted to postpone it. Why wouldn't he agree to her request if he was sure about them?'

'Maybe he's not sure about them.'

'Then what's he doing?' The lump in my throat is back.

'God knows,' Bridget mutters. 'I still don't know why you don't just hook up with Lachie. That would take your mind off Alex.'

I roll my eyes. 'That's wrong on so many levels. One, I'd be using Lachie to take my mind off Alex, and two, I'd feel completely shit when he sleeps with me and moves on to the next chick.'

'Do you think he's like that?'

'Don't you?'

She frowns. 'I don't know. I'm not sure.'

'Yeah, well, I'm not about to risk it for the sake of a twenty-four-year-old guitar bum.'

She laughs. 'He's not a guitar bum.'

'If you like him so much, why don't you sleep with him?'

'Alright then, maybe I will,' she replies flippantly and I stare at her in shock. She smirks at the look on my face. 'I'm just joking.' She points her forefinger at me accusingly. 'I *knew* you liked him.'

'I don't.' I frown. 'Not really. Not like that.'

'Well, he likes *you*, not me, anyway,' she points out.

I pull a face. 'Do you seriously think he does?'

'Yeah. *Obviously!*' She gives me a 'duh!' look. 'But whatever. If you're not attracted to him . . .'

'I didn't say I wasn't attracted to him.'

'Oh?'

'Who isn't?' I say.

'Fair point,' she concedes.

I sigh and get up from the bed, stretching my arms over my head and yawning loudly. 'I'm going to see if I can fall asleep now.'

'Alright. Night-night, Bronte.'

'Night-night, Bridget.'

I walk out of the door, but she calls after me, 'Night-night, Mary Ann!'

I call back, 'Night-night, Billy Bob!' I turn into my room.

'Night-night, Suzie Lynn!'

I smirk. 'Night-night, Sally Jo!'

'Night-night—'

'Shut up, Bridget!' I cut her off and slam my bedroom door.

She cracks up laughing and I do too.

CHAPTER 23

Monday rolls around quickly. I'm nervous as I travel into work, wondering how Alex is going to be around me.

For the first time since I saw him on the up escalator when I was going down, our paths cross over in Tottenham Court Road Tube station.

'Hi!' he exclaims with surprise as we pass through the turnstiles next to each other.

'Hi yourself,' I bat back, feeling myself blush. I must've walked straight past him on the escalator – I'm in my own little world today. He adjusts his bag over his shoulder as we make our way to the stairs. I'm still a little out of breath and I feel awkward. I don't know what to say so I hope he does.

'Did you speak to Polly?' he asks.

'No.' My mouth turns down. 'Couldn't face it.' I glance at him. 'I guess that makes me a bad person.'

'Never.'

We spill out of the Tube station and into the cold, wet street. I run for cover under the Centre

Point overhang as the rain pelts down with a vengeance.

'What happened to summer?' I mutter as Alex joins me, shoving his damp, dark hair off his face. It's still only mid-August. I pull my super-light-weight umbrella out of my bag. Since moving to England, I've found it as essential as my Tube pass.

'At least it was nice yesterday,' he says as we set off towards Covent Garden and our magazine offices. I'm holding my umbrella over both of us, but we're not huddled together so his right shoulder will be getting wet. 'I went to see my sister and her husband in St Albans,' he reveals.

'Is this Jo and Brian?'

'Yeah.' He smiles down at me. 'Your memory is amazing.'

I shrug. 'Yeah, it's pretty shit-hot.'

He laughs and the sound fills me with warmth. I like making him laugh.

'Do you have a photographic memory?' he teases.

'I wish. No, I usually only remember the things I want to fff—'

He finishes my sentence for me. 'Forget?'

I try to laugh it off, but the sound catches in my throat. I nod instead.

Yes, there are definitely some things I'd rather forget.

★　★　★

When I start up my computer a familiar name jumps out at me from my inbox. I click on the message from Lily and squeak.

Elizabeth Rose Whiting arrived on Sunday 17 August at 7.15 a.m. weighing 3.3 kg. She was two weeks early so Ben is hoping this is a sign that she won't keep us waiting (up all night) in the years to come. Mummy thinks Daddy's dreaming . . . I'm recovering well after a relatively easy labour – no, I never thought I'd utter those words either! (Thank you Dr Gowri and your hypnosis CDs!) Pictures of our beautiful little girl attached. We are so in love right now xxx

I put my hand to my mouth as I stare at the photographs of the tiny baby. She is so adorable. I can't wait to meet her.

The latest issue of *Hebe* lands on my desk and I look up at Simon.

'Thanks,' I say. He pauses and smiles, seeing the baby snaps on my screen.

'Who's that?' he asks.

'My friend Lily had her baby,' I tell him.

'The Lily who got us the Joseph Strike pictures?' he asks with interest.

'Yes.'

He leans forward and peers at the pictures. 'Aah. She's cute. Why don't you get Sarah to send her some flowers from us? That baby bump issue is still our highest-selling issue of the year.'

Followed in close second place by the Joe Strike baby issue.

'Aw, thank you, I will.'

How sweet is that? I get up and go to speak to Sarah, the editorial assistant, who's only too happy to oblige. She's still super-keen and efficient, but I wonder how long Simon will be able to hang onto her before she moves onwards and upwards.

A week later, Nicky resigns. I seem to be the only person in the office who is shocked.

'She was pushed,' Russ whispers gleefully when we're in the kitchen.

I frown at him. 'What makes you say that?'

'It's obvious, isn't it? She's rubbish.'

'Russ,' I tut, rolling my eyes.

'Good riddance,' he adds.

'She's not that bad.' I can't believe I'm defending her. If she had superpowers, her evil stares would have bored a huge hole right through my head.

Simon calls me into the back office for a meeting later that week.

'As you know, Nicky has resigned,' he says.

There's still no clear indication of whether she was pushed. She claims she wanted to take a break and spend some more time with her ageing parents.

'Yes.' I nod.

'It's company policy to advertise, but I've spoken to Clare and she agrees. We'd like you to step up.'

My eyes widen as I stare at him. Just like that? They're not going to make me jump through horrible interviewing hoops like they usually do? My face breaks into a grin.

'It takes a certain person to be able to deal with celebrities and get them to do the things that you want them to do,' he says with a smile. 'Some of these people are very, very difficult to deal with. You have to be extremely tactful, you can't upset or annoy them, yet all the time you have to still, *somehow*, convince, cajole, and do whatever's necessary to get them to deliver. Nelly Lott is a very good example of how you achieved that.'

'Well, that was mostly Alex,' I say automatically. 'It was a joint effort,' he insists, and I can't argue. He continues. 'As Picture Director, you'll also have to manage the budget and negotiate big sets of pictures, which means handling large amounts of money. We'll send you on some courses, including one for management, because you'll be in charge of two people. I know you've covered for Nicky before, but it would help for you to shadow her before she leaves, so you can learn the ropes properly.'

It goes without saying that I'm not overly keen on this idea. 'Will she be okay with me doing that?' I ask tentatively.

'Absolutely.' He sounds very confident. Then again, if she wants to leave with a good reference . . . 'Helen will move up and we'll advertise for a picture assistant.'

'Okay,' I nod, still trying to take all of this in.

'Happy?' he asks.

Surely he can tell by my face that I am. Very. 'Yes!' I enthuse. 'Thank you!' But hang on . . . 'What about my visa? It expires in March. I'm supposed to be going home. Is this just temporary?'

He appears thoughtful. 'I'd forgotten about that,' he admits.

My heart sinks, but he doesn't look perturbed.

'Would you consider staying here in the UK?' he asks.

'Can I just do that?'

'I don't think it will be a problem to extend your visa, if that's what you'd like?'

Is that what I'd like? I think so.

'I'll speak to Clare about it,' he says of the publisher. 'She's handled visa situations in the past. She'll know what to do.'

'Thank you.'

'Either way, I still want you to step up,' he says. 'Even if we only have you for another six months or so.'

I grin. 'Cool.'

'I'll make the announcement on Friday, so please keep it under your hat until then.'

'I will.'

The meeting is over, but an idea comes to me. 'Do you have anyone in mind for the assistant job?'

'No.' He shakes his head. 'Do you?'

'I was wondering about Sarah?'

'Our editorial assistant?'

'Yes. She's shown an interest in pictures, and I think she'd be great.' She was intrigued to know that my first job in the magazine industry was editorial assistant, too.

'Let's talk to her together,' he says.

Everyone in the office cheers on Friday afternoon when the announcement is made. Three of us are stepping up: Helen, Sarah and me. Sarah was absolutely ecstatic to be given the opportunity, which was lovely. Simon is advertising for a new editorial assistant position and he'll be inundated with applications.

It's a given that my friends and I will all be heading to the pub. Alex seems genuinely proud of me when we chink glasses.

'You deserve it,' he says.

'Thank you.' I purse my lips at him, cheekily. 'I think it was that Nelly Lott shoot that swung it, so thanks for that.'

He looks perplexed. 'Why are you thanking me?'

'You were the one who convinced her to pose in her dodgy PJs without any make-up on.'

'There's no way I'm taking credit for that,' he says resolutely, shaking his head. 'You convinced her, too. You were amazing on that shoot.'

I smile at him. I thought the same about him.

'Aren't you going back to Oz in March?' Lisa interrupts us. Simon didn't go into details about my visa, so I relay the developments to my colleagues.

Clare thinks we won't have too much trouble getting an extension.

'So you're staying in the UK?' Alex asks, shocked.

'Looks like it,' I reply.

He seems taken aback, but he quickly recovers and appears happy. 'Well, cheers to that.'

We chink glasses again. 'How are the wedding plans coming along?' I ask Russ.

'Service is booked in,' he tells us. 'Who's sorted their flights?' He stares around the table with purpose and then points at each and every one of us in turn.

'I'm doing it at the weekend,' Lisa replies.

He skips over Pete who looks a little shamefaced. 'I know you're not coming.'

'Sorry, we can't afford it,' he makes his excuses. 'The wedding wiped us out.'

'The flights—'

'I know you said they're really cheap, but it's all the other costs. Anyway, Sylvie can't get any more time off work.'

'Fine.' Russ sighs melodramatically and turns to me. 'I know you're coming,' he says with a grin.

Despite my objections, Russ and Maria paid for my flight, Rachel's and, I assume, Lachie's too. I haven't spoken to him since the Friday before last.

'I'm booking mine tomorrow,' Alex promises, snapping me to attention.

'Yay!' Russ holds his arms aloft like a champion. 'Zara as well?'

'She can't. She's in New York again that weekend,'

Alex replies, and it feels like someone has removed my heart from my body for a second before putting it back in again. Zara's not coming, but he is?

'She's always in bloody New York!' Russ exclaims. 'Can't she go another week?'

Alex shrugs. 'Nope. Her boss is pretty full-on.'

Russ moves on to the next person at the table, Tim. I hear him say he's got his tickets booked, but I'm still pondering Alex's revelation. He's coming to Russ and Maria's wedding – alone.

CHAPTER 24

'Hey,' Lachie says with an easy grin, getting up to greet Bridget and me. We've met up in the departure lounge of Stansted Airport. I give him a big bear hug – I haven't seen him since that weird night with Polly, but I'm so pleased he's here. He pulls away and smiles affectionately down at me before turning to Bridget. I greet everyone else, but it's the sight of Alex that makes me the most jittery.

The flight to Bilbao is short but sweet. Some of Russ and Maria's other friends and close family also joined us at the airport and there's a fun feeling of camaraderie between all of us.

When we arrive in Bilbao at just after one o'clock in the afternoon, the skies are mostly blue, but a few clouds are hanging over the mountains by the time we get to our destination just over an hour away. Maria's grandfather's property is in the foothills of the Pyrenees. The villa itself is sprawling and a little bit random, stepped down in several levels over a steep incline. At the higher end of the large property there are three two-bed apartments, separated from the main villa by a driveway.

Russ has reserved these for his family and some of his and Maria's close friends, while Maria's family are staying with her grandfather in his separate apartment at the lowest level of the villa.

Her grandfather and parents are waiting on the drive when we pull up, and there's much hugging and kissing and talking in Spanish – which sounds very welcoming, although I don't understand a word of it – before we're allowed to take our bags inside.

The ramshackle main body of the house has been built above the apartment and that's where the rest of us are staying. We enter into a large kitchen with a long wooden table that seats twelve. A few steps down take us into a TV room, then more steps take us further towards the back of the house where two double bedrooms with balconies look out at the gorgeous, tree-covered mountains. Russ dumps his bag in the larger of these two rooms. He has a huge south-facing balcony that looks over the swimming pool and grassy lawn below. A white marquee has already been set up on the lawn and the sight makes Maria squeak with delight. Despite the fact that she's pregnant with his child, Maria's parents were allegedly aghast at the thought of her sharing Russ's bedroom. It's bad luck to see the groom before the wedding, anyway, so tonight she's staying in the apartment downstairs and tomorrow they'll sleep together as man and wife.

Maria directs Bridget and me into the room next

door, which has a smaller balcony facing east. Because we're excited and curious to see the rest of the house, Bridget and I follow the others up the second set of stairs leading towards the front of the house. There are three more double bedrooms at the top. Alex and Lachie are in the only twin.

'At least you won't kick me this time,' Alex muses drily as he drops his bag onto the bed nearer the window.

'Yeah, but I'll still have to put up with your snoring,' Lachie replies, propping his guitar case against the wall.

I think he's joking. To my knowledge, Alex doesn't snore.

Lisa, Tim and their partners are in the other two rooms. Rachel is staying in the more private apartments with a couple of Maria's friends who she knows well.

We go to explore. A side door from the villa takes us down some steps to a barbeque area with a round, stone table surrounded by enormous hydrangea bushes with large pink, purple and blue flowers. More steps lead down to the expanse of grass where the marquee has been erected, and to the right is the pool. The sky may be a little overcast, but the air is decidedly warm. Tiny sparrows flit from branch to branch and large, brilliantly striped dragonflies hover over the pool.

I hope Maria and Russ have some swimming time booked into their plans for the day.

'Swim?' Russ suggests as he rubs his hands together with glee.

'You read my mind,' Bridget speaks before I can.

We return to the house to get changed and on a whim I grab my camera and fit my staple 35 mm to the body. I got this lens when I bought my camera a couple of years ago, but I also recently invested in a couple of new whizz-bang lenses of my own: a 200 mm and an incredible but astronomically expensive 85 mm F1.2. It cost almost two thousand pounds. My promotion comes with a pay rise.

Nicky's last day is today. I feel bad for not being around to suggest we go out for farewell drinks – but not that bad. She's never shown any interest in joining us on Friday nights and I doubt she'll start now. Shadowing her was nowhere near as bad as I thought it would be. In fact, she's been more relaxed in these last few weeks than I've ever seen her. She's taking a break to go and spend some time with her parents in Wales, but she says she'll come back to London soon and try to find work on a monthly magazine. She claimed to be a bit 'over' weeklies.

I gave her a good luck card yesterday before I left and some chocolates, but I haven't forgotten how unpleasant she's made work for me at times. I can't say I'm not glad to see the back of her.

'Come on, Bridget!' I urge as she tries to decide which of her three bikinis to go for. I'm wearing the only one I own and it's red. I slip a sheer, white kaftan over my head to cover myself up. I have a pretty good figure, but I'm not about to run around practically naked.

'The green one,' I tell her and she makes a snap decision, bolting into the bathroom.

'Wait for me!' she shouts. I roll my eyes and go to stand on the landing outside our room. Lachie jogs down the stairs wearing hot pink surfer-style board shorts and nothing else. His tanned chest is perfectly cut and an involuntary rush of breath escapes my lips. I'm tempted to take a photo of him right then and there. He nods at the camera hanging from a strap around my neck. 'You working already?'

'May as well.'

Alex follows a moment later. He's wearing navy swimming trunks and I'm struck by a memory of the last time I saw his lovely, lean body. It's been two years, but he still feels scarily familiar to me. He's not as broad or muscular as Lachie, but he's toned and fit and gorgeous and I can't believe those thoughts are going through my mind. I shout at Bridget to hurry up.

Lachie peers past me towards our bedroom, where Bridget is knotting a black sarong around her waist. 'I cannot believe you chicks are sharing a bed together,' he murmurs, his eyes shifting back to mine as he gives me a suggestive look.

'Here we go,' Alex says jokingly, sounding as if he has the weight of the world on his shoulders.

'Like you don't find that thought hot?' Lachie

teases him with a grin, leaning against the wall and folding his arms. The posture makes his biceps bulge. I glance over my shoulder in time to see Alex roll his eyes. I smirk back at Lachie as Bridget joins us.

'What's hot?' she asks innocently.

'You and Bronnie,' Lachie replies, pushing off from the wall.

Bridget looks amused, but confused.

'Us in bed together,' I explain.

'Ooh. You want to join us?' she jokes seductively.

'Stop encouraging him,' I snap as she laughs loudly.

I turn around to see Alex open the door and hold it back with a wry smile on his face. Lachie, chuckling, follows me outside.

Down by the pool I have second thoughts about bringing my camera outside. What if it gets wet? What if it gets broken? I decide to take some photos now – I'll put it back in my room when I'm done. I catch Alex in mid-air doing a perfect dive into the deep end. He emerges and flicks his dark hair out of his eyes. I click off some shots of Lachie picking up a protesting Bridget and dumping her into the pool before jumping in after her. I capture Russ bringing a cool box full of ice and beer bottles down the steps, flanked by his brother and best man, an old friend of his from home. And I snap Maria standing arm in arm with her grandfather as they laugh from the sidelines.

Russ opens bottles of beer and hands them out and a dripping-wet Lachie climbs out of the pool to take one. 'You should really put that down,' he says to me with a cheeky grin, taking a swig of his beer as rivulets of water stream down the length of his hard body.

'You stay away from me,' I warn, impulsively clicking off a shot of him.

'You like this, do you?' he asks me provocatively, dragging his hand across his abs.

'You're an idiot.' I try to keep a straight face.

'What did you call me?' He looks mock-horrified as he slowly and purposefully places his beer bottle onto the mosaic-tiled table top.

I lower the viewfinder from my eye and back away from him. 'Don't you dare.'

He steadily walks towards me.

'Don't. You. Dare.' I say again. Still he comes. 'Lachie, don't.' I feel a little panicked now. He wouldn't, would he? 'You'll break my camera!' I cry with alarm.

He stops suddenly. 'As if I'd throw your camera into the pool,' he berates me and I can't tell if he's genuinely hurt or if he's still winding me up. He turns his back on me and I stare at him, unsure. Then he returns to the table and picks up his beer bottle. I feel a bit thrown. I decide to go and put my camera inside anyway.

Rachel and a few more of Russ and Maria's friends have joined the pool posse by the time I get back, and there's a real party atmosphere.

Maria has agreed to be the designated mini-van driver tonight. We're all going out clubbing in nearby San Sebastian, and she's not drinking, obviously.

'I can't believe you're having a joint hen and stag night,' Lachie complains.

'Well, I can categorically say now that we won't be out too late. I've got a wedding tomorrow,' she replies.

'Aw, but you're such an excellent make-up artist,' Bridget says, passing me a beer. 'You'll easily cover up your dark circles.'

Lachie is standing nearby and I gently chink my bottle against his. 'I know you wouldn't really throw my camera and me into the pool,' I say quietly.

The glint in his eyes instantly returns. 'I didn't say I wouldn't throw *you* into the pool.'

'Oh, shit.' How dumb am I?

I dump my bottle on the table and run. He catches me quickly, scooping me up in his arms from behind. I squeal as he carries me to the pool and throws me in, kaftan and all. I come up gasping and spluttering.

'Me Tarzan, you Jane!' he yells, flexing his muscles. I can't help but laugh. Bridget sneaks up to him from behind and I try to keep my eyes trained on Lachie so as not to give her away. It works: she shoves him and he goes flying. Moments later, everyone else joins in.

★ ★ ★

That night, Bridget and I get ready together. I know how long she takes in the shower so I go first, then choose a thigh-length black and white shift dress with high heels. I leave my hair loose and borrow some of Maria's make-up. She always has the best stuff. She takes next to no time to get ready too, so I join her, Russ and the boys on their balcony for a drink while we wait for the others. Lachie and Alex have made a big bowlful of sangria, using red wine, lemonade, Cointreau, lots of freshly squeezed orange juice and lemon and orange segments. Lachie ladles some into a glass for me. He's wearing black trousers and a black shirt that hugs his broad frame. His sandy blond hair is still damp from the shower. He's made a bit of an effort for a change. Alex gets up and gives me his chair – there are only four around the table, but there's a bench seat near the wall. He's wearing a more casual cream linen shirt with a silver pinstripe and grey trousers. His sleeves, as usual, are rolled up.

'Thanks,' I tell him with a smile as I take the seat he's offered. 'I'll save my feet for dancing later.' I kick my heels up and he grins, staring down at me.

'Dancing, hey? Planning on getting wasted, are you?'

I shrug and take a sip of my drink. 'Whoa! I don't think I have much choice,' I exclaim, holding the drink away from me.

Lachie and Alex laugh. 'Is it strong?' Maria asks.

319

'Just a bit,' I reply.

'Oh, I wish I could drink,' she moans. Russ rubs her shoulder in a consolatory gesture.

'Sorry,' he murmurs.

'Yeah, you *are* to blame,' she bats back.

'Hang on, it wasn't my idea to swap tents!' he exclaims, holding his palms up.

'Actually, I blame Bronte,' Maria says with a smirk. 'If you hadn't decided to turn thirty—'

'Oi!' I interrupt. 'If anyone's to blame, it's Bridget. She organised that trip.'

'What are you blaming me for now?' she cries, coming out onto the balcony, looking sexy as hell in a tight, red, backless dress.

I point at her. '*You* are responsible for *their* baby,' I say.

She grins. 'In that case, I'm responsible for this goddamn amazing holiday that you're all on, and for that, I demand free drinks all night. Starting now.'

Lachie gets her a drink before sitting back down again and patting his knee. She gladly perches.

'Nice dress, Bridgie,' Lachie murmurs appreciatively, drawing a line across her bare back.

'Why, thank you, sir,' she drawls over her shoulder. 'You can come again.'

'I might just do that.' He chuckles and she giggles.

I inadvertently sigh and glance at Alex, who has moved to sit on the bench against the wall. Rachel and one of Maria's friends appear. I get up to join him, making space at the table.

'Have you seen Polly recently?' he asks me quietly as the others chat and laugh amongst themselves. Rachel is now sitting on Lachie's other knee.

'No. We've texted each other. No mention of that night. I doubt she remembers.' I should speak to Grant about an intervention, but I haven't been able to bring myself to call him. I'm not proud, but there's so much history between Polly and me that it's almost going to make confrontation harder. I don't know what she'll throw back at me if I tell her *she* has a problem. The truth is, I'm scared.

I mirror Alex's body language and lean forward, resting my elbows on my knees.

'It's so beautiful here,' I say.

In the distance the mountains fall away to the ocean. The clouds are glowing orange in the pale blue evening sky and the sunset is lighting up the trees as though they're on fire.

'Apparently you can walk to a waterfall over there.' He points at the mountains to our left.

'I'd be up for doing that.'

'Maybe Sunday? Before we fly home?'

'Sounds like a plan, Stan. Have you brought your camera with you?'

'I have,' he says with a nod.

'Aha! Finally I get to see some of your shots.'

He laughs. 'They're nothing to write home about.'

'You're so creative.' I elbow him in his ribs. 'I bet they're brilliant.' He leans back in his seat and shrugs casually, playing it down. 'What sort of thing do you like photographing?' I ask.

'Mainly landscapes. I don't really do people.'

'Not likely to ever become a wedding photographer, then,' I joke.

'I think we can safely say you've got that covered.'

'Mmm.' I lean back in my seat, suddenly feeling preoccupied. 'I'm a bit nervous about tomorrow,' I admit.

'You're not, are you?' He looks taken aback. 'Why? Because they're friends?'

'Yeah. It feels like more pressure.'

'Don't stress. You'll be fine. More than fine. Amazing.'

'Aw.' I blush and glance at him, meeting his beautiful blues straight on. Oh, why do I have to fancy him still?

It hurts.

He looks away and clears his throat. We fall into a slightly awkward silence. I'm the one who breaks it.

'How's it all going with Zara after, you know . . .' The pregnancy scare.

'Okay. She's been really busy at work lately.'

'Is she very career-driven?'

'Extremely,' he replies.

I hesitate, but curiosity gets the better of me. 'Whatever happened with that colleague of hers?' I'm talking about the man she was allegedly interested in when she and Alex were on a break.

'She says nothing ever did.'

'Did you ever tell—?' I clamp my mouth shut. I can't believe I was just about to ask him if he told her about me.

'Right!' Russ, luckily, distracts everyone with a clap of his hands. 'Let's get this show on the road.'

It's still light when Maria drives us – a little erratically, it has to be said – into San Sebastian. She takes us on a brief tour of the city before parking the van, and then we wander en masse through the pretty streets, which are an interesting mix of old Spanish and innovative new-build architecture. Eventually we arrive at the large, sweeping Bay of La Concha, which is surrounded by three colossal mountains. Santa Clara islet protrudes straight out of the middle of the bay in front of us, and a huge statue of Jesus Christ stares down at us from the top of Mount Ulia to our right. Maria says he's supposed to protect the city. She's quite religious, unlike me.

Bridget knows the names of all the mountains – I sometimes forget that she is a travel writer, and now her knowledge impresses me. She says that La Concha beach is often featured in travel magazines as being one of the best urban beaches in the world.

Because of the sangria we had at the villa, we hit the ground running, starting with a tapas bar crawl. By the time we reach the club, it can safely be said that I am drunk. Maria appears to be having the time of her life, despite the fact that she's driving, and even Rachel, who never seems to drink much, is well on her way to being smashed.

The club is hot and the music is loud. Lachie and Bridget are at the bar, lining up shots, which we definitely do not need, and I'm leaning against a column and taking a breather because my feet are killing me. I don't know where Alex is.

Lachie brings me a shot, but I shake my head.

'Come on!' Bridget shouts at me, knocking hers back. Lachie does the same with his, and then gives me one last chance to take mine.

'No, thanks!' I say, wobbling slightly. He shrugs and knocks mine back too.

'This feels oddly familiar,' Alex says in my ear as he joins us. He accepts a shot and knocks it back.

'Doesn't it just?' I give him an amused look. His eyes are darker again in this light. He reaches past me to put his shot glass on the bar, brushing my bare skin. All of the hairs on my arm stand on end. I shiver, trying to snap myself out of it and turn to speak to Lachie.

'Are you looking forward to going home at Christmas?' I ask him, trying to be friendly. I have to lean in close and shout in his ear.

'Yes and no.' He smiles. 'Feels like I haven't been here long enough, but it'll be good to see my family. And who knows, maybe I'll come back again.'

'What will you do when you go back?'

'Dunno.' He shrugs. 'Carrying on gigging, I guess. I don't have any big career plans.'

It amuses me that he's so laid-back. 'I'm going to miss you!' I impulsively loop my arms around his neck and give him a friendly hug, wobbling slightly in my inebriated state.

He pulls away and frowns down at me. What did I do?

'Let's dance!' Bridget shouts, dragging me away before I can ask.

Later, with the soles of my feet burning beyond help, I search for somewhere to sit down. Spying Alex with a few of Maria's friends, I go and join him. He scoots over on the bench seat to make room for me, but it's still a squash.

'My feet are killing me,' I complain. 'Why do I always wear stupid heels?'

He grins and tucks a strand of hair behind my ear. It's a far-too-familiar gesture and my eyes widen.

'Sorry,' he says, appearing equally taken aback.

I shake my head quickly and then a song comes on that obviously means something to Maria's friends because they rush onto the dance floor, leaving us alone.

'Did you ever think about me?' The question is out before I can stop it.

He turns his head to look at me and his expression is tortured.

I know it's wrong, I know that I'm drunk and I should get up and walk away. Or *he* should get up and walk away. But he doesn't, and I'm glued to my seat.

He nods slowly, his eyes never leaving mine. 'All the time.'

My heart crashes against my breastbone and I can feel my pulse throbbing in my ears.

'What happened after I left?' We're sitting close together and we're far away from the speakers so we don't have to shout.

'We pretty much picked up where we left off.' He sighs heavily. 'You were gone.' His arms are folded, as are mine, and the fingers of his right hand suddenly brush against the fingers of my left. He doesn't move away, and neither do I, and the contact feels electric.

'I looked for your name in magazine mastheads,' I tell him.

'I worked for a newspaper.' He gives me a sad smile.

'I know.'

He shifts his hand closer and links his fingertips with mine. It feels so right. The rest of the room melts away around us.

I'm in love with him. The instant realisation makes me want to cry.

'Why didn't you wait at the top?' I ask him, my nose beginning to prickle. 'When I saw you on the escalator?'

'I wanted to,' he says. 'But I thought about Zara and just . . . couldn't.'

Hearing her name makes me reflexively close my fist, the motion taking my fingertips away from him.

'Bronte . . .' he murmurs. And then I look up to see Lisa coming towards us. Her smile falters slightly when she notices how closely together we're sitting. Coming to my senses, I quickly edge away.

'Hey!' I exclaim brightly. 'Having fun?'

'Yeah, you?' She sits down next to Alex and that's the end of our conversation. For now.

Later, back at the villa, Russ and Maria call it a night, but Bridget persuades a few of the others to have a nightcap at the stone table by the barbeque. I find myself staring at the starry night sky. A far-off satellite is circling the earth and it looks like a shooting star in slow motion. The fresh air is clearing my head a little and I know I should go to bed. Rachel has already turned in and we both have to work tomorrow. Guessing what Bridget's reaction will be to me leaving, I quietly slip away.

It's stuffy in our bedroom, so I open the doors to the balcony. Now that I'm alone, my head has the space to contemplate what happened earlier with Alex. My mind begins to race again and I know that trying to sleep is futile. I take off my heels and step outside onto the balcony. The terra-cotta tiles under my feet have a sprinkling of sand which I imagine is always there, no matter how many times they're swept. I rest my elbows on the wrought-iron railing. The mountains in front of me are dark, but pinprick stars light the sky. I almost don't hear the knock on my door.

'Hello?' I call, turning to peek into the room. The door opens and Alex walks in. He looks around the room.

'I'm out here,' I call quietly, my heart racing as he comes out onto the balcony.

'We didn't finish our conversation,' he says, joining me at the railings.

'Did you ever tell her about me?' I ask him outright, now that we're alone and finally speaking openly.

He hesitates a moment before answering. 'No.' He sighs. 'I didn't think there was any point in hurting her. It wasn't like I was ever going to see you again.'

We both regard each other hopelessly. If only we'd known. Would we be in a different place right now? It's too hard to say.

'I couldn't believe it when I saw you on that escalator,' he tells me.

'I ran back to the top. I looked everywhere for you,' I whisper, remembering how much that search hurt.

'I'm sorry. I just . . . freaked out. I could barely think straight when I got to work. I was starting a new job and I was a mess. And then when I arrived at the shoot and you were standing there on the pavement . . .' He shakes his head in disbelief before staring up at the stars in silent contemplation. I see him swallow, his Adam's apple bobbing up and down.

'I can't believe you're getting married,' I say in

a small voice, and as I fight back tears, I'm struck with the horrible thought that I am a *bad* person. I don't deserve love. I don't deserve him. He doesn't belong to me. He belongs to Zara. He belonged to her for years, well before I came along and confused things.

Alex turns to face me, slowly reaching out to draw his fingers across my temple. There are so many butterflies in my stomach that I think I'd be able to hear them fluttering if it weren't for the loud beating of my heart.

'I don't know what I'm doing,' he whispers.

I love him. And it's killing me.

He pulls me into his arms and I'm helpless to stop him. I close my eyes as he holds me tenderly, his hand cradling my head as I rest my face against his warm chest. My hands are clammy and my heart is pleading for some let-up. Tears spill out of my eyes and roll down my cheeks.

He pulls away a little and looks down at me. 'Hey,' he says with dismay, brushing away my tears with his thumbs.

'You should go,' I say, placing my hands on top of his and gently lowering them from my face. 'The others might come looking for us. I think Lisa already suspects something.'

'We're not doing anything wrong.' He frowns and lets his hands fall to his sides.

I give him an odd look and he sighs. 'Okay.' But he seems reluctant to leave. 'Come here,' he says, pulling me in for another hug, but this time it's less intense and more friendly. 'Are you okay?' he asks into my hair.

'Yeah.' I pull away from him. 'I should get some sleep. I have to work tomorrow.'

'So you do.'

He follows me back into the room and I dust my sandy feet off before seeing him to the door. I open it up and peek out, but all is quiet. 'See you in the morning,' I say as he walks through. I start to close the door but he turns around and puts his hand on it, locking eyes with mine. He looks torn.

'I don't know what I'm doing,' he says in a pained voice. In that moment, I'm certain he's going to kiss me and I know I'm going to do nothing to stop him. The door to the outside opens behind him and I jolt as Lachie comes in. He looks shocked to see Alex and me facing each other in the doorway to my bedroom. My reaction is instinctive and I don't think twice about shutting the door in Alex's face.

CHAPTER 25

If I didn't have a wedding to photograph, I think I'd be on the next plane home. Alex and Lachie are sharing a room, so I dread to think what they said to each other behind closed doors last night. Maybe they said nothing, but I'll be surprised if there's not an atmosphere between them today. Hopefully it will only be clear to me.

Bridget hasn't asked me where I disappeared to last night. She's so hungover, I don't think she cares, if she even noticed. I heard her come in in the middle of the night. She crashed onto the bed without even getting undressed and I had to shake her awake this morning so she could get ready in time. She swore at me repeatedly.

I assist Rachel with the bride preparation photos downstairs in Maria's grandfather's apartment and it's good to have something to take my mind off last night. Maria is glowing, despite her serious lack of sleep. We photograph her applying her own make-up.

'How are you feeling?' I give her a warm smile. It's a question I've heard her ask so many brides.

She giggles. 'Better than you.'

331

'I don't doubt that. Did you have fun last night?' I ask as Rachel takes a photo of the pair of us talking to each other.

'I loved it. Best hen night ever.'

I grin. 'Do you think Russ enjoyed himself?'

'Yeah, he had a wicked time. I bet he's feeling rough today, though.'

Maria and Russ are getting married in the next town, just down the hill from here. Russ's dad is ferrying everyone to and from the church in the minibus. Rachel checks her watch.

'Do you think I should go?' I ask her reluctantly.

'It's probably time.'

I stand up unwillingly. We agreed that I would photograph the guests boarding the bus, but I really don't want to face Alex and Lachie.

It's a bright and sunny day, which according to Maria is not as normal as you'd think for northern Spain. Apparently it rains a lot up here. Then again, it is very green.

My head is pounding as I walk up the stairs to the drive where I can hear the murmur and chatter of happy people talking and laughing. I see Lachie standing with Bridget. She's wearing dark sunglasses and seems a bit the worse for wear, even though she looks lovely in a floaty, knee-length emerald-green dress. Alex, I notice, is standing on the other side of the drive with Tim and his girlfriend. He's wearing a suit and my heart hurts to look at him so I don't. I soon discover that he's avoiding eye contact with me anyway. He's not the only one. Lachie won't look at me, either. Even as he boards the bus and sits at a window on my side, he keeps his eyes trained forward.

My face burns as the bus pulls away. I should be relieved that they were the first to go to the church, but my stomach swirls with nerves and nausea, which I'm pretty sure is not alcohol-induced. It will be at least fifteen minutes before the minibus returns for the next load so I go for a walk and take some photographs of the marquee. Really it's just an excuse to get away from all of the people. I take a deep breath and try to settle my stomach. Today is going to be tough.

Russ comes out of the villa with his best man and I force a smile back onto my face as I capture him for posterity.

I'd love to see Maria board the bus, but I have to go with Russ to the church, so I hurry down to the apartment to wish her good luck. Rachel is lacing up her corset while Maria's only bridesmaid – a friend of hers from school – stands helplessly by. Rachel has had a lot of practice. My eyes prick with tears and I photograph the sight with blurry vision. Hopefully it's my eyes and not my lens which is unfocused. I laughingly brush my tears away and try again to make sure I'm not messing it up.

Maria looks absolutely beautiful in an elegant cream-coloured silk gown. She's not starting to show yet – well, only slightly, but the way the skirt flows from the bust downwards makes it a perfect choice for hiding a little bump.

I give her a kiss good luck and go back upstairs to join Russ on the minibus.

The church is constructed of red brick and slightly crumbling grey stone and I'm not entirely sure it's safe. Russ seems nervous, but for entirely different reasons. I photograph him and his best man as they kick up dust with their black shoes on the stone path outside the church. Eventually they go inside and my stomach churns as I follow them. This time it's not the church that's the problem; it's the people sitting in the dark wooden pews. I focus on my job and photograph the pretty, simple hydrangeas attached to the ends of the pews, while Bridget teasingly tries to distract me.

'Take your glasses off, you idiot,' I mutter at her. She's still wearing them indoors.

Lachie is sitting beside her, studiously looking at his fingernails. I click off a shot of Bridget and then move up to the front of the church. I say hello to the Spanish priest, who doesn't speak a word of English, so I hope we're going to get on. He seems friendly enough. I wonder who's going to translate the service to Russ and the rest of us.

I step up towards the altar rail, tensing when I see the old pipe organ. I photograph it quickly and then turn around to see Russ taking his place next to his best man. I click off some shots of them before flipping the focus to capture his mother dabbing at her eyes in the pew behind him. I lower my camera and my eyes lock with Alex's. He averts his gaze immediately.

I could cry. Things are going to be weird between us from now on, I just know it. It's hard enough that I've admitted to myself that I'm in love with him. I lift my camera up to hide my face, forcing myself to photograph the simple, stained-glass windows before calling it quits. I go outside to wait for Maria.

She arrives on time and looking beautiful, wearing her late grandmother's veil. Rachel helps her to adjust it as I lean against the heavy wooden church door and fight back tears. I know it's normal for people to get emotional at weddings, but it's not normal for me. I take a few photo-graphs, even though this part is Rachel's bag, and then move into the church. Rachel pats my arm and I see her eyes are shining too as she moves past me into the church. The organ starts to play and I photograph Maria taking a deep, calming breath while she braces herself. Her father looks grave as he offers his arm, and then she fixes me with a confident smile and walks steadily towards me.

She is really going through with this. I wasn't sure if she would. They barely know each other. It blows my mind that they're about to commit to a life together. My attention shifts to Russ. His nose goes bright pink when he sees her and I notice him swallow, but then he smiles bravely, happily, and there isn't a shadow of doubt in my mind that he loves her and wants to be with her.

I hope with all my heart that they'll be very happy together.

Bridget manhandles me later when we're back at the villa having a champagne reception around the pool. 'What the hell happened last night?' she mutters under her breath as she pulls me behind a hydrangea bush.

'What are you talking about?' I ask wearily.

'You could cut the atmosphere between you and Lachie with a knife. He disappeared and then I realised you were gone, too.'

'I went to bed,' I tell her.

She looks away from me. I can't see her eyes behind her dark glasses so I don't know what she's thinking. At a guess though, she's hurt because I'm not confiding in her.

I sigh. 'Alex came to find me.'

She looks at me sharply. I tell her everything.

'Holy shit,' she murmurs. 'And Lachie saw you?'

'Nothing happened,' I reply.

'He doesn't know that.'

'No,' I admit. 'But I'm sure Alex told him.'

'I doubt he would have believed it anyway, if he saw Alex nearly kiss you. Fucking hell, Bronte, what if he'd been Lisa or Tim? Don't they know Zara?'

I blush furiously. She has every right to tell me off, but I'm still trying to come to terms with what happened myself. I think she realises. 'Do you want me to speak to Lachie?'

'No.' I shake my head. 'I'll tell him if he asks. I'm sure he won't say anything to anyone.'

'I hope you're right.'

We manage to get through the group shots before the wedding breakfast and then Rachel and I take the happy couple off for their private shoot. And they are happy. Blissfully. We photograph them with the mountains as a backdrop.

Rachel and I may be working, but for once, we don't take our break in private. We sit at tables with the other guests, although neither of us is drinking. My friends and colleagues, on the other hand, are navigating their way through their hangovers by the hair of the dog method and they're coming out the other side laughing. I watch with relief over the course of dinner as the atmosphere between Lachie and Alex dissolves. They're sitting on a nearby table – the food is a buffet with no seating plan – so Rachel and I are with Maria's friends from home who had space on their table. Bridget pulled a face at me when I didn't sit down next to her, but I think she understands it's probably best that I keep my distance.

The speeches take place when coffee is being served. Rachel and I get back to work. Maria's father is the first to speak, so my focus is on Maria's mother and her table of close relatives, while Rachel concentrates on Maria and her father. I get some lovely shots of Maria's mother looking quite emotional as she smiles with pride. Despite the circumstances of the more pressing, er, biological issue that has sped up the proceedings, she seems genuinely delighted to see her daughter tying the knot.

Russ speaks next, and his speech has everyone both sniffing and cracking up with laughter. I hold my breath when his best man speaks. Maria and her immediate family didn't come clean to her more elderly relatives about the reason for her hasty nuptials, but although the best man makes insinuations about a tent in the Lake District, most of Maria's relatives can't speak a word of English anyway. They can count to nine though, so they might get a surprise in approximately five months' time when a baby is born.

The tables are cleared soon after the speeches and I watch Lachie distractedly as he sets up. He has studiously ignored me all day long, and I feel sick and sad as I see him plug in his beloved guitar to the amplifiers brought in by Maria's DJ cousin. I'd like to speak with him, but it will have to wait until I'm officially off duty – which may not be tonight. It's time for the first dance so I move closer to the dance floor. It's only when I'm already in position that I realise Alex is close by. My skin's burning all over as I pretend to fiddle with my zoom, but he sees me, and buoyed by alcohol perhaps, he comes over.

'How's it going?' he asks.

'Fine,' I reply. 'Good. It's been a good day, hasn't it?' I keep my voice sounding casual.

'Great.'

Lachie starts to play Noah & The Whale's '5 Years Time' and I smile as I click off some shots of Maria and Russ doing an impromptu but gorgeous dance on the dance floor. I zoom in on Lachie and catch him looking super-cute as he plays his guitar and smiles while he sings about drinking stupid wine, getting drunk and having fun, fun, fun. He looks into my camera lens and to my relief his smile doesn't drop even as his lyrics change to love, love, love, but then his eyes move to my left to where Alex is standing and his gaze hardens. He returns his attention to his hands on his guitar, and my heart sinks. I step away from Alex and photograph the smiling crowd.

When the song finishes, everyone claps and cheers and Russ and Maria kiss before turning to give Lachie a round of applause. He grins and casually tips an imaginary hat to them.

A short while later, Rachel places a glass of champagne in my hand. 'Cheers,' she says with a grin, taking a sip from a matching glass.

'Where did you get that from?' I ask. I thought the champagne ran out ages ago.

'Maria saved us a bottle,' she tells me with a smile.

'B!' Bridget shouts, appearing with a glass of white wine in her hand. She's cheered up a whole lot since this morning. Maria leaves Russ behind to join us too, and Rachel, ever the professional, snaps a shot of the three of us with our arms around each other. We stand together and watch Lachie along with pretty much every other girl in the vicinity. I think he likes the attention. He grins over at us a couple of times.

Eventually I bow to Rachel's insistence that she can cover the rest of the night – she really is the loveliest boss and mentor. I take my camera inside to my bedroom and freshen up a bit. I'm wearing a yellow halter-neck with a ruffle hem that falls to just above my knees. I find the length easy enough to work in, although usually I wear smart trousers when I'm running around with my camera. Not today though, because I'm a guest as much as I'm a photographer. I tidy my hair, reapply a little make-up and return outside.

The sun is setting and ribbons of colour streak across the sky: mauve, grey, orange, yellow, white, and high above my head, light blue. I pause on the steps and take a moment to stare at the view. I shouldn't have put my camera away quite so quickly, but the colours will have faded by the time I go back inside to get it.

I walk down the steps and falter when I see Alex standing with his camera by the pool. I hear his shutter going off as he photographs the sunset. He turns around and sees me.

'Hey,' he says quietly, putting his camera down on the mosaic-tiled table. 'I was coming to look for you. Can we talk?'

I cautiously agree, wondering what he's got to say to me now after practically ignoring me all day.

He glances towards the marquee to check we're alone before nodding towards the pool shed. I follow him around the corner of the small building and into the darkness of the leafy green trees. He thrusts his hands into his pockets and turns to face me.

'I'm sorry about last night,' he says seriously. 'I was drunk.'

I flinch slightly, hating hearing him use that as an excuse.

'Forget about it,' I say. 'I was, too. Let's just move on.' I go to turn away from him, but he grabs my wrist and stops me. I look up at him, startled.

'Bronte . . .' He shakes his head, looking anguished. 'I'm pretty fucking confused right now.'

The look on his face makes my heart melt. But I don't want it to melt. I want it to toughen the hell up and let me walk away from him.

'I'm sorry,' he says sincerely, letting go of my wrist and touching his fingers to my face. 'I . . .' He swallows and I can see he's finding this difficult. 'I care about you.'

I regard him with uncertainty. 'Why do you want to marry her?'

From the look of surprise on his face, he wasn't expecting me to ask that.

'I . . . Zara and I have been together for years.

I always wanted to settle down, have kids. It's how I was brought up. I know you don't believe in marriage—'

'It doesn't mean I don't want those things, too,' I cut him off.

'But you're going back to Australia.'

'At the moment I'm planning on staying.'

He shakes his head with frustration and begins to pace the start of the forest floor here behind the pool shed. 'Who knows what would have happened if we'd had more time together when we met. I'm not sure I would have gone back to Zara.' I hold my breath, waiting for him to continue. 'But we didn't have more time,' he says finally.

'She texted and you had to go home.'

He looks utterly lost. 'I really liked you.' He shakes his head. 'I *still* really like you.'

I close my eyes briefly in resignation. 'I really like you too,' I say.

No. I love him.

He stops pacing and stares at me intently. It's so dark under here. Only the twilight sky peeks through the leaves above our heads.

I don't think I've ever wanted anything as much as for him to kiss me right here and right now. The realisation makes my eyes sting.

'Bronte,' he says sadly, seeing my expression. He steps towards me and takes me in his arms. I'm so tense. He pulls away and looks down at me. I'm almost too scared to meet his eyes. He cups my face with his hand and rests his forehead against mine. His breathing has quickened. His lips are only inches away and oh, I remember what an incredible kisser he was. I put my hand on his chest, feeling the warmth of his skin searing my palm. He breathes in sharply and very slowly drags his nose down across my cheek until his lips are resting against my neck. I feel like my heart is going to peter out.

'Alex,' I murmur, knowing he has to stop but wanting him to do anything but. I feel the heat from his mouth against my skin as he takes ragged breaths. I can't do this. I can't stop. I turn my face towards him and then jolt violently as his lips find mine. He kisses me like there's no tomorrow and at this moment, I almost wish there weren't. I clutch the fabric of his shirt with my fingers as his tongue delves into my mouth. My hands fly to his face and feel his five o'clock shadow beneath my fingertips as he slams me back up against the pool shed. I want him so much. I want to feel his naked skin against mine again. We were as close as it's possible for two people to get – no barriers, nothing. I want to be that close to him again. But oh . . . It's not going to happen.

He wrenches himself away from me and looks absolutely horrified. His expression changes into one of disgust, even though I know it's directed at himself, not me.

'Oh Christ, Bronte,' he exhales in a rush of air. 'I'm so sorry. Fuck. I'm so sorry.' He's mortified as he shoves his hands through his hair and clasps his head in disbelief at what just happened. 'Oh, fuck. Oh, fuck,' he mutters over and over.

I watch him with distress as he paces the ground. I slowly drag the back of my hand across my mouth to wipe away the feeling of his lips on mine. I feel numb.

'Go,' I say. He looks wretched as he stares back at me. 'Go!' I say louder. I want to be alone. Grief is etched across his features. 'Please just go,' I whisper. He nods abruptly and stalks quickly away.

My head is spinning as I watch him leave. He can't marry her. He can't. I'm in love with him and I know he feels something profound for me too. With severe effort I gather myself together and go back to the party. I can hear Lachie singing a heartfelt acoustic rendition of 'Love is Blindness' as I walk towards the marquee. It doesn't seem like the most appropriate wedding song, but everyone is in high spirits, anyway. Alex is nowhere to be seen. I join Bridget and a couple of Maria's friends who are fixedly staring at Lachie. I shakily pull up a chair and sit down.

'Where have you been?' Bridget asks me.

'Just taking a breather,' I say blandly. I've never been a very good actress, but I really don't want to face an aptly named Spanish Inquisition tonight. 'I think last night might have caught up with me.'

'Ouch. I told Lachie, by the way.'

'Told him what?' I glance at her, confused.

'That nothing happened between you and Alex. That you were just talking.'

'Oh.' Her information is a little outdated, I think in a daze. 'Thanks.'

Lachie finishes his song and tells everyone that he's taking a quick break. Music starts to play out of the speakers, courtesy of Maria's DJ cousin. I notice Lachie go to the bar and get himself a bottle of beer before scanning the crowd. Spying us, he comes over.

'Mind if I join you?' he drawls, glancing down at me. He still has a hard look to his demeanour. I'm not sure he believes what Bridget said, and I'm not about to try to persuade him. Not now that it's a lie.

'Of course not,' I reply, forcing a smile as I move to make room. He drags a chair over from a nearby table. 'That was great,' I tell him as he sits down.

'Yeah? You missed most of it.'

'I went to put my camera back inside.'

'Did you.' He takes a swig of his beer, and I answer his question even though it came without a question mark.

'Yes.'

'Where's Alex?' he asks, his eyes flicking to meet mine.

'Urgh, give her a break, Lachie,' Bridget snaps, getting to her feet. 'I told you nothing happened. I'm going to the loo.' She pats him slightly conde-scendingly on his shoulder and sets off through the crowd.

'Yeah, she told me nothing happened,' he says. 'Did she? Good.'

'I don't buy it.' He fixes me with a hard stare. 'And I hope you don't mind me saying,' he starts in a reasonably calm tone before it transitions to anger, 'but what the fuck are you doing?'

'Stop it.'

'He's getting married in three months.'

His cold blue eyes are making my insides feel like ice.

'Do you think I don't know that?' To my horror, my eyes well up with tears, and because I can't sit here blubbing, I get up and walk out of the marquee.

Unfortunately, he follows me.

'Leave me alone,' I say hopelessly as I head behind the marquee where I hope it will be private.

'I'm sorry,' he replies gruffly. 'I didn't mean to make you cry.'

I bite my lip and turn to face the mountains. '*You're* not making me cry.' No, he isn't. *Alex* is.

'What are you doing, Bron?' he asks again, deeply perplexed. 'You seem pretty smart. I don't get why you'd go for a guy who's about to get married to another chick.'

'You think I have a *choice*?' I ask him tearfully. 'Do you think I wanted to fall in love with him?'

He recoils. It's a moment before he speaks and when he does his expression is a mixture of shock and horror. 'You're in love with him?'

'Surely that's obvious?'

He turns away from me, resting his hands on the wooden fence surrounding the property. He shakes his head in disbelief. 'In that case, I really can't help you, can I?'

'Lachie . . .'

'I knew you liked him, but I didn't think . . . Fuck.'

My heart goes out to him and I suddenly think that Bridget might be right: his feelings for me go deeper than just the surface. Instinctively, I reach out and put my hand on his arm, wanting to comfort him.

'Do you *want* a man who cheats?' he asks me with disbelief.

I slowly let my hand slip to my side. 'Of course not.'

'If he does this to his fiancée, how could you ever trust him?'

I shake my head. Alex isn't a cheater, not really.

'Once a cheat, always a cheat,' he adds bitterly.

'That's not true.' I raise my voice. 'This is . . . different.' I look at him defiantly. 'He's confused. He doesn't want to feel like this. If he could stop it, he would.'

My words bring with them a horrible sense of déjà vu. I jerk violently as a memory filters through to me.

'I'm confused. Bronte, darling, please. I'm so confused. I can't help it. I can't help myself. If I could stop it, I would. Please don't tell your mother . . . Please. Come.

Come here, darling . . . I can't help how I feel. Please don't tell your mother.'

I stare at Lachie with wide-open eyes as my stomach clenches with nausea. He gives me an odd look, sensing something is very wrong. 'What is it?'

'Nothing.' I try to say the word but no sound comes out.

'You're shaking,' he says with concern.

He's right. I'm shaking all over. A cold sweat passes over my body, and then I'm reliving the last conversation I had with my mother. She told me I needed to come home, that it was important. She wanted me home for Christmas. 'It could be your last chance,' she said. 'March might be too late.'

'I'm not coming home in March,' I told her. 'I've got a promotion. I'm staying.'

She said she'd book me a flight home, ignoring my protests about having to work. 'You'll have time off at Christmas. Everyone has time off at Christmas,' she said. 'You need to do this. I need to see you. He needs to see you. It might already be too late.'

Calm settles over me as I stare ahead in a daze. 'I have to go home,' I murmur to Lachie.

'It's only one more day.'

'Not to the UK. I have to go home to Australia.'

He gently rubs my shoulder. 'It might be for the best.'

I turn sharply to look at him. 'This is not to do with Alex. I'm coming back. I just need to go home for Christmas.'

He looks baffled. 'What are you going on about? That's almost four months away.'

'I know.'

'Fuck, you're so confusing, Bronte.' He buries his face in his hands, then makes a frustrated noise deep in his throat before literally shaking himself out of it. 'You're all over the fucking place,' he mutters, unable to meet my eyes. He turns away from me. 'I've gotta get back to work.'

I watch him go. He's right. I'm a screw-up if ever I saw one.

CHAPTER 26

Somehow I manage to pull myself together and return to the marquee for another hour and a half, before slipping away to bed at an acceptable time. My head is buzzing and when I finally do manage to doze off, I have a fitful sleep plagued with bad dreams and childhood nightmares.

I wake up early in the morning. Bridget is sound asleep beside me after hitting the sack at one o'clock when the DJ music finally piped down. I was wide awake when she came in, although I pretended not to be.

I throw on some clothes and leave the room. The house is silent. I pad barefoot to the kitchen. The early morning light is cold and grey. I fill up the kettle and flick it on, then jolt when the front door opens. Alex comes in, his head down, deep in thought.

My heart speeds up. 'Hi,' I say, and he nearly jumps out of his skin.

'Shit!'

'Sorry.' I give him a small smile.

He looks abashed. 'I thought everyone was asleep.'

'They are. It's just me.'

He nods, not meeting my eyes.

'I'm making tea,' I say, trying to sound normal. 'Do you want one?'

He hesitates a moment before replying. 'Sure.'

'Have you spoken to her?' I ask steadily.

'No.' He shakes his head. 'It's the middle of the night in New York. There's no reception here so I walked up the road to check my messages.'

I take the tea things to the table and sit down. 'Were there any?'

He nods. 'Yeah. She called yesterday.'

When you were kissing me? I keep that comment to myself. I don't think it would help to say it out loud.

I pour tea into the two cups and push one towards him. I add a dash of milk to mine, watching as the white liquid swirls around the dark water like a miniature storm cloud.

'A storm in a teacup,' I murmur.

'What?' His voice is barely more than a whisper.

'The teacup. Look.' I pour some milk into his tea and watch another cloud shape form. 'I've never realised where that phrase comes from before. A storm in a teacup,' I say again, putting the milk down on the table. I look up, right into his eyes. He looks anguished. He reaches over the table and takes my hand. His touch sends a shock zipping right up my arm and I want to slide my fingers along his forearm and hold more of him.

'I'm sorry,' he whispers.

351

I shake my head. 'I'm not.'

He doesn't speak, but his brow furrows slightly. If I don't tell him now . . . I'll regret it. He can't marry her. He can't. My eyes fill with tears that start trailing down my cheeks as I bare my soul to him. 'I love you.'

He draws a sharp intake of breath and inadvertently tightens his grip on my hand.

'I love you, Alex.'

'Bronte, don't.' He shakes his head at me and releases my hand. 'I can't.' My insides freeze.

'I know you feel something for me, too,' I say with more certainty than I feel.

He meets my eyes, but he looks torn. His face is pale and washed-out. 'I do. I care about you. We have chemistry. But Zara and I—'

I flinch.

'We have history,' he finishes his sentence. 'I have to go home and speak to her.'

Fear and dread fill my heart. 'Will you tell her about me?'

He closes his eyes, resigned. 'I don't know,' he says eventually. 'But we obviously have issues for this to happen.'

This? Him and me?

'You can't marry her.' I don't want to beg him.

'Bronte,' he says reluctantly, not able to bring himself to look me in the eye. 'I don't know what to do. I can't be with you. I can't be near you. I need some space to sort my head out.'

He presses the heels of his palms into his eyes

and rubs for a few seconds before letting his hands fall.

'What are you saying?' I ask as the dread in my stomach grows.

'I need to speak to Simon.'

'Alex, no.' I'm begging now. 'Don't leave. Not because of me. It will be okay.'

'I'm sorry,' he says again.

'Stop saying you're sorry,' I raise my voice. 'I don't want to hear it.'

'Shh,' he urges me to keep my voice down.

I shove my chair out from the table and stand up. 'You can't . . . You can't just kiss me like that—'

'I won't kiss you again,' he cuts me off. 'I need to go home and put this right. I feel like a bastard for even talking to you right now. I'm going to ask Simon if I can work on a special project. He told me Tetlan is launching a new magazine, wanted me to consult on it. It will give me space to sort myself out.'

I bite my lip, but it doesn't stop the tears from falling. I angrily brush them away, but the stream is relentless.

'I think you're making a mistake,' I whisper, turning to look into his deep blue eyes. I'll never forget the look of doubt on his face as I turn and walk away.

I barely see Alex for the rest of the day – he doesn't come to the beach with us, and his claim that he has a stomach virus means that everyone leaves

353

him well alone. I don't know how I get through the day before boarding the plane that night. Turns out I'm a much better actress than I thought.

I force myself into work on Monday – it's my first day as Picture Director and I have no idea how I find the internal strength to not just throw in the towel. I have a backstage shoot to organise for a major music awards ceremony next week. *Hebe* is effectively the official photographer for the TV channel – we'll be shooting dozens of celebrities – and the shots will appear in the magazine in a few weeks' time. Alex is supposed to help generate ideas for the various backstage sets we'll be using, but in meetings he avoids eye contact with me, and it's much worse than it's ever been between us. True to his word, he asks Simon if he can work on the new, top secret magazine that our publisher is launching. And even though the awards ceremony backstage gig is hugely coveted and only attended by a lucky few, he lets Tim go in his place. The following week, I come into work to see Tim sitting in Alex's chair and a part of me dies. I sob my heart out that night. He may as well have pried open my ribcage and broken my heart up with his fingers.

I tell Bridget everything. It would be impossible not to. I put a brave face on it and stumble through my days at work, but my mask slips by the time evening comes around and I can't hold it together.

Work is busier and harder than ever. I have to organise and art-direct shoot after shoot, which means liaising with celebrity PRs, negotiating timetables and handling many tricky personalities. I have to book locations and studios, call in styling and hair and make-up artists, and come up with countless concepts for original photo shoots. And Simon is a tough boss. He's even more of a perfectionist than I realised, and week after week, it's a strain. I know that if Alex were here, he would help me deal with the extra responsibility, nurture my creativity and brainstorm with me for shoot ideas. But he's not here. I'm on my own and I'm really feeling the pressure.

The days turn into weeks. September passes into October. The green leaves turn golden and slip from the trees, and I agree to my mother's request that I'll come home for Christmas. I miss a couple of calls from Polly, but I can't yet bring myself to call her back. And then one day she gets hold of Bridget.

'Polly's going to AA,' Bridget tells me that night, dropping her bag on the floor.

'What?'

She slumps onto the sofa, frowning at the music coming from the stereo. It's 'Love' by Daughter and I've been playing it on repeat because it reminds me of Alex.

'She rang me at work,' Bridget continues. 'She said she keeps calling you, but you haven't rung her back.'

'I can't face her,' I say with difficulty. 'She's going to AA?'

'She said Michelle and Grant forced her to see that she has a problem.'

'Michelle?'

'It sounds like they hosted an intervention, like you said we needed to do.'

It hits me that I've failed my friend. I'm a horrible person. My face crumples.

'Okay, that's enough,' Bridget says sharply.

Her tone snaps me out of it somewhat.

'You've got to stop feeling sorry for yourself,' she continues crossly, grabbing a handful of tissues from the nearby, nearly empty box and throwing them at me. 'I've had enough of it. Stop playing this depressing song. Get over it. He's not leaving her so you've got to move on. Get back on the horse. Find another man, someone who you don't have to share. Lachie—'

'He won't be interested,' I cut her off. 'Not any more.' Not after seeing the mess I was in at the wedding.

'Lachie *is leaving* in a couple of weeks. That's what I was going to say,' she continues determinedly. 'Let's go and—'

'What?' I instantly feel cold. 'Where's he going?'

She looks at me like I'm a bit dim. 'Travelling,' she states purposefully. 'He wants to see Europe before he heads home. You *know* this,' she adds with irritation. 'Oh no, that's right, you've been too caught up in Alex World to remember what your friends are doing.'

'Lachie is leaving in two weeks?'

'Yes. And despite what you say about him not being interested, he does still care about you, Bronte. He's been asking after you.'

'Has he?'

'Yes.'

I've stopped going for Friday-night drinks, but Bridget hasn't.

'He's doing the wedding on Saturday,' she tells me with meaning. 'One last gig.'

'I'm not sure I can—'

'For pity's sake,' she snaps. 'Don't be another Sally. Rachel is depending on you. You've already let her down once this month.'

It's true. I couldn't face the last wedding I was scheduled to do, so Sally had to step in in my place. Made a change.

I nod, still feeling tearful. 'Okay.' I dry my eyes and blow my nose loudly. 'Polly's really getting help?'

'Yes.' She nods, but there's a wariness to her expression. 'I told her you were having some personal issues. It's why you haven't called.'

'Thank you,' I reply quietly.

'She asked if it was to do with your dad.'

I give her a guarded look. 'Did you tell her no?'

She looks at her hands and doesn't answer.

'What did she say?'

'I didn't know,' she replies quietly. 'About your dad.'

'What about him?' I ask dully, wondering just how far back Polly went.

'She said he's sick.'

I nod. 'He is.'

'And she said you had a difficult childhood,' she adds carefully.

I swallow. 'I don't like to talk about it. And Polly should know that. She does know that, usually, when she's not off her face on alcohol. I thought you said she'd stopped drinking?'

'She has. She was stone-cold sober.'

'Then what the hell is she doing spouting off about my family?' I ask angrily, getting to my feet. 'If I want to talk about what happened, I'll talk about it. I don't need that silly bitch bringing it all up again!'

From the look on her face, I've done the impossible: I've shocked Bridget.

I storm into my bedroom and slam the door. I'm shaking all over – violently. I want to break something, but the feeling doesn't last too long. It's a good half an hour before Bridget dares to knock on my door.

'Come in,' I call.

She does, warily.

'I'm sorry,' I say bluntly, sitting up on my bed. I'm still angry, but I know it's not Bridget's fault. 'I just can't believe all that shit followed me around for years, and Polly *knows* that. The talk, the rumours, the weird stares. It's why I left my little beach town in South Australia. I couldn't wait to get away from there. She used to understand that.' Sudden sadness crushes my anger and my bottom lip begins to tremble. 'Oh God, not more tears.' I sniff back my snot and reach for another tissue, and Bridget ventures into the room and perches on the end of my bed. 'I felt like a leper at school,' I tell her miserably. 'Polly was my only friend. I thought it was just a matter of time before she ditched me, too, but she never did. I thought she'd be glad to get rid of me when I moved to Sydney, but the stupid cow followed me there a year later.'

I laugh disconsolately and dry my eyes. Bridget regards me with compassion.

'She always was a bloody nightmare,' I mutter. 'I don't know why we were friends in the first place. I don't know why we're still friends.'

'You have history,' Bridget says gently.

'We have chemistry. But Zara and I . . . We have history.'

I shake my head. No. I will not bawl my eyes out again. 'Yeah, and she still didn't ask me to be a frigging bridesmaid.'

Bridget starts to laugh, and I do, too. 'Not that I wanted to be a frigging bridesmaid!' I cry, bordering on hysterical. 'Did you see what a nightmare she was? Poor Michelle!'

My laughter dies eventually. 'I guess she made the right choice in the end. Michelle was there for her, when I wasn't.'

'Polly's not here for you, either,' Bridget says quietly. 'She hasn't been here for you for a long time. Whatever history you have . . . I know you feel loyal to her, but sometimes friendships are meant to go their separate ways.'

I nod shakily. 'If I hadn't come to that wedding, I wouldn't be in this place right now.'

'Don't you think you still would have gone for that job at *Hebe*? If you had, you and Alex would have still crossed paths.'

I contemplate this and realise she's right. And I'm pretty sure we still would have had chemistry. 'But I might not have met you,' I say as a fresh bout of tears fills my eyes.

'Well, in that case, I'm glad you came to the wedding.' She sniffs as I witness another first: Bridget crying.

'I'm sorry, Bridge. I know I've been a nightmare to live with. I'm sorry I've been moping about Alex. I promise to pick myself up and get on with things now.'

'Starting with the wedding this weekend,' she says firmly. 'Don't turn into another Sally.'

I nod quickly. 'Okay.'

CHAPTER 27

'Hey, you!'

I smile at Maria's warm greeting as I climb into the back seat. 'Hello!' I reply as I put my kit bag on the seat next to me and lean forward to give her a kiss on her cheek. 'Wow!' I spy her baby bump – and it's grown.

'I know!' she puts her hands on her belly. 'It seems to have doubled in size overnight.'

'Not quite,' I tell her, buckling my seatbelt as Rachel sets off. 'But you're definitely looking pregnant now.'

'It feels like ages since I saw you,' Maria says, swivelling in her seat to face me. 'Where have you been?'

'Really busy at work,' I reply apologetically.

'Russ said you haven't been well?'

'Not that great, no, but I'm much better now.'

'But you've still been at work?'

'Yeah.' My health problems are mental, not physical. 'I just got a promotion, so I've been pushing through it.'

She looks concerned. 'Take it easy, though. You don't want to wear yourself out.'

'Thanks. I'm fine now,' I reiterate. 'It'll be good to get some fresh air this weekend.'

My eleventh wedding – tenth without including Pete & Sylvie's – is in Rachel's home town of Bath. The journey is about two hours' long, and we're setting off early on Saturday morning and staying the night in a B&B.

'You look well,' I say to Maria. It's true. I didn't think her hair could get any glossier, but the proof is right in front of me.

She smiles. 'Thanks.'

As Rachel drives into Camden, my nerves kick in. I haven't seen Lachie since Maria and Russ's wedding two months ago. He may have asked after me, but he hasn't tried to contact me, and he hasn't attempted to see me. If my friends and colleagues have caught up with him, it's because they've gone to his pub. Considering how easily he came to be a part of our crowd, it's strange how far he seems to have withdrawn.

'Can you run up?' Rachel asks me, as she pulls up on double yellow lines outside Lachie's place. 'I might have to go around the block.'

'Sure.' I prepare myself for seeing him again.

Lachie lives in an apartment within a town-house which is not unlike the converted house where Bridget and I live, although Lachie's could do with a coat of paint. I've never been inside, so I climb out of the car and walk up the broad grey steps leading to the property's front door. There's a keypad with four buttons on it. I can't see Lachie's name, but I remember his flatmate is called Dan. I've met him at the pub in the past.

I press the button with Dan's name on it and a moment later, the door buzzes. I push it open, and hesitantly step inside. Which one is his apartment? I hear a door open on the first floor, up the communal stairs.

'Come up,' Lachie calls.

The hallway is littered with junk mail. I step over it and climb the grubby stairs past the cream-coloured walls stained with years of handprints and who knows what else. One of the two doors at the top of the flight of stairs is ajar, so I tentatively push it open.

'Lachie?' I call, peeking my head around the door.

'Bron?' He appears in the hallway, looking surprised to see me.

'Weren't you expecting me?' I ask, walking inside.

'Well, you didn't come to the last wedding, so I wasn't sure. I'll be with you in a sec.'

My eyes scan the room. It's tidy, but not too tidy, and there's not a lot of furniture apart from a comfy sofa, a big flatscreen TV with a PlayStation set up in front of it and two remote controls on the smudged glass coffee table. You can tell two guys live here.

'I didn't know you did that last wedding?' I say. Rachel didn't mention it.

'Yeah.' He gives me an odd look and then shakes his head, chuckling under his breath as he zips up his backpack. 'I thought you must've been avoiding me.'

'No,' I say resolutely. 'No. Not at all.'

He slings his backpack over his shoulder and turns to face me. 'How are you?' His question is packed full of meaning.

'I'm alright,' I say unenthusiastically.

'How's Alex?' His tone is dry, but there's even more meaning crammed into this question.

'I don't know,' I tell him truthfully, my mouth turning down. He raises one eyebrow in silent query. 'He's been working in another building. I haven't seen him since just after Russ and Maria's wedding.'

'Oh.' His blue eyes study me. 'And are you alright with that?'

I shrug. 'I'm trying to be,' I answer truthfully.

He snatches a set of keys from the kitchen countertop and stuffs them into his pocket before grabbing his guitar case.

'Ready.'

I lead the way back down the stairs, past the scattered piles of junk mail and out of the front door. Rachel is nowhere to be seen. Then she appears around the corner and pulls up.

'Quick!' she shouts through her open window. 'Police car behind me.'

She screeches away from the kerb. There's not a lot of room in the back and the whole of Lachie's left-hand side is pressing into me.

'Are you alright there?' Maria asks him

apologetically. 'Sorry, sitting in the back makes me feel sick at the moment.'

'I'm fine,' Lachie says before glancing at me. 'Will my guitar fit in the boot?' he asks Rachel.

'I don't think so, sorry,' she replies.

'Don't worry about it,' I tell Lachie, but he takes my kit bag from my lap and finds room for it under his guitar case.

I'm still not feeling very chatty, so I listen while the three of them make conversation before switching off and staring out of the window.

I finally spoke to Polly yesterday. She admits that she has a problem and she's trying to combat it, with Grant's – and Michelle's – support. She apologised to me for mouthing off at the pub that night – Grant told her all about it. She tried to strike up a conversation about me going home for Christmas, but I'm still not ready to open up to her about that.

Lachie's body is warm and comforting against my side and I suddenly feel very tired. I close my eyes.

I'm playing the organ, my small fingers tripping across the keys. I can't believe I'm making this big sound – me! All by myself! Pride swells inside my heart as my feet press on the pedals below. It's only a simple tune, but surely Daddy will be proud of me. Oh, please let him be proud of me! I just want him to love me. Then suddenly he's there, staring down at me, but he's not proud, he's not happy. He's angry. My fingers falter, my feet freeze, and then his hand closes over my wrist and he drags me off the stool.

The dream jerks me awake, and Lachie jerks in turn. He sleepily unfolds his arms and looks down at me, blinking slightly as he comes to – he must've drifted off as well. 'What's up?' he murmurs. Rachel and Maria are talking, oblivious to the two of us in the back.

My pulse is racing and my heart has sped up.

'Hey,' he says gently. I grab his hand and squeeze it tightly, pressing my eyes closed to block out the memories, but I can't.

My schoolmates are pointing at me, sniggering and whispering. Their expressions are hateful as they revel in my discomfort. I'm not doing anything to deny the rumours are true . . .

I want to shove open the door and get out of the car, but we're travelling at such speed, it would be suicide.

'Bad dream?' Lachie asks me and my eyes fly open.

I nod quickly and reluctantly let go of his hand, placing it back on his lap. But he shifts and puts it around me instead, pulling me into the crook of his arm. The gesture makes me want to cry. He's so kind to me, so sweet and gentle and funny. I don't deserve him. But I don't want to let him go, either. I turn into him and bury my face in his chest and he holds me tightly as my breathing regulates. His hand moves up to stroke my hair and I turn my face so I can breathe more easily, but I don't want to move away. His lips press onto my forehead and my breath does an about-turn, quickening instead of calming down. I pull away and look up at him. If Alex's eyes are the same shade as a cool blue ocean, Lachie's are the colour of a summer sky. My gaze drops to his lips and I remember the passionate kiss we shared at Pete and Sylvie's wedding. He removes his arm from around me and that snaps me to life. He slowly rests his head back on the headrest, but his eyes never leave mine. His face is full of regret, but I drag myself away and turn to look out of the window. I'm attracted to him. I've always been attracted to him. But whatever Bridget said about me jumping back on the horse, I can't do that with Lachie, even if he wanted me to. He deserves better than to be my rebound guy.

We're staying in the same B&B as the groom, so we check in and drop our bags off before going to the bride's parents' house.

I don't pick up on the atmosphere at first, but after a while it becomes clear to me that we do not have a happy bride on our hands. Her name is Hester and Rachel flashes me an apprehensive look when she tells Maria she doesn't mind whether she wears her hair up or down.

It's not that she's being easy or simply bowing to the expert. She doesn't care. Her mind is on other things. And no matter how much we try to cheer her up or tell her she looks beautiful, the most we get is a distracted smile.

'Didn't Maria have a practice run with her?' I ask Rachel.

'No. She said she didn't want one.'

I have to say I'm worried when I set off to the church.

The groom, Billy, is in much higher spirits, and I try to convince myself that his bride-to-be is just nervous as I take a deep breath and get to work photographing yet another old English church. The flower arrangements are especially beautiful and bursting with autumnal colours: yellow sunflowers, red chrysanthemums and orange freesias. I jolt slightly at the altar when I see the organ. I run my fingers over the cream-coloured keys as I remember the little girl from my dream.

I wonder if he ever feels sorry. I wonder if he feels anything at all.

'You must be the photographer.'

I jump as the vicar appears at my side. He's a young man with a warm, open face. I nod quickly, swallowing to try to keep my tears firmly at bay.

'Yes. Hello. I'm Bronte.'

He holds his hand out and shakes mine. 'Father Phillip. Pleased to meet you.'

'We'll keep out of your way,' I start to say.

'You don't need to do that,' he says. 'The bride and groom want you here, and that's good enough for me.'

'Thank you.'

'Do you play?' he asks me, indicating the organ.

I nod, biting my lip.

'The piano?'

'No, well, yes.' I clear my throat. 'I play the organ, too. At least, I used to.'

'How interesting,' he says. 'Not too many people choose it as an instrument these days.'

'My dad was an organist.'

'Was he?' He smiles with pleasure. 'Oh, here's Nicholas, our organist, now!' he exclaims brightly. 'This young lady plays the pipe organ,' he calls to Nicholas as he approaches.

'I'd better keep going,' I say quickly. I can feel the vicar's confused gaze following me as I hurry away.

I haven't photographed the stained-glass windows, but it's too late because the bridal party is here. I hurry out to the porch in time to see Hester's three bridesmaids climb out of the car wearing long, flowing floor-length gowns of cherry red. I risk a quick glance over my shoulder at the vicar. He's talking to the groom, smiling and nodding and putting him at ease, no doubt. He seems like a nice man.

I breathe in deeply and inhale the damp scent of my surroundings. I used to love this smell. I think back to how panicked I was at my first wedding this year – Suzie and Mike's. It all feels a little surreal now. I don't mind the smell so much any more – at the very least, it doesn't give me chills.

Once upon a time, I used to love being in church. I loved the vast, cool, beautiful spaces – a guaranteed haven in the hot Australian summer, a place for quiet contemplation. No matter what was going on at home, I could come to church and feel at peace.

I turn to see Hester coming towards me. She looks absolutely beautiful in a strapless sweetheart corset studded with sequins and pearls. She's wearing a veil and as she turns to the man beside her and allows him to take her arm, something dawns on me. That's not her father – he's much younger. Her brother perhaps? Has her father passed away? Is that why she's not smiling?

Rachel pulls a face at me as she passes. 'Here goes nothing,' she says worriedly.

I get into position as Nicholas starts to play Wagner's infamous piece.

I click off some shots of Hester as she passes, but she's still not smiling. I capture Billy turning around and giving her an encouraging nod, and I wonder what Rachel's book will look like with the complementary shots next to each other. I have my doubts that these pictures will be some of this bride and groom's favourites.

Hester continues her march to the front, the overhead spotlights causing the diamantés along the hem of her veil to sparkle beautifully like tiny flashguns going off. As the music dies down and the vicar starts to speak, Hester backs away from her groom.

'Hess,' Billy says, his expression turning into one of horror.

Even from back here, I can see her shaking her head. He holds his hand out to her in a silent plea and a murmur passes over the congregation. 'I can't,' she mumbles, and then she turns and runs back down the aisle, carrying her long skirt as she goes.

'Shit, really?' Lachie's face is a picture. 'Fuck. Where's the poor guy?'

'Downstairs,' I tell him.

'In the bar?' he asks with surprise.

I nod. I've just given Lachie the news. He was chilling out in his room, reading a magazine on his bed when I knocked on his door. He wasn't due to play at the reception for another few hours.

'What happened?'

I fill him in on the morning's proceedings, trying not to be distracted by his biceps. He's still only wearing a short-sleeve T-shirt and his tan is relentlessly clinging on from summer. He's the most warm-blooded person I know.

'So what now?' he asks after he's muttered a few profanities on behalf of the jilted groom.

'I don't know. Rachel and Maria are downstairs.'

'Let's go, then,' he says, touching his hand to the small of my back before instantly snatching it away. 'Sorry,' he mumbles as I jolt in surprise.

What, so now he thinks he has to apologise for

touching me? I hate that I've made him feel that way.

Downstairs, the bar is full of wedding guests. Probably about one fifth of the people who attended the service are here, groom included. Rachel and Maria are at the bar.

'What are you drinking?' Rachel asks us as we approach.

'Are we staying?' I reply in confusion. I kind of assumed we'd drive back to London.

'May as well. We have rooms. Also, Billy and his family asked us to join them, and I feel like I need a drink after all that.'

'I know what you mean,' I agree.

'Great,' Lachie says. 'What shall we go for? Bottle of red?' He glances at me.

'Sure.' My eyes scan the room to hunt out the groom. He's sitting hunched forwards in an armchair. His mother is kneeling at his feet with her hands on his knees. She's taken her hat off but she still looks resplendent in a long, silvery-grey skirt and matching blouse. I don't know what she's saying. We're outsiders looking in, not privy to personal details – at least, not many. Chances are we will never know why Hester left Billy at the altar. And we have to let it go – that's our job, however much the curiosity might kill us. But whatever Billy's mother is saying to him is making him nod. Lachie nudges me. He has a bottle of wine in his right hand and three wine-glass stems protruding from between the knuckles of his left. Maria is on the soft stuff.

There's a small table free in the corner so we go over to it and squeeze around it.

It's a strangely heart-warming evening, considering the sad events that have led us here. It's hard not to get swept up in the emotion of it all. We watch as the members of Billy's extended family and not so close friends disperse, until finally it's just the groom, his parents, his close family and friends remaining. They laugh, they cry, they smother him with love and affection, and after a while we join forces with them and become part of their gathering. Well into the evening, someone suggests to Lachie that he get his guitar. He's happy to oblige, and when he returns, the accommodating hotel manager closes up and we have our very own lock-in while listening to Lachie's deep, tuneful voice. He avoids his more upbeat wedding collection and instead sings slow, soulful songs about love and loss and everyone has to get more tissues out. It's strangely cathartic though – even I have a little cry.

Maria calls it a night first, slipping out quietly so as not to disrupt Lachie's private concert. Rachel goes next, patting me gently on my back. 'Don't stay up too late,' she warns with a mischievous glint in her eye as her gaze flickers towards Lachie. I'm feeling slightly dazed as my attention refocuses on his toned arms, watching his muscles flex as he plays his guitar. He's singing a stripped-back version of The 1975's 'Sex' and it's so sexy. *He's* sexy. Suddenly he looks at me and a bolt of desire shoots straight through me. I can't tear my eyes away from him. His blue eyes are smouldering, scorching, burning into me as he sings 'talk about sex'. The way he says that last word makes me want to have some with him.

Seriously, if he wants to sleep with me tonight, I'm his. Without a shadow of a doubt. A tiny, less drunk part of me realises that this is probably a Bad Idea. But I don't care right now. He gives me a quizzical look as he strums a fast acoustic section. His hands are wasted on his guitar. I want his fingers to work their magic on *me*. I'm so jittery, so on edge and completely turned on when he strums the last chord and calmly meets my eyes.

'Thanks, folks,' he says, breaking eye contact with me as everyone applauds, as they have done for all of his songs so far. He stands up. 'I'm going to hit the sack.'

With me? Please with me. I haven't had sex in way too long.

He shakes hands with Billy. 'Good luck, mate. It's going to be okay. You've got good people around you.'

I'm so breathless I can barely speak, let alone commiserate with the groom again. But I've done plenty of that throughout the evening, so I give him what I hope is an encouraging smile and make my way to the door. I turn around to wait for Lachie. He's packing his guitar away. He snaps the case shut, smiling and saying goodnight to everyone as he passes. As he walks past the last table, his eyes meet mine and my breath quickens.

'Okay?' he drawls, looking down at me.

I nod quickly and move to the stairs. I'm intensely aware of his body right behind me. I go straight to his room.

'Aren't you down the hall?' he asks me wryly, leaning against the wall in the corridor. He reaches into his pocket and brings out a key, then he opens the door and holds it back for me without saying another word. I'm taking this as a very clear, very welcome indication that he wants me too.

He closes the door behind me and locks it again. I take a step towards him, my gaze fixed on his lips. His hands come to rest on my waist and I suck in a sharp intake of breath. He stares down at me.

'You only ever want to kiss me when you're drunk,' he says in a low voice.

'That's not true.' I shake my head. 'I wanted to kiss you in the car.'

'Did you?'

Even with all the debilitating alcohol running through my veins, I blush my response.

'Then why didn't you?' he asks, and the feel of his thumb stroking my waist through the flimsy fabric of my shirt is distracting.

'I want to kiss you now – isn't that enough?'

'We're there now, are we? Just as I'm leaving? Is that what you do? Go for people you can't have?'

His words floor me. I shake my head, speechless. Is he right? *Is* that what I do?

'Why?' he asks quietly. 'Why do you do that? Don't you think you deserve to be happy?'

'Stop,' I say, squeezing my eyes shut. 'Just stop.' He's only twenty-four. How does he come out with things like this at his age?

'I'd give anything *not* to fall for someone I can't have, Bronnie,' he says sadly, and then he asks me the question I really didn't want him to ask me. 'Are you still in love with Alex?'

The sound of his name breaks my ribcage open again and my heart is bare and bloody and broken. I force myself to answer him, putting my hand on his chest and gently pushing him away. He lets his hands fall to his sides.

'It's been almost two months,' I mumble. 'I haven't seen him. I don't know. I've been a mess, but I'm feeling better. I'm a lot better.'

I dare to look up at him and when I do, his eyes are full of sadness and pain and something else – compassion?

Maybe not the last one, because he knows his next words will hurt me. 'Rachel told me she saw him and Zara recently.' Rachel always catches up with her brides and grooms at least twice before the service – she wants them to feel as relaxed around her as possible. 'She said they seemed happy. More than ready to tie the knot.'

He may as well have torn into my heart with his teeth. I wince and turn to put my hand on the door.

'Come here,' he says, drawing me back into his strong embrace. 'I'm sorry. It's going to be okay.'

I take a deep breath and relax against him. He's so comforting.

'I'm sorry for asking you difficult questions when you're drunk,' he says into my hair.

Yeah. Bastard.

'But I know I'll get an honest answer out of you.'

On the plus side, my desire to have sex with him has flown right out of the window. No morning-after regrets for me. I slowly break away from him.

'Guess I'd better go.'

'Stay,' he says, his hand on my arm.

I give him a perplexed look. He's got to be kidding, right? After all of that?

'Sleep with me,' he says casually.

I shake my head.

'Just . . . *sleep*,' he says more firmly.

Yes. I do want to be held by him, more than I want my PJs or my toothbrush, I realise. And it does feel like a choice. He takes my hesitation as a yes and holds my hand, leading me to the bed. He pulls back the covers and kicks off his shoes. I wobble slightly as I do the same, which he seems to find entertaining. And then he pulls his T-shirt over his head and my mouth falls open. Obscene. He throws the T-shirt at me and I catch it in a daze. He jerks his head towards the bathroom and then at the garment in my hands. 'PJs,' he says with amusement.

Mmm. Yes, I'd be quite happy to wear this to bed. I go into the bathroom and strip off everything apart from my knickers. I pull his T-shirt over my head and feel the cosiness of it engulf me. Still warm. Always warm. Then I return to the bedroom. He's switched off the lights and I can barely make out the shape of his body as I slide under the duvet. His arms snake around me and I snuggle into his chest. He kisses the top of my head.

'Night-night, Bronnie,' he says in a deep, sleepy voice.

'Night,' I murmur.

I lie there for a long time, listening to his breathing slow down and become long and steady. But I can't fall asleep to save my life. His skin is soft under my palm. I slide my fingertips across his chest and down to the hardness of his ribcage. I run my fingers along the length of his bottom rib. He catches my hand. Oh dear, I've woken him up.

His breath is hot against the top of my head. It's less slow and steady and more short and sharp. His fingers ensnare my wrist, but I flatten my palm and place my hand against his stomach. He makes a strangled-sounding noise at the back of his throat.

I tilt my face up and kiss the place where I think the sound came from, and then I run my tongue across his skin. That's it for him. He crushes his lips against mine and as I straddle him, he slides his T-shirt up and over my head in one smooth movement. A shiver goes down my spine, partly because of the cold, but mostly because I'm suddenly so turned on I can barely contain myself. Only his boxers and my knickers separate us from each other, but I can feel him, and I want him. *So* much. He puts his hands roughly on my hips and pulls me hard against him and I gasp into his mouth.

'Fuck,' he curses. 'Jeans.' He smacks my bum and pushes me off him. Jeans? Oh, condom. I feel dizzy as he gets off the bed and retrieves his wallet from his jeans, snapping it open. He finds what he's looking for and returns to the bed. Moments later, he flips me onto my back and hovers above me, but he hesitates. I slide my hands down his broad, muscular back, willing him to take me. Isn't this what he wanted? He bends to touch his lips to mine and his ensuing kiss is so sweet and so full of love and longing that it makes me feel strangely emotional. He keeps his lips on mine as he pushes into me, and the raw sensation damn near takes my breath away. And then we begin to move together as one.

I fall asleep in his arms afterwards with my head on his chest and I wake up with his arms around me, his body spooning me from behind. My head is throbbing, but as I lie there, slowly coming to, I realise I don't have any regrets. Last night was amazing. Breathtaking. His right hand is cupping my breast and his arm is heavy as I try to extract myself. He murmurs as I slip out of bed and go into the bathroom. My mouth tastes disgusting. Urgh. I rinse it out with water and borrow some of his toothpaste, but it's not enough. Finally I grab his toothbrush and think to hell with it. I brush my teeth. He doesn't need to know. I look around for a robe, but there isn't one. Bath towel? No, I'll look ridiculous and he's still asleep anyway.

Oh. No, he's not. I run back to the bed and climb under the covers and smile at him as his arms encircle me again.

'I thought you'd gone,' he murmurs with a sleepy grin.

I shake my head and kiss him.

'Mmm, minty,' he says in a deep, warm voice. 'Wait, did you use my toothbrush?'

I can't help but giggle.

'Sneaky,' he mutters, but he's grinning when he kisses me and our teeth knock together. He pulls me against him and I murmur with pleasure at all of our bare skin contact. I slide up his body to reach his lips and feel him *fully* wake up.

'Can't,' he murmurs against my mouth.

I pull away and look at him.

'I only had one condom,' he explains. I may be on the Pill, but we're still practising safe sex. 'But we can do other stuff,' he tells me with a suggestive look before my disappointment can sink in.

We do 'other stuff' for most of the next hour.

Finally we realise we should probably show our faces and work out what Rachel and Maria are planning to do today. Rachel wanted to go and see her parents, seeing as she's nearby, and Maria had been talking about getting started on her Christmas shopping. By some miracle, I manage to make it back to my room without being seen. I have a quick shower and get dressed in jeans and a jumper before going downstairs to the dining room. Lachie, Maria and Rachel are already sitting at a table together. The sexy look on his face as I approach them makes my face heat up again. How embarrassing. Rachel purses her lips and my colour deepens – I'm sure she's guessed. And by the end of breakfast, Maria knows, too. Might have something to do with Lachie grabbing me at one point and kissing me smack on my lips.

I find the whole thing slightly mortifying, but Lachie just seems amused.

We make a plan to meet up at the B&B for a three o'clock departure and then go our separate ways – although Lachie stays with me. We spend the morning wandering around the pretty spa town, looking at the architecture and going for lunch in a gorgeous pub. He's even more tactile with me than usual and it's lovely. I like him. A lot. And the fact that he's leaving next week has not failed to escape my notice.

We sit cuddled together the whole way back to London. Rachel is planning to drop me off first, but as we approach my street, Lachie turns to me.

'Come back to mine?'

'I have work tomorrow,' I tell him regretfully.

'Grab what you need?'

'I'm happy to wait,' Rachel says with a look of amusement.

'I'll be really quick!' I promise.

I unlock the door of my apartment to see Bridget sitting on the sofa, reading a book.

'Hey, how did it go?' she asks casually.

Er, I have a lot of explaining to do. And I don't have time for that with Rachel pulled up on a busy road downstairs.

'Really well,' I say. 'Um . . . I'm going to stay at Lachie's house tonight,' I blurt out.

'What?'

'I . . .' Argh! 'We slept together.'

'You did *what*?'

'We . . .' I wave my hands about. 'You know!'

'You screwed him?' she asks incredulously.

'Well, if you want to put it that way,' I reply, escaping into my bedroom. She's hot on my heels.

'Oh my God!' she squawks. 'How did that happen?'

'Rachel's downstairs,' I say apologetically as I flap about trying to decide on an outfit to wear to work tomorrow.

'Tell me quickly,' Bridget demands, snatching a woollen shift dress right out of my hand and slamming it onto the bed. She goes to my drawer and pulls out a matching pair of tights while I fill her in, emptying my overnight bag onto the bed and repacking it with toiletries and fresh clothes.

'Do not make any plans for tomorrow night,' she says sternly while pointing at me. 'I want a proper lowdown.' Then she grins and gives me a hug and sends me on my way.

'Sorry,' I apologise as I climb into the car. 'Bridget wanted to talk to me.'

'Did she now?' Lachie murmurs and I smirk at him.

We arrive at Lachie's flat to discover that his flat-mate Dan has company. Dan and another guy are sitting on the floor in front of the TV playing the PlayStation, while two more guys sit on the sofa drinking beer.

'Hey,' Lachie says when we walk in, me a little on edge. I wasn't expecting to have to face anyone.

He's greeted with enthusiasm by his mates, which swiftly transforms into surprise when they see me. The two guys playing on the PlayStation pause their game.

Lachie rests his hands on his upright guitar case. 'Guys, this is Bronte,' he says, using my actual name for a change.

'Hi,' I respond to their cheerful hellos and put my bag down. A couple of pairs of eyes follow the progression of my bag and then look with puzzlement back at my face.

'Catch you in a bit,' Lachie says casually, not explaining my reason for being here. He indicates the door to the small hallway so I pick up my bag again and follow him, awkwardly. He opens the first door on our left and I walk through to his bedroom. It's small – there's barely enough room for his double bed – and he has one chest of drawers but no wardrobe. The drawers are half open, with clothes spilling out. I can see the straps of an enormous backpack peeking out from underneath the crumpled cream-coloured duvet resting on top of the bed – it's a sudden, painful reminder that he's going home soon. He puts his things down and turns to face me.

'Sorry it's a bit of a tip,' he says, looking a tad sheepish.

I don't care about the state of his room. A lump has formed in my throat. 'I can't believe you're leaving next week.'

'I did tell you,' he says with a small smile as he places his hands on my waist. 'But I'm going to Europe, first. I'm back here for a few days in December before I fly home.'

My heart lifts a little. 'Did you know I'm going home for Christmas now?'

'No.' His eyes light up. 'Are you? Will you be in South Australia?'

'Yes. Just for a couple of weeks, then I'm back over here again.'

'Oh. Then you're back to Sydney in March?'

I shake my head. Didn't I tell him? 'No, I got a promotion. I'm coming back here.'

His face falls, but his grip on my waist tightens. 'You're coming back to the UK?'

'Yes.'

'I thought you were going back to Sydney.'

'No. I was, but not any more. I thought I'd told you.'

'No.' He shakes his head, looking anything but happy for me. 'You didn't.'

I realise with a jolt that I'm getting him confused with Alex. It was Alex I told.

Lachie goes to sit on the bed. His mood has taken a dive. He smooths his palm across his crumpled duvet cover. 'I was sort of thinking about coming to Sydney,' he says quietly.

'Were you?' I can't hide my surprise.

'Well, I didn't think you'd be moving to Perth any time soon.' He glances at me with a wry look on his face. 'I know where that suggestion got your last boyfriend.'

He's my boyfriend now? I'm not sure how I feel about that. But he's leaving next week and I'm staying. There's nothing long-term about us. I go back to feeling sad.

'Guess we'll just have to make the most of the time we have, then,' I say as I put my hand on his shoulder. He kisses me gently, twisting his body so that the weight of him presses me back onto the bed. I'm vaguely aware of gunfire and the grunting shouts of soldiers coming from the PlayStation in the living room as his kisses begin to get hot and heavy. I can't help smiling.

'What?' He pulls away and stares down at me. His eyes are burning into mine and it's such a hot look that it almost whisks my doubts away.

'Do you think we should go and chat to your mates for a bit?'

He groans and kisses me one more time before climbing off me, holding his hand down to me.

★   ★   ★

I like his friends. They're all Australian with the exception of one, and they're all young guys in their early twenties. I feel a little old in comparison. We order in pizza, drink a couple of bottles of beer and are sociable until about nine thirty, when Lachie tells them that he's 'tired'. From the looks on their faces, they don't buy it, but I don't care any more. His thumb stroking my waist has been severely distracting all evening.

I'm jittery by the time we reach his bedroom. He kisses me slowly, gently, and undresses me without saying a word. He pulls his T-shirt over his head and I kiss his neck and run my hands over his perfectly cut torso and down to the waistband of his well-worn jeans. His breath hitches as I work on his buttons, his heavy breathing causing the muscles on his chest to ripple. Once naked, we climb into the cold bed and let our bodies heat each other up. Our kisses become more passionate, but I'm still too aware of his mates on the other side of the thin walls. He makes a guttural sound when I slide my hand down across his stomach and I smile against his ear and tell him to 'Shh.'

He kisses me hungrily, his hands suddenly getting very busy, and I'm almost losing my mind by the time he takes me. The awareness it takes for me to keep quiet makes the whole experience feel incredibly intense and almost unbearably erotic. His lips are on my mouth when we finally find release and I gasp against him, trying not to cry out. Then he collapses on top of me, hot and heavy, while I try to catch my breath. He's crushing me, but when he tries to move, I hold him still. I like the weight of him.

We make love two more times before finally succumbing to sleep, and in the morning he gets up to make me breakfast before I go to work. The flat is silent – Dan must still be in bed, which is good because I'm not sure we were that quiet the last time.

'What are you doing tonight?' Lachie asks between mouthfuls of toast.

'Bridget wants me home,' I tell him with a smile. 'What about you?'

'I've got a shift at the pub.'

'Do you want to come to mine afterwards?'

He looks pleased. 'Sure.'

He kisses me goodbye at his doorway, and would have followed me downstairs in his T-shirt and boxers if I hadn't stopped him with a giggle.

'See you later,' I tell him.

I smile the whole way into work. On the walk to Camden Town Tube station, on the steps down into the depths of the Underground, and throughout the entire jam-packed journey. I'm still smiling as I walk into the office, and then I see Alex sitting at his desk and the smile drops from my face.

CHAPTER 28

He looks up as my footsteps falter. 'Hey,' he says.

'Hi.' I put my head down and hurry past him to my desk. There are too many of our colleagues nearby for me to do anything else, but my heart is racing as I sit down.

I can't concentrate at all. I force myself to move things around on my desk to make it look like I'm working, and I even manage to smile at Helen and Sarah as they arrive, but mostly I keep my head down. I'm sitting in Nicky's seat now, by the window, and if I look over my computer I can see Alex's perfect profile. I mean, Alex's profile perfectly. But oh . . . I risk a glance at him and his profile *is* perfect. His strong jawline, his straight nose, the way his hair sometimes falls down across his forehead before he thinks to push it away, which he just has.

I bite my lip until I draw blood. The taste of it on my tongue takes me a little by surprise, but it serves me right. I am not going there again. I steel myself to be professional and eventually my racing heart settles to a normal pace and I start to feel okay again. It helps when I think of Lachie. I take a deep, slow breath and remember him smiling at me while taking a bite of his toast this morning. I close my eyes briefly and then open them again and get on with my work.

By the time ten thirty rolls around, I'm desperate for a tea. Sarah has taken to bringing in coffee from the café across the street and Helen usually has one too, so I'm on my own when it comes to tea these days. Eventually I succumb to my thirst and walk past Alex with my head held high.

A moment later, he joins me in the kitchen. I almost swear at him. Why doesn't he just leave me alone?

'I didn't know you were coming back to the office this week.' I manage, with an astounding amount of effort, to keep my voice sounding neutral. 'Are you back permanently?'

'Yeah.'

I don't look at him as I set about making tea.

'Hey,' he says gently, touching his hand to my arm. I snatch it away.

'Just. Don't,' I say through gritted teeth.

He looks anguished. I was hoping to never have to lay eyes on him again. Just then, Russ comes into the kitchen. I hear Alex's sigh as I hurry up with my task and leave them to it.

Alex sends me an email shortly after I return to my desk.

Can we have lunch?

I stare at my screen in disbelief and then look over the top of my computer, but he doesn't meet my eyes. I angrily tap out a reply.

Are you for real?

I watch his jaw twitch as he reads my response, then I see him sigh and start to reply. After a while, I realise he might not be replying to me because he's taking for ever. I'm about to get on with my work as I suspect he has done, but then an email from him pings in.

I'm sorry. I know I've screwed up. I just want to apologise. It might seem like a pretty crazy concept right now, but I was hoping we could be friends. I still care about you.

My breath catches as I read that last sentence. I'm too stunned to reply. Another message pings in.

I don't mean it like that. Please can we have lunch?

I angrily reply.

No. I don't want to have lunch with you. It's bad enough that I have to see your stupid face from here. In fact, I'm thinking about moving back to my old desk.

I start to smirk to myself as I type that out. I continue:

> Whatever you have to say, you can say it now.

I almost delete the first part of my email but then think, fuck it, and press send. It gives me great pleasure to see his eyes widen as he reads my message. He stares at his computer screen and I start to regret being so impulsive. I regret it even more when Simon comes over to speak to him. I type out another message.

> Forget I said that. We have to work together, and maybe one day it won't be so awkward, but I still don't want to have lunch with you. I hear you had a good meeting with Rachel? All going well?

I see Alex's eyes dart to his computer as my message hits his inbox. He has to force himself to concentrate on Simon, but as soon as our boss heads back to his desk, he replies.

> Thanks for saying that. Things were a bit rocky for a while but I think we're going to be okay.

My chest tightens. But I'm going to be okay, too. I force myself to think of Lachie as I reply.

I'm glad to hear it.

It's a lie, though.

I spend every night that week falling asleep in Lachie's arms. It helps. The weekend is our last one together, but unfortunately, it's also my last wedding of the year that I'm doing with Rachel. I'd rather spend my time with Lachie, but Rachel needs me, and she's already promised to give me more weddings next year if I want them.

Luckily, the wedding is in Totteridge in north London, so we're done in time for me to return to Lachie's pub for last orders. I sit on a stool at the bar and watch him work while fending off the attentions of a multitude of attractive, flirtatious girls. I'm pretty sure he could have his pick of them. Why does he want me?

I go with him to help him gather empties once the lights in the pub have gone on. The drinkers are slowly dispersing.

'How was it?' he asks of the wedding.

'Fun,' I reply. 'Fancy dress.'

'Really?' He looks interested.

'Well, not fully.' I smile as I tell him about the bride and groom and their guests, who wore full wedding garb from the neck down – a black morning suit for the groom and a cream-coloured silk skirt and corset for the bride, although later she swapped her long skirt for a shorter one with burnt-cream-coloured ruffles peeking out from underneath. The fancy dress part came from their hats – the theme was outrageous headgear. The groom wore a Roman centurion helmet with a red Mohawk-style brush spanning from the front of the shiny silver helmet to the back. As for the bride, she wore a bird's nest. Yes, really. But it was no ordinary bird's nest. Hers had two silky-looking magpies sitting on the back of it, looking down at a nest crammed with glittering jewels. The photos are going to look amazing.

'Last wedding of the year, right?' Lachie checks.

'Yep.' I smile at him. Needless to say, I don't think I'll be invited to Alex's.

He gives me a tender kiss and we carry the empties back to the bar.

I told him Alex was back at work this week, and while the news put him into a pretty bad mood on Monday night, as the week has progressed, he relaxed.

As have Alex and I. In fact, I even had an amusing conversation with him yesterday about the two charismatic gay guys who are doing the flowers for his wedding. They're partners at home and work and their relationship is tumultuous to say the least. Alex wouldn't be surprised if they fell out and he and Zara ended up with no flowers at all on the day.

'Time's up, people,' Lachie calls to a few stragglers as he wipes down the bar. I wish they'd hurry up and leave. I want to take this gorgeous guy home to bed.

'You can go, Lachie,' his boss says to him with a smile. 'See you on Monday?'

'Sure thing.'

'Thanks for all your work.' They shake hands, warmly. 'You'll be missed.'

Tonight was his last shift. He leaves on Tuesday morning, but he's having a few drinks here on Monday night.

He grabs his chunky black coat from behind the bar and shrugs it on over his red T-shirt. The weather has suddenly become very cold and even his astonishingly warm-blooded body needs proper help fighting the chill. We walk past a couple of girls who look downcast to see Lachie leaving with me.

'Looks like you've got some admirers there,' I whisper to him as we step out onto the icy pavement.

He smirks. 'They're always in here.'

Hmm. 'Not tempted?' I can't help but ask.

He frowns at me, not dignifying my question with an answer.

'What do you see in me?' I ask him outright.

He reels backwards slightly in surprise. 'You need to ask that?'

'I'm a bit confused,' I admit, shivering slightly because it really is freezing cold. He wraps his arm around me.

'Well, you're beautiful. And funny. And smart. And really fucking good in bed.'

I whack him on his chest and he laughs and pulls me tighter to him.

'I'm going to miss you,' I tell him, swallowing the sudden lump in my throat.

'I'm going to miss you, too.' He's no longer smiling when he kisses the top of my head. 'But I don't want it to be goodbye when I go.'

I let his comment rest in my mind. I'll have plenty of time to ponder the future when he's gone.

On Monday, Russ is by my desk when Alex walks out of the meeting room.

'You coming tonight?' Russ asks him, making me tense up.

Alex's brow furrows. 'What's happening?'

'Lachie's leaving drinks.'

'Oh. I didn't know he was leaving?'

Russ glances at me, expecting me to elaborate as Lachie's girl, but I don't speak so he fills Alex in.

'Yeah, he's off travelling for a bit before returning to Australia.'

'Oh, right.' Alex nods. 'Sure. I could come for a couple.'

My heart sinks. I don't actually want him there, and neither, I imagine, will Lachie. But I can't very well tell him he's not welcome in front of Russ. When Russ disappears, I type Alex an email.

You don't need to come tonight. Lachie won't expect it.

I watch his perplexed expression and then he taps out a reply.

Would you rather I didn't come?

I sigh. Do I really want to go into this? I'm not even sure Alex knows that I'm seeing Lachie.

I just don't think there's any need.

I feel a little bad when he replies with a simple 'OK', but I really don't think Lachie will be happy to see him, and this is his night.

By sheer coincidence, Alex is leaving work at the same time as Russ and me. Russ is meeting Maria at Lachie's pub and Rachel and Bridget are also coming. We all walk to Tottenham Court Road station together. I think Russ assumes Alex is coming with us and they chat amiably about Russ's current flat hunt. He and Maria are still living with Rachel, but they're searching for an apartment to move into together.

'What about you, mate?' Russ asks him. 'How are the wedding plans coming along?'

'Yeah, it's all fine,' Alex replies a touch stiffly, probably because I'm there. 'Although I kind of wish we'd just done it like you. Zara's driving me insane going through all the details every night.'

'It'll be worth it,' Russ tells him as we walk down the stairs into the station. 'I just hope Maria doesn't regret not having a big do in the future. She's been to so many weddings, she really knew what she wanted.'

'Your wedding was stunning,' I chip in. 'One of the nicest I've ever been to.' Even if it did have its ups and downs.

'I thought so, too,' Russ says with a smile.

There are often buskers standing at the bottom of the escalators so I don't pay any attention to the sound of distant guitar strumming as we pass through the turnstiles. Then I hear his voice and I let out a little cry of delight.

'It's Lachie!' I squeal.

I step onto the left-hand side of the escalator and crane my neck to try to spot him rather than walking down like I usually would.

'No way,' I hear Russ say with a laugh as Lachie comes into view.

He grins widely when he sees me. He's playing 'Sympathy for the Devil' by The Stones and I have to stop myself from laughing. His smile wavers slightly when he sees who's behind me, but as his eyes rest on mine again, he perks up again. It would be hard not to – my enthusiasm is surely infectious. I spill off the end of the escalator and he stops playing mid-way through the song, grinning and swinging his guitar behind him so he can engulf me in a hug. I reach up, take his face in my hands and give him a long kiss smack on the lips.

'Hello,' he says warmly, looking down at me with a twinkle in his eyes.

'What are you doing here?' I ask gleefully.

'One last busking session. Which, coincidentally, happened to be at the station you go home from.'

'I don't believe in coincidences,' I tell him with a grin.

He stares past me. 'Hey.' He lets me go to shake Alex and Russ's hands. I glance over my shoulder to see Alex looking a bit shaken.

'You coming for a few drinks?' Lachie asks Alex. I doubt it's obvious to anyone other than me, but his tone is less warm than usual.

'I've got to head home,' Alex replies awkwardly.

'What?' Russ exclaims, staring at him in confusion. 'I thought you were coming?'

'Uh, I can't.' He glances at Lachie. 'I heard you're leaving tomorrow?'

'For a bit, yeah, but I'm coming back.' There's a definite hardness to his tone.

'Are you?' Russ asks him with surprise.

Lachie shrugs. 'Yeah, for a bit in December.'

'So are these leaving drinks just another excuse to get hammered?' Russ asks with a grin.

Lachie rolls his eyes and then smiles down at me. 'Shall we go?'

'Yes.'

I step away from him as he collects the coins from his guitar case and packs his guitar away. 'See you tomorrow, then,' Alex says to Russ and me.

'Yep. Bye,' I reply curtly. I swear he looks a little pale as he walks away.

★   ★   ★

398

A lot of people turn up for Lachie's farewell drinks – I never knew he had so many friends. It hurts to think of the time we've wasted not getting to know each other when we had the chance. I'm also sorry that he felt he had to withdraw from my friends and me after Spain. There are so many things I wish I could change.

I'll have him to myself tonight, so I retreat a bit and let him enjoy the company of his mates – and an unsurprising number of females.

'Are you going to miss him?' Bridget asks me as we sit at the bar.

'Yes,' I reply dejectedly.

'What's going to happen now?' she asks, giving me a significant look.

'I don't know,' I murmur.

'Do you think he'll come back over to England?'

'I'm not sure he can,' I reply as I watch him huddle close to his mates and laugh at something one of them has said. 'He had a one-year visa. And I know he misses home and his family.'

'Would you go back?' she asks probingly.

My response is automatic. 'Not now that I've got a promotion. Anyway,' I wave her away. 'We've only just got together. It's too soon to be making plans about the future.'

She cocks her head to one side, thoughtfully, but she doesn't pry any further. I'm relieved.

Our lovemaking that night is sweeter than ever before, but no matter how tired I am, I can't fall asleep in his arms. Eventually I leave him in the bed and go out into the deserted living room. It's freezing cold, and I'm shivering as I sit down on the sofa. Lachie's guitar case is propped up against the wall, where he left it before we went to the pub. I sit in the darkness and let the tears slide down my cheeks, too miserable to wipe them away. The rational part of my brain tells me to go back to Lachie in the nice warm bed, but it's only a whisper inside my head. The more dominant part tells me firmly to stay where I am in the cold. That part wants to punish me for daring to fall in love.

Love? Who am I in love with?

His face is lit by sunlight pouring in through a crack in the curtains. I prop myself up on my elbow and watch the whizzing, circling, silvery flecks of dust caught in the bright shaft of light.

Alex murmurs and I glance down at him.

'Wow, your eyes are really blue,' I say with surprise, my voice coming out sounding huskier than usual.

He smiles sleepily up at me. 'What time is it?' His voice is thick with sleep and alcohol abuse.

'I don't know. I think it's late morning, judging by the sunlight.' I turn my head back towards the curtains. 'Look at the light shaft. The dust motes are like fairy dust. They're magical.'

He frowns. 'What are you going on about?'

'Can't you see them?'

'No.'

'*Maybe you have to move out of the light to see how beautiful it is,*' I muse.

'*You're beautiful,*' he says.

Emotion bubbles up inside me and I can't hold it back. I cry silently, muffling my sobs with my arm as tears trek down my cheeks. And then Lachie's words come back to me and I cry even harder.

'*I'd give anything not to fall for someone I can't have, Bronnie.*'

When Lachie finds me, I'm shivering uncontrollably.

'What the hell are you doing?' he gasps in dismay as he scoops me up in his arms. 'Come back to bed.'

'I'm sorry,' I say. 'I just can't . . .'

'Shh,' he silences me with his kisses and I find myself melting into him, desperate to escape my memories.

I wake up suddenly in the morning and stare at the wall for a while, just thinking. A minute or two later I realise that Lachie is also awake. I turn to face him, as humiliation washes over me. He looks concerned as he regards me. I don't know how long he's been awake.

'Are you alright?' he asks me.

'Yeah.' My face heats up. 'Bloody hell, that was a bit melodramatic of me, wasn't it?' I try to make a joke of it.

He doesn't smile. 'I'm worried about you,' he murmurs.

'Don't be worried about me,' I brush him off and sit up in bed. 'I'm fine.'

'You see, I just don't think that you are,' he replies quietly, looking up at me.

'Oh Lachie, stop it,' I say with a little frown. 'I'm sorry, I don't know what got into me last night. Please just forget about it. It's embarrassing.'

He sighs and reaches up to pull me down into the crook of his arm. I go, a little reluctantly. 'I was thinking. Maybe I shouldn't go travelling. I could stay here until next month. Maybe we could even fly home together.'

'Don't be ridiculous,' I snap, feeling him tense up at my tone. 'Sorry, I don't mean you're ridiculous,' I quickly apologise as I raise myself up on my elbows to look at him. 'But I *really* don't want you changing your plans for me. There's no need. Go have fun. It's a once-in-a-lifetime opportunity.'

'That's not necessarily true.'

'You know what I mean. I just . . . Please. I *want* you to go.' I put my hand on his chest in what I hope is a reassuring gesture, but I feel his body stiffen even more. I'm not doing very well. 'I don't mean I *want* you to go. Of course I don't. I'm going to miss you.' I lean down to kiss him, but his lips are rigid. I pull away again.

'Stay away from Alex,' he says warningly, with a defiant, direct stare. My eyes widen. He's bordering on angry as he continues. 'I saw the look on his face when you kissed me at the station. He wasn't expecting that. You didn't tell him we were together?'

'No, I . . .' I blush again and I realise this makes me look guilty. 'I've barely spoken to him!' I can't help raising my voice as I try to defend myself. 'I'm avoiding him. I *am* staying away from him,' I try to convince him, but I'm not sure I'm going to succeed. 'Lachie,' I say with disappointment as he breaks eye contact with me to glare at the ceiling. 'He's getting married in three weeks. You have nothing to worry about.' I put my hand on his chest, hoping to soothe him. 'I really . . . like you,' I tell him, but I'm not sure it's enough. My hand rises and falls with his heavy sigh. 'I really do,' I add.

He briefly covers his face with his hands and then pulls himself together. 'I guess I'd better get ready,' he says eventually and my heart sinks as he climbs out of bed.

I don't have time to dwell on his mood, though. I have to get ready, too.

He sees me to the Tube station. His flight isn't until later. We walk in silence and I feel very flat, very morose. I turn to face him on the bustling pavement. The twinkle from his blue eyes has gone – he's not smiling, and neither am I. At that moment I feel more than just 'like' for him, but I'm still not sure it's enough – and it's too late anyway.

'I'll see you in December?' I stare at him with regret.

He nods, but doesn't reply.

'Will you text me from Europe? Stay in touch?'

'Yeah,' he mutters.

'Lachie, please,' I say, taking his hands and fighting back tears. 'I care so much about you. I'm going to really miss you.'

His eyes meet mine and my sadness is plain to see. Finally, he takes me in his arms and I hold him as tightly as I can.

After a while his chest vibrates against mine as he chuckles. 'You're crushing me,' he murmurs into my hair.

'Really?' I grin up at him. 'You great big wuss.'

He grins down at me and I stand on my tiptoes to kiss him. But his arms hold me in place and he deepens the kiss as his lips move against mine. My knees go weak as I slip my arms around his neck and kiss him back.

It's only the sound of someone muttering, 'Get a room,' that makes us break apart.

'See you soon,' I say, giving him one last quick, tight hug before turning away. I swear I hear him say he loves me as I hurry into the Tube station.

CHAPTER 29

Coincidentally or not, Alex and I bump into each other again at the station.

'How was last night?' he asks me on the walk into work.

'Fine,' I reply, staring ahead glumly as we pass St Giles Church on our right. 'I'm going to miss him,' I admit, swallowing.

'I didn't know you guys were . . .' His sentence trails off.

'Yeah,' I reply quietly.

'When did that happen?'

I frown at him. 'Does it really matter?' I can't help sounding touchy and he looks shifty.

'No, of course not,' he replies a little defensively. 'I'm just happy for you, that's all.'

He doesn't sound very happy.

'Thanks.' I try to sound gracious but fail miserably. 'Don't be too happy for me, though. He's gone now.'

'Not for long.' His arm bumps me and I think he's trying to cheer me up. It's not working. But at least he's making an effort for things not to be strained between us.

★　★　★

I do as Lachie suggested and stay away from Alex as much as I can. Lachie texts me regularly to let me know where he is and what he's doing and his messages are always the highlight of my day. As Alex's wedding day grows closer, our working relationship becomes easier. It still hurts to look at him sometimes. It doesn't help when he wins a design award at our publishing awards ceremony, clearly I'm not the only one who thinks he's clever and talented. It still makes my heart clench when I breathe in his aftershave in the morning when he comes into the kitchen to make tea. I don't want to listen to our colleagues discussing all of the last-minute wedding details with him, and I don't want to hear all the gory details from Russ about Alex's stag do. Sometimes I feel his eyes on me and I wonder how he really feels. But by choice or not, I'm moving on. And I know that he chose to do that some time ago.

He works right up until his wedding, and on his last day, we all go out for lunch. I'd rather not be there, but it would be weird for me not to go. So I sit and chat to Lisa and Esther about anything other than weddings until the hour is up and we have to return to work. Somehow I find myself walking back alongside Alex as we cross over Soho Square.

'Well, good luck for tomorrow,' I say, folding my arms across my chest to try to keep out some of the cold.

'Thanks,' he replies quietly.

'Rachel will be there so you're in good hands.'

'Feels kind of wrong that you're not going to be there,' he says.

'Does it?' I let out a slight laugh and give him a sidelong look of disbelief.

'Yeah,' he says a little defensively. 'I know you wouldn't want to be—'

'I wouldn't care,' I cut him off. 'It's all fine and anyway, it's just work.'

We walk a few steps in silence.

'It's freezing,' I mumble. 'I'm actually starting to look forward to going home for Christmas, and I never thought I'd say that.'

He frowns slightly. 'Why is that?'

'Long story,' I brush him off.

It occurs to me that he knows nothing about me, and I know nothing about him. Not really. I haven't met his family, I haven't met his sister, his mum has never cooked me one of her famous roasts. I know nothing about his dad. Are they close?

It's ridiculous to think that I could have ever taken Zara's place – like he said, they have history. We just have chemistry. And I'm not even sure we have that any more.

'Where are you going on your honeymoon?' I change the subject.

'Austria. Then we're driving to Switzerland via Italy.'

'Sounds nice.' Sounds cold.

'Hopefully will be.'

'How long are you going for?' I ask casually.

'Two weeks.'

'Oh, so I won't see you after today for quite some time.'

'Why's that?' He looks confused.

'I fly to Australia before you return.'

'Oh, right.'

I'm taken aback to see Polly waiting on the pavement outside work.

My footsteps falter and Alex notices. Following my line of sight, he spies my friend. 'You weren't expecting her?' he asks me.

I shake my head as my body goes rigid. 'No.'

I haven't seen her since that night at the pub where she embarrassed me in front of everyone. And apart from that one time we spoke on the phone, I haven't attempted to call her, either. I know that's wrong. I know she's going through a lot. But I can't help but still feel angry at her.

'Do you want me to tell Simon you'll be a little late?'

'Yes, please.'

I break away from him and go over to her. She looks different – sheepish for one, but also I see that she's lost weight again, although not nearly as much as she had before her wedding. She looks . . . well.

'Hi,' she says. 'I had to come in to do some Christmas shopping. I thought I'd pop in to see you. Your boss said you were probably on your way back from lunch so I thought I'd wait.'

'Oh.' I shift on my feet. 'I'm afraid I've got to get back in there.'

'Bronte,' she says hesitantly. 'Can we grab a quick coffee?'

'Erm . . .'

'Please,' she says.

We go to the café across the road.

'You look well,' I tell her. 'How are you? Are you still going to AA meetings?'

'Yes.' She nods.

'That's great, Polly. And how are things with Grant?' I ask, taking a sip of my tea.

'Really good.' It's her first genuine smile and despite my wariness around her, the sight lifts my spirits.

'Really?' I ask.

'Yes.' She smiles warmly, but her expression changes almost instantly and her eyes fill with tears. 'He's been a rock.'

I reach across and take her hand. I hate seeing her cry.

'I'm so sorry, Bronte,' she whispers. 'I know I've been a shit friend. Grant told me some of the things I've said to you. Bridget did, too. I'm so sorry I brought up your parents in front of your work mates.'

I stiffen and let go of her hand.

'I know how much it hurts you to talk about your childhood and that was unforgivable.' I brusquely nod my acceptance of her apology. 'I know you're going home at Christmas, and I just wanted to say I hope it all goes well.'

409

'Thank you.' My tone sounds sharp.

'My mum—'

'Polly, I don't want to hear what your mum thinks,' I cut her off. Her mouth falls open.

'I just wanted to—' She hesitates, seeing my face. I feel sick inside. I wish she didn't know everything about me. I wish she'd never moved to England. I wish I'd never followed her. 'I wanted to warn you,' she finishes.

My nausea intensifies, but curiosity is a strange emotion, one that cannot often be tamed. 'Warn me about what?' I snap.

'Mum saw the priest. You know. The one.'

My breath catches. 'When? Where?' My voice doesn't sound like my own.

'He's at a church in the city.'

'Does my mum know?' I ask, feeling the blood drain from my face. He moved to Queensland. Why has he come back?

'I'm not sure,' Polly says. 'But I can't believe she doesn't.'

No. Not much stays quiet around our parts. But she's not finished yet.

'She also saw your dad,' she continues reluctantly. 'He's not good.'

'Mum has told me,' I reply in a shaky voice.

'I just think you ought to be prepared.'

I don't want to know any more. I'll be there in person soon enough.

Polly walks me back to the office. 'Can we catch

up again?' she asks me. 'Come over for dinner sometime?'

I nod.

'Bronte, I'm sorry,' she says sincerely as we come to a stop outside my office block. 'You're my oldest and dearest friend. I don't want to lose you.' Her eyes are brimming with tears.

'You're not going to lose me,' I say gently, giving her a hug. 'I'm your oldest friend, but surely not your dearest,' I chastise her gently.

She pulls away and looks at me with confusion.

'Michelle is, now,' I point out casually.

'Michelle's a good friend, but she's not my best friend.'

I give her a wry look.

'Is this because I didn't ask you to be my bridesmaid?' she asks with a sniff.

I laugh. 'No,' I lie, feeling embarrassed. 'Forget about it.'

'Bronte, you hate weddings!' she exclaims, grabbing me by my arms and shaking me slightly. 'I couldn't actually believe it when you said you'd come!'

'Really?' I'm blushing furiously.

'I thought you'd absolutely kill me if I asked you to dress up in watermelon!'

'It was fuchsia.'

'It was watermelon. It had green sleeves.' I start to laugh. 'Michelle still hasn't forgiven me.'

'Oh Polly, you crack me up.' I grab her and give her a hug as she laughs into my shoulder. 'I've got to go, but I'll see you soon. Let's catch up in January when I get back.'

'Definitely,' she promises, brushing away her tears.

My phone buzzes to let me know I have a text message. I pull out my phone as I walk into the lobby, fully expecting to see it's from one of my colleagues chasing me up. But the message is from Rachel. My heart nearly stops when I read it:

> Sally has flu. Please, please, please tell me you're free tomorrow?

I stare in shock at the message. I walk on auto-pilot into the lift and press the button for my floor. What do I do? What can I say? Rachel has no idea at all what she's asking me. I've never told her about Alex. What did he say to me on our walk back to the office? That it feels wrong that I'm not going to be doing his wedding? Does he mean that? And what did I reply? I wouldn't care – it's just work. Do I really mean that? It's a stupid question. Of course I care. But could I do this? What if I say no? Rachel will have to handle things by herself. That's not true. Maybe Maria can help out. Oh no! No, she can't. She and Russ are visiting her parents this weekend. What the hell am I going to do?

The lift doors open and I step out onto the landing and return to the office. Alex glances up to see the expression on my face.

'What?' he mouths.

I crouch on the floor beside his chair. Then I show him the message. I watch his face closely for his reaction. His eyes widen, he swallows, and then he looks at me.

'Are you?' he asks me.

'Am I what?'

'Are you free tomorrow?'

I stare at him with confusion. 'Yes, but . . .'

His expression softens. 'If you meant what you said . . . If you're okay with it, of course I'm happy for you to do my wedding.'

It's not what I expected him to say. I stare back at him for a few long seconds. 'Okay.'

His smile wavers. I get up and go back to my desk, my heart racing.

Lachie calls me that night after Bridget has spent half an hour laying into me. I excuse myself from her tirade to answer the call.

'Hey, beautiful,' his warm voice spills into my ear, but I'm icy inside. 'How are you?'

He is going to kill me.

'Um, I'm alright,' I say hesitantly.

'I was just wondering what you're doing tomorrow?' Does he know? He doesn't sound like he knows. 'Because,' he continues amiably, 'I had an idea. I'm in Paris and I wondered if you fancied jumping on Eurostar and coming out to spend the night with me?'

I can't begin to describe the strange mix of emotions competing with each other inside my stomach.

'The tickets are really cheap on a Saturday,' he tells me, his tone becoming increasingly cautious as he realises I'm not jumping at the chance.

'I . . . can't,' I tell him, my voice coming out in a whisper.

'Oh.' Pause. 'Do you already have plans?'

'I have to work.'

'Work? With Rachel?' He sounds perplexed.

I squeeze my eyes shut. 'Yes.'

'I thought you'd done your last wedding of the year?' In the time it takes for me to find the words to explain, he answers his own question. 'You're doing Alex's wedding.'

The deadly tone of his voice sends unpleasant chills shivering down my spine.

'Sally has flu,' I tell him in a pained voice.

'Are you out of your fucking mind?' he asks me with barely contained fury.

'I'm beginning to think that I am,' I reply quietly. 'But I have to do this.'

'No, you don't,' he snaps. 'It's the stupidest thing you'll ever do.'

'It will give me closure,' I tell him. It's an argument I used on Bridget, but she didn't buy it either.

'You're a fucking idiot,' he says angrily.

'Lachie!' I exclaim.

'Out of your fucking mind,' he says again. 'I'm starting to think I should have you committed.'

Is he only just now starting to think that? I've been thinking about having myself committed for some time.

'Please don't be angry. It will be okay. I'll just get it done and then I'll go.'

'What did Alex say?' He's incredulous. 'Did he agree to this?'

'Yes.'

He lets out a snort of utter disbelief.

'He wants me to do it. He trusts me.'

'He wants you to do it?' He can't believe what I'm telling him. 'Oh my God. That *guy*!' I've never heard him so angry. But it doesn't matter. Nothing he says will change my mind.

'I have to do this, Lachie. I'm doing it.'

'You really must fucking hate yourself, Bron,' he says. 'I'm done with watching your car crash. *We're* done.' And then he hangs up on me.

THE THIRTEENTH WEDDING

I wake up early in the morning after one of the worst night's sleeps I've ever had. I can't cope with Bridget's ongoing diatribe, so I get ready as quietly as I can and then slip out of the house before she wakes up. I hop on the Underground with my kit bag and change trains at Kings Cross to take the Piccadilly Line to Covent Garden.

Alex is getting married in St Paul's Church in the piazza at midday and I have hours to kill. Needless to say, I'm leaving Rachel to handle the bride prep shots.

I walk through Covent Garden's cobbled streets in the dim light of early-morning London, passing by shops that are yet to open, in search of a café to spend a couple of hours in. I find one just around the corner from the church and huddle at a table in the corner, shivering and accepting that I won't feel warm at all today.

At ten o'clock I get a text from Lachie. I cringe as I open it.

Are you really going through with it?

I reply with nothing more than a yes, and don't expect to hear from him again.

Bridget also tries calling me, but I divert her calls three times before she settles on a text, too:

I just wanted to wish you luck. I'm thinking of you and I have a bottle of vodka waiting to be drunk when you get home.

My eyes sting as I reply with a thank you.

At eleven o'clock, with nausea swirling in my gut and nerves that are far worse than anything I've ever had to endure, I force myself back onto the cold, sunny streets of Covent Garden. The beautiful, seventeenth-century church is on the west side of the piazza. By the time I arrive, a crowd has already congregated in the piazza behind the church, and I can hear their cries and cheers as a busker on a unicycle performs. I walk past them in a daze and take the few stairs down to the churchyard. I don't know how I'm going to do this.

My legs feel like lead as I force myself up the steps to the glass front door. I push it open and go inside. The interior of the church is a single space, undivided by piers and columns. Nicknamed The Actors' Church, its connection to the theatre is illustrated by memorials to famous actors and actresses along the walls. The flowers are a sea of red winter berries, dark red roses and green pine hanging from every pew. There's a guy in a

417

morning suit up at the altar, kneeling down to light dozens of pillar candles in tall clear vases. I force myself to go up to him.

'Hi, there,' I say.

He looks up at me. Oh! It's Brian – Alex's sister's husband from the stag do. He frowns slightly, trying to remember where he's seen my face before. I put him out of his misery.

'I'm Bronte,' I say. 'The assistant photographer. We met at your stag do.'

'Oh, right!' He stands up and shakes my hand. 'That's a coincidence!'

'Mmm. Do you mind if I take some shots of you lighting those?'

'I'm not sure I'm very interesting, but go ahead.'

'These sorts of shots look great in the overall picture. Just carry on doing what you're doing. It's better if they look natural.'

I get my Canon out of my kit bag and set to work photographing Brian before moving on to the flowers. I can hear the cheers of the crowd behind the church in the piazza through the stone walls and stained-glass windows. It's not going to be the quietest ceremony. The vicar appears so I go to introduce myself and then capture a few early guests arriving. Brian, I take it, is one of two ushers. I'm just about holding myself together when Alex's parents arrive.

It's immediately obvious to me who they are: not just because Alex's father is wearing a red rose and red berry buttonhole, but because he looks like his son: tall with a chiselled jawbone, perfect, straight nose, and dark, albeit greying hair. As for his mother, I nearly jolt in shock when I see her eyes: as blue as the ocean on a summer's day. She smiles and approaches me and it takes quite a lot of effort not to turn and run. What if this woman can see straight through me? What if she can tell that I'm in love with her son?

'Hello there,' she says warmly. 'I'm Clarissa, Alex's mother. Are you here to do the photos?'

'Yes.' I smile nervously.

'Silly question. I can see that by the contraption you're holding.' She reaches out to shake my hand.

'I'm Bronte,' I tell her.

'Best of luck,' she replies, turning to lead her husband to the front of the church. I watch her in a daze.

I'm just Bronte. Here to do the photos. I'm an employee, on the outside looking in. I'm not part of these celebrations, not part of this wonderful, supposed 'best day of their lives'. She has no idea who I am or what I mean to her son.

I don't even know what I mean to her son.

I don't think she'd like me very much if she knew the truth. The realisation makes me feel dirty and deceitful and makes me really not like myself very much.

I shouldn't be here.

No. I am here because I'm doing Rachel – and Alex – a favour. I'm not a bad person. I'm not. With that in mind, I get on with my job.

419

The church has filled up considerably and it's almost eleven forty-five, but there's still no sign of Alex. After snapping lots of shots of the guests, I go outside to check the churchyard for him. Where is he?

The wedding starts at midday – he's bordering on late.

What if . . . What if he's changed his mind?

Despite my internal pep talk of only minutes ago, hope surges through my heart.

I *am* a bad person. Who am I kidding?

It occurs to me to wonder what I would do if Alex called it off, if he said he wanted me and only me?

Several thoughts fly through my mind at once: I'd be the one who split him and Zara up, the bitch who stole someone's boyfriend of almost a decade. His mother, his father, his friends and relatives wouldn't like or trust me. We'd start off on the wrong foot from the very beginning. Maybe Alex would come to regret his decision, maybe we'd discover we don't have that much in common. But of all these thoughts, the one that fights its way right to the forefront is the idea of never seeing Lachie again. The pain as this thought takes hold is so intense that it takes me by surprise. Last night he told me we were done. I haven't let that fully sink in, but now I'm overwhelmed with sadness. It hurts so much more than I ever could have anticipated.

The rational part of my brain tells me that he

said we were done in the heat of the moment, that I can still change his mind – if I want to. Do I want to? Yes. Without a doubt. But that still brings me back to my initial question: where is Alex? Is he having second thoughts? And do I want him to be having second thoughts?

For the first time, I think the answer might be no. But it's a shaky no.

And then I see him in one of the side entrances to the churchyard, in a dark alley walkway that cuts under the buildings surrounding the churchyard. My heart jumps and then freefalls: he's here. He's going to go through with it. A wave of grief engulfs me all over again. But he's not coming this way. He's with someone else: another man in a morning suit. I catch a glimpse of his friend's face and he looks concerned. What are they talking about? *Is* he having second thoughts?

This is unbearable. I feel so confused. My head feels like it's in a vice and I almost wish someone would crank up the pressure and put me out of my misery once and for all.

Without thinking, I start to walk their way.

'Alex?' I ask as I arrive at the alleyway.

His head shoots around to stare at me, and I've never seen him look more torn or anguished. He doesn't speak, but his best man – if that's who he is – looks straight at me.

'We'll be there in a minute,' he says firmly, encouraging me to go away.

Alex turns back to him and mutters something and his friend's face drops off a cliff.

'What are you doing here?' the friend asks me in what is barely more than a whisper.

'I'm photographing the wedding,' I reply, holding up my camera.

He stares at Alex, incredulous. 'She's photographing the wedding?' he asks in astonishment.

'I'm Bronte,' I tell him, still unsure what's going on.

'I *know* who you are.' The way he says it tells me that he not only knows who I am; he knows *everything*.

It's a sickening realisation, but it's Alex I care about. He's shaking.

'Are you okay?' I ask him with concern, keeping my distance outside the alleyway. 'It's almost midday.'

He nods quickly, but he's unable to meet my eyes.

'Just give us a minute, would you?' the best friend who I've never even met says in a tone that is bordering on anger. 'Why the hell are you even here?'

'Ed,' Alex warns sharply, turning to look at him. 'Maybe you could give *us* a minute?'

'Mate, what are you doing?' he asks with genuine distress. He checks his watch. 'Zara's going to be here any moment.'

'Do you think I don't know that?' Alex says. 'Please. Just give us a minute.'

Ed flashes me a hard look as he stalks past me. I quickly check over my shoulder to make sure no one else has exited the church to search for us. Alex doesn't make any move to come out from the dark alleyway, so I venture in towards him. His eyes never leave mine.

'I'm so fucked up,' he whispers, tears welling up in his eyes.

My heart goes out to him and at that moment I want nothing more than to put my arms around him and try to take his pain away. But I stay exactly where I am and wait for him to speak.

'This morning I went into the living room and there was a shaft of sunlight coming through a crack in the curtains. It lit up the dust flying around.'

A cold chill settles over me because I know exactly why he's telling me this. He's remembering the morning after we first met. I just don't know why it's relevant.

'It's what you said to me: you have to move out of the light to see how beautiful it is.' Tears spill down his cheeks. 'I couldn't see it, Bronte. I still can't see it clearly enough. There's been too much pressure. Too much focus on Zara and me this year from all our friends and family. This whole engagement – it's all been so confusing. I just want to press pause and take it all in. But I can't. It's all going too fast.'

'Alex,' I murmur, not daring to touch him.

'I love you,' he says hopelessly.

A little gasp slips from my mouth, and everything inside me hurts.

'But I love Zara, too.'

Through the fog of agony, I see with extreme clarity that he's not the only one who's in love with two people.

'ALEX!' Ed's voice reverberates loudly around the alleyway. 'Zara is here.'

Alex and I meet each other's eyes, but all I see is terror. I shake my head and back away from him. The decision has to be his.

Back in the church and so full of dread I can barely function, I realise that the decision is not just his. It's mine, too. Lachie or Alex. I don't know. I still don't know. The light is on all of us and it's so intense and bright that it's hard to see straight.

I'm vaguely aware of a hushed murmuring passing over the congregation. The groom is still not at the front and news that the bride has arrived has reached some of the guests. I see Alex's mother craning her neck towards the back of the church, worry etched across her features. And then her face breaks into a smile.

I smell him before I see him, his aftershave wafting by as he passes. I watch in a daze as he and his best man take their positions at the front, while some of the guests break into spontaneous applause and Ed takes a jovial little bow. Alex does nothing. He's staring straight ahead. And then the organ starts to play.

'All set?' I'm vaguely aware of Rachel patting my arm as she passes by in good spirits, oblivious to my inner turmoil.

My hands are shaking as I lift my camera up to my face. I can't turn around. I can't bear to see her. I don't want to see what she's wearing. Rachel better have got enough shots to suffice because photographing her is one thing I cannot do. I hear the gasps of delight and I know that she's behind me. But my main goal is to do what I always have done as Rachel's assistant: to capture the groom's reaction to seeing his bride for the first time. My hands become steady as I zoom in. I can see him clearly and he's still facing the altar. Out of the corner of my eye I see a flash of white moving by. In what feels like a strange out-of-body experience, I will him to look at her, to let me do my job to the best of my abilities, and then his head starts to turn. I click off several shots, not wanting to miss the moment that his eyes meet hers, but he doesn't look at Zara. He looks straight down my lens. *Click*. His blue eyes pierce right into my soul. *Click*. Ed's expression is alarmed as he realises who has Alex's attention. Then, a moment later, Zara joins him. He breaks out of his spell and turns to look at her, smiling in a slightly dazed way as though she's a long-forgotten friend bumping into him on the street. I snap off a single shot.

She can have that one.

But the others are mine.

★   ★   ★

I don't know how I get through the next half an hour: the prayers, the hymns, the introduction and declarations. When Alex declares his desire to marry her, I die a little inside, but it's far from being over. A reading . . . The address . . . The vows . . .

'*I do . . .*'

It's killing me.

And then the vicar says in a loud, clear voice: 'What God has joined together, let no man tear asunder.'

A shiver spirals uncontrollably through my body and I can't stop shaking. I feel like I'm going to be violently sick. I can barely stand, let alone focus a zoom lens, and how would it look if I did throw up?

My kit is too heavy as I turn and walk quickly out of the church and past the huddled bodies of tourists sitting on the churchyard steps.

The camera bangs against my chest and I have an overwhelming desire to stuff it into a bin or smash it on the ground. I know I'm not thinking straight, but I feel like it's infecting me, suffocating me – I don't want it anywhere near me. But I have to get the bride and groom's exit.

Just then, someone shouts my name from the direction of the church.

'BRONTE!'

Alex?

No. I see him standing there on the steps and he's not a tourist – at least, not really. My face

426

crumples as Lachie jogs down the stairs towards me.

His warm, comforting arms ensnare me and I give in and sob into his shoulder. I'm vaguely aware of the guests singing 'All Things Bright and Beautiful'.

'You're shivering. Fuck me,' he murmurs into my hair.

'I don't think I can do this,' I say.

'Of course you can't!' he snaps, not unkindly. 'Where's your coat?'

Trust Lachie, the warmest person in the world, to think of my coat.

'In the vestry,' I manage to say past the enormous lump in my throat. 'Leave it,' I try to hang onto him as he pulls away from me.

'I should let Rachel know you can't go back in,' he tells me reluctantly, before breaking away.

She's going to kill me for letting her down. But I feel dead already.

I watch Lachie as he jogs back into the church and slowly pushes open the glass door, letting the sound of the organ rush out before it's engulfed by the door swinging shut again. Less than a minute later he re-emerges, picking up an enormous backpack from the steps and shrugging it onto his shoulders as he walks. He helps me into my coat like I'm a small child and ushers me, still shivering, across the churchyard and out onto the road.

He holds me the whole way home in the taxi,

but doesn't say a word. I'm too exhausted to contemplate what's going through his mind. The morning's events ebb and flow within my consciousness, and sometimes I can't help shuddering. He just holds me tighter and strokes my hair.

Outside Bridget's apartment, he has to take my bag from me because my hands feel too weak to find my keys, let alone unlock a door. In the back of my mind I'm aware that my behaviour will be scaring him away – who can cope with their girlfriend being an emotional wreck over another man? But there's nothing I can do about it. I'm lost.

I barely have the strength to walk up the stairs, while poor Lachie lugs his heavy backpack and carries my kit bag, too. He knocks first before entering, and in that time, Bridget has come into the hall. Her face pales when she sees the state I'm in.

'Oh, Bronte,' she murmurs with dismay.

Lachie ushers me inside and she gives me a hug while he takes his backpack off and gently lowers my camera and kit bag to the ground. I'm too tired even to cry. The three of us go to the living room and I sit on the sofa, huddled against warm, lovely Lachie who I may only have for a short time longer. But I'm hanging onto him while I can.

'He married her, I'm guessing?' Bridget asks quietly.

In my side vision I see Lachie nod. Bridget sighs.

But he told me that he loved me first. I can't say it out loud. I don't want to say it out loud. I'm not sure that I ever will.

Bridget puts the telly on because I'm in no state to talk, and after a while she gets up to go and make us something to eat. I'll have to force food down, but I haven't eaten since yesterday.

As soon as Bridget has left the room, I pull away and look up at Lachie. He glances down at me, a combination of sadness and wary restraint on his features.

'I love you,' I whisper, staring into his light blue eyes.

He turns his head slightly away from me, but I can't read his expression. His chest under my hand has tensed up.

'I want you to know that. And it's not because he married her. I loved you before.'

'Don't talk about it now,' he says in a tight voice. 'I can't . . . hear it.'

I watch with despair as he returns his focus to the telly. 'I'm sorry,' I whisper, tearfully. I lean up to him and press my lips against his neck. 'But I do love you. And I'm sorry.'

I nuzzle my face against his neck until Bridget returns and only then do I pull away. By then, he's relaxed again, but only slightly. I don't know if he'll ever forgive me. *Is* it possible to forgive someone for falling in love with the wrong person?

Suddenly I'm prickling all over as the enormity of this question sinks in. And I'm not thinking of

Lachie any more. I'm not thinking about Alex. I'm thinking about someone else entirely.

I have another bad dream that night and I jolt awake, gasping for air. Lachie stirs beside me and a moment later I feel his hand on my arm.

'It's okay,' I say. 'Just a bad dream. Go back to sleep.'

His hand slides away and I lie there in the darkness with my eyes open, just staring at nothing as I try to process the previous day's events.

Alex is married. He told me he loves me. He told me he was confused. And I could see it – I could see it in his eyes. But I did nothing to stop him, to convince him not to go through with it. Should I have done? Would he have chosen her anyway? It's too late now and the thought of seeing him again is hell. I don't know how I will ever get over this. How will I ever return to work in the New Year after Christmas? I don't think I will ever forgive him.

'What was your dream about?'

Lachie's voice cuts into my thoughts. I assumed he'd gone back to sleep.

I hear him sigh.

'Why don't you tell me about it,' he says after a moment.

I go rigid and don't reply.

'Bronnie,' he urges, gently. 'There's so much I don't know about you. I know you had a difficult childhood, but I don't know why. I know your dad was an organ player. I know you have a fear of churches.'

'Not so much any more,' I interrupt him. Although yesterday might have put me back a bit.

'You say you don't believe in marriage, although I'm not sure I believe you.'

'Why?' I'm curious.

'The way you reacted yesterday. If you didn't believe in marriage, you wouldn't have got so freaked out.'

'Alex believes in marriage,' I tell him quietly, and that makes yesterday feel overwhelmingly significant.

'Don't get me started on Alex,' Lachie mutters, his grip on my hand wavering. I tighten my hold. 'What you said earlier,' he says in a strangled-sounding voice. 'Did you mean it?'

'That I love you? Yes.'

He exhales loudly. 'Do you trust me?'

I frown. 'I think so, yes.'

He shifts on the bed. A moment later my bedside table light comes on and I flinch at the brightness. Lachie turns back towards me. He places his hand on my cheek and stares steadily into my eyes.

'You can trust me. I love you.' I see his eyes fill with tears just before my vision goes blurry. I wipe away my own tears and lean forwards to kiss him on his lips. He kisses me gently, then retreats. 'You can trust me,' he says again.

I take a shaky breath. 'What do you want to know?'

'What happened when you were growing up? What are your nightmares about?'

'I never talk about this to anyone,' I tell him.

'You can talk about it to me.'

'I don't even know where to start.'

'Start with your dream.'

I take a shaky breath. 'It takes place when I'm nine years old.'

He reaches over and takes my hand, holding me reassuringly.

'Mum and Dad were not happily married, although no one would have ever known it. They were very religious and we'd go to church every weekend and Mum would smile proudly when Dad played the organ and pretend that they were a happy couple. But at home they never laughed together. Mum was always crying if she wasn't shouting or screaming. But Dad would never shout back. He just took it. He and I didn't have a relationship growing up. He didn't even seem to like me. The only attention he ever gave me was when I showed an interest in learning to play the organ. I used to find church services boring, but when Dad started taking me to church after school to teach me, I saw the church in a different light. Sometimes I'd meet him there and wait in the cool, beautiful space and it would clear my head. It was one of the only times I felt at peace – away from all the shouting and crying at home. The only time he ever seemed to smile was when I was playing the organ. But at home he just seemed like a shadow of himself. He barely spoke to either of us. He was a shell and no matter how much Mum tried to get a rise out of him, it wouldn't work. Then he started to get funny about even teaching me to play. He kept brushing me off with excuses, telling me he didn't have time to teach me. Sometimes I would go to church anyway, and if it was deserted, I'd pretend to play and just hope that he would show up. One night Mum was crying – I could hear her through the walls. She didn't even try to cry quietly. She didn't care that her sobs were like nails being driven into my heart,' I say bitterly and Lachie squeezes my hand. 'So I took off. I snuck out. I was only nine.' I take another deep breath, because this part is from my dream. 'I went to church, wanting my dad, wanting him to come home and stop Mum from crying because sometimes – and only sometimes – he could. I don't know what he'd say to her then, but I wanted him to say it to her now. There was no one in the church so I went and sat at the organ. I was too scared to turn it on, so I pretended to play.' My breath catches. 'I heard something. It sounded like someone was hurt.' This is so hard to talk about. 'I looked around the corner of the organ and saw my dad and the priest. They were kissing.' I cringe at the memory and stare straight past Lachie as my voice drops to a whisper. 'I had never seen anyone kiss like that. It was like they were eating each other, devouring each other. Now that I look back I can see that they were just kissing incredibly passionately, but I was only nine.' I return my gaze to Lachie, but he's just listening, not reacting in any way. 'I didn't fully understand what I was seeing. The priest had only moved to South Australia recently. He seemed quite young – I think he was probably in his twenties. But he was very popular and kind and everyone seemed to like him. I liked him. And my dad clearly did.' I swallow and Lachie reaches over to stroke my cheek. 'Anyway, they started to take things further. I don't think they were going to have—' I can't say it. I can't talk about sex and my dad in the same sentence.

'Sex?' Lachie has no problem saying the word.

'Yeah. I don't think they were going to do it at the altar, but they had their hands up each other's shirts, were clasping hold of each other's bodies. It looked . . . painful.' I pull a face, still disturbed by the memory even though I have a better under-standing of it now. 'Then I cried out.' Tears prick my eyes.

Lachie strokes his thumb soothingly along my jawline.

'They heard me. They jerked away from each other and my dad came storming towards the organ. He never got angry,' I whisper. 'Not once with Mum, never when she was calling him wet and a terrible excuse for a man. But when he saw me sitting there and knew that I knew . . .' I gulp in a breath. 'He wrenched me off the stool and I banged my head hard on the wall. That hurt, but it wasn't enough for him.' Tears slide down my face. 'He smacked me across my face and called me a stupid little girl. He shook me and kept calling me a stupid little girl, over and over. But he was crying. I had never seen him cry. The priest pulled him away from me and held him back. But my dad just kept shouting, 'You stupid little girl!' over and over. The priest tried to calm him down and as soon as I saw my chance, I ran. But he caught me. I was *terrified*.'

'Poor thing,' Lachie murmurs.

'He locked me in the vestry in the dark and I really, honestly didn't know what he was going to do to me. I had never seen him like that – ever. I was so scared.' My bottom lip starts wobbling. 'Eventually – it seemed like hours – he came into the vestry alone. He'd calmed down and was so sorry, but I was very frightened. He begged. He pleaded. He was deeply distressed, crying and sobbing and asking me not to tell my mum. I swore to him that I wouldn't. I still didn't understand what he was doing with the priest. It was all so confusing. Now I get it.'

'What do you get?' Lachie probes gently.

'I get that he was gay. He is gay. He wasn't in love with my mum. He married her because he felt he had to. He got her pregnant and it was the done thing,' I say. 'But really he was just a coward. He should have stuck with the one he loved and left Mum and me in peace if he hated us so much.'

'I don't think he hated you,' Lachie says gently.

435

'It felt like he did. After that day, he couldn't even look at me. But I never breathed a word. Mum continued to cry and he never said a word to defend himself. And then the rumours started to hit. I presume my dad carried on with his affair because the priest stayed in town for almost a year after I saw them together, although he never said another word to me. At church that Sunday, my mum even pointed out the bruise on my face to him, from where I was banged against the wall and then smacked by my dad. She smiled and apologised for my appearance and said I was clumsy and had fallen over. And he never said a word. Bastard,' I hiss. 'Having an affair with a married man.'

Lachie stares calmly back at me and the double standards of my sentence sink in. 'It's not the same,' I say. 'He had a child. Me! And Alex wasn't married. I would never—'

'What happened afterwards?' he interrupts.

'The rumours started spreading. I went from being a happy – albeit quiet – girl at school with several friends, to having just the one: Polly. Other kids teased and bullied me and called my dad names. It was a small-town mentality and they were very unforgiving. Polly was my only friend, but even she made me feel like I owed her, like I was indebted to her. I went through years of that agony. The priest left, another came and more rumours circulated. As far as I know, Dad never came clean to my mum. But I am certain beyond

436

a shadow of a doubt, that she knew . . . She *knew*,' I say pointedly. 'And she stayed *married* to him!'

This is what I will never understand.

'Why didn't she get a divorce? Why live a lie? Why make themselves miserable? It was a complete and utter farce!' It makes me feel angry. 'I think Dad wanted to get a divorce. I heard him mutter something about it to me once, but Mum would never let him. Just before I left home, I asked her why she didn't leave him if he made her feel so unhappy? Do you know what she said? She said: "I married your father under the eyes of God and in His eyes we will always be unified." What a joke!' I exclaim. 'They made a mockery of marriage. They never should have married in the first place, let alone stayed married. They are *still* married!' I exclaim, feeling slightly hysterical. 'And he's gay! My dad is *gay*! What the hell was he thinking?'

'Have you asked him?' Lachie asks.

Now my lip is wobbling very dangerously indeed. I shake my head. 'I can't.' I sniff loudly. 'The thing is, I've been thinking recently that I might be able to forgive him – not that he's ever asked for my forgiveness. He wouldn't look me in the eye when I last went home – even now, he can't look at me. I hate going home,' I say vehemently. 'I avoid it at all costs, but my mum puts such guilt trips on me to get me there. I can't believe I'm going back for Christmas.' I rub my hands over my face.

I'd almost rather stay here and welcome Alex

back from his honeymoon. I feel a sharp pang at the reminder that he married Zara yesterday.

'You said you thought you might be able to forgive him,' Lachie brings me back on track as I take my hands down from my face.

'Yes. He did so much wrong. The way he handled it, the way he was with me, the way he never seemed to forgive me for discovering his secret. But at the end of the day, he fell in love with the wrong person.'

Lachie tucks a strand of hair behind my ear. 'Are you sure about that?'

I look at him, confused.

'Maybe he fell in love with the right person. Maybe the priest was the right person. Maybe they would have been happy together. Maybe *he* could have been happy. Do you think you could have accepted it? The fact that he's gay?'

'Of course I could have. I know he can't help it. It's not a decision. I understand that, even though some of the small-minded people that I grew up with refused to accept it. It's the thought of a happy dad that I can't come to terms with. I can't imagine him happy. Seeing him kissing that priest . . . It was disturbing seeing my dad doing that with anyone. I'd never even seen him peck my mum's lips. But that kiss . . . That was the most alive I had ever seen him. He was like a whole different person. He was a stranger to me. And that was scary.'

'I can't believe he and your mum are still married,'

Lachie says. 'No wonder you think marriage is a farce.'

'I know it's not a farce for everyone. I know some people are happily married their entire lives and that's great.'

He looks amused. I almost sounded sardonic, but I didn't mean to.

'I just think that you should be with who you want to be with. And if you don't want to be with them any more, then don't be. You don't need a piece of paper or a blessing from God. You just need to love each other. And if you decide to have children, then love them, too.'

I sniff and wipe away my tears.

'I'm sure your dad loves you, Bron,' Lachie says sadly.

I stare back at him. 'I'll probably never know.'

CHAPTER 30

Lachie doesn't return to Europe. He says that if I'm going to be living in London for the foreseeable future, then he'll come back as soon as he can and maybe we can do Europe together. The idea makes me smile, but neither of us knows when that will be and the thought is sobering. He stays with me at Bridget's, and knowing that I have him to come home to helps, but I seriously struggle through that last week at work. After managing to change our flights, Lachie and I travel back to Australia together. He offered to come home with me for Christmas, but I'm not ready for him to meet my family yet. Our relationship is already on shaky ground, although to my eternal surprise, he is still with me and is heart-warmingly positive about us. In the end, we part ways in Sydney and then fly on to our destinations separately.

The sun is shining on Adelaide when I touch down. I cleared immigration in Sydney, so my mum is waiting in the domestic terminal ready to greet me as soon as I step off the plane. I don't recognise her at first. Her normally mousy, long hair has been cut to a shoulder-length bob and is highlighted. Her skin is glowing and she looks fit and healthy and very, very different to the last time I saw her: washed out and weary, her face carved with worry lines.

I stare at her with astonishment. 'Mum?'

'Hello Bronte.' She smiles and gives me a stiff hug. Nothing's changed there, then. 'How was your flight?'

'Fine,' I reply, still staring at her with amazement. 'You look so different.'

She smiles and shrugs in a strange, carefree way. Who is this woman?

I grew up in a small beach town about an hour and a half south of the city, but the way my mum drives, it's likely to take closer to two hours to get there. We potter through Adelaide's suburban sprawl at an excruciatingly low speed, passing a myriad of single-storey delis, dry cleaners, charity shops and hairdressers. We make awkward small talk about work and my life in the UK, and eventually settle into a comparatively comfortable silence. I must doze off, because when I wake we've left suburbia behind and are surrounded by the muted bush tones of grey, green, yellow and brown. The road is dwarfed by enormous yellow-brown hills dotted with green pines and eucalyptus trees. The ridges on the hills created by years of driving winds and rain remind me of ripples on the water, and as we pass a deep gully, I catch a glimpse out of my mum's window of the sparkling blue-green ocean beyond. I'd almost forgotten how beautiful my home is. I can't help but smile as I look up at the blue sky to see an enormous flock of white cockatoos pass overhead.

We continue to drive along the winding road for a while, past glittering lakes, dry creeks edged with big, old gums and farms filled with sleek horses, hot cattle and dusty-looking sheep. One colonial-style house nestled in the hills is fronted with white rose bushes. White roses will always remind me of my dad, who took so much pride in his.

Ten minutes later when Mum parks her red Kia on the driveway, I'm shocked to see that all of Dad's prized rose bushes are dead.

'What happened to Dad's roses?' I ask her with a frown, also noting that the once green lawn is yellow and dry.

She shrugs defensively. 'I don't have time to garden.'

'Is work particularly busy?' She helps out at a library a few towns away.

She ignores me and climbs out of the car. I follow suit, standing and staring for a long moment at the small, cream-brick, brown-tiled Seventies bungalow that I once called home. The blue and white striped canvas awnings are pulled down and in place, shading the windows. I always hated how dark and dingy they made my bedroom feel.

Mum unlocks the door, and rests her hand on

the handle, seeming to hesitate before pushing down.

'I've decided to sell the house,' she blurts out. 'I wanted to tell you when you were in England, but it's so hard to get hold of you.'

And I tend only to call her on Saturday evenings when it's Sunday morning in Australia and I know she'll be at church.

But I know from the look on her face that not being able to get hold of me is just an excuse.

'I don't have a problem with you selling the house,' I say calmly.

'Don't you?' Her relief is palpable.

'Why would I? I haven't lived here in years.'

'I just thought . . . Never mind.'

Does she think she needs my permission because Dad isn't around to agree or disagree with her any more?

She opens the door and an achingly familiar smell wafts out as I follow her inside. I look through the open living-room door on my left to see boxes piled up. She's already got started on the packing.

'I haven't touched your room, yet,' she says warily. 'I thought maybe you could sort out your things while you're here?'

My parents never touch my room, so it always looks exactly the same as when I left it at the age of seventeen and I'm always too depressed to do anything about it on the rare occasions I do venture home.

'I don't want any of it. We can give it all to charity.'

She looks taken aback. 'You don't want to keep anything? Not even Monty?'

Monty was my favourite cuddly toy when I was growing up. He and I went through everything together. He knows all my secrets.

'No,' I reply bluntly. 'Although I don't imagine the charity shop will want him, either, so we can just bin him. I'll put my bags in my room.'

My bedroom is the first door on my right. I feel increasingly deflated as I take in the pink walls, which still look lurid, even though the curtains have been drawn and the outside awning is stealing much of the rest of the sunlight. The walls are partially covered with bleached-out magazine posters, the cheap bookshelves are packed with neat rows of colourful children's books and Bible stories, and the crappy brown wardrobes and matching chest of drawers no doubt still hold a few dowdy jumpers from my teenage years. My eyes fall on the neatly ironed lilac bedspread and the ratty-looking dog in pride of position resting against the pillow. I let my bags fall to the threadbare carpet with a thud. Then I go and sit on the bed.

Monty gazes at me dolefully with his one glassy black eye, which lost all of its shine years ago. I pick him up and stare at him.

Okay, so maybe I'll take Monty with me. He hasn't done anything to deserve being binned. But the rest of it can go.

There's a knock at my door.

'Come in?'

'I'm putting the kettle on. Would you like one?' Mum asks.

'Sure.'

I get up and follow her to the back of the house where the orange lino-floored, yellow melamine-cupboarded kitchen hasn't been updated in forty years. Damn, it's depressing. I pull out a chair at the kitchen table and slump into it. Mum puts a packet of Yo-Yo biscuits in front of me and that perks me up slightly.

'I have a friend coming over at one o'clock,' she says in an oddly breezy tone that immediately gets my hackles up.

'Oh?'

'Yes. He's helping me take some of these boxes to the charity shop.' She goes bright red.

I stare at her, deadpan. 'He?'

'His name is David and he's just a friend,' she says defensively.

I feel cold inside. 'Polly told me you had a male friend.' I try to sound neutral, but it's a struggle.

'He's just a friend,' she says again, but her blush is not reducing.

'When was the last time you went to see Dad?' I ask her, a strange emotion forming inside me.

'I see your father all the time!' She raises her voice at me, reminding me more of the mother from my childhood and less of her glossy, bronzed, highlighted current self. 'I've given him everything!'

she cries. 'I gave you both everything! Now it's time I took care of myself!'

I stare at her and then get up and walk out of the room.

'Bronte!' she shouts. 'Come back here!'

No. I can't. I grab my handbag from my bedroom and walk out of the front door.

I turn left and set off at a fast pace, slinging my bag over my shoulder and crunching over the brittle, dead eucalyptus leaves scattered across the baking hot path. I don't know where I'm going, but I can't be there with her. I just can't. Friend! She's lying. She gave us everything? She gave me an unhappy childhood. And as for Dad . . .

The sun beats down on my pounding head and my body feels like it's been emptied of its contents and filled with sand by the time I come to my destination. And I didn't even know it was my destination until I'm standing in front of the little church built out of bluestone rock. The tin roof gleams silver in the sunlight and the white wooden cross above the small bell tower looks even brighter than usual. I wipe my nose on the back of my hand and walk up the path, trying to ignore the dead pine needles slipping into my sandals and pricking my feet.

The door is open so I walk straight in, barely faltering as the familiar smell assaults my nostrils. I walk with determination up the aisle, past no more than ten pews, and come to a stop in front of the organ. In a daze I sit on the stool, my memories washing violently over me. I can *hear* my father and the priest, I can *see* them, and then they see me and my head relives the memory with me, as a painful throbbing pierces the right side of my face, just above my eyebrow where my head hit the wall. I press my cool palm to it and try to calm down.

I don't know what I'm going to do now. I really don't want to go home. I could call Lily and Ben. I wonder if they would let me stay with them for a few days. I know they have a tiny baby, but maybe Lily would appreciate the help.

My eyes fall on the door to the vestry and I instantly feel a little claustrophobic.

'Bronte?'

I sigh wearily. She's found me.

'Bronte?' Mum asks again, coming up the aisle to see me sitting there desolately at the organ.

'Just leave me alone,' I murmur, suddenly too tired to argue with her.

'Please come home,' she urges, looking around fearfully. God forbid anyone should see us here and *talk* . . .

'I don't want to come home,' I tell her. 'I don't know why I came here at all. I should have stayed in England.'

Alex's blue eyes stare back at me from inside my mind and I wince. No, I don't want to be in England, either.

I should have gone with Lachie to Perth. I jolt. I *could* go to visit Lachie in Perth! I don't have to stay here. I'm not a child, she can't make me.

'I need to talk to you about your father.' Mum's words quash my hopeful thoughts.

'What about him?' I say dully.

'He's not good, Bronte.'

'I know. You've told me. Polly has told me. What do you want me to do about it?' I slowly lift my eyes to meet hers.

She looks shaken. 'Do you want to see him?'

'Not really.' I stare back at her, feeling like I'm not really there inside my body as I watch her reaction. 'But maybe we should just get it over with.'

Mum has embraced the digital age since I last saw her and she uses her new mobile phone to call her friend David or whatever he is to postpone their trip to the charity shop. I wait in the car while she calls, but I can hear her high-pitched weirdly girlish tone as they speak. He is more than a friend. I stare out of the window as she drives me to the home, then I get out of the car and tell her through gritted teeth that I don't want her to follow me.

'I'll wait—'

I slam the door on her sentence. I breathe deeply and erratically as I walk up a path lined with purple agapanthus to the front door. I need to calm down before I go inside, but it's so hard with her sitting there watching me. So I push ahead and approach the reception desk. A middle-aged woman with a permed bob and an unflattering shade of orange lipstick looks up at me.

'Can I help you?' she asks pleasantly.

I tell her I'm there to see my father, Terrence Taylor. Her eyes widen and she smiles widely. 'You must be Bronte!'

I nod.

'And you're here all the way from England?'

'That's right.' Mum must have told her I was coming.

'Oh, how wonderful! When did you arrive?'

'Just today,' I say, in no mood for conversing with a stranger.

'Oh well, that's wonderful.' Her smile fades slightly, then slightly more, until her face changes into an expression of compassion. 'He might have changed a little since you last saw him,' she says gently.

'I know. I've been warned.'

'He has his good days and his bad days,' she explains kindly. 'Sadly the good days are getting less and less. He seems quite perky today.'

I just want to get this over and done with. 'Where is he?' I ask.

She looks down briefly. 'He's in the communal room to your left, through the double doors.'

'Thank you.' I turn away from the sympathy in her eyes.

I push open the doors and the sound of tinkling piano music instantly reaches my ears. Frowning, I walk towards the sound, coming out of the corridor into a large room. There are dozens of brightly coloured armchairs, many of which are occupied by elderly residents staring into space, although a few of them have what I assume are family members visiting. One ancient old lady has hair the same colour as the purple agapanthus lining the outside path, but my focus is on the man playing the piano.

A lump forms in my throat as my feet glue themselves to the carpeted floor. I can't move an inch, so I just stand there staring. I recognise this song. He used to play it when I was growing up. I don't remember what it was called, but it's a difficult piece and his fingers dance across the octaves as he bows his head and occasionally nods along to the music.

He's greyer than I remember and his hair is too long, but he really doesn't seem too bad. He's playing the piano! What's he doing in a home?

My feet carry me on autopilot over to him. I stand at his side, watching him hesitantly as I wait for him to notice me. But he just carries on playing.

'Dad?' I ask tentatively after a minute.

Still he continues to play.

'Dad?' I say again more loudly. I put my hand on his arm. His fingers continue to play, seemingly with a mind of their own, but he slowly turns his face to look at me. Nothing. No sign of recognition.

'Dad, it's me,' I say, a tightness in my chest. 'Bronte.'

Again nothing. He's an empty shell. A vacant

vessel. He turns back to look at the piano, his fingers merrily tripping across the keys.

'Dad,' I say again, shaking his shoulder.

All of a sudden it hits me. He's gone. I'm too late.

But no. He can't have left already. I'm not ready for him to leave without saying goodbye. I've got to get through to him.

I shake his shoulder gently and once more he meets my eyes, but this time he just looks more confused.

'Bronte? Bronte, dear.' I spin around as someone touches my arm and I come face to face with a middle-aged, kindly-looking nurse. 'Will you come with me, dear?' She pries my hand away from my dad's shoulder, and he never stops playing, not once. The sound of his music is ringing in my ears as she leads me to a small office, shutting the door.

'He's deteriorated far more quickly than we expected, I'm afraid,' she says softly.

'But how can he still play the piano?'

'Alzheimer's is a strange thing. Pre-learned music can remain until quite late in the illness because of the area of the brain involved. I'm sorry, dear.'

I walk out of there in a daze. A single tear rolls down my cheek.

So I will definitely never know if he loved me. He doesn't even know who I am.

Mum regards me with a mixture of trepidation and sympathy as I climb back into the car.

'Is it true? Is he in Adelaide?'

She looks confused for a moment, not sure who I'm talking about.

'The priest? Is he back?'

She instantly looks shifty. Is she, even now, refusing to accept that it ever happened?

'I want to see him. Do you know where he works?'

'Don't be ridiculous!' she snaps.

'If I can't ask Dad any more, then I want to ask him.'

'Ask him what?'

'How it happened! How did my father end up having an affair with him?'

She recoils and I shake my head at her. 'Dad is *gay*, Mum. Why didn't you divorce him when you found out?'

'Marriage is sacred.' She looks uneasy.

I regard her with disbelief for a long moment. 'How can you say that when you've got yourself a boyfriend?'

'He's just—'

'*Don't* tell me he's just a friend!' I interrupt her, losing patience. 'Stop lying to me!'

She looks away from me. Her voice wavers when she speaks. 'I was scared. And I was miserable.' Tears stream down her cheeks, cutting through her foundation like new rainfall coursing through a dry Australian riverbed. 'The whole sorry episode was so embarrassing. I was ashamed. People were talking and I just wanted to bury my head in the sand and shut them all out. I wish I'd been stronger.' She meets my eyes. 'You're right about David. I'm in love with him.' I sharply inhale. 'And I know that makes me an adulterer, just like your father, but I love him. He makes me happy. And I want to be happy, Bronte. I've had a lifetime of misery and I want to be happy.' She starts to sob as she holds her hand out to me, asking for my blessing.

Compassion sweeps through me and I reach over and take her hand, squeezing it tightly.

I just wish Dad could have been happy, too.

We can't help who we fall in love with. She can't. Dad couldn't. The priest couldn't. And neither could Alex, Lachie and I. Sometimes it all just comes down to chemistry.

Suddenly I feel very, very tired, and maybe it's jetlag, but all I want to do is sleep for a week.

'Can we go home?' I ask quietly. 'I'm so tired.'

'Will you ever forgive me?' she asks worriedly.

'Of course I will, Mum,' I reply. 'I already have.'

CHAPTER 31

In the end I do go to stay with Ben and Lily in their warm and cosy home in the hills for a few days, and it's a relief to be away from Mum and David. David's friendly and seems fairly decent, but I'm still coming to terms with Dad's illness and I can't yet bring myself to get to know him. Mum has continued to pack up the house – she's downsizing and moving closer to the city, where David lives, and I'm glad she's having a fresh start away from gossip and the rumour mill.

I visit my dad again, and I'm told he will only deteriorate further from here on in. So my last hope of finding out what went down all those years ago ends with the priest. Polly manages to uncover where he works. I have no doubt that my asking her will eventually find its way back to my mum's ears, so I take the opportunity to go and speak to him before my mum can intervene.

Lily drives me down through the beautiful, winding Adelaide Hills to the city, and it's comforting and heart-warming hearing the sounds of her tiny baby cooing in the back seat. She parks in the church car park and we make a plan to hook up at a coffee shop in half an hour before she sets off with baby Elizabeth in her baby carrier for a walk around the shops.

I'm on edge as I look up at the daunting gothic-style, brown stone church with its tall, pitched roof and spires piercing the sunny sky. I walk through the groomed churchyard to the front door and enter into the cavernous space. There's no one in sight so I look around for the vestry and spy it to the right of the altar. I knock on the open door and call, 'Hello?' and a moment later a man in a cassock with a white dog collar appears in front of me. 'Can I help you?'

He's older – about twenty years older, to be precise, with middle-aged spread and greying hair – but he hasn't changed as much as I have, and it's unmistakeably him.

'Father William?' I ask shakily.

'Yes?'

'Can I talk to you?'

His brow furrows. 'Of course.'

He waves his hand with a flourish, encouraging me to enter. I perch on a new and quite uncomfortable armchair and he takes a seat opposite me.

'You probably don't remember me,' I start. I'm not as nervous as I thought I would be. 'My name is Bronte.'

The look on his face . . . All of a sudden he knows exactly who I am.

'I don't want to cause you any trouble,' I say as

his face drains of blood. 'My dad is not well – he has Alzheimer's.'

A flicker of pain passes over his face.

'So I can't ask him anything.'

'What do you want to know?' He sounds reluctant, like he's forcing himself to speak to me.

'I don't know,' I admit. 'I'm trying to understand how it happened.' I want to tell him how their relationship affected my life, how nothing has ever been the same and I'm only now facing my demons. But there's nothing he can do about that, and I'm not here to blame him or to cause him misery. I don't doubt that he's had more than his fair share already.

He blushes at the idea of telling me how it 'happened' and I regret asking the question. 'Can you tell me about him?' I ask in a small voice. 'What was he like?'

He regards me with an odd look. 'Well, he was kind and talented and a good friend,' he admits carefully.

'*Was* he kind?' I find myself asking. 'Because I don't really remember that.' My eyes fill up with tears. 'All I remember is how miserable he always seemed, how he never seemed to like Mum and me, let alone love us, love *me*.'

'Of course he loved you,' William says quickly, reaching forward as though to take my hand but thinking better of it. I wouldn't have minded. 'He was a very confused man.'

I don't doubt it. 'He was obviously gay—'

'Not gay,' William interrupts. 'Bisexual.' His flush spreads to his neck.

'I don't know how he ended up with my mother. They didn't seem at all well suited.'

He remains respectfully silent. I doubt he disagrees with me. 'That night . . . The night when I saw you . . .'

He draws a sharp breath and nods quickly. 'I'll never forget it,' he says in a tight voice. 'I never stopped thinking about you,' he adds to my surprise. He never stopped thinking about me? 'I am so, so sorry about what happened, what you saw, how your father reacted, and how I handled things afterwards. I have asked for God's forgiveness time and again. You shouldn't have had to lie for us and I am so sorry.' His eyes well up and tears spill down his cheeks. 'I loved him,' he says. 'A part of me loves him still. He's in my prayers every night – him and you and your mother.'

'My mum is seeing someone else,' I tell him. 'And Dad is in a nursing home and he doesn't know who I am.' A thought comes to me. 'I don't think he'll know you either, but if you'd like to see him . . .'

He regards me for a long moment and then nods, tearfully. 'Thank you.'

I give him the address before making to leave.

'Please come back any time,' he says. 'Any time. If you ever have any more questions about him, I'll help in any way I can.'

'Thank you.' I get to my feet. 'One question. Why did you come back here? To South Australia? I thought you moved to Queensland.'

'Sometimes you have to go back to be able to move on,' he says.

I smile sadly and nod. I know exactly how he feels.

Lily and Ben say I can stay with them for as long as I like, but I have other plans, and now that the idea of seeing Lachie has come to me, I can't stop smiling. But before I can tell my mum I won't be joining her and David for Christmas this year, I have to speak to my gorgeous guitar guy. His phone goes straight through to his voicemail so I leave a message, asking him to call me back. I need to check that his parents will be okay with me gate-crashing his family gathering. The thought of being in his arms again fills me with happiness.

Happiness which is snuffed out when I answer the phone to an unknown number and hear Alex's voice at the other end of the line.

'Bronte?'

I freeze all over.

'Bronte?' he asks again. 'It's Alex.'

I find my voice, and when I reply it sounds as icy and cold as my insides feel. 'What do you want?'

I'm in the living room with Ben and Lily. We were hanging out and watching telly while Lily feeds Elizabeth. They both glance at me with concern. I get up and go to my bedroom and close the door.

I hear him sniff. His voice sounds strained and quiet and utterly desolate. 'I've broken up with Zara.'

I inhale sharply and sink onto the bed.

'I told her everything,' he says. 'I'm so sorry. I never should have gone through with it.' He breaks down.

Goosebumps appear all over my body and I choke back a sob. I can't speak so it's just as well he has more to say.

'I'm so sorry I put you through that at the wedding. When you walked out of the church . . . I knew how much you were hurting and I couldn't do anything about it. I just felt numb,' he says.

I'm distraught listening to him speak.

'It was all so surreal. I was sure I'd made the right decision about marrying her. It was actually a relief, after Spain, when I went to work in the other office,' he reveals. 'Even when I saw you again, I felt like it was all going to be okay, that I was doing the right thing. And then I hit a brick wall on the morning of the wedding. Suddenly I was there at the church. The thought of calling it off, *then*, with all of our friends and family sitting there waiting, it was just too much. But I hated myself.'

My chest tightens as he continues.

'Things haven't been good between Zara and me this year. It felt like the right time when we decided to get engaged, but then you came back into my life and threw things. Bronte. Please say something.'

So I say something. 'I'm in love with Lachie.'

'Oh God, please don't say that.'

'I'm sorry but it's true!' I cry. 'It's too late.'

'No. It's not too late,' he says fervently. 'You're coming back to London; he's staying there.'

'I've just told you I'm in love with him!'

'But you love me, too. Don't you?' He sounds panicked. 'Please tell me that you still love me.'

'Part of me does, but oh, Alex, that part is poisoned! You poisoned it when you chose to get married to Zara. Even if I didn't love Lachie, I don't think we could ever start afresh.'

'Don't say that,' he pleads. 'When are you back? Can we talk? Face to face? I know this is too much to land on you like this, but I just miss you so much.'

'I don't know,' I say in a small voice. 'The thought of seeing you again has been agony. I haven't known how I'll ever cope with it, but Lachie has been helping me.'

It's a while before he speaks and when he does he's contemplative. 'Maybe I should have waited until you got back to tell you in person, but I didn't want you to go through another day without knowing how much I love you. Sometimes it scares me how much. But we can't deny it. *You* can't deny it. When you see me again, you'll know. We're meant for each other.'

I squeeze my eyes shut and then ping them open again. Suddenly everything is clear.

EPILOGUE

'I'm coming! Sorry, I got held up at work,' I say in a rush to Bridget, who's calling me to find out why I'm so late for our lunch together. 'People are eyeing this table like they're vultures and I'm road kill, so get your butt here ASAP.'

'I'll be there in five,' I promise, ending the call and waving to the receptionist in the lobby, who has her head buried in a bridal magazine. I hear her boyfriend has just proposed.

I look out of the floor-to-ceiling glass and sigh when I see it's pouring with rain outside. I shouldn't be too surprised: it's typical weather for March. Luckily I have my lightweight umbrella in my bag, so I get it ready and push out through the revolving doors onto the pavement. My phone rings as I'm putting it up. With the rain pelting down around me, I dig out my phone from my bag and smile when I see who's calling me.

'Hey,' I say.

'Hey yourself,' he replies warmly. 'What are you up to?'

'Off to meet Bridget for lunch.' I set off at a quick pace, struggling to hold my bag, the umbrella and my phone to my ear. 'I'm late so I've got to rush.'

'Busy morning at *Hebe*?' he asks over the sound of drumming rain on my umbrella.

'Crazy.'

'Does that mean you'll be late tonight?' His voice is tinged with disappointment.

'I'll be home before they arrive, I promise,' I reply with a smile. I haven't forgotten that we've got his new boss coming for dinner.

'Good. Love you.'

'Love you, too.'

I end the call and hurry across the road. A few minutes later I arrive at the restaurant, smiling at the sight of Bridget sitting there in prime position at the window. Trust her to get some of the best seats in the house.

'Hello!' I call. 'I'm so sorry!'

'Don't worry.' She brushes me off, leaning over the table to give me a hug. 'Just been sitting here admiring the view.' She looks pointedly across the room at two gorgeous guys sitting at the bar.

'And there's me thinking you might be talking about the Sydney Opera House,' I say sweetly, glancing out of the window to indicate the white sails of the famous landmark just a few hundred metres away.

'Yeah, yeah, bit bored of it now,' she jokes, waving me away. 'And what the hell is with this weather? I thought Sydney was supposed to be hot!'

'It's autumn, you idiot.' I roll my eyes. 'Come back in summer.'

'Don't joke about it,' she says, quite seriously.

I'm in Sydney and Bridget is visiting. I didn't go back to the UK. I didn't go back at all. I spent Christmas with Lachie in Perth and as soon as I saw him my world spun just a little more steadily on its axis. He centres me. So in between Christmas and New Year, I called Simon, *Hebe*'s editor, and came clean to him about everything. It was a horrendous, difficult conversation, but I needed his understanding before I could ask for his support. Even if Alex weren't a factor, I wanted to be closer to home to help Mum and look out for Dad. I don't know how much time he'll have left.

Although naturally disappointed, Simon agreed to let me stay in Australia instead of insisting I return to London to work out my notice.

Bridget was devastated to hear I wasn't coming back. She's been the best flatmate, but more importantly, the best friend I've ever had. I knew I'd miss her terribly, but she said she understood – and vowed to wangle a press trip to Australia as soon as she could. She stayed true to her word. She arrived a week ago, laden down with excess baggage, including an extra suitcase with the rest of my things. She's enjoying herself so much, she's contemplating staying for a bit. As a freelancer, she could certainly eke out her fair share of Australian-based articles.

After New Year, Lachie and I packed up and said goodbye to his funny, friendly, warm and slightly wacky family and set off to Sydney on an adventure of our own. We found a one-bedroom apartment in Manly near the beach and I spoke to all my old contacts to try and line up work on various picture desks. To my amazement, I found that my *old*, old evil boss at *Hebe* Australia had handed in her notice. So I applied for the position of Picture Editor – and got it. Lachie, meanwhile, landed a job on a building site to bring in some cash, which he plans to supplement with busking and gigging.

We've been in Sydney for just over two months now and life is good.

But I still think about Alex. It's hard not to when he emails me every day. One morning, I'm certain I will arrive at work to find my inbox empty, and I'm not yet sure how I will feel about that. For now, when I see his name, I freeze, wondering what he will say to me next. This morning it was: 'I love you. I'm not giving up.'

Father William came back to South Australia because he said that he had to go back to be able to move on. Maybe there's something in that. Maybe I have to go back to London to see Alex before I can truly move on. But I'm not ready to do that yet. If I see him again, I may cave. The chemistry between us is overwhelming and I don't think it's healthy: sometimes chemistry can be toxic.

When I'm thinking clearly, I don't think we could have ever had a fresh start. Our relationship would have always been built on shaky ground. He needs time to adjust without Zara in his life, and for now, I need to be with someone who makes me feel happy and loved and secure. But that's when I'm thinking clearly.

When I'm not thinking clearly, I still love him. Even despite the pain he has caused.

'You're going to be around tonight, aren't you?' I say to Bridget.

'Yeah, why?'

'We've got Lachie's boss and his wife coming over for dinner. I'd love you to meet them.'

'Cool, okay. Are they nice?'

'Very. I've got a good feeling about them. I think they could be friends.'

'I can't believe you're not coming back,' she says suddenly, sullenly.

'I miss you, too,' I reply quietly. I miss all of my friends and colleagues. Russ and Maria had a baby boy in January and are still going strong. Polly and Grant are tighter than ever and she remains off the booze. Rachel's assistant Sally split up with her boyfriend, which is sad for her, but at least increases her levels of reliability for my friend. Rachel was upset to lose me, even after I let her down so badly during that disastrous thirteenth wedding. She kindly told me that I got the shots she required of the church and the groom for the portfolio – but in the end, none of our shots were needed because the bride and groom split up before Rachel had even put together the final package. She wasn't surprised. She could sense both in the church and at the reception that Alex was there in body, but not in spirit, although she didn't understand why he seemed so detached until I finally told her the truth about us. She was stunned that I agreed to do his wedding in the first place. I have to keep reminding myself that I did it for the right reasons – that he was a friend and I didn't want to let him or Rachel down – but Lachie still wonders if I have sadomasochistic tendencies.

Rachel sent all of Alex and Zara's photographs to them anyway – including the shot I took of him looking at her when she reached his side. But I never gave Rachel the ones of Alex looking at me. I've filed them away. I know I should delete them. But for now, I can't bring myself to.

Maybe Lachie's right. Maybe I do have sado-masochistic tendencies. But for now, those tendencies are pretty much suppressed.

My mum is still seeing David, and my dad is declining steadily. I speak to the nurse occasionally to get medical updates, and she tells me that Dad is occasionally visited by a priest, who I'm assuming is Father William. Even he doesn't seem to spark off any memories, as far as the nurses can tell, but apparently the priest seems to find it comforting to just sit there and listen to Dad playing the piano, which apparently, he does often.

'Have you thought any more about doing some part-time wedding photography?' Bridget asks me after the waitress has come to take our order.

She suggested the idea to me, wanting to put me in touch with the Australian version of the bridal magazine where she worked in London, just in case they had any advice.

'I'm not completely closed off to the idea,' I reply. 'Lachie's lined up a wedding gig for next summer,' I reveal with a smile.

'You two should open up a wedding business,' she says eagerly. 'You do the pics, he does the entertainment, quids in!'

I laugh. 'Maybe one day I'll look into getting another assistant job, but I just want to settle into life in Sydney and not complicate things.' I also need to let my heart recuperate.

'I think you should get back on the horse pronto,' she says in her usual straight-talking manner. 'And bollocks to assisting – Rachel thinks you're good enough to run the show. You should get *yourself* an assistant,' she says firmly. 'In fact, what about Lachie?'

'What?' I pull a face.

'You could teach him how to take the pictures of the groom and the church, then take over at the reception when he does his bit.'

Her suggestion makes me think more of Alex than Lachie.

'What?' Bridget asks, seeing my cogs turning.

'Alex is the one who's into photography,' I say bleakly.

She leans back in her chair and makes an exasperated sound. 'Enough about Alex,' she snaps. 'What did today's email say?' she demands to know.

'It doesn't matter,' I reply, not wanting to set her off on another rant. She is *not* happy that Alex continues to email me.

'I can't believe, after everything he's done, he's still at it!' she erupts.

'Leave it, Bridge,' I say wearily.

'Seriously!' She's not going to leave it. 'You're happy with Lachie! What the hell does he think he's doing, still chasing you? He needs to let you go, let you get on with your life. He's done enough damage.'

I sigh.

'And *you*,' she starts in an accusatory tone, making me stiffen, 'need to stop encouraging him.'

'I'm not encouraging him!' I'm outraged. 'I never reply to his emails!'

'Exactly,' she says with the satisfaction of someone who feels they're in the right.

I eye her with trepidation.

'You're not telling him to stop contacting you,' she continues sternly. 'It's not fair on Lachie, and even though I think he's a total arse, it's not fair on Alex, either.' She leans across the table towards me and gently takes my hand. 'You need to let him go,' she says imploringly. 'It's about time.'

I leave Bridget in a pensive mood. I know she's right. If Lachie had an ex-girlfriend who was emailing him every day, trying to win him back, I'd go mad. Lachie's not even aware of the extent to which Alex still emails me. If he kept something like that from me . . . Dread surges through me, quickly followed by guilt and finally, resolve. I huddle in a doorway, out of the rain, and get out my mobile. Without letting myself think about it too much, I dial Alex's number. It's pretty late on a Thursday night for him, so I hope he'll still be up.

'Hello?'

My heart clenches at the sound of his sleepy voice, but I force myself to harden up. 'It's Bronte.'

'Bronte!' He sounds shocked. 'What are you— Where are you?'

'Sydney. Alex, you need to stop emailing me,' I say in as firm a tone as I can muster. 'I'm with Lachie,' I continue. 'I love him. It's over between us.' It never really started in the first place, but the sentiment is true.

There's silence on the other end of the line, and for a moment, I wonder if he's there, but then he speaks. 'I'm sorry. But I don't believe that's it. We can't be done.'

'We are.' I force myself to say the words. 'You'll never change my mind.'

I hear him sigh heavily. 'Okay, Bronte,' he says softly. 'If you're sure that's what you want.'

'I am.'

A long pause follows, and then he says, 'Okay,' with an air of finality. A lump forms in my throat. 'I'll look out for your pictures,' he says. 'Maybe you'll get to do a royal wedding one day.'

'Maybe.' Tears start to roll down my cheeks. I don't tell him that I'm not doing any weddings at the moment. I'm sure I will start up again soon.

I don't want to break down on the phone to him. As Bridget said, I need to let him go. It's about time. 'I've gotta get on,' I say. 'Goodbye, Alex.'

I close my eyes and wait for it, and finally it comes: 'Bye, Bronte.'

I end the call and dig into my bag for a tissue, giving myself a moment in the dark doorway to gather myself together. But by the time my mobile is back in my bag and my heels are clicking along the pavement, a weight I didn't know I was carrying lifts from my shoulders.

I brush away the last of my tears and take a deep breath. That was the right thing to do.

I speed through the rest of my day at work and catch a JetCat to Manly, staying inside the cabin to avoid the relentless rainfall. The grey sea is rough as the ferry surges away from Circular Quay, leaving the Sydney Harbour Bridge and the Opera House far behind as we descend on Manly. I join

471

the hordes of commuters stepping off the boat and then set off at a brisk walk to our apartment near the beach. My legs are wet through by the time I arrive – autumn has well and truly come and I really need a bigger umbrella. It's a dark day and as I look up at the two-storey apartment block and our small balcony with a wetter-than-wet wetsuit draped over the railings, I can see that the lights are on inside. Lachie is home. I don't imagine he got much work done today on the building site, but I'm pretty sure his new boss Nathan won't hold it against him. In fact, from the sight of the wetsuit on the balcony, I'm guessing the pair of them have been surfing again. Nathan is coming for dinner tonight with his wife, Lucy, who I really like. Oddly enough, when I told Lily about them, she said they used to be her friends, although they haven't stayed in touch for one reason or another. It's a small world. She thought it was quite a coincidence.

But I don't believe in coincidences.

Before I can unlock the door, it opens, and Lachie – my gorgeous, sexy, lovable boyfriend – is standing there with his arms open wide. I laugh and step into them, dropping my dripping umbrella to the floor. All of my chills are soothed away and replaced with the warmth I always find in his arms.

'You're soaked,' he murmurs into my hair, knocking his bare leg against my drenched one. He's wearing board shorts – another sure sign that he's been surfing. The weather may be bad, but the swell is good, and he doesn't care if it's raining. I worry about him out there in the ocean, but he says he's surfed all his life. There's certainly something very sexy about watching him ride the waves. Now I know where he developed his long, lean, muscular body.

'Let's get you out of these wet clothes,' he murmurs in my ear.

I don't argue with him. 'How much time do we have before Nathan and Lucy arrive?' I ask as he swiftly unbuttons my black shirt. I pull his orange surfer T-shirt over his head and murmur my appreciation as I run my hands over his lovely chest.

'Just enough,' he replies, kissing me urgently as he moves us to the bedroom. 'I don't know about Bridgie, though,' he says.

'Forgot about her.' I giggle, sidestepping her suitcase by the sofa bed, which still has to be returned to its sofa position before our guests arrive. 'I thought she'd be here?'

'She wanted to do some writing at a coffee shop,' he tells me between kisses, hurriedly unbuttoning my jeans and hooking his thumbs into the rear to slide them down along with my knickers.

'She could be back any minute,' I point out, laughing as he pushes me onto the bed and yanks off my rain-soaked clothes.

'We'd better make it quick, then,' he says with a mischievous grin as he steps out of his board shorts.

Mmm, now *that* is a view. He climbs onto the

bed and hovers over me, his light blue eyes twinkling moments before he claims my mouth with his lips as his body claims the rest of me. I love the feeling of this warm, kind, soulful man.

I still don't believe in coincidences. And I don't believe in God. I'm not sure if I believe in marriage – it's certainly not for everyone, but for some it works. As for love, well, I definitely believe in love. My heart is full of it.